TIM KINDBERG

# VAMPIRES OF AVONMOUTH

NSOROMA
Press

Vampires of Avonmouth

Print edition ISBN: 978-1-8381142-0-6

E-book edition ISBN: 978-1-8381142-1-3


Published by Nsoroma Press

Bristol, UK

www.nsoromapress.com


First edition: November 2020

1 $i$ -1 -$i$ 1 -$i$ -1 $i$ 1

A CIP catalogue record for this title is available from the British Library.

*For Gene, born a century before*

*Deep under the city's deepest stone,*
*This grinning sack is bursting with your blood.*
Ted Hughes, *Vampire*

# PROLOGUE

Accra.city, 2080

After his wife died, David drew his daughter, Yaa, even closer. Or tried to.

They had stopped for breakfast at a food stall on their way to her high school, both sweating in the heat. He watched as she bit into a slice of melon. A trickle of juice escaped down her chin, which she wiped distractedly with the back of her hand. A smear remained. She was probably full, he thought, of wondering about her best friend and the sensa they had been telepathically exchanging that morning via their beads. Images, sensations and thoughts sent by one appeared almost instantaneously like tiny dreams in the mind of the other. The mental link was supposed to be unobtrusive, but he could see the arrival of the other girl's transmissions reflected on Yaa's face. He would have turned off the wireless connection if he could.

As the traffic of market-goers passed them, he tenderly wiped her chin with a corner of a serviette. Last night he'd dreamed that she was taken from him, kidnapped. And when suddenly, in the bustling reality of that morning, a young man pushed by them quickly through the crowds, his detective's instincts bristled. But the man disappeared as quickly as he had arrived.

"Da-aad!" She grimaced as David turned back to dab at a spot of juice he'd missed. She was still embarrassed by him, no matter what he did, at age sixteen. "Leave me here. I'll make my way by myself. It's not far." She looked at him imploringly, peering round to see if any of her friends had observed them together. She wore a silver choker with an adinkra medallion which he knew to be Nkyin kyin, symbol of twisting and versatility. And in that choice of jewellery she followed her mother. She was tall like her, too, with cascades of fine curls and intelligent, liquid eyes. He wanted to pinch himself every time he looked at her, every rare time she confided in him. He wondered how long it would be before she left him altogether to go her own way. Twisting, versatile.

"No. You're not going without me. Ready?"

Yaa pouted, but she never disobeyed him. She tossed what remained of her melon slice into the bin. David knew only too well that dangers lurked in Accra.city, especially since his promotion from beat policing to tracking down the renegades – criminal hackers, that is, who had turned against the government. David could never tell Yaa about the lengths to which they would go for a piece of the government's profits.

David and Yaa didn't speak for the rest of the way, as they crossed streets nimbly, carefully avoiding the swarms of bikes and tro-tros filled with passengers. After he'd left her at the school gates, David switched on the beads embedded in his left wrist. He left them disconnected whenever he was off-duty, sometimes even when he was at work. He sent a telepathic message of love like an intuition to Yaa. It was no surprise when she didn't respond. He couldn't bring her mother back, just as he hadn't managed to heal their estrangement before she died a year ago, however hard he had tried. Yaa had wanted so much for them to be reconciled. Her mother's loss was still fresh within her. She felt it with the keenness of her age.

Loosening his tie in the damp, oppressive heat, David decided to take a few moments to himself on a bench in the shade of tall wawa trees. He looked up into the spreading foliage before taking a seat, then clutched his hands together, tense about the case he was working on. David's job was to hunt the renegades down, and there was one particular individual whose scent he had caught. At the thought of this man, who was known to have tortured anyone who got in his way, David rose and moved on, unable to sit still.

All that day, he flashed his badge and made enquiries, repeating the same questions endlessly, receiving the same practised blank stares. Accra.city knew better than to rat on criminals whose technologies were so far ahead as to be indistinguishable from magic – dark magic like electronic voodoo. The figures that had started to appear in the city's trees over the last six months were a grizzly testament to their powers. As he followed his investigations, taking tro-tros from one part of the city to another, David hoped he wouldn't see any of them. Yet he felt compelled to look upwards on his journeys.

These unresponsive, void-staring husks of human beings climbed into the branches instinctively and tottered until, finally weakened, they fell like empty, wing-clipped angels into the Accra.city streets. He had seen one fall with his own eyes but hadn't been able to get a close look. Agents of Special Branch, who appeared on the scene as soon as the first reports came in, kept him back along with everyone else while they took the corpse away. No one – outside Special Branch, anyway – knew much about what had happened to the fallers, or why. It appeared that they had had their minds removed. By all accounts they were people with no known criminal connections: ordinary folk in sales, finance, energy, as though they had been picked at random. Everyone knew it was the work of the renegades, who maybe were not entirely in control of their experimentation, for all their vaunted abilities.

When he left his former department a couple of months ago, his colleagues had joked about being careful not to lose his mind in the new job. He had laughed too; now it wasn't so funny.

That night, David might have found out a great deal more about the type of experimentation the renegades were perpetrating on their

3

victims had he remained conscious after he knocked on the door of a dilapidated address in East Legon. Had the careful blow to the back of his head, struck immediately upon entry, not been followed by a series of electro-biological keyhole surgeries performed on his brain over the course of two weeks. The renegades' purpose was to implant something never before attempted: an entity that could impress itself upon his mind like a message through his beads. Except that this entity was an internal being, an agent within his mind – the ultimate hack in a world of mental content, of sensa.

When, finally, he woke up alone, flat out on a bench in the shade at midday, in a part of the city he'd never been to before, he was surprisingly clear-headed. Switching on his beads in the hope of finding out what had befallen him, he was met by hundreds of increasingly near-hysterical attempts to contact him which Yaa had made over the course of two weeks – not to mention the messages from his colleagues. Alongside this mental content – he tried hard to deny it but couldn't, any more than one could deny the existence of pain – was the presence of an inhabitant like a weight inside his mind. It was blurry, but he could just about make it out, a muscly shadow which watched the operation of his mind from close quarters. It seemed more or less static. David eventually understood why: it appeared to be behind the door of a mental prison cell.

Special Branch came and took David back to an area of security HQ where he would normally never be allowed. An extensive medical examination revealed no ill effects, physically speaking, except for three small holes drilled in his cranium. There was no shadow on the MRI to show anything interfered with or planted inside his head. His beads, on the other hand, had been hacked beyond recognition. They had to be reset.

For three days they questioned him, let him rest, then questioned him again. An agent calling himself Detective Inspector Kojo was insistent, to the point of spitting, desk-thumping brutality, that he give them answers. David wondered, sweating and fevered with worry, whether Kojo was going to hit him. David was lucid about his activities and movements, apart from the missing two weeks. He could remember nothing after entering the house in East Legon – which Special Branch had found empty and wiped clean of any traces of occupation.

All this time his occupant stared coolly through what David could now clearly see, in a waking nightmare, were the bars of its mental cell, apparently listening to his thoughts and trying to peer through his eyes to the world outside: the special agents, the chairs, the coffee cups, the boards mounted with pictures of suspected renegades and the tumbledown house where he had been operated upon.

Had the renegades implanted it to spy on his unit? Or was he only imagining that it was looking and listening? And communicating? But then, what was it there for?

A hundred times David tried to formulate the words to describe what was happening inside his mind, to tell his interrogators. But they would think him mad. Get rid of him altogether. He would have to find a way to purge it by himself.

In the meantime he thought of the empty figures fallen from the trees. Something had taken their minds. Was this thing the perpetrator, or another like it? Was it waiting to consume his mind? Or someone else's? It stared impassively when he looked at his colleagues, seemed unable to get beyond the bars of its cell. It didn't even try. But what if that changed? What if the cell door opened?

The fear that choked him only increased. After the first day he was having trouble speaking.

On the fourth day they released David and told him to get some rest. He was desperate to see Yaa, even though he could tell her little that would make any sense. He had already had to lie to her telepathically, about an undercover operation that was keeping him away. It would soon be over, he told her.

Instead of returning home, he took a room in a hotel on the other side of the city. For several days he wandered the streets with a gun in his pocket. If the thing stirred towards anyone, he told himself, he would put a bullet through his head there and then. Nothing happened, despite many encounters with the denizens of Accra.city. The thing remained impassive and mute in its cell as he bought provisions, ate in cafes. He was expecting it to speak, for someone to contact him through it. To reveal whatever horrific plans they had for him.

Eventually, he couldn't stand not seeing Yaa any longer.

He didn't want to walk in unannounced in case he shocked her, so he sent a telepathic message ahead that he was coming back and knocked on the door of their home. When she appeared, tearful and angry, he reached out a hand. Then stopped. Almost immediately upon the sight of her – upon the rush of love he felt for her – the thing's cell door started to open. It was pushing its meaty hands through the gap.

"Yaa. I'm... I'm so sorry, Yaa. I love you. I can't explain what's happened. I don't want to go but I can't stay. Go to your uncle. I'll be back when I can."

He felt for the gun in his pocket and turned. Ran.

# PART ONE

## Nkyin Kyin

The twisted pattern.

Changing one's self, playing many parts.

# CHAPTER ONE
## David

Avonmouth.city, 2087

No flesh were present. Within the anonymous shell of the port's controlnode, lying in the near-above, a group of bodais ignored the clear view over the docks to the estuary and moved between the displays that told of ships' comings and goings. If flesh had been there, the bodais' attention to the consoles would have seemed farcical. For only flesh needed screens and controls to marshal the maritime trajectories and schedules. The bodais wore glassy expressions, registering one another, seeming to converse. Practising flesh-like interactions was part of their training: a way to pass the time as long as their algorithms handled the moving blips satisfactorily.

But on that day an anomaly occurred. A ship entered through the radar horizon that should not have been there and did not exist in Big Mind. The ship was headed directly for the port, crossing dangerously close to other traffic.

This was highly unusual, and triggered an exception. The bodais engaged in protocols to identify the ship, to contact those on board. All attempts failed.

A threshold was soon reached. They called for flesh.

The deputy harbourmaster, Stevens, entered with an assistant. Stevens ignored the bodais, the screens and the controls, and marched straight to the window overlooking the busy port.

"Bearing?"

His assistant read from a screen. Through powerful, ancient binoculars, Stevens examined the approaching ship.

"What the fuck is that?" He passed the binoculars to the assistant, who whistled when he saw it.

"Like something out of another time. Cute cranes on board. Is there any part of it that *isn't* rust? And it's doing fifteen knots."

"What do we know about it?"

"Nothing. It's not online and it doesn't correlate in Big Mind."

"You've already sent an intercept, right? Call them."

The assistant touched the beads on his left wrist, which reconfigured. The sound of a speeding boat's watery concussions, filtered through mild static, filled the control room.

"Lenczyk, talk to me. Can you give us a visual?"

"Sorry, no, some of my systems have started playing up. But we have a good view. I'd say two to three thousand tonnes, cargo. Never seen anything like its condition. All broken-up rust. Maybe someone found it on the bottom, patched it up."

"Any response from its crew?"

"None. Offline. No sign of anyone. In complete breach of ID laws."

"Is there *anything* to go on?"

"Well, a name. You can just about read it through the rust."

"And?"

"*Mek... Mekhanik Pustoshnyy*. If my Russian's any good."

"And where the fuck has it sailed from? Who does it belong to?" Stevens was getting nervous. The ship was not far now.

"Still can't find anything in Big Mind," the assistant said.

"You mean we're going to have to look it up in a book?"

The assistant peered round at the bodais, who were standing awkwardly behind them. "Shall we ask them?"

Stevens turned to them. "Locate the logs. All of them. The physical logs. From – when, Lenczyk?"

"About a hundred years ago, I'd say. Elizabethan times. What do you want me to do? It's not slowing."

"Please repeat," one of the bodais said.

The assistant rolled his eyes. "It's headed for an empty section of the quay now," he said to Stevens. "And with a bit of luck it's going to miss that container ship – by a hair's breadth. Shall we wait?"

"Or do what? Blow it up? Yes. We'll wait."


The call came early in the morning. David's desres, a modest one-bedroom affair in a byway of the near-above, woke him, speaking into his earpiece of details already sent to his beads. The port authority had taken possession of an errant ship. Officers had found sixteen Westaf flesh on board, suspected of class-A ID crime. There were rumours that it was actually class A*, but then flesh liked to talk these things up without really meaning it. A* was notional, could never be attained.

He gathered himself from the disarray of sheets, dragged himself up. Ignored the mess, again. Forewent breakfast. Put on the one remaining clean shirt, the same suit. Didn't shave, leaving stubble across the hollow cheeks. His eyes were switched off for now. He donned the shades that would cover them when the vodu came alive.

Rocking slightly as the N-car's snake of carriages swept beneath its monorail through the near-above, David looked out. They passed one of the logos dotted around. The only signage allowed was that of IANI, the supreme network authority which had been known in Elizabethan times as IANA. No one had suspected that the Internet Assigned Numbers Authority could have been used as a launching point for totalitarian control. Transmuted into IANI, its logo was written *I&I*.

Not *Us*, which would have meant togetherness, not *You and I*, which would have connoted a difference in knowledge between the self and another, but *I&I*, a collection of Is living in almost mutually aware co-existence by dint of the network and its capabilities for delivering sensa. This state of collective consciousness he was supposed to think was worth defending. In Westaf, where the genpop's existence was more a case of "us", he had served with pride. Not here. Never here.

Flashing by him through the window, the graffitied phrase that had begun appearing lately: *Last Few Days*. This time it was sprayed on a wall, not an N-car. There was a time when graffiti was rife, up to the quashing of the rebellion that came after the Disruption. When *Last Few Days* could have been a declaration – a hope – that the Disruption would end, or the name of a band of musicians, or a gang. But he hadn't seen graffiti since he was a boy – since, along with all the other flesh, he'd started to receive sensa through his beads.

He was ten years old when the very first sensa hit him in 2050, along with the rest of bead-wearing humanity: the realisation that an image in his mind had not derived from him but was miraculously conjured from afar. *Fill your mind with joy*, it said in magisterial lettering, signed *I&I*. The phrase had moved across his field of vision then seated itself in a corner of his consciousness before disappearing altogether. A few days later a taste appeared in his mind, the sweetness of a chocolate bar, part of a sales campaign whose banners were all over the internet. Then, one boiling summer's day, a new facility appeared: person-to-person telepathic transmission. Before long he was exchanging sensa with his friend, Mikey.

After just a few months, whatever the passionate – and violent – responses for and against, sensa were a fact of most people's mental life. No one – no one except the powers that be – could turn IANI's stream off. You could switch off friends and family, and many did after a row or two. But somehow they found themselves turning them on again. At that point, humans had become the fleshwork. And the power of the network over them was complete.

Now, in the new order of 2087, David wondered where the graffiti writers had found the spray paint. It represented highly unusual interest in the physical world, a departure from the collective consciousness. And what did it mean? Undercurrents were always stirring, new rebels of the Between, as they styled themselves, their mantra "The truth is offline." A bunch of would-be nons causing minor trouble, hustling to disconnect. They were like flies to IANI. More would-be than actual nons, the ID police – and that included him; it was how low he had fallen – always picked them up, nipped them in the bud. David could never tell anyone, but he didn't blame them for not wanting sensa from multinats and other flesh playing in their heads whenever they weren't at work. The rebels considered the sensa to be an unreasonable intrusion. And that was where David would have stood – against it all – if he weren't an ID cop with the stream switched off when he wanted. If he were himself again. If he hadn't been numbed, overcome by the trauma of the vodu's implantation and losing Yaa, he'd be hustling against it too.

But the incident with the ship didn't sound minor. He felt an unusual stirring at the coming challenge of the investigation. More than that: an instinctive feeling, whose origin he couldn't put his finger on, that the ship carried cargo from Westaf which would bring a change.

Telling himself not to manufacture false hopes, he looked around at his fellow travellers, felt some of them through his beads. All online, the fleshwork connected to the network, felt telepathically, propagating and receiving sensa, mind to mind and IANI to mind. But they couldn't feel him, the ID cop. One of them, a boy in his late teens, was looking back at him. David loosened his collar. The sunlight filtering through the near-above was oppressive, its heat trapped in the clammy air. He thought of Yaa, back in Accra.city. She wasn't much older than this boy. What was she doing at this moment? He stared back until the boy averted his eyes.

After climbing for a while beneath its monorail, the N-car came to a stop at an intersection. Flesh and bodais milled on the pristine platform, many of the faces incurious, sensa flickering within minds as they transited between nodes, psychblood running in veins. The glass, concrete and metal of the nodes all around was winged with the outspread lattices of solar panels. Despite the panels and the wind turbines, the risen water heaved against the reinforced quays in the down-below.

Cities had contracted laterally into themselves, fearful of migration and the rising seas. The multiple fortified tiers which David watched being constructed for the more wealthy became known as the near-above: a lattice of repurposable, logistically reprogrammable nodes for living, entertainment and work, all connected by transitways. They were a shiny escape from the climate-induced trauma of what had raged beneath. The nodes were all cuboids of varying proportions, some with Gothic touches in the shape and surrounds of their entrances and windows. The supposed nearness of their elevation was misleading double-think: despite the scaffolding that connected them, for all but essential purposes the nodes were isolated from those struggling beneath. Algorithms policed this plan of vertical segregation.

IANI had restored order in the down-below too, shadowed by the near-above. Nowadays it wasn't so different from how it had been in the early part of the century. There were old-fashioned terraces of renovated brick desreses and carless streets of tarmacadam in an atmosphere of numbed peace, without a trace of the mid-century carnage that was the post-Disruption years. Equally, there were no longer any parks, gardens, galleries or museums, since those could be virtually, telepathically experienced via sensa delivered at optimum times.

In the late twenty-first century, flesh and bodais moved freely between the near-above and the down-below, going about their network-driven business. IANI excelled at order. Bodais kept the physical world of Avonmouth.city, one of the remaining habitable pockets of the still-overheated planet, perpetually clean and tidy while the network hummed. Unused bods leaned in charging bays arranged along the transitways. One of them emerged, readied with an AI, a female model in overalls carrying a toolkit, to board the N-car.

David's gaze alighted upon a reflection that turned out to be his own, thermally quivering in the polished glass outside the carriage like a phantom haunting him. Tall, thin in suit and shades. Rough around the edges. Saddened. The reason for cutting himself off from his precious daughter, Yaa, here in Avonmouth.city, thousands of kilometres from his Westaf home and completely incommunicado from the only person left alive he loved – the reason for his exile stirred itself.

Inside his mind, the vodu turned its back on him.


The ship that the sixteen crewed – if that could be said of people dressed in a grubby negation of smart casual wear, possessing little idea of how a ship functioned – was the *Mekhanik Pustoshnyy*: a 2,500-tonne cargo vessel built in the last century which had once plied its way around the Baltic. It was fetched up against a corner of the Avonmouth.city docks. The sixteen had sailed it unladen and it sat high in the lapping water, a long, rust-coloured hull reaching ahead of a scrappy white superstructure at the stern.

Due to the unresponsive and errant nature of its arrival, Stevens, the deputy harbourmaster, had reported a suspicion that the *Mekhanik Pustoshnyy* might be part of a physical – as opposed to cyber – terrorist attack, the type that used to take place in the early part of the century, still Elizabethan times – part of the disorder that existed then in the fleshwork.

However, despite the crew's claim that the ancient radio had broken down, eventually, in the final moments of their approach, the group had responded to the port authority's calls. They replied severally and incoherently, as though they had selected whoever had some idea of how to answer each question put to them.

And the ship, clearly steered by novices, came round in a path of wildly varying curvature and stopped offshore, amid approaching supertankers and cruise ships. The boarding party had found sixteen flesh waiting for them, one of them female.

David, the senior officer assigned to the case, was to interview the boatload of them. His intuition told him to start with her.

He entered the interview room where she was guarded by a bodai. In the terrifying final days he had spent living underground in Accra.city, consorting with witch-technologists and necromancers in a desperate attempt to find a way to rid himself of his own inhabitant, David had learned something about the horrific nature of what he learned were called vodus, derived from an ancient spirit term. This woman had been squatted by one, he could tell at once. That is, they could tell: the vodu inside him, too. First, her eyes, live with mentalmagic. The veins on her bare forearms were another giveaway. Like a man's, only more: they almost-blued and snaked beneath the glistening black skin of her arms, in an apparent effort to escape from her inhabitance. She had been beautiful, though, with spiralling locks, fine brows capping a sculpted visage; her teeth were perfectly white, if animal-sharp – sharper than when she had been all human. It was the tongue, though, that one had to watch out for.

He had the hots for her, he suddenly realised, for this young woman across the desk in the interview cabin. Well, David thought, that is how it works for us upon recognition. Only it doesn't last. How could it, given what would happen if union took place?

The crew had been discovered in a state of exhaustion. Except for her. David knew her to be incapable of tiring, however fleshly she had presented herself to the boarding party. They were from Westaf. What was she doing here, in Avonmouth.city?

Recognition was quite possibly mutual. David was covered up in a suit, the Avonmouth.city ID cop in shades. But you never knew. She was smart with mentalmagic. Maybe she had other ways of sniffing him out.

"What do you call yourself?"

"Obayifa." The way she said it, looking straight at him, it was her real name, whatever she was to the network.

He looked at her beads, the bracelet of moving dots implanted at her left wrist. He felt towards her, straining with the beads on his own wrist. Nothing. Really, nothing; just as a vampire has no reflection in a mirror.

She stared through him, projected a thin, mocking smile. He was sweating, faint. The A/C had broken down, was breathing warm air into the cabin. I can't do this, David thought. Not now.

The vodu inside him concurred as to his weakness.

"Take her," he commanded the bodai, "and make sure that only bodais supervise her and not flesh, understood? She's not to come into contact with any flesh." She couldn't fuck with a bodai – at least, as far as he knew. A bodai would be like a stone to her, an object without psychic contents – without food inside.

He watched her being led away, cuffed. There wasn't much he could do about her, a case of mentalmagic such as those he had experienced in Accra.city: her vodu driving her inexorably. If she got the chance, who would she take with her? Some soul. He meant that close to literally, give or take a philosophical nicety. And there was no room for niceties anymore.

At the same time, an instinct gripped him, as when he first heard about the ship's arrival: somehow there was a connection between

Obayifa and the trauma of his inhabitance, he was sure of it. Or perhaps he needed to make one. He couldn't return to Westaf in his current state and imperil Yaa. But Westaf had come to him.


David went out for air. He stood in the heat, if only to escape from the cabin and the claustrophobia she had instilled in him, and looked around. This wasn't a place, like his haunts as a boy in Liverpool.city, or the compounds he'd known in Accra.city; it was yet another node where ones and machines flowed. There was loading and unloading all about him.

A module swooped from above, sleek and highly manoeuvrable, with IANI insignia and tinted windows. You had to be important or at least on official business to ride a module and not an N-car. The chief climbed out. A chief. For this one was not flesh but a bodai. An artificial I assigned to a bod, the bod to a module, the module dispatched to David and consequently to this node. Anyway, there he – it – was.

"I need your report ASAP."

"You'll have it today." David deliberately looked as though he didn't mean it, a casual and common expression of fleshly dissent that had stayed with him from his youth. The bodai probably wouldn't recognise David's mild disrespect, and what did it matter if it did?

"Who have you talked to?"

"Just network and her." He gestured at the departing detainee. The chief didn't look.

"Flesh."

"Yes. Why?"

"Like you."

"Indeed."

There was a pause. One might have said there was a rumination on the chief's part, a pondering on the role of flesh in the network and what the chief could expect from David, especially in the way of intuition, which lay beyond them. Bodais relied on flesh to interpret flesh. But could they trust flesh?

In fact, the pause was just a timing routine, a ruse to slow them down so they could talk to flesh, and not freak flesh out with sheer speed. David sensed this one might be a little iffy on the network-to-fleshwork interface.

"Give me headlines," it said.

He cringed at the phrase. "From somewhere in Westaf, is all I know – suspect, anyway. She's the first of sixteen. Long day ahead of me. What they're doing in a crate like that fetching up in Avonmouth city, I have no idea. Flesh travelling that far should be taking modules, right? Not getting wet. It's not as though they don't have them out there."

"You've been."

"You could say that."

Another timing routine. The uncanny blankness of a bodai pause, despite the engineers' best efforts.

"I spent my twenties and thirties there," David continued, as if to himself.

"Send me your report."

This one had a peculiar gait. If he'd been flesh David would have said he grew up on the street. Off he went to be sliced, rebodded, reassigned, moved, whatever. The combinatorics weren't worth thinking about. That was what the network was for.

But why this interest from the network? More specifically, something told him it came all the way up from IANI. As a result, his curiosity was pricked all the more. He was so used to the bleak impassivity by which he had just managed to survive since his arrival in Avonmouth.city, the dull ache of self-exile from Yaa, the denial of any emotion towards those around him lest his vodu escape to ravage.

Did he have it in him, he asked himself, to rise to the ship's incursion, and more to the point, Obayifa?

Above him, wind turbines whumped against the hot white sky.


At least you could say it was better than going home.

It took until night-time to interview the remaining fifteen crew, the sky filling with blinking craft, the muddy smell of the estuary drifting across the plots, bays and warespaces and in through the window of the stuffy cabin.

The fifteen males ranged from late teens to fifties. None of them was squatted like her, Obayifa, and, David noted, none of them mentioned her. How many days had they spent together in that ship, the *Mekhanik Pustoshnyy*? Each claimed not to know anything about anyone else. None had a valid ID.

"So you left Port-Harcourt city a month ago," David said, disbelieving the last of them, as he had disbelieved all the others. The previous member of the crew, if you could call them that, had said they'd left Majorca.island, en route from where he wouldn't say, six weeks ago.

"Correct, sir." Like the others, this detainee was flesh and smelled from weeks without washing. The female was in a boiler suit when they found her, but the men had all worn the semi-casual dress of business people: suits but no ties, pale blue or pink shirts, Oxford shoes. The shoes were scuffed, their clothes bore greasy dirt marks from the journey. It was as though they had left a corporate meeting to immediately board a boat – however strange a choice the *Mekhanik Pustoshnyy* would be – for an away day, but something had gone terribly wrong.

"And you were headed for...?" The man smiled senselessly at David, but didn't respond. David continued. "You came to shore in Avonmouth city, wherever you were headed. Why here? If you were in trouble – and you aren't a trained crew, so you must have got into difficulties in a craft like that – there were plenty of opportunities to land before now, surely. Or stop and radio for help."

The man shook his head. "The ship malfunctioned. No radio. The engine would work for a while, then cut out unpredictably. We'd drift, then make for land when we regained control of it. A zigzag. None of us are—"

"Sailors? Whose idea was it to get into a ship without anyone who could sail it?"

The man shook his bent head. He closed his eyes. David had noticed him before they were taken away for processing, or rather he had noticed the expensive-looking watch that showed from under his filthy cuff. The watch was on the right wrist, of course; beads were on the left.

"Tell me about her."

"Who?"

"You know who. The female with you on the ship. Obayifa."

"Obayifa?" Evidently he had not heard the name before. "We never spoke."

"How many days on board, and you never spoke? What was her role? What do you know about her?"

The man did not reply, his face scrunching.

"You're afraid of her."

He gave an almost imperceptible nod.

"That'll be all for now."


The following morning. Visiting time. Conversation in the carie was proving difficult. All the wing-backed chairs around them were occupied by residents and family. Mr Charles was in too much pain to move to a quieter corner, so they'd had to remain where he sat, and David had to stand. David did his best to talk with his friend from long ago, despite the stares and half-cocked ears, the occasional yelps and muffled incoherencies around them: emanations from demented brains. Dems, they called them.

There was a long pause. David looked across the room. A smell of sour milk invaded his nostrils. A young woman in the blue uniform of the carie had spotted him before he noticed her. She quickly looked away, busying herself with the slouched gentleman she was attending to.

David tried to think of something to say to Mr Charles, a friend of the family who took an interest in him when he was growing up without a father in Liverpool.city. In a fit of loneliness as much as in friendship, David had looked Mr Charles up on returning to UK.land, as soon as he'd learned he was living in Avonmouth.city.

"Don't worry about it," Mr Charles said, seeing the struggle on David's face. "The Lord looks after me here. Me and all these good people." He swept an arm feebly round. Mr Charles – as David had always called him – was the only non-demented resident in the carie, brought here for a reason David could not determine, a glitch in the network.

"I need to get you out of here, David said. "You shouldn't be here. You should be in a…"

"'Gated community'? There's no bytecoins for that." Mr Charles tried a smile.

"No, not a gated community. Of course not." David pictured the last such retirement resort he had visited, on official business: full of the well-heeled, barred away from the likes of Mr Charles – or David, for that matter. As full of faltering minds as the carie, only with more freedom to roam. Many of them weren't much older than David and some were even younger, in their early forties, smitten by the dementia plague that had spread backwards like a wave through earlier and earlier stages of life.

"Where then?" Mr Charles' eyes flashed. He held a small framed photograph of a woman he had never talked about, which he always carried with him. David tried not to look at it. It seemed to stir the vodu's interest when he did.

There was a commotion in the adjacent lobby. A group of bodais were bringing in a fresh group of residents-to-be, taking them firmly but gently by the arms according to protocols and passing them to flesh. The incomers were dressed smartly. It wouldn't be long before the carie's entropy would take hold: their clothes would be mixed up, ill-fitting on the wrong bodies, like the assortment flapping or fitted too tightly on those in the chairs around them.

David looked back to the young woman, but she was gone. Mid-twenties, slightly older and shorter than Yaa, but with strikingly similar almond eyes.

"Still have your eye for beauty, then," Mr Charles said.

"No, it's not that. I..." He had never told Mr Charles about Yaa, much less the reason for abandoning her: that he was terrified of what the vodu trapped in his mind might do to her if it escaped. Mr Charles, too: what if it squeezed through the bars right now – what would it make him do to the old man, his only friend? And yet it did not escape. He had learned to harden his heart, to keep it locked up. But his daughter was another question. The cage had begun to open when he saw her, when the intensity of his love for her showed. It opened by just a chink, but he could never take the risk.

"You don't have to explain, David. A pretty girl's a pretty girl. And you're a single man, aren't you? A bit old for her, mind! Such things keep us flesh together. We know what it's like to inhabit skin – real skin – together with the Lord. Anyway, you'd do all right with that one. She's kind. She looks after me."

"I wish you wouldn't say that."

"What, now?"

"I wish you'd keep the Lord out of it."

"And let the network have it all? Even faith?"

David looked at the beads on Mr Charles' wrist. They had been deactivated, as had those of the dems around him. Beyond a certain point, the network deemed flesh unsuited to connection. Conversion to sales was unlikely, maintenance and psychblood were hardly cheap, and how to filter what came from their minds?

David said, "There are other, real things to vest our faith in."

"Like what? You talk to me of faith? You? You're devoid of it, David. If you'd take those stupid sunglasses off I'd see in your eyes what I know about you in my heart. Where is the David I knew before he went to Westaf? He never came back."

"I have to go," David said. "Never mind me. It's you I'm worried about. Your mind is intact but you're surrounded by—"

"The lost and the fractured, the broken. It's the beads that did it, accelerated the onset of their dementia. I'm sure of it. I'm fortunate. Shall I come to live with you, then, David? Me and my pain and my aloneness and the Lord?"

"No, I—"

"No, indeed. They have cures for everything nowadays, except dementia and old age. They don't know what to do with the broken but undemmed, so they act as though I'm one of my brothers and sisters here."

"Look." David was deeply uncomfortable by now, a product of the connection he both tried and tried not to sustain with Mr Charles. "I have to go." All conversation around them had stopped. Other visitors were listening in, to gain respite from the unsettling talk of their relatives and spouses.

"Very well." Mr Charles cast his eyes back down to the photograph and, without looking back up to David, said, "I'll see you next week. Take care now."

She had made herself scarce. She'd spotted him, the ID cop, he thought; that was the look he'd seen on her face, wariness behind a practised facade.

# CHAPTER TWO
## Pempamsie

Berekuso, Westaf, 2066

I had made a contraption – a toy, I suppose you would call it. The robots had received instructions in relation to me, instructions that were incomprehensible to one aged eight, although I now know what they must have been. They waited with me in the compound, ready to stop me running away. And I, snotty, tall for my age, acting out a contrived interest in the contraption – I, Pempamsie, stood with my heart beating hard. I sensed that I was in almost all respects beyond the ken of their algorithms. These robots were of a type unknown to me: glassy, mock-skinned; making small movements in crude emulation of flesh.

Father was arguing with the flesh who had brought them. Mother came from her office to argue with them too. There was a lot of shouting through the open front door. Both my parents were violent of tongue at the best of times. They would have been wrangling about the price being paid for me. The visitors didn't shout back. As I later realised, they didn't need to. They had come to state certain facts established within the network and not the business of the fleshwork, especially not in Westaf. To this day my parents could never have known about the exact nature of their only child's exploitation – by

IANI, as it would transpire, not some mere multinat in the pyramid of the Between.

The flesh left in their module, and the robots took me away by the wrists in theirs.


IANI North, Arctic circle, 2076

I lived at one of the two shrinking ends of the earth. As the multinats extended their digital reach, which became telepathic reach, so they shrank their physical domicile to the poles. They made the robots to walk among the genpop on their behalf. Bez chose the North Pole, where I was, and sent his minions to the Antarctic. At each pole, a single station sprawls upon the ice sheet, surrounded by server farms whose hum is inaudible beneath the wind. The cables from the Between ultimately end at both poles. Exactly how symmetrical are IANI's icestations at the North and South Poles is a subject of some thought but no discussion. Those who visit one of them never go to the other. However, their roles in the network are thoroughly understood: the two poles are a failover pair: if one were to cease to function, the other would continue. No one has told Nature not to claim both of them.

Bez died in 2050. I never came across anyone who had met him. But he was everywhere. In the long dormitories where we slept. In the vast corridors and atria we commuted through, from training session to training session. I and others like me who were kidnapped and brought there.

Bez existed still in the mentality by which IANI functioned, the total belief in algorithmic supremacy, despite its manifest inadequacies; the provision everywhere of robots and automation for the merest tasks that might interfere with profitable user journeys, for the greatest efficiencies; Bez fostered the coldness beneath the forced, conforming good humour with which all was transacted.

My parents named me after an adinkra. I, Pempamsie, am that which cannot be crushed. I studied these symbols of my people when I was a child, each perfectly memorised in shape and meaning.

The instructors at the icestation showed me how to tone my body and taught me, and I obeyed. There was too much blood when I didn't. Theirs and mine. Blood in the icestation, surrounded by howling wind and contracting ice.

Odenkyem: the crocodile lives in water, yet it breathes air. I trained in Bez's icestation and I obeyed, yet I breathed the adinkras.

My teacher, Emmanuel, wore a white one-piece suit like me. His head was shaven like mine. His skin was pink and delicate in the whiteness all around us. He was flesh. I, black flesh.

"You'll be sent back," he told me soon after I arrived. "You'll be sent back to the Between when you're ready."

"When I'm ready," I mimicked back to him. "To stem the threat. The threat to order. To content delivery. To sensa. Mental content is king. All is known."

"All is known." He smiled at me.

Whence does Pempamsie derive her strength? From my parents' treatment of me, to be sure. But also from somewhere deeper. From the bowels of the earth, spinning, magma-filled; its twin tops, the diminished poles, squatted by IANI; IANI, which lives in fear of what would happen if there were to be a loss of user satisfaction.

Apart from my sessions with Emmanuel, I trained with the others alongside robots and their flesh handlers. I didn't talk to these others. I didn't know where they were from. We spent hours exercising, reaching physical perfection. We learned to make algorithms. And to crack algorithms. They pitted us one against the other and against the robots. Day after day went by, learning efficiencies, information flows and server architectures; cost structures and statistical models of

28

interaction with flesh; learning, above all, how algorithms seep into minds and extract data via beads and psychblood. I, Pempamsie, watched and learned. I was careful not to challenge. I was Pempamsie inside. Odenkyem.

If there is one thing Pempamsie truly understands, it is that they believe their own mantra: that they reach inside every corner of every mind. Whereas Pempamsie knows that they merely pass vapid sensa telepathically, to and from the minds of Betweeners: a software-controlled hallucination over the network that pleasures them and causes them to buy. The Betweeners are mere data feeds to IANI. But human consciousness, like true intelligence, remains beyond their grasp.

Sunsum: the soul.

All is known.

One day, Pempamsie was called to a meeting. Only flesh were present, Emmanuel and others I didn't recognise. Pink flesh dressed in white. They told me it was time. My training was done. Time to re-Between me.

I asked them for my task.

They said there was no task.

Where was I to go, then?

Home. To Accra.city. Not to my house. I was never to see my parents again.

I asked when I was to report to them.

They said they would let it be known.

I examined my beads, none of which were the ones implanted at birth. Since I had arrived at the icestation, no messages had played in my head. Would they start again?

What would I do?

You will integrate, they said.

I re-examined my beads.

What am I? I asked.

They smiled. You are Pempamsie, they said.

# CHAPTER THREE
## David

David decided to interview the fifteen males a second time. The female could wait until he had worked out what measures he could possibly take against a vodu-driven creature. Especially here, where vodus were not known at all – unlike in Westaf, where the effects of their psychic vampirism, at least, were known only too well: the fallers from the trees, their minds consumed.

There was a knock. A young female officer entered without waiting to be asked. Not flesh, but a relatively good simulation. More bio than electro in the mix. She looked from the interviewee to David, and back again.

"Can I help you?" David was annoyed by the entrance.

"Reporting for duty."

"And your flesh is?"

"You."

"Indeed." He could do with all the help he could get, even a dopey bodai. "And what do I call you?"

"Breakage."

"Breakage?"

The rarer nouns weren't all that uncommon as names, but this choice was particularly random. She didn't respond, not hearing the question mark. He changed his mind.

"I think I need to work with flesh on this case."

"Not available. Can be helped by Breakage."

"Sit." She pulled up a chair beside him, across from the interviewee. David motioned to her. "Go ahead."

Breakage faced the man from the Mekhanik Pustoshnyy. He was filthy and unkempt. She wouldn't be able to smell him like David could.

"What is your name?" she asked.

The man ignored her, looked at David and said, "I'm tired. I have been through an ordeal. Weeks at sea. I have rights."

"We don't know who you are," she said. "One or more ID crimes suspected. You cannot be processed until."

The man continued to look at David, waiting for her to finish her sentence, which she didn't.

"Until what? Go ahead and do whatever it is you've decided to do. Deport me. In the name of—"

"Where do you come from?" Breakage asked. She sat stock still, supposedly about twenty-five years old, neat in blouse and baggy trousers. David's beads told him she worked for the ID police like him; she would have the same circuitry to pick up his beads but had failed momentarily to tell whose emanations were whose between the two flesh when she entered, a common inability of the artificial.

"Look," he said to David, smiling defiantly. "I won't talk to your robots, to anyone who's not flesh. Can I rest now? Don't you have somewhere to take me where I can sleep? And shower?"

David said, "Give me something about her. I know a lot about her, including what she is capable of. I think you do too. But I need more. You need to give us a cause to keep her locked up. What if we were to let all of you go? What if she was loose, in a position to do to you what she has not done so far only because your mission is not complete?"

"Mission?"

"Yes. Don't try to tell me you don't have one. What did they do to you to get you on board? Were you press-ganged, or your family threatened, or both? Was it total loss of data? Was that what they said they would do to you or someone you love if you didn't go along with this charade?" David made as if to slit his own throat with his finger. Total loss of data: in network terms, the most serious ID crime of all. They used to call it murder.

"I know of no mission," the man said. "We were sailing the ship for pleasure. I do know that the pleasure is not over. Hers, that is."

"Oh? What do you mean?"

"Let us all go and you'll find out. I wouldn't frustrate her, if I were you. It's better to let her take her pleasure and leave. You won't regret it. Her leaving, I mean."

"I'll do what I fucking well please. You're all mine at this moment, and I intend to keep it that way until I find out what you're up to. Take him," David commanded Breakage. "But we're keeping them separated. And I'll get them all legal representation. Do you know anyone here in UK land?"

"No. Of course not. Not in this forsaken place." The smile disappeared, but not the defiance. This one was strong, David thought; he wasn't scared. The other males were afraid, were doing what they'd been told. By him, or Obayifa, or their masters?

"Breakage take?" The bodai had risen, expressionless, in her immaculate pink top and pinstriped trousers – in the bod that had been found for the AI expediently, transiently, optimally, according to the logistics of which bods, of which types, were needed where.

"Breakage take. And make sure they are all run by Parkin in ID Forensics. We need the details on their ID infringements."

33

David needed to have a look at the *Mekhanik Pustoshnyy* for himself. Lenczyk, the harbour cop who took David on board later that night, was the head of the boarding party who had arrested the crew.

"They were just standing there on the bridge," Lenczyk told him as they entered the spotlit hulk. "We've searched. No one else was on board. No cargo, either. They wouldn't speak to us but they gave themselves up calmly. They'd shut everything down, engines and comms. We couldn't ID them. The ship was hacked, so we didn't even know when they came on board.

"Fifteen men and one woman," he continued. "None in crew uniform, like they'd walked on board off the street, or from some office meeting more like. You couldn't tell them apart in terms of rank, nothing in the body language to suggest who was the leader. Proper bloody anarchists if you ask me, bloody throw-backs to just after the Disruption. Most likely Westafs, the lot of them, but since they didn't speak we couldn't be sure. We don't know what sophistication of ID infringement there's been, but it's major. We left that to you, the experts. I assume you're running them by forensics. And you might want to talk to Afripol."

Which David had once worked for. "And the ship?" he said.

"The ship came from nowhere. Supposedly scrapped in the twenties. It's ancient, late-twentieth-century construction. Look at the state of it. I'm amazed it's afloat. It's a big bastard. Where would you put it and have no one know about it all this time?

"Tell me about the female," said David.

"Well, what can I say... quite something, isn't she. Of course, we wondered at first whether they... whether the men had kidnapped her, used her – but it soon became clear she was wrapped up in it just like they were. Poker-faced like them, i.e., zilch for us to go on. Except... oh, never mind."

"Go on."

"No, it's nothing."

Breakage returned with Lenczyk's bodais.

"Sleeping quarters for ten, all used. Less than sixteen. Also blankets for one in cargo hold. No changes of clothes. No belonging items. In the galley, many opened cans."

"And they were sloppy buggers." One of the officers was flesh after all. "Not much in the way of washing-up."

David raised an eyebrow, but at the thought of his own desres, which he had stayed away from since two nights ago. He had been with one of the girls at the Royal, the hotel in what they used to call The Village. He'd allowed himself to go there, thought better of it as soon as she had come to the door, but then entered the room in a driven gloom of weakness, his vodu's weight in his mind. She was pretty, and solicitous. She'd let him stay afterwards, for a price he couldn't afford, but he couldn't go back to his desres and have to face himself alone, not that night. With her arms around him, they had slept awhile. With his vodu inside him, they had slept awhile. Before he had even closed the door, there was the rush of shame. And on the way back, a good self-beating in response, a promise to himself not to do it again. The clammy feeling on his skin, the thought of a hot shower, drove him quickly home. He made himself recall the girl's face on the way back: she was a person, however trammelled by sensa, and didn't deserve a life of being fucked by strangers. It would be easy to blame the vodu for his visits to the Royal: the vodu inside him, with its coal eyes. Well, it was true that without the vodu he would be back on the leafy streets of Westaf, with Yaa. And none of this would be happening. He could choose not to go whoring, he told himself. But he chose not to stop. His promises didn't work. He carried a monster, was a monster. Could not allow himself to feel.

He returned to the present moment. There, before him, was the bodai, waiting.

"Breakage, you're to organise a more thorough search. There must be clues somewhere on board. Some indication of what these people are doing here."

Lenczyk said, "What they were doing here on the ship, or what made them come to Avonmouth city?"

"We don't know whether they came here by accident," said David, "or if they have designs on something or someone here. I'm waiting for forensics to report, but so far there's nothing apparently unusual in their user journeys apart from the voyage, no sign of criminal activity." Apart from her, with no user journey at all, with her vampiric absence of reflection in the network. "Equally, nothing links them. What we did notice was that they didn't all go offline at the same time – maybe some were picked up along the way."

"You think they're just obeying orders?"

"Hard to say. If anyone's got a mind of her own, it's that female."

More than a mind, David thought, in the usual sense of a unitary consciousness. She was capable of extracting the minds from flesh, of that he was sure from his Accra.city days. He needed to find a way to neutralise her. But how? Even back there, in the land of electro-psychic sorcery, any reins upon her would be of dubious value.

"I know this is vague," said Lenczyk, "and I wasn't going to mention it. But there was something about her I couldn't quite put my finger on. I had the sense that she was trying not to draw our attention to something, something festering when they wanted everything to appear innocent. Like she'd just dumped a body overboard and she was specifically not looking where she'd pushed it over. Do you know what I mean?"

"But what could it have been?"

"I've no idea. I'm sorry, probably should have kept that to myself."

Above Avonmouth.city, the sky was white and low with heat. The wind turbines rolled around, only just. Everywhere, concrete, steel and tarmac exuded a dull skin prickle of thermal radiation; solar tiles did their best to absorb it. Of vegetation there was none.

David's inhabitance had sucked almost everything out of him. He was lost, belonged nowhere, to no one, to none of the flesh and bodais standing around him in the cafe where he had dragged himself, his face puffy from sleeplessness and his frame heavy and weary. He had left himself behind in Accra.city, with Yaa. He existed here and that was all, a ghost impelled to live amongst the denizens of the network intersection that was Avonmouth.city: the birthplace, his deceased mother had once told him, of the father he had never met.

He bought an espresso, sipped its frothed bitterness.

"So, what have you got for me?"

This morning his assistant was a young man. That is to say, Breakage was assigned to the bod of a young man. A substitution had been made in the night: either the network was replenishing his previous bod of a young woman or another AI had needed to utilise it.

The young man had been waiting outside David's desres, at the top of the concrete stairs. David knew it was his bodai assistant because of the scan he made with his beads and, to be sure in these early days of their association, the bodai's passphrase, which matched the words mellifluously delivered into David's earpiece: "I want to rain in the water."

David couldn't quite put his finger on why, but somehow the male embodiment suited the AI better. Breakage was a "he", whatever bod was assigned to him.

Breakage said, "We got them all up in the night."

"And?"

"Nothing new, except for one thing."

"Tell me about 'one thing'."

"The female wants to see you."

"Did she say what about?"

"No, but she said it was urgent."

Hence the desres had woken him from the final few dregs of sleep by letting in the light. The sheets were tangled around his sweaty body, the sun's white rays burning on him. He'd sat on the bed's edge, head in hands, staring first at his toenails, which needed a good trim, then the calamity of his piled possessions on the floor, things he'd purchased but without knowing why. And that was even without the urgings of telepathic commercials.

"I'll be along," he said. "What did Parkin in forensics say?"

"Female illegally nonned, category A. Others have fabricated IDs, category C. All is known. However, he requests to speak with you."

She was a category A* non, but that was deemed not to exist, would not be admitted. "No surprise there. But I'll see her first."


The A/C had broken again. Through a window opened just a notch, hot air blew into the interview cabin, carrying its molecules of evaporated Severn, distending the brown curtain with its draught.

The attraction was stronger. Lusting after suspects was part of the job for David, with the incontinent, ruinous libido that had risen inside him as a response to the vodu, but she had her volume cranked up to maximum. He let out a sigh, told himself to get a grip. His vodu, from its internment, watched in its constant silence. If the renegades had implanted it as a spy – always supposing it could communicate through his beads – there had been little in his routine policing life in Avonmouth.city for it to spy on. Until now. Did it, too, know what she was? Lying there poker-faced, he couldn't be absolutely sure whether it heard his thoughts or saw what he saw. Whether it only felt to him like it did.

The renegades must surely have meant the vodu's release from its cage to be triggered by something other than love, by some other phenomenon more in line with their fuckery. Whatever it was, their botched electro-psychic algorithms had conflated it with tenderness for someone physically present. For Yaa.

Sometimes he wished it would speak up. Speak its mind – no, speak itself, since it was a mind within his own mind. An aschizophrenic inhabitant. Aschizophrenic: that wasn't a word; it hadn't been needed before. His vodu was a silent implant, not a second voice, in the head of a flesh, formerly known as a human being.

David said, "Please, sit up straight. In your chair." She had arranged herself seductively, leaning, chin propped on forearm, eyes bright with mentalmagic, lips full with malevolence. In control. She didn't move.

"What do you want to tell me?"

She didn't respond.

"I have things to do and I'm not going to waste my time." He stood up as if to leave, paused, placed himself behind the chair, shifted it, its legs scraping on the floor. "Come on, tell me. I'm not about to play games with you."

She raised herself. My God, he thought. Maybe I should just find a pretext to free her, then deal with her in the way only I know how. Kill her, that is. Smash her brain to a pulp.

These Avonmouth.city cops knew nothing of vodus. He really didn't give a damn anymore. The vodu inside pulled itself around; he could feel a tiny twist.

"Sister," he said. "Let's not do this."

"Do what, Detective?" She pulled up her sleeves. Her veins were a river system of tumescence.

He took a sip of his cold coffee, its taste now cardboard.

"You told the bodai you had something to say to me. Well?"

Her face suddenly lost its sexy languor, and the veins grew a little more under the fine skin. The pressure inside her, he thought, the pressure inside her. A hunger, to feed on minds. He adjusted his shades.

"I'm going to count to ten, then I'm leaving." He made a point of yawning, feeling ridiculous as he did so. Then, embarrassing himself further: "You're making me want to do something exciting, like read you the officer's code." Elizabethan cop talk.

"I want to tell you about the ship, about why we were offline. We could go offline now, too. You and I."

"You're so online now, sister, as am I, at this moment."

Breakage entered, closed the door softly, stood by the table so that they faced one another. He was a child now, aged about ten.

"We won't be needing you, Breakage."

"But protocol—"

"We won't be needing you."

"Noted. Logged. Reported."

David smiled at the bodai, who looked uncannily embarrassed, and waved him out. Breakage clicked the door softly behind him.

"The truth is offline," she said. Her tongue came out a little too far between unnaturally incisive teeth, drew back and rested on her lip.

"You're not seriously going to try and convince me you're one of the rebels, are you?" he said. "Spare me, please. I may not know who you are, but I know what you are. "

"No, our truth. You and I. It's offline, isn't it?"

David, as an ID cop, had the authority to null his beads and hers temporarily, to take them both offline. He did so, pressing the swarm of them on his wrist. It would be noted. He would have to submit a report. It had better be good: the code was insistent that offline was merited only in rare, justified circumstances.

But he didn't give a damn, not a damn anymore. He'd had it. Once his daughter, his only love, was lost to him, there was no one to be faithful to, certainly not IANI and least of all himself.

He said, "When you say 'truth', according to which algorithm?"

"None," Obayifa said. "Semantic truth. Facts."

"And you'd like to lead me to this truth, no doubt. Alone, perhaps?"

"Yes."

He gave in to a reckless urge. "Then we'll go."

She stood in her orange jumpsuit, nearly as tall as him. He handcuffed her. She looked intently at him, standing a shackle away. They left to stares from his fellow officers. Breakage, the child, was waiting outside to report to him. With an exaggerated motion of his hand, David bade him to remain. They climbed into a module and sat in adjacent chairs.

"You're squatted," she said.

"I've no idea what you're talking about."

"Can I speak to it? It appears to be in some sort of confinement."

"Go ahead." David assumed she was like the vodu-inhabited he had come across in his last days in Accra.city: they were unable to enter or remove his mind, since he himself was squatted by a vodu. It appeared to be a universal rule: a vodu cannot or will not fuck with a vodu. Were he free, on the other hand, she would have a choice: either to extract his mind or to invade him, leaving one host for another.

She lifted his shades, stared directly into his eyes. "There's something wrong with you. What are you? Impure. Broken. You've been—"

"What have I been?"

She drew back into her chair. At least it was confirmed, so far at least, that she wasn't going to try and steal his mind; he was immune to her. Unlike the genpop of Avonmouth.city, to whom he owed a duty of protection. Duty? He was going through the motions. He no longer knew what the exercise of authentic humanity could mean. To work for the network was to maintain the fleshwork as walking autobiographies, emitting and consuming sensa.

He headed out along the coast, leaving Avonmouth.city to fall away behind them. David felt even more reckless. He did not know what he would do next, and it was exhilarating. She was exciting him, instilling a primitive and wild urge in his being without lifting a finger. He flew them through the above, like two ids in the collective unconscious.

"I'm not," she said, "whatever you assume I am. Not like the others of my kind. And not like you, in case you're wondering. They know about you, by the way. IANI knows. You think they don't, but they know. They'd never tell you, would they, they'd just observe. And now you've gone offline with me: it will just confirm it. You need me. Stop here."

"Obayifa, I'll stop if you tell me your mission. Otherwise you leave me no alternative."

"Than to crash the module? Kill us both? Do it, Detective."

"I mean it." He did. Oh, to die with someone who was his own kind, however repulsive he knew she was beneath the sexual magnetism – to put an end to his meaningless, Yaa-less life. He was no better than a bodai. In his vodu-ridden condition, exiled from his daughter, there was nothing left.

She gave him a long look. "Very well. Stop and you shall be told."

He landed on a patch of stubble between two lots.

"I've come for you," she said.

"No. I'm nobody."

"Release me. I'm here to take you back."

"You're lying."

"To your own kind. You'll be free. Free to be what you really are. To nourish and fulfil yourself. It's no different," she scoffed, "to the system you are part of now, which mentally rapes the genpop and convinces them it's what they want."

Obayifa put her hand on his arm. "Come. Only those who did this to you can release you."

David suddenly realised she wasn't talking to him. She was talking to the thing inside him. It was pulling on the bars that constrained it inside his mind, wrenching like a starving dog slavering for a bone.

A cold light came on in his head, a tube flickering into dismal illumination. What had he been thinking? He hadn't. He was altogether lost, his centre unheld. He turned the module back for Avonmouth.city.


"We have to let her go."

Avonmouth.city's ID police had no headquarters. The relevant ones – flesh and bodais – had been called to a hotnode on the thirteenth floor of a tower belonging, via a chain several levels deep of pyramid ownership, to one of the multinats. There was David, Parkin from ID Forensics, Breakage and the superior flesh who was addressing them, stiff in his drainpipe uniform, his collar pointing up into his crew-cut hair.

"But she's a non. They were all offline without permission. At the very least," said David, "she's one of a group of sixteen afloat in a vessel that surely had no permission to sail."

"And to whom did the vessel belong?" The superior's brows knitted in impatience.

"We don't know."

"So you don't know they didn't have permission to sail. That's your presumption."

"True, although I haven't searched Big Mind thoroughly yet. And certainly they were offline."

"Certainly? Certainly who was offline? You know as well as I do, Detective, that these are not always simple matters to establish. You checked the ship, correct?" The superior looked at Breakage, who was a child again, like one of the plastic characters who used to populate model railway sets.

"Comms were down," said Breakage in schoolboy tones. "Faulty. Or hacked."

"And when had they last been active?" The superior appeared to be going through the motions, thought David, wanted to be gone. Flesh could be so difficult.

"Too old to know, very old technology. All is known," said Breakage.

"They were knowingly disconnected from the network," said David. "Their beads would have warned them."

"Knowingly," said the officer. "But willingly?"

"We can't tell because they won't answer our questions. Which is suspicious, wouldn't you say?"

"Or indicative of fear, Detective."

"There's no fear in that female, with all due respect."

"Well, I have my instructions. No crime has been committed beyond doubt, and we are to let her go."

"You really want me to—"

"Yes, Detective, I do."

"Parkin," said David, "you found her to be a non, category A, correct?"

"Yes, although I couldn't positively say it wasn't a malfunction."

David looked in disbelief at Parkin, to the superior and back again, causing Breakage to do the same, clumsily.

"You're changing your story."

"Am I? I'm not aware that I have given you any contradictory advice on this matter, Detective."

"You told Breakage—"

"The bodai. Yes. Not you. A preliminary observation."

"I see." David looked at Breakage. "And the fifteen others?"

"We'll let them all go," said the superior. "Orders from the ID Prosecution Service. We'll have their IDs reset and hardened. Job done."

David had never encountered this superior before. He had the confident, suave look of one who really belonged, more net than flesh. David's vodu was eyeing the superior too. The man's bead reading was exemplary, no dross, no dirty bits, true Is and zeroes. The vodu never showed its thinking, but the time it spent regarding him was information in itself: evidence of his significance, in whatever universe of considerations it had. Breakage, meanwhile, bore a stupid look aimed firmly below what had passed over his AI's head, a look rendered more pathetic by his schoolboy embodiment.

"Breakage, come," said David. "I take it you won't be needing us further, sir?"

"Indeed, Detective. Thank you for your time."

This flux that was the network. It made your head swim sometimes. David was thankful suddenly for what little in the way of constancy there was in his life. Mr Charles, however awkward were his visits. Going back to the same desres, whatever he thought of it. Now it seemed like a sanctuary. Even the girls in the Royal: his addiction was at least a known.


David had Breakage organise the release of the men. But he interviewed Obayifa before he had her discharged. He motioned for her to sit across from him at the table.

"We're letting you go. You're free."

She stared back at him, amused. He'd brought Breakage in, who stood and stared straight above them.

"Oh, that's nice," Obayifa said with menace.

"But I'll be keeping an eye on you," he said. "I don't know what led you to sail that ship so recklessly, or why you landed here, but I'm pretty sure there is something here you came to find."

"I told you: it's what you've got in there that I came for." She tapped her temple.

David was acutely aware of what she might reveal about him. Thankfully there was no technology to resolve thoughts in the connected mind, but everything else was being logged. He pushed his shades up against the bridge of his nose. The cabin's A/C, which had stuttered into action, chilled the sweating nape of his neck. She had her hands below the table. His beads were picking her up now, but something was wrong. He couldn't put his finger on it. She was supposed to have been reset. There was a new ID, which should have been clean. Yet it didn't smell right, already. There was a perturbation of some kind, one he hadn't encountered before. A stench of rot. She brought her cuffed hands up and spread them flat on the table, her toned, dark arms stretching from the short sleeves of her orange inmate's uniform. She smiled with meaningless glee.

"Now if that is all, Officer, I believe I am to be discharged."

All attraction for her had gone cold. He saw her in that moment purely as a mind-sucking vampire: a creature who would evacuate and lick clean the minds of those she needed to feed upon.

"I expect to be hearing from you," David said. "Since it's me that you're after. But you don't frighten me. You know you can't get what you want." Vodu plus vodu equalled mutual annihilation.

"Can't I?"

"What do you mean?"

"Oh, only that it was surgery that implanted it. Surgery can remove it."

Maybe they could remove it. But at what price? "Tell them I'm not interested. There's no way in hell I'm going back to Westaf."

"Would that be because of a certain someone?"

A chill went down his spine. Was she bluffing? He had wiped all connections with Yaa, got her a new ID. "I don't acknowledge anything that you're saying. Log this," he said to Breakage. "I consider this detainee to be mentally disturbed, and dangerous. I am releasing her under protest."

"It'll be so nice to be free. I have things to do here in Avonmouth city. A little… sightseeing. But you're right. You will be hearing from me. I'll be sending you messages in a particular way."

"What is that supposed to mean?"

She stood up, held her cuffs out for unlocking.

"Uncuff her," David ordered Breakage. "I have a guard on the *Mekhanik Pustoshnyy*," he warned her. "I'm tracking you."

"How long can you keep that up, since your superiors have had you overruled?"

She walked up to him, examined his forehead.

"It must be so tiring, must take so much energy to constrain what should be free."

"I haven't said you can go."

She left. On a mission he could only guess at. One that IANI wanted her to fulfil. Or at least to observe her in the attempt.

# CHAPTER FOUR
# Pempamsie

Accra.city, 2086

"Pempamsie?"

There was a man beside me. Long, waking seconds elapsed until I recognised him from the night before. I returned my head to the pillow.

"Pempamsie? Hey, girl. How are you this a.m.?"

I slept with them from time to time, when the ache had grown so much. This man had no idea that I would go no further.

"You can leave now." I shoved him from the bed with my foot and turned over. He cursed and complained. I waited for him to finish.

Suddenly I was jolted. There was a sensation through my beads that I had never before experienced. Nothing to do with the man. From afar.

"I said you can leave now."

I would not show him my discomfort. Pempamsie is patient. After he had left I rose and opened the blinds to look out the window. The bolt of sunlight made me squint. I felt its burn on my skin. For a moment, I relived the pleasant temperatures inside the icestation.

Then the hand opened. A key lay there. I memorised it.

I, Pempamsie, had been living quietly and carefully. Akoko nan tiabe na enkum ba: a hen treads upon chickens but does not kill them.

Then the new sensation reasserted itself.

It existed both where the bead terminals buried into my wrist and inside my mind. Like a hand. A touch at one moment, then a grip the next. Physical and mental. Located, and not.

It was them. They were reaching me from the icestation.

The key opened the message via an old robotic toy I kept in my flat. The little robot signalled to me, ultimately an analogue signal borne on a digital and mental carrier, digitally perturbed psychblood. I, Pempamsie, at last understood my mission.

I was there to silence those in the Westaf fleshwork who would overturn the glorious user journeys, the striving for conversion that the network fosters. Sepow: the knife thrust through the cheeks of a man about to be executed, to prevent his invoking a curse on the king.

I, Pempamsie, was the knife. And Pempamsie now knew whose curse she must quash.

I, Pempamsie, was free only to the extent that I must obey them. If I defied them, they would terminate me. Pempamsie does not fear death. But my body would be brought, mutilated, to my parents' home. I could not allow that to happen.

My beads had become quiet again. All of us in the Between – even in relatively clement Westaf, and I, too, though I was the agent of IANI – were slaves. Epa: handcuffs. You are the slave of him whose handcuffs you wear.


I had heard Ako-ben, war horn. The call to arms or duty. I received instructions in relation to officers of Westaf's Agency for Technological Interventions. I was to disable them: to visit their houses of hackery, Mframa-dans – built to withstand treacherous conditions. Always they worked alone in these isolated nodes, subverting the algorithms of IANI. Pempamsie was to break in, destroy their equipment and take them to a rendezvous where they would be transported, ultimately to the icestation.

One by one, Westaf's technological capability was to evanesce. That was IANI's plan, and I, Pempamsie, was there to implement it. The firewalling of Westaf from Big Mind was to be undone.

The first two times, all went as I was told to expect. I took them to the hills outside Accra.city. They were drugged through a psychblood cocktail, no ordinary electro-chemical mix but an active compound that turns the brain a uniform yellow under a neuro-imager.

But that was only the first two. The third time, I hacked the target's door, crept inside, approached from behind as he sat at his machine and worked on somebody's beads – or was it their profile in Big Mind? – from far away. I, Pempamsie, was masked and nonned to all but IANI.

But then, as if in mid-step, the course of my memory became blank. Until I saw him afterwards. He lay back slumped in his chair, his machine fallen and smashed. And I, Pempamsie, was holding the knife. Blood. A pulsing stream from his throat. The knife, in my hand, slick and warm with it.

The next time was similar except that a gun was used. Blood. It poured from his chest. The gun. In my hand. Smoking.

Neither time had I taken a weapon, of course. Both times I was alone at the scene with the victim. I strained a thousand times to remember who had given each weapon to me. Or had I found them there?

And had I in fact sliced with the knife, pulled the trigger? Or were they placed in my hand afterwards?

Despite their edicts, despite all I was taught, they did not mean mere silence or reform, but death. IANI was supposed to be above murder: there is a self-imposed decree against total loss of data.

I tried not to think what IANI had done in the icestation to those first two, the live victims. But these others: had I been intoxicated, like the alleged killers of King Duncan, and some Macbeth the actual perpetrator? Or was I remote-controlled to find the weapon, in each case hidden in the hacking house, and to use it against the targets, who kept it for defence?

How could IANI control Pempamsie's mind thus?

Pagye: striking fire with a flint: war.

And I, Pempamsie, an instrument of their war.

The little robot signalled to me again. This time it held an ink pen and wrote, like a character from another age. Once it had finished its script, it lay down the pen and folded its arms. It was no bigger than the sheet of paper.

I left my flat.

But this time, this time I stopped dead in the street. Pempamsie did not move for a long time.

Sankofa: turn back and fetch it. You can always undo your mistakes.

Fofoo: a small yellow flower which later turns into a spiky black seed.

I, Pempamsie, was fofoo.

The morning sky burned like a wound. A bank of cloud, like a vaporous bandage, half covered it. Pempamsie stared up, ignored the flowing of ones and tro-tros all around her.

It had to end. There and then. The silencing.

Pempamsie could hide in the physical world. But how to hide in the network? The longer she was live in the network, the more certain it was that she would end up dead herself.

Pempamsie disconnected herself: an act sometimes permitted to agents but which was allowed to last for but a limited time. I turned to take a tro-tro to the Dame-Dame Towers.

# CHAPTER FIVE
## David

The N-car swayed slightly as it climbed through the near-above. David grasped the rails that hung from the ceiling as he walked along the carriages. Now that Obayifa and the rest of the crew had been taken from his remit, he was back to mundane policing. This meant passing among the genpop, who only ever congregated at work and in the transit systems. The genpop used filters to enhance what they telepathically transmitted about themselves, and they fabbed their profiles. There was a huge market for legitimate filters and fabs, but Westaf made its money trading in hacked and stolen ones. As far as IANI was concerned, the genpop could augment themselves and lie to one another with their sensa and profiles as much as they liked, but its imperative was to ensure that this did not stray into the territory of broken IDs: of misidentification with respect to the network itself. IANI fought a constant cyberwar with both the government and renegades of Westaf to maintain the network's integrity. David's duty was to ensure the uninterrupted flow of IANI's sensa into the minds of the fleshwork, to safeguard its telepathic feels of their mental metadata.

Algorithms constantly crawled the intersections of flesh user journeys, looking for ID crime: illicit or stolen sensa filters and IDs, and far more serious attempts to disconnect altogether. David's role as an ID policeman was to spot what algorithms were blind to, by feeling with his beads and watching the body language. As in the case of the young man his eyes alighted upon, who was looking shifty. Without a word – he was still angry and frustrated about being overruled – David seized the youth's wrist, examining his beads. They swam and reconfigured there, suspended on a band bedded into the flesh, the boy's veins running like rivers beneath.

Prompted algorithmically by David's interest in the boy, another young man approached, dressed flamboyantly, a cravat plump at his shirt's wide collar. It was Breakage.

David looked unflinchingly into the fleshren boy's eyes while addressing the assistant bodai.

"Battery charged?"

"Check."

"Psychblood levels?"

"Adequate."

"System integrity?"

"Fail."

David shook his head.

"He's in breach of which ID statute?"

"Theft, fabrication."

The boy, in his late teens, gave David a defiant look. David could feel the animosity through his beads. He sighed within. Once teenagers really had been rebellious. David almost felt contempt for the superficiality to which the genpop tended, stupefied by the sensa playing in the corners of their minds. A trace of sympathy touched David at the same time, nonetheless. This boy would have experienced sensa since he was a toddler, when the first beads were implanted around his left wrist. There was no way for him to disconnect.

"Whose ID did he try to steal?" It was theatre. David could feel the answers to his questions through his beads.

"Acquaintance," said the bodai. "Terry Van Damme. All is known."

"All is known," David repeated to the boy, staring deeper into him. "Terry has some good gear, does he?" He glanced at Breakage. "And the fab? Attempted fab, that is."

The bodai called up a user profile, manipulated to enhance the sensa the boy had sent to his friends – without payment.

"What would IANI say?"

Going back to being the ID cop had acted as a distraction from his troubles, but David now felt distaste, the words sticking in his mouth. Had he really been reduced to threatening youths guilty of ID misdemeanours? The kid looked scared now.

David thought back to the beginning, about his friend Mikey and the sensa they exchanged when the facility for inter-personal telepathy first appeared. You could choose from a library of smells, tastes, feelings, ironies, amusements, or capture whatever you were seeing, feeling or thinking as if with a mental camera, and send it to another person. It appeared in their minds, wrapped like a package they could decide whether to open, in a blurred representation of the contents. But first the recipient had to decide to friend you telepathically, an act of connection so intimate that its initiations and withdrawals brought about a massive disruption in human relations – a whole new class of negotiations, of delicacies, of deliciousness, of hurts. David fell out with Mikey when he telepathically unfriended him. They didn't speak to one another for several weeks.

David released the youth's wrist. This boy could make out nothing about him. Like every ID cop, David was officially nonned to civilian flesh, in order to perform his duties. It was how the boy knew him for what he was: a blank over the network, apart from his badge number. But physically present.

"Deal with him," he instructed Breakage, and walked further along.

In the next carriage he paused beside a group of strap-hangers to watch a purchase. One of the N-car bodais had approached a smart man in his fifties, to fulfil an impulse following pleasurable suggestions in his sensa. David could feel these facts through his beads in an undercurrent of data. In physical space, the fleshren who had sat rocking beside the purchaser got up to make way. The bodai opened its jaw. Through his beads, the man transferred bytecoins, which he earned as a sensa editor in an officenode. The bodai shut its jaw as soon as the payment was made, and squeezed his arm gently. It handed him a quaint printed receipt for what David could tell in metadata was a cologne to be delivered to his desres, and said, "All is known."

David had watched many such transactions before, but this one only increased the distaste he was feeling more and more for his working existence. The network had impregnated the man's mind, and the bodai was sent to make the sale. In principle the bodai was there to provide information about the product and a notionally personal service. In fact, it was an intimidating agent, an obtuse presence that would prove difficult to send away in a public setting.

David missed his job and his colleagues in Westaf. He thought of his life as a beat policeman there, before his promotion to detective, working against the renegades. How much happier he had been before the vodu had changed everything. He cast his mind back to patrolling the fronded byways, beneath the wawa trees, where disconnection from the network was routine and humans locked eyes. The Westaf government, whatever he thought about its monolithic rule, at least allowed the people the dignity of their fleshly selves. It left the population to use sensa in the collective consciousness as it saw fit, even though he had hated Yaa's acceptance of it. And most importantly the government kept IANI away.

Here IANI's propaganda was everywhere. Sensa were charming and opportune, the mantra went. Psychblood had been a marvellous invention. Only the dems went without psychblood's benefits; there was nothing to be done for them. One could always take oneself off for the Beautiful Alone, for a break from the telepathic connection. If one really wanted. During regulated times. They were sure to miss the sensa from the network after a little while, to want to be connected again.

David had no need for the Beautiful Alone. It was a sop to those without his official advantage: being able to keep the stream turned off.

Obayifa's arrival had brought David's discontent with the status quo into new focus. He had been so caught up in his own lostness that he had tried not to notice that everyone else was too. The flesh he policed had been subjugated. Psychblood was a drug. Sensa entailed cognitive impairment – when the network desired it. How could one function while the sensa played, no matter how muted or peripherally placed in the mind? The stream of sensa displaced artistry and radicalism such as could still be found in Westaf. How could you know and realise your own human nature when the stream trammelled you?

After the sale had taken place, David watched a seedy character occupy the seat next to the purchaser and engage him in conversation. Something wasn't right. Mr Seedy was obviously bothering him. David felt him through his beads. He was fabbed to high heaven. His ID was impure, its Is and zeroes tainted. There was something brash about the fabbing. What was he? Maybe a creation of Westaf's Agency for Technological Interventions, to stoke demand for the hacks they sold in the Between.

David walked over as the N-car came to a stop. Mr Seedy spotted him and dashed onto the platform. David thought about following, but he had no further stomach for it after cautioning the young man in the previous carriage. He decided not to act – not even to call it in. The man soon disappeared, shouldering his way through the crowd towards the nexus of pathways.

Breakage appeared stiffly, sporting his cravat.

"Problem in the carie. All is known."

"Breakage. Why are you even here? The case was closed. You're no longer assigned."

"Breakage remember from detective profile. Remember detective personal connection."

"Personal connection? What are you talking about?"

"Mr Charles. Total loss of data. All is known."

"Mr Charles? But he's had his beads deactivated anyway. So what data? What do you mean?"

"Total loss. All is known."


The beginning of thunder-rain: the drops sparse & heavy, splatting into the greenery and ringing on stone.

Mr Charles had been in immense pain – those idiots could never plan his medication right – but certainly had not been ready to die. And here was his body, entering the earth. David was glad the old man was back in Bristol.city now, Arnos Vale. Free at last of the carie in Avonmouth.city, where some clueless bodai or, worse, careless flesh had had him ensconced. His friend's mind had been sharp and gentle at the same time: kind but no fool. Uncomplaining.

David guessed it was loneliness that killed him, even though the medical certificate said heart failure. For Mr Charles had no other visitors. Mostly when David went to see him, Mr Charles would be next to the white woman he jokingly referred to in her absence as his mother. He would always speak gently to her, despite the curses she spat at him. Her personality was melted by dementia; she was sometimes confused, babbling. At other times, like a lamb, occasionally exclaiming about a memory that had returned from an indeterminate point in her past.

David had observed Mr Charles' aloneness keenly. Exiled from Yaa, his only family, he wondered whether he too was headed for continuing isolation, or the frenzied, cold encounters that the vodu had in store for him if it got its way. The strain of hardening his heart, so that it couldn't, had told on him. The thought of dementia cast a gloom: that he himself might be headed that way before long, at forty-seven. Or, like Mr Charles, he might remain mentally intact for some time but surrounded by dems when he retired, struggling to maintain his sanity.

The rain was soaking through his suit. His shades were doubly out of place in the clouded darkness, where death demanded disclosure. David wondered who the other mourners were, given that Mr Charles had told him everyone he knew had passed away. There were just a few of them, standing around the grave but apart – strangers to one another. All flesh: no bodai would ever appear at a funeral. And among them was the carie nurse: the probable ID felon who Mr Charles had said was kind to him.

David approached to take a better look at her. Once again, her resemblance to his daughter struck him, tenderly; he wondered what Yaa was doing at that moment.

He was pretty sure the nurse was an illegal, but he decided to let it go – in Mr Charles' memory, since the old man was fond of her, but equally, he realised, for his own sake. In Westaf he'd have turned a blind eye, seeing that she did no real harm. That was who he used to be.

She raised her head and their eyes met for a second before she looked back at the lowering coffin. When he first saw her it had occurred to him that she might have been inhabited, such was the furtive, clever look in her eyes. But no, it wasn't mentalmagic. When she had rolled up her sleeves to help an old man in pyjamas from a winged armchair, the veins had lain flat beneath the flesh of her forearms.

She had seemed caught up in her task, but David could tell she was sensitive to his presence. She had the network to contend with, for sure. If you were genpop, the network was processing you, running in and out of your beads, storing you in Big Mind and analysing your user journey. A fugitive like her would just have to hope she remained below the statistical threshold for attention from the ID cops. Her covert vigilance was the animal instinct of flesh. She would be looking out not only for ID cops but for whoever else might hold something against her: hiding from everyone, all flesh, however close – although David suspected there would be no one close. You had to be good to get away with it, to live with a criminally fabbed ID. You could never take anyone around you for granted. Yes, the bodais were mostly clueless, and the genpop so preoccupied in sending sensa to one another, half the time they were generally too incurious to be a danger. But there was always the prospect of someone you hadn't spotted, someone for whom you were not too small a fish.

When the ceremony ended, David moved towards the nurse to accompany her, but she pulled up her collar and headed down a puddled path through the trees. As he walked around the grave her pace quickened. He called to her, but she left him behind and he stopped, the cold rain continuing to pour through the warm air.


The twilight soon fell after Mr Charles' funeral, and the near-above was filled with a swarm of vehicle lights like gnats around the nodes as David entered its sprawl. Riding above the Parkway in an N-car from Bristol.city to Avonmouth.city, David's thoughts returned, with a mixture of fascination and revulsion, to Obayifa. She was the only one aboard the *Mekhanik Pustoshnyy* of any real interest, that much he had surmised. Not that the others were to be taken altogether for granted, given their notably independent accounts of the voyage together.

Why had they ordered him to let them all go? And who, exactly, were "they"? The chief, who had definitely carried the requisite authority, whoever he was, had said the ID Prosecution Service had ordered it. But there was no such thing as a unitary authority. Everything in the network – and in the terrestrial material world – everything below IANI was owned and operated by a collection of multinats. Nothing, in fact, was unitary: even IANI, the supreme issuer of multinat licences, was fissioned between the poles, straddling the Between and in complete control everywhere except Westaf.

The chief and the rest of David's ID department were just obeying orders, he was pretty sure. They didn't even know what they were doing. With no idea of what David knew – that she was a vodu-inhabited creature, a feeder upon minds – they had forced him to let her loose. Who else would recognise her for what she was, apart from someone like him who was vodu-inhabited? To be fair to them, all the flesh who had come into contact with her had mentioned there was something nefarious about her, even if they couldn't put a finger on it. Like David, they weren't sure her mission was in common with the rest of the sixteen. The fifteen males – also free now – were highly suspect, but David's instinct told him they were just doing what they'd been told to do. And they were not the thing she was. She had her own agenda. Any vodu had. To persist, a vampire consuming conscious energy, leaving a trail of devastation behind her. A victim of vodu inhabitance himself, he had no idea what he could do to limit her.

And what else did she have in mind, so to speak?

A strap-hanger was looking fixedly at David. She made her way over to him, edging past fellow travellers.

"I'm to come back with you," she said into his ear.

David didn't answer. He looked out of the window as they left Bristol.city behind. Eclipsed by Avonmouth.city as a side effect of the Disruption, Bristol.city lay drab and dilapidated, unrecognisable from its days as a centre of creativity and technology early in the century. Now it was little more than a collection of cemeteries. They left the uninhabited suburbs, soaring above the fleeting landscape. The Avon, with its crinkly mud walls at low tide, snaked back to the Severn Estuary beside them.

She put her arm through his. He removed it. She smiled. David wondered who was making the call. It would be to do with the case. Unusual interest, it meant. In Obayifa.

They left the N-car and walked to his desres, the quarters of a chief detective in the department of ID crime. Not much, but a place to doss when exhausted by his job, his vodu and his addiction. His clothes were strewn and washing-up was piled in and around the sink. He wondered how he lived like this. It wasn't always so. He was too fucked up, he reflected, to keep himself together enough to buy washing-up liquid.

She sat on the crumpled bed, hands on knees, looking at him in that uncanny way that some bodais had, ones like her built for intimacy. She was attractive, and David felt himself stirring. Then he thought of Obayifa, ready to suck the consciousness out of anyone in her path. Then he thought of the prostitutes he used, then the carie nurse, then Yaa, then his vodu, like a flick through a deck of Tarot cards. The stirring stopped.

She said, "David, we're worried."

There was no way of knowing precisely who "we" were. But he guessed it was IANI. Why would they contact him, a lowly ID cop?

"You need to get to the bottom of this," she continued, "and soon. What do you think so far?"

David's desres told him the clearance level of any bodai or flesh within it, through sound. He was supposed to trust her, the way the desres had almost silently purred when she entered. But that didn't mean he knew where the words originated from, only that he was allowed to reply. He recalled the screech from the desres when he had let in a sex worker the previous week. It had almost put him off.

She said, "What do you think? You know as well as I do that sixteen flesh had been intentionally offline for some weeks at least. One of them class-A nonned. And now they are all at liberty."

"But I was told to let them go! Why didn't you stop the prosecution service from making their determination?" Could a multinat be exceeding its privileges, going against IANI? In a world mostly operated by AIs, a cock-up was quite possible. But he sensed the decision had been purposeful.

She rose and stood close to him. Her breath would have been on his face if she were flesh.

"That wasn't us." She smiled. Suddenly David realised she was an agent of Westaf, despite everything his beads told him. His mind flashed back to the officials he had worked closely with in Accra.city. Good people he hadn't wanted to leave without saying goodbye to, but he didn't want even them to know his destination, in case they tried to persuade him back. He had obfuscated his trail to Avonmouth.city in every way he knew, and crafted a new ID. Given their abilities, it was no great surprise that they had seen through his ploys.

"And the female, David. What about the female?" Of course, Obayifa was their real interest. A vodu whose presence was no doubt connected to one of their renegades.

"Obayifa? Oh, she's maybe cleverer than the men. Look, what do you want me to do?"

"We want you to continue pursuing this case, by all means necessary."

He was hard again. She saw, and lay on the bed.

David raised himself from his pillow. The messenger had left. A clinging, sweaty sheet was swathed around him as always, no matter how much he needed a peaceful sleep, what candles he lit or other measures he took to achieve rest. The desres was making tiny animal sounds of concern, an expression at odds with the scene around him of clothes discarded on the floor and draped over the furniture, of smeared crockery on whatever surface had been at hand and half-unpacked boxes of belongings – he could barely remember what remained in them – left in corners. Memories of Elizabethan detective stories flooded his mind, books he'd enjoyed back in Accra.city before his inhabitance. The PIs always lived in a state of some dishevelment, lived broken lives. He was carrying the torch for them, but if only they could see what had become of their world.

There was a faint knocking at his front door. Nobody knocked at a front door. From his early youth, lost words came to him, suddenly remembered: *neighbour, neighbourhood*. Once, neighbours might have knocked. Nowadays, there were flesh who lived in adjacent desreses as a matter of physical fact, but the concept of neighbourliness – linked to nearness, distance – was irrelevant to those who were either telepathically linked or absolute strangers. Neither were there neighbourhoods as such in Avonmouth.city. The city's regions were but topological contingencies of the built environment, without individual character. And yet flesh sometimes referred to parts of the down-below with the names of streets as used to be: Merebank, Kings Weston, Ironchurch.

His head ached as though he'd been drinking heavily the night before. But he hadn't. It was simply the damage from an endless cycling of the same thoughts, clattering like bricks in a washing machine. And the vodu – his vodu – looking on from its mental enclosure, learning about him.

The desres raised the lights softly as he got up into the darkness of what he now saw was five a.m., written in green script on the wall.

"Shut up," he said. Its mewling ceased. The knocks were now accompanied by a voice.

"A little boy's told me! He's told me. The little boy!" It was a middle-aged man's voice. The projection David switched on confirmed it. Late middle age in a smart maroon dressing gown over pyjamas patterned with small grey diamonds. Bare feet. Bare chest. His hair ruffled, by sleep perhaps. He was flabby. Childish terror contorted his face. But there was something familiar about him. Then David realised he had been at the funeral.

David couldn't remember when he'd last had a visitor at his door. Not flesh, anyway. The screen and the intercom system were only for a security situation like this. Ones joining you by agreement would be let in by dint of bead protocols. Otherwise, some solecism or act of criminal intent was in progress.

"Hello?" David said through the intercom. "I don't know what you're really saying but I do know you've got the wrong place. If you're locked out, call the network. It will sort you out."

The man knocked harder.

"Château-d'Oex," he said. "Château-d'Oex!" He was smiling now. "I'm going skiing in Château-d'Oex!"

The man's helpless state made David think of his father, whoever he had been; a question crossed his mind fleetingly about how his father had ended his days.

Except that this visitor might not have been helpless, of course. An ID cop had plenty of enemies. The man was looking upwards, hands shoved into the pockets of his dressing gown. What did he have in there?

"Desres? What is happening?" The mewling began again. The man must have come from the carie. Or had escaped at the funeral after David had left. David looked beyond him as though searching for the path he had taken in the horizontal and vertical expanse of Avonmouth.city, visible at this hour only as points of light, surfaces falling into the distance.

The man's eyes suddenly turned to the side, then back to the door.

David opened the door.

The mewling of the desres became a loud whistle of alarm. David overrode it with a gesture. The desres switched on the morning news and further lights shone up the walls from recesses.

The man at once put on a sickly smile.

"Bastard!" he said. "Fucking cunting bastard!"

David stepped out towards him, careful to check to the side as he did so. The desres registered only one presence outside, but the man had looked at something and you couldn't be sure.

The concrete immediately sent coldness up through his bare feet. Avonmouth.city rumbled and whirred softly in the dawn, its nodes busy in the network, unfortunate flesh up all night attending to it. Even at this early hour, the air was tepid.

Two flesh in dressing gowns facing one another, bleary.

"Get away, you cunt! Stay away, bastard!"

This was a man, David told himself. Flesh like him. He had heard many times in the carie, when visiting Mr Charles, the rapid transition from childishness to curses. Dems could hit too, hard. The man's hands were still thrust into his pockets.

David said, "I'll get someone to help you. You don't need to worry. Breakage," he continued through the desres. "Breakage, come."

The desres turned down the news so that Breakage could answer him, an unfamiliar voice. "Five minutes."

"Wait out here," David said, and turned to go back inside. He didn't know why, but he'd needed to see him in the flesh, in the open air; had felt a basic urge to go back offline. Not that either of them was offline; their beads would report the encounter. Seeing the actual, unpixellated texture of the man's puffy skin, feeling the very faint heat of his body close by – nothing could reproduce that.

"David," the man said.

"What did you say?" The cold seeped deeper into David's feet, numbing the bones. Mr Charles must have told him his name.

"David." The man seemed to be preparing himself to say something further, his jaw tightening and opening, chewing air slightly. Behind him, Avonmouth.city was starting to crystallise with the dawn, new thwacks and electric engine sounds starting up somewhere nearby, carried in the ever-bath-time air, a billion coils turning on axes through magnetic fields.

Just then Breakage appeared at the top of the stairs, a beefy middle-aged man. He came and stopped just behind the visitor at David's door, who was looking ever more the product of an unhealthy life, decades of the wrong food and lack of exercise, of toil in the fleshwork for the network. And all for what? To blather in front of a stranger's door, his mind dissolved in psychblood.

Except that he knew David's name.

"David a good boy," he said, looking down at Breakage's hand on his arm. "David will want to see juju."

"What is juju?" David said.

"Good boy," the man said. "Cunt. Good cunt. Fucker."


Seven a.m. David made enquiries of the carie and waited outside for her to finish the night shift. The carie was a forlorn, single-story node surrounded by warespaces in the down-below. Birds sat in the few scrappy trees around it, not singing. Forests covered vast swathes of UK.land, but in cities the trees were few and far between. The only sound was the whine and sweep of N-cars and modules in the near-above, their tones changing as they climbed or descended between nodes. Everything was squeaky clean, scoured overnight by an army of bodais. What appeared to be public streets were owned by multinats. It had rained heavily in the night. Puddles of pseudo-tropical rain evaporated from the immaculate pavements in the morning's white glare. David was starting to sweat in his suit.

When she left the building she saw him without seeming to. An expert, he thought, as he strode to intercept her.

"Hello," he said. He had researched her easily despite her fabbed ID. Mary was the best he could arrive at by way of a genuine name. David looked at her, serious Mary in her blue uniform, her crisp ironed blouse, her hair in a bun beneath a tam-o'-shanter. Schooled in Nairobi.city, holding a PhD in he couldn't remember what, working in a carie, a home for those in their forties and above with dementia. Like many others with or without a doctorate, she performed duties that no bodai was capable of and no one else in the fleshwork would do. Her willingness to do the work was deemed to outweigh her transgressions.

She finally looked at him. "I'm just having to rush somewhere, if you don't mind."

"I do mind," he said.

"Oh, I'm sorry to hear that, but I really must dash. Nice to meet you."

"Wait—"

"I've heard it. What you're about to say. Not interested. Now, I'm tired. It's been a long night."

"I wanted to talk to you about Mr Charles."

"We're not allowed to talk about the residents. Unless you're a relative."

"I'm not."

"No, of course you're not. In that case I can't help you."

"Look, it's not a professional matter."

"What isn't?"

"My talking to you."

"You're talking to me unprofessionally?" She walked on. He was going to let it go, but he followed swiftly and walked beside her, the only two around.

"How did he die?"

She stopped. "If I tell you about it, will you leave me alone?"

"Sure."

"We don't know."

"He was buried. There must have been a cause of death."

"There was, only it wasn't what they recorded."

"Then who certified it?"

"You'd better ask the network."

"And what makes you say they lied?"

"I didn't say that."

"But he died in the carie, right?"

"Someone did."

"What on earth do you mean? It might not have been him?"

"He had a visitor. Who took him out for the afternoon. Afterwards it wasn't Mr Charles anymore. As though everything had been sucked out of him. They found him dead on the ground next to a dresser in his quarters. He appeared to have fallen off."

"Mr Charles? In all that pain? How could he have climbed onto a dresser? Look. If this is some kind of joke then you'd better stop. You know what I am."

"Yes, Mr ID Policeman. I know what you are, all right. Sorry if I'm confusing you. Sir. But you asked me. Sir. And I'm telling you."

"I don't want to take you in for questioning, but I will if I have to. Be more specific."

"He was all sweaty. I don't know where he'd been taken but he had been through exertions. I washed and redressed him. His skin was strange, pale like porcelain. He wouldn't speak. Didn't blink – his eyes were wide open."

"You make him sound like a doll."

"Yes. That's what he was like. I don't think he saw or recognised me. When I took him to his room the only thing he seemed interested in was climbing."

"Climbing?" David pretended not to recognise what had become a familiar story in his last Accra.city days.

"On the bed. He tried to stand on it. Then he eyed the taller furniture in the room. I never thought he'd—I never imagined he'd have the strength to climb anything higher. You know what pain he was in, despite the medication. It was the end of my shift. I had to go.

No choice but to leave him. One of the others brought him tea later and found him."

"The visitor. What do you know about him?"

"Her, not him. I'd never seen her before. The profile said she was his niece but—"

"You didn't believe her. Why?"

"Instinct."

Mr Charles had no relatives. And he was the kindest man he had ever met. There was no one who could possibly want to harm him for any straightforward motive. It must be her, Obayifa, the thing from the *Mekhanik Pustoshnyy*. David resolved not to report what the nurse was telling him. He would investigate the death himself.

"Go on," he said.

"Well, Mr ID Policeman, it's what she said, okay, that she was his niece and that's what the carie said she was. She took him out for lunch – that was what she told us. I wasn't comfortable with it, but what could I do? When she brought him back it was obvious something was wrong, so I asked her what had happened. She just shrugged, waved at him, one of those tiny waves like to a child."

It was a message. For him, David.

"The carie read her beads and said she was his niece when she couldn't have been."

"Yes, I told you. The carie's been acting up. I've reported it. You can look in the logs. No one listens to me."

"She's beyond the powers of any carie. Don't worry. You won't get into trouble for this. I'm sorry."

"Sorry for what? Can I go now, Mr ID Policeman?"

David didn't want her to leave. He tried to keep her straight in his mind, distinct from Yaa. The physical resemblance wasn't strong but was close enough. It was how Yaa talked to him when she was feeling bolder. Yaa also thought he was being interfering, wanted him not to be so close. And now he was far.

Loneliness hit hard. Yaa was lost to him; Mr Charles gone. And this young woman was departing. Mr Charles had meant something to her; it made him want to spend time with her even more.

But she couldn't wait to get away from him. And he could find no words of his own to persuade her to stay, only the commands of an Avonmouth.city ID cop that he couldn't bear to pass through his lips.

He stopped and watched Mary go. Through his beads he scanned the carie records and saw Obayifa dropping off Mr Charles.

Why had she done this? To get his attention. Well, she had it, all right. Now it was personal.

# CHAPTER SIX
## Pempamsie

Cocooned in a glass elevator, I ascended the thirty-seven floors of Dame-Dame Towers with the group of men who had met me, pushing up its outside flank into the white sky. They had Ohen Tuo symbols stitched into the lapels of their baggy black suits, the skyward guns of the king, and flaunted the Chanel beads – as if! – living on their wrists. There were four of them, four pairs of eyes turned who knew where behind shades. I didn't know anything about them, really, beyond the little Kwame had said, or rather implied – and I wondered for a second if these men weren't going to non me, which was the idea; I wondered if they were going to try to assault or even rape me. I readied myself in defence. These were renegades from the government of Westaf, after all, and their beneficence to the people was lacking, to put it mildly.

There was no turning back, so I did my best to put the thought aside and not let it disturb my composure.

The lift doors swished to let us into impossibly ice-cool air beneath sheets of glass, the sun hammering photons down on an open floor of low couches and tables, empty except for a waiter leaning against a bar. Then, after I'd concluded his was the only presence, there was a figure who must have risen from one of the plush settees.

As we walked towards him in the wide space, I noticed signs of hackery – tiles and hatches moved aside or opened, the original devices removed or replaced with others patched in. The man had been basking in the sun's rays, but the skylight filters turned on, dimming the scene slowly as we entered; my eyes, which had been screwed up against the white intensity, gradually relaxed.

The waiter came to take our order. I became calmed, the rape threat evanescing as I sensed the authentic Nsaa nature of the scene, its excellence.

"Respect," I said to the man, who was emblazoned in a scripted suit of swirling shapes. "I, Pempamsie, would be a non." I stretched out my right arm. We touched beads. They swam and mutually configured, wrist to wrist.

I couldn't help thinking about what he was equipped with, all wrapped up in that suit. The shifting patterns, like clouds in a sky, accentuated his muscular frame, crawling over the big shoulders, drifting down towards his groin and veering away. If these Ohen Tuos weren't around, why I'd...

"You waan me fi non you, sistah?" A boomerang: his ancestors sold from Westaf to Carib, and now he had come back to the homeland. He sounded almost jolly but didn't smile. "Dassa whole heap a credits, y'know." The Ohen Tuos stood behind me in an arc. "Show me da bead ting again," he said.

He held me by the tips of my fingers and turned my wrist around, examining my configuration closely.

"You can replace them, correct?" I said.

He made a clicking sound of contempt.

"Surgery. Electrobihalogical. Me can do it yes but it nah perfek. Seen? A wha ya tek me for, now? Anyway, what da sistah need nonning for? A wha she do?"

"You don't get to ask me that question. You were saying, about the surgery?"

"Tek more dan dat. Depen' who she a non to, y'understan'? Wid de surgery, she be a non to a likkle donkey. But not to multinats wid a special interest in her, ya see? Not ta mention IANI. Dem have fi dem algorithms, we have fi we algorithms, we mix dem up. But only so far if ya just change da beads. Ya get me?"

"So, what, you want to change something in the rest of me? Cosmetically? Are you joking me?"

"Nah, nah, don't get me wrong now. We all know da old-fashion' disguise be useless, although if it's flesh you a hide from, a nuh nuttin' to change ya face, ya breasts, fuh example." He took a good look. "But child's play fuh dem algorithms to see through it. You know it. I know it. Ya tink me nah fuh real now?"

"You're also saying it's pointless to non my beads – then what can you do?"

"Don't get me wrong, we'll non ya beads, it'd be good so far fuh some tings. Mebbe not the big boi dem as I was sayin'. But here, ya came to us, right, not to dem others all over town? Here, we got speciahlism."

The Ohen Tuos left me near Independence Square, melting away into the crowds. I touched my beads, wondered whether he could have interfered with them in any way, reprogrammed them somehow with his beads or that hacked-up penthouse res of his.

I took a three-car tro-tro back to James Town, swishing through the Accra.city streets overflowing with my people, streaming past the Chinese robots standing around, delinquent and menacing. Bad robots, cut off from the motherland, stitched in a pirate network. We leave them to their fuckery, or deal with them in our stride. The fleshwork is Nkonsonkonso, human links in a chain, never break apart. The telepathic traffic of messages is entirely under the people's control and relatively light compared to the rest of the Between.

But I, I couldn't swim as I in these streets. Not for long. Hence the visit to Mr Swirling Suit, he of drifting shapes, atop the Dame-Dame Towers, hunkered up for all to see and yet invisible. He'd let me know a plan. To be nonned: that is, proof against the algorithms of all entities that would ID me. Multinats and, yes, IANI. He had a specialism all right, one I'd never come across before but which my ancestors would have shaken no leaves at.

I received a message instructing me to rendezvous at an address in East Legon. The tro-tro dropped me off at a half-finished building, like a relic of the old days: its ground floor comprised an anonymous, seemingly respectable business premises; above it rose bare concrete pillars that might never be completed, like a wish that someone had uttered.

A girl came to the door, little more than a child, naive and blank-looking, showing little comprehension of what went on inside. It occurred to me that I was venturing where no one knew my whereabouts, consorting with men whose honour I could hardly rely upon.

She left me in a room that smelled of damp. In my bag was a disabler I was prepared to use if it became necessary. I thought about the semblance of a life I had cultivated in Accra.city: the veneer of a highly successful business woman, my reputation impeccable. Men wanting me, like children. A life that meant nothing to me.

And now: waiting to be nonned, to leave it behind. In this room whose walls were rough plaster, its door and windows constructed with crude carpentry. The few pieces of furniture hailed from another age. Wall hangings were suspended in dust. Blinds let in little of the searing light outside. It was quiet.

I touched my beads. Nothing since our last meeting had led me to believe that Swirling Suit had tampered with them. I had no idea what his price would be. I would listen and agree.

The girl had shown her beads on her bare arm and I had sensed them when she showed me in. The sensation was gone. Had she left, then? I had not heard the front door.

After about five minutes I heard it open, a heavy approach of steps. The door to this room swung clear.

"Sistah!" He was wearing the same suit, only now there were birds flying across the material, from cherry blossom branch to cherry blossom branch and soaring to cloud fragments.

He was carrying a case.

My beads still sensed no one around me, and lay still. In the Dame-Dame Towers they had responded to him and his men, although I had not trusted what they were given to sense.

Sense-data. Intuition. In the icestation they had taught me to feel through my beads the ones around me. To feel their real data, beyond any paid-for facade they presented in the genpop. They also taught us how, in probing, to keep secret both ourselves and the presentiments of the network.

He made a point of showing off his beads. They configured and even glowed.

But, at the same time, they were not there.

He smiled, knowing I felt an absence.

"A me sistah! Ya got me!"

I said, "What's in the case?"

"Nuttin' ya need fi ask about. A fi me business."

"I don't want to be like you, absent. It's creepy. I said I wanted to be nonned – to be someone but no one."

"Nah, it's necessary for da procedure, yah understan'? First me have fi do dat ta yah, too."

"How are you going to do that?"

"Me tek ya offline wid a sign-out, one a them maintenahnce protocols, seen? I an engineer, first class. Me have privilege. Ya nah go tah none a dem bead clinics? It's what dey do, sistah, only dem nah tell you."

He looked at me with blood-shot intensity. What did he know of me? Not that he was facing an ex-agent of IANI. He trusted that I was not undercover. If I were still an agent, everything he thought he knew of me would be meticulously and convincingly contrived. It was a dangerous game he played.

I said, "Why do you trust Pempamsie?"

"Trust who now?"

"Me." Like any other, mine was merely a name uttered in the fleshwork, of no great significance in his domain.

He laughed momentarily then looked at me with deadly seriousness.

"Yah tink me trust you? Sistah, me nah need no trust. No trust in my game at ahl. Assume da worst a what me a say."

"Can I have a glass of water, please? It's hot in here."

There was no A/C and only a thin breeze puffed occasionally from behind the slatted blinds. He looked at me quizzically. The birds fluttered among the cherry blossom branches while he held himself still, gazing into me. He was a little shorter than I remembered.

I, Pempamsie, would be a non. I, Pempamsie, needed to have faith in myself. And yet faith was draining away from me, now that I was mentally, if not yet in practice, removed from the icestation's remit. I wanted to run. I didn't know where.

Still he stared at me strangely, pondering and motionless. Could he be a robot? Surely not. Apart from anything else, I could smell him: his male fug in the hot room, the sheen on his dark skin.

One of the Ohen Tuos – he looked like one of the men from the Dame-Dame Towers – came in with water. Swirling Suit had not, apparently, beckoned him.

The Ohen Tuo handed me the glass and closed the door softly behind him, as though there was someone nearby who slept and must not be wakened.

"Nah, drink ya water an' we start."

He opened the case. In it were parts of what appeared to be a human skeleton: a skull and bones, part of a ribcage. A tracery of wires connected them.

His suit suddenly switched; the blossom, birds and sky vanished, to be replaced by a texture of grey blanket.

I put down the glass and extended my beaded arm.

# CHAPTER SEVEN
## David

"Discovery on ship. Flesh remains. Circuitry." It was noon. Breakage was a middle-aged man, this one balding. "I absolutely feel sure that's what they found."

"You what?" David was swilling the last of his espresso down. The red sun was climbing behind the blades of a wind turbine, ascending to where soon it would be swallowed by the thickening white vapour that was the late twenty-first-century Avonmouth.city sky. Flesh shuffled in and out of the Spoons. He sat next to the window with his coffee, looking out. A man pushed a baby past in a buggy. David was reminded of the youth he'd cautioned a few days ago on the N-car. As soon as the buggy's occupant could walk, the man would take his child to have beads fitted, and the two would begin to communicate as much through the telepathic stream as they did offline. One day the child would find itself experiencing sensa from IANI, from every channel it could wish for, every sweetener to its humdrum physical world. Just as one day it might fall in love with the wrong person. And so its mental subjection would begin, with full parental consent.

Beyond them, two-cars and three-cars glided, ferrying flesh from node to glass-and-concrete node.

David's beads registered like dull thoughts; he was struggling against his exhaustion. The vodu had been pacing in its cage all night, tapping around and making sleep impossible.

*I need help.* Someone to talk to about Obayifa and what she had done to Mr Charles. David had no fleshren colleagues in the ID police. Like other flesh detectives in the force, he was kept largely isolated: granted the services of bodais as and when he needed them but limited in his contact with flesh, rationed to particular needs. He worked for the force, but that meant only that he was an instrument in an algorithm.

He couldn't stop thinking about Mr Charles. His only friend, gone. Mind-sucked by that creature. Dolled. And he had no idea what to do about the perpetrator, Obayifa. A sweet pain lay in his stomach. The vodu pricked him. He thought about having a girl at the Royal. He tried to pull himself together, to draw himself back to Breakage, waiting beside him in a warped simulation of patience. If Breakage had replied, David had not been paying attention.

"I'm still trying to understand why you're working with me, Breakage. Don't you have another case to work on? Anyway, since you're here: where were they found, these remains?"

"Ceiling cargo bay. In hull. Dogs found them. Barked upwards. Twenty metres."

"And just who ordered a dog search? I didn't."

"Breakage. Initiative."

"You don't have initiative. You're not supposed to have any damn initiative."

"Suggestion appeared for Breakage. Can't find in logs."

"Oh, nice, so you have intuition now. I'm proud of you, Breakage." He examined the balding head, resisted a pat. "Why were these not found before?"

"No dogs before. Not available. Wrong node. Wrong time."

"What condition are they in?"

"Dogs well."

"I meant the remains."

"Bones. Circuitry. In case. Took to forensics. Parkin."

Parkin. Who had conspired in Obayifa's release. Obayifa. He had sensed it was her real name when she first uttered it, but maybe it was a meaningless appellation, like a label in a surrealist painting. How to find her? The new network ID they had given her, supposedly hardened, was laughable given her powers, dissolving even during her detention. She'd nonned herself again, to class A*, vampire levels. Untraceable by network search, she would have to be physically found – an archaism in 2087. In his favour was the sheer intensity of her physical presence, which would get her noticed by flesh, at least. He could not help but think about her sexually, despite or because of her vodu nature: her limbs long and toned, her eyes a liquid swivelling towards the unknown, uncoupled from her actual thoughts, highly intelligent. Mentalmagicked. She wasn't particularly strong physically, he guessed, but she would dominate any situation. David imagined her keeping her white-collar crew in line on the *Mekhanik Pustoshnyy*: not averse to slapping them, then aloof at the bow. He thought of her eyes piercing him, in the humid hut where she had answered none of his questions, and in the module, on the mad ride he had let himself be reckless enough to take with her.

Then she had dolled Mr Charles. Fuck her. He was going to get revenge.


Parkin looked pleased with himself, happy to have been part of wresting Obayifa out of David's hands: a conspiracy whose real nature David could only guess at. And now he was clearly ecstatic to have received this new evidence from the *Mekhanik Pustoshnyy* before David knew anything about it.

And here David was in the copnode, humiliated. Parkin smiled at his victim's exasperation. Then he twitched his nose, as he often did. David had no idea why he had become the enemy of this calculating man with cropped blond hair, but he wished he was not, wished he had not spurned him without realising it.

"I'm taking them with me," David said, and coughed. He could feel a tightness in his throat, strangling the words as he tried to utter them. The vodu was wide awake. "This is none of your business. Breakage—"

"Breakage followed protocol," Parkin interrupted. "Brought the evidence to the forensics officer assigned to the case."

An aluminium attaché case lay on the desk between them. It was ribbed and rugged, big enough for some human bones, some of them intact, perhaps. How many were in there? And what had Breakage said about circuitry? David wanted badly to open the case for examination, but didn't want to give Parkin the satisfaction of watching his reaction to what he, Parkin, had already seen.

David said, "The investigation of the crew is over, as you well know. However, as senior detective in connection with a crime scene, the *Mekhanik Pustoshnyy*, where these bones were found, I've decided that, due to developments only I am party to, I need the remains to be examined by a specialist. Now hand them to me."

Parkin looked at Breakage. Flesh deferring to the network when it suited.

Don't you dare, David thought. Breakage would be the network's mouthpiece.

"Protocol states—" Breakage began.

"Protocol states," said David, "that you will consult with your detective flesh and not take any initiative. You used initiative, which is forbidden to a bodai. Now." David turned to Parkin. "I'll have those remains."

"All is known. Error. Give," Breakage said to Parkin, who, after an insolent pause, pushed the case across the desk towards David. Then he twitched his nose again.

"This isn't the last you'll hear of this," Parkin said, drumming his fingers.

David took Breakage on a five-car that trundled up as they left the copnode. It was a relief to board. Parkin had looked as though he wanted to murder David and trash the bodai.

The five-car rose to the level of turbines and silos. Huge ships sat moored or sailed to and from Avonmouth.city, letting out low moans. The *Mekhanik Pustoshnyy* lay out of view, awaiting the network's logistical decision as to its fate.

The find lay in the attaché case on his lap. He was still anxious to open it, to see the cause of this new fuss, but there were passengers' eyes upon him. The case might in principle have been unrelated to the sixteen crew, a relic from some earlier voyage. But he didn't believe that. A gap appeared in the vaporous manifold of the sky, and sunlight fell suddenly like a bolt of gold cloth onto the case, as though to affirm its significance.

And there was something he couldn't put his finger on about the readings from his beads since he had collected it.

Breakage stood along the car from him. Bodais didn't sit, by default. When they considered it appropriate to do so, they were often wrong.

After two stops the balding middle-aged man disembarked to fulfil a logistical calling, and a young woman came on board. Breakage stood in the same place in this form, holding on to a strap and looking directly at David. The young woman bore an expression of near reproach, as though the scene with Parkin in the copnode had caused embarrassment that this female bod could sense in a way the man bod couldn't. Which made no sense, since the same AI, Breakage, operated the two.

David got off and walked the transitways to another Spoons. His life seemed to consist largely of N-cars and Spoons. Breakage followed.

A few moments elapsed before Breakage realised he was expected to come closer to talk to David. David always sat by the window, mildly claustrophobic at the best of times and not least since his inner space had been invaded by a vodu. He placed the case between his feet. A spotty young bodai took his order. To his left, a flesh messily ate an unmeatburger in a hurry.

Close up, you could see the sheeny plasticity of a bodai's face, the nearly imperceptible stepper motor shifts of mouth, eyes and skin distenders. It was always embarrassing to be this close to one, to see them looking around as though they meant it, or addressing you as though they wanted to. David forced himself to keep looking at Breakage. It was mind-boggling to talk to them if you thought about it, as though faced with the unknowability of your own self.

The vodu stirred, shifted in a pretend sleep; its whole body was a blur of twisted meat.

"Breakage." David looked around to see if Messy Eater or any other flesh was witnessing the awkward, compelling spectacle of flesh and bodai in conversation. "Breakage, who told you to search the ship again, and to take what you found to Parkin?"

Breakage pretended to think and then said, "Network."

"I see." Of course network did.

"What agency?"

"Unknown. Graph and crypto complexity exceeded. All is known."

"Yes. Quite," David said. This was pointless, wasn't it? He went on, nonetheless. "What do you intend to do, now that I've contradicted the network?"

"It is for ID detective to—"

"No, you are listening to network too. Are you working for me – really working for me?"

"Yes. Network too. Always. All is known."

"Breakage, I want you not to listen to the network." David felt Breakage with his beads as he said this.

"Very well."

"What?"

"When network calls, will consult David first."

"Are you sure?" Stupid question.

Breakage said nothing, took to looking around falsely, now at the flesh walking outside, now at the bustling interior of the Spoons. He even looked at Messy Eater.

David picked up the case. "Are you sure there are bones in here?" Without waiting for the answer, he opened the case just enough to see what could be a ribcage, embedded in packing material. And something else, more solid.

"Certain. Identical as found."

"Where should we take them? Parkin will have alerted the rest of forensics to treat them like a case of plague."

"David say."

"Give me options."

Breakage blinked once. "Option. Professor Dirac."

David almost smiled. He'd heard about the professor, who assisted in investigations with technical advice, but never met him. Dirac's reputation, passed unreliably through the scattered flesh within the ID police, was for a dark, brooding brilliance. It was said that as the father, the inventor, of psychblood, he had run rings around the network. Hence the network had demoted him and stripped him of most of his resources, assigning him to a low-level technical role within the ID police, based at an out-of-the-way labnode.

"That's what I hoped you'd say. We'll go. It's late now. Tomorrow."

Should he not look Breakage, this gift robot, in the mouth? Not as long as he was useful. But he must remain wary. The vodu tapped an alien rhythm on the bars of its cage.

The hot soup that passed for air slicked all around him, instantly producing sweat as he walked back to his desres, soaking his clothes. Reluctantly he entered the swarm of ones milling along the pavement, hundreds of flesh and bodais marching or shuffling incuriously. A module swept up, looking for his interest in a lift, accelerated away when David waved it along.

He found himself alone on the transitway as he neared his dwelling. The case, becoming heavy in his hand, was producing the faint, unusual feeling through his beads again.

When he climbed the steps to his desres there was a group of men in dressing gowns waiting by his door. He recognised one of them as his recent visitor, the dem who had come knocking. The others looked as though they could have escaped from the same carie. Some were muted, staring into space or at their feet, standing unnaturally still; others were muttering, restless.

The first one to spot him yelled, "It's the bastard!" The others looked with varying degrees of befuddlement; some shouted, hurtling expletives at him. He stopped a few metres away, two of them shaking their fists now, between him and his front door.

Then they saw his case.

"When can we go home?" one said. "Pack and go home? When can we go home?"

A group of bodais arrived swiftly upon his call. They took away his visitors with gentle but firm grasps, immune to the curses that a greyed, frail woman spluttered at them. Why the interest in his desres? Or was it him the men had waited to see? David was perturbed by these gowned escapees. In his loneliness, their visits were salt upon his wounds.

When David entered, carrying the attaché case, the desres was mildly alarmed. It bleated that someone unidentified was entering along with him. David had to override its concerns, but that fact would be logged in Big Mind. David reported a malfunction. This would not stand up to forensic scrutiny. Why was he behaving like someone with something to hide? He laughed mirthlessly to himself. You ask yourself that, you with a vodu caged up inside your mind?

The vodu was standing, its bare arms raised up along the bars of its cage, clutching their cold solidity.

David opened the case. There were indeed bones inside: parts of a human skeleton, packed closely and carefully in protective foam. There was an almost complete skull, the radius and ulna of a forearm and the upper half of an otherwise intact ribcage. Harnesses of intricate wiring connected them. The skull's look landed on him as soon as he opened the case, as if reproaching him for meddling, expecting someone else. Beads encircled the radius and ulna at the wrist. Presumably the beads were the source of the emanations, although he needed to check everything in the case. The assemblage appeared to be a circuit of some kind.

The attaché case was of robust construction, its shell apparently double-walled. Carefully, David lifted out its contents. He took the empty case back out into the hot night air and placed it in a recess a few hundred metres away. No one else was around. Next to a column, a figure appeared. Yaa, in the blue dress he had bought for her twelfth birthday, the last time he had ever successfully chosen a garment for her to wear. Her hair was braided. Sometimes he couldn't help himself, allowed himself to conjure her for one brief second in his loneliness. The vodu shifted hungrily. He quickly thought of Obayifa, to drive the vision away.

When he returned, he asked, "How many ones in desres?"

"Two," it replied.

The desres was not capable, as far as he knew, of detecting his vodu: only he perceived its caged presence within his consciousness. Its reply therefore confirmed that the emanations came from the circuit of bones rather than the case. He left his desres again to fetch the case, wary lest the vision of Yaa should return. It was eerie to leave something with a macro-identity in his home. What was it capable of?

His vodu shifted as he thought these thoughts. It was a swirl of articulated lines, like a painting of exposed flesh. Was it aware of the ID emanating from the bone circuitry? How was he supposed to know what it knew or did not know, except the fact that he loved Yaa? He only thought he could recognise, sometimes, its reactions to the world.

"Desres," he said into the air, "who is with me?"

"Unknown entity," it replied.

"Has it been here before today?"

"No."

"Who was here yesterday?" The messenger girl. Not a girl at all.

"Unknown."

"Suppress emanations to the outside from the one inside that is not me." Better not to have anyone poking their nose in.

"Unable to comply."

And this was the desres of an ID cop. He thought, by contrast, about the relatively puny improvised Faradays used by ID felons in the genpop: desreses hacked to prevent their owners' beads from revealing something they didn't want the network or fleshren enemies to know. It was a futile act of desperation. Offline was online: an absence of a known ID in the network was detectable as much as a presence. An algorithm would detect the anomaly and signal an alert. A swift visit from a bodai dispatch team – and an ID cop like him if the felony was serious – would lead to their arrest.

"Desres, tell me when someone leaves or enters."

In the night, Yaa haunted him, begging him to look at her, but eventually he managed to sleep. The desres woke him.

"One has left, one has arrived. Without door."

He checked his small desres just to be sure: the bathroom, the kitchenette he never used, behind the sofa. Was the bone circuitry transmuting its own ID, then? Perhaps Professor Dirac would know.

# CHAPTER EIGHT
## Pempamsie

I, Pempamsie, wanted to become a non. To disappear, beyond the knowledge of the icestation. And Swirling Suit obliged. Expertly.

However, the bytecoins with which I paid him were not what they seemed to be. They looked like the sum we agreed. It was a good rendition. You don't mess with a man like that. Never kid a kidder, they used to say.

I may look like a million, and yet, detached from IANI, I was almost destitute.

I left that half-building in the outer suburbs of Accra.city, that impromptu surgery of his; I said goodbye to its pink facade and the sky-pointing girders of its undone upper floor, to be gone. Really gone. A non. The very thing he made me helped me get away from him. Not offline, online – but not me.

Such an old trick: what seems to be data is code. Once I had left, my payment spun itself into his systems and, just as the coffers of Swirling Suit opened to swallow it, wiped away not only itself but the fact of its non-existence.

IANI would assume I had defected to Westaf, the cyber-engineering workhorse of the world, which left Silicon Valley behind in its wake long ago.

Reality: I, Pempamsie, was now sought by both IANI and Swirling Suit, the Westaf renegade. I had no bytecoins. I had never had friends.

But my eyes were opened. I had seen the fleshwork in the vast Between for what it had become: the living data factory of the multinats. The earth was a hothouse of purchases driven by telepathic advertising and shoddy algorithms.

Westaf: at least they see futility for what it is and waste no time on such puny algorithmic dreaming – except to make money by opposing it. What they understand above all is Nkyin kyin: the twisted pattern, changing one's self, playing many parts.

I, Pempamsie, wished an end to the tyranny that started with IANI, this oligarchy stretched between the poles, and equally the now spirit-inflected hackery that rose from Westaf to meet and profit from it. I wanted back what they used to call humanity.

I, Pempamsie, was now a non. My true presence in the network had disappeared. For I was inhabited by another. A vodu. Which perturbed every digital emanation from my beads and spun a fabrication in my stead, superior to the algorithms of IANI. It was a conscious being, like me. That Swirling Suit had made or captured. I know not which.

And was I, Pempamsie, still I? That which cannot be crushed?

Yes, and no. I was Afuntummireku denkyemmireku: the plural-headed crocodile with a single stomach.


And so I walked, a walk that felt more like swimming, swimming in the murky heat of Accra.city.

And then a Chinese robot approached me. They all had a certain look about them, not Chinese but an unsubtle representation of us. Robots are stupid and always will be, their utterances and actions statistical cusps in a rush of integers. No match for the brains of flesh, our symbolic sensibility. The multinats peddle the old fantasy that software will develop into true intelligence. They act as though they really believe it. I, Pempamsie, knew this to be a fantasy. Owuo atwedie baako nfo: all men shall climb the ladder of death.

And yet, they are creatures who converse with us.

"I know you," it said.

"You are mistaken."

"Are you flesh?"

"Surely."

It came closer. Menacingly. The Chinese introduced thousands of these robots at the tail end of their economic colonisation, a venture that came to no good as we lifted ourselves by our digital bootstraps and ejected all foreign investment. Their robots all went offline at the same time, frozen. Then they came back online under the control of an unidentified entity, who kept them on the streets, hanging around in public places like gangs of teenagers up to no good. I hated them.

The robot stood stock still. It felt me through its beads as with a cold hand, in a silent digital appraisal. One or two flesh from the current of ones around us slowed, wondering at our stand-off.

I, Pempamsie, walked on. I made for a one-car tro-tro a few metres ahead. Bad move. Two more Chinese robots were strap-hanging, and my accoster followed me on board. Bodies, flesh and bod, were packed close. The density and the white rays that pierced even the filtered glass were too much for the tro-tro's A/C. The smell of flesh clung in the air.

I felt the beads of all around me, and they felt me: as we flick our eyes over those around us, looking for what piques us as flesh: danger signs, sex signs, curious demeanours.

I had the Chinese robots' interest, that was for sure. Had Swirling Suit cheated me? Had he already taken his revenge for my non-payment? I should appear so ordinary that you could not tell me apart from the crowd. Background.

The robot who had accosted me shouldered its way towards me, like a bee seeing in bit-light instead of visible light, casting around with its imperfect algorithms. It stood with its mouth as close to my ear as it could manage, which was next to my shoulder.

"Don't you wish," it said, "for a quiet life?"

I, Pempamsie, disdained from placing my gaze upon this robotic creature, did not meet its icy stare.

I said, "I do not know of what you speak." The other two made their presence known through my beads. All the flesh around us were oblivious to our exchanges, caught up in their thoughts, some with sensa from their fleshren flickering inside, as the tro-tro pulled through Accra.city.

Then the vodu came alive inside me, like a shadow that pulled itself up from its recline and loomed.

The vodu played upon my emanations, replacing me with another identity. Even as the robot felt me. Robots are incapable of emulating the double-take of surprised flesh. But in their circuitry they were dumbfounded as the vodu impressed another self on them. Their digital grip fell away.

I left at the next stop. The Chinese robots, still minus comprehension, remained on board.

I wanted to engage with the vodu itself but could not. Swirling Suit said it would do its work but not communicate. It was a shadow, subtly and indistinctly present. A co-existent self inside me. A mild visitor, he told me. Not a Mr Hyde who I would become, oblivious. Not a guest who arrives and tumbles the company, makes them wonder who invited him, so limp do they become in the wind of his energy, his mad voice.

No, it was subtle, he said – just enough to send me through the gaps in their algorithms when they felt me with their beads or from the poles.

I wondered, if I had a familiar, nay, a lover, would they notice something different about me, ask what was wrong? I felt the same inside. I had entered, to the outside, the Incognito Divide. Courtesy of

Swirling Suit, and his vodu. A living mental transfusion via software and psychblood.

But I suspected it cut both ways, that the vodu was not entirely neutral. It would have needs too, perhaps.

And the man who engineered my inhabitance was now my enemy. I had no one to extract my squatter, should I want that. Equally, I wondered if it had a way to leave of its own accord, or if it would ever want to leave. Except, of course, when I died.

Hungry, I entered a shopnode for food. I had found a few fake bytecoins stashed away: the purest, crispest, newly minted bytecoins that may cause consternation in the network after use but which could not be traced. Thank you, IANI.

My basket was full. I didn't seem to have thought through where I was to eat. I packed the items and made to leave. An alarm sounded.

A robot appeared at once. My ears became hypersensitive. I thought I could hear its mechanisms, the multitude of electric motors humming and whining within.

The robot blocked my path.

And flesh arrived, dressed in an exaggeratedly militaristic uniform.

"Contravention, ma'am," he said, looking bored. The robot stood precisely still, looming.

"I don't know what you mean. Look in my bag."

He poked in it with his truncheon, not looking. Chuckled.

"I don't need to look. The system says contravention."

"Contravention of what?"

"The code."

"What code?"

The robot spoke up. "Unexpected item."

I felt a noumenal stirring within my soul, an unexpected touch on my spine. From within. Something moving, beyond my control. I was like a child taken by the hand, going along with its holder to an unknown destination.

"Is that better?"

The flesh, in his hugely peaked blue cap crested with a *Best One* badge, looked at the robot. The robot turned to him with an inaccurate swivel.

"All expected items. Error. All is known."

I, Pempamsie, my soul churning, walked into the stream of flesh outside.

Swirling Suit told me not to worry, that the vodu would operate only in the network, not the fleshwork. To IANI, from which I had to remain hidden, network is all: the fleshwork is the substrate, a petri dish.

He lied.

How did I, Pempamsie, discover this?

In the shopnode and on the tro-tro with the Chinese robots, all was as Swirling Suit had said it would be. The vodu stirred, I projected someone else. I triggered not recognition but interest. My inhabitant's operation had not been smooth, but probably it was learning its shadowy trade.

However. I had begun to feel, undefinably, that I was not as I used to be. Pempamsie's mind was altered.

I sat in a tree-shaded square and reached in my mind for what could comfort me against the unknown journey ahead. I reached for a memory from my childhood. But I could no longer remember my mother and father. There was a hole where their memories used to be. Paths led to that hole in my thoughts, presentiments of what I would find when I thought of them. But I reached only a chasm. Names: gone. Faces: gone. Words they spoke to me: vanished.

I girded myself. Again walked the path within my mind. Nothing. I had been orphaned, cut off from the two people I had never seen since my abduction but the memory of whom had kept me true to myself.

And what was that truth? That however I was forced in the icestation to become IANI's agent, however I was compelled thereby to relinquish all but the most perfunctory interaction with other flesh, my parents were where I came from. They occupied such an important place in my freezing heart. But I couldn't picture them anymore.

Swirling Suit, in implanting the vodu to alter my network emanations, had cut away a part of me. Redacted it, cast a shadow over it. I knew at once that I must eject the vodu. I had to remove its spell. I didn't care anymore what became of me: why should I, if "me" was to be no more?

And the next day it took me over, more and more. It nonned me, yes, but it went beyond. In the mirror, sometimes, for a moment, a stranger faced me. A stranger with a scar running down from her left eye whose origin had become obscure.

Pempamsie's hair was coiled up. Her lips were full, eyes wide, brows strong. She was tall, yes. Strong, yes. The strange scar seemed to attest to a fight, not weakness. The gazes of men and women still swivelled her way in the fleshwork of Accra.city. And yet.

Clouds loomed where Pempamsie's clarity used to be. A minuscule difference in the set to my mouth, to my eyes, to my thoughts. And then I looked at my bare arms: the veins had started to run thickly towards my wrists, visible as never before.

What had I done to rid myself of IANI? What compromise had I made? I, Pempamsie, had no one. My greatest fear was that I would not even have me.

I had made a mistake.

# CHAPTER NINE
## David

Dirac's labnode stood at what used to be called the seaside, an off-car zone reachable only by module. Seagulls cried around it. The sea made its waves in partnership with the wind, utterly alien to what had come to exist on land: the network incarnate, lattices of concrete, steel and glass. Farms of wind turbines spun offshore. Ships, many of them under sail, began or ended their voyages. Further away, the thin line of the tidal barrier stretched across the estuary. David felt a moment's concern for Breakage: the maritime environment would rust bodais. At least Breakage didn't have to bear the heat, though. As they walked up to the labnode, there was no relief from the infrared that pummelled down from the low sky. The gulls made circles, as did the blades of the turbines. Once, in Elizabethan times, flesh would have sat and played near here, or walked their dogs. Flesh who were at that time entirely undistracted by sensa.

Professor Dirac appeared at the door. He had lost, blue eyes. A long upper lip told of his intelligence. David's research had confirmed some of what people said about Dirac. His scientific practice had been taken away from him. Science was now the preserve of the inner nodes of the multinats. He did what he could to make a living as a technical assistant to the ID police. He was reputed to be brooding and bitter.

"Professor, how good to meet you at last."

"A pleasure, Detective," Dirac said coldly.

"I'll get straight down to business. I'd like your opinion on what's in this." David handed him the case.

"I see. And what exactly am I looking for?"

"I don't know. Anything unusual."

Dirac opened the case, regarded its contents in silence for some time. "I'll need a while. Will you wait?"

"Of course."

David left the labnode to take the air, instructing Breakage, who was in the form of a natty office professional, to remain. The wind tugged at him as he walked on grass and sand down to the beach. No one else was there but the thing was inside him, so solitude was impossible. He felt trapped, wanted to disappear. If he couldn't be with Yaa, he could be on a sailing ship, perhaps, in a far corner of the ocean.

He walked along by the waves, lost in thought until he realised he'd been called and saw the silhouetted figure of Breakage beside the squat labnode. The bodai could not come closer to sand and water. David returned.

"The bones" – Dirac's spidery hands were trying to follow swift thoughts – "date from before the first human. They are parts of the skeleton of a member of a humanoid species for which there is no record. Where did you find them?"

"On a ship. Which came from Westaf: probably from Accra city or Port-Harcourt city. But we can't be sure."

"There's DNA within them of a type not known in Big Mind. Something's very strange about them altogether. Not to mention the beads and the circuitry that connects them."

"Do the bones actually do anything?"

"To be honest, I don't see how. But the wiring is intricately attached to them. The forearm, with its beads at the wrist, seems to be an interface to the rest of the world for the skull and ribcage. I will get to the bottom of it. You know, I am sure, that I have certain interests and specialisms here, Detective."

"Psychblood. I know about you and psychblood, Professor."

"Your tone disappoints me. You speak of it as though it were witchcraft. Psychblood is being released into you and modulated through your beads as we speak, is it not? Yes, you can override its effects as an ID detective. But does the network not bind you to charging your beads with electricity and psychblood like the rest of us? Systematic, algorithmic manipulation of the genpop's consciousness." The words rolled from Dirac's mouth like the carriages of a train. "I conduct experiments, and as part of those investigations I measure… emanations, presence." Dirac touched his beads. "Such as those of beads but also other configurations of matter. And these bones with their circuitry, Detective, are emanating their calciferous little hearts out."

"You say they predate the earliest known human to date, but are they human?"

"I said humanoid. But they will cause quite a stir."

"Any stir will have to wait, because they are evidence in a case."

"Oh, and what case is that?"

"We'll get to that in due course."

Breakage stood stock still beside them. David suddenly became conscious of his assistant observing their conversation, causing Dirac to throw a glance at the bodai.

"Consciousness is in this circuit of bones but not in you, Mr Robot," said Dirac.

"Consciousness?" said David. "But you're surely not suggesting this bone circuitry is alive. It's simply matter. Sophisticated matter, no doubt assembled in Westaf, but matter nonetheless."

"And you know all about that difference, do you, Detective? I tell you, whatever the effects of this circuit of bones are, they are not precisely digital or analogue."

"What else is there?" said David.

"What are you?" Dirac said. "What am I? What is flesh? Conscious."

"To say that is not Turing, is it, Professor. All is algorithmic, as we know. Everything is ultimately reproducible by an algorithm running on machines. A machine at the poles, to be precise. Do you not agree? All is known." David reproduced the network's teaching with a mild sneer to let Dirac know what he thought of it. He became conscious of the vodu inside him, of another consciousness within his own, far more sophisticated than the sensa ferried by the multinats into the minds of the genpop. And at least sensa were benign in themselves. The vodu was a spirit, however mute: it had agency; was synthesised at least partly through software although not necessarily under the implementor's control.

Dirac, who was watching him closely, said, "You are correct. It is not Turing. But it's true. Are you going to arrest me for it?"

"No, Professor." David threw Breakage a forbidding look. "We won't be arresting you. We need your help."

Dirac said, "Think of your beads, which communicate with others' beads and with transceivers all around you. Correct? Are you listening to me, Detective?"

David forced his attention back into the labnode again, the bodai next to him and the professor looking at him with a new focus now, beyond a lonely man's ambivalent interest in whatever half-intelligent beings came his way; looking at David as though he had caught sight of something new about him.

"I'm listening, Dirac."

"Our beads are relatively old hardware, servicing constantly evolving algorithms."

"Why are you telling me what you know I know? Anyway, you don't know how they work, do you, Professor, because that would be illegal, wouldn't it." David gave Breakage another look. The natty professional stood down.

"Of course, Detective. But I do know them from outside, so to speak, just as you do. And they, with their manipulations of psychblood, are the most psychically integrated technology that exists, are they not?"

"Your point, Professor, is what?"

"My point is that greater psychic integration with matter is theoretically possible."

"Theoretically?"

"Yes, theoretically. Detective, how could I possibly speak of more than that?"

David considered Dirac's existence by the sea, surrounded by measuring devices in his technical outnode, with few opportunities to engage his prodigious brain – reduced to forensics and crash investigations.

"I need a second opinion."

"Naturally. Why should the ID police accept my word?"

"Especially when you're making two highly contentious assertions: that the bones predate all known human remains, and that they are associated with a mental presence."

"Did I say 'mental'? Did I go that far? I suppose I said 'conscious', didn't I. Anyway, you are so right, Detective, to speak to someone else. Exactly what I would do, if I were in your shoes."

There was sarcasm, yes, but Dirac touched his beads as he spoke, tugged at them like a shackled man. "I expect you will take them to an inner-network scientific authority regarding the first question. And ignore the second."

That thin, super-intelligent, unmeant smile again. And the eyes. There was almost a touch of mentalmagic. David's vodu was pondering Dirac too. But no, that wasn't what was in the eyes. At least David didn't think so.

"Would you do me a favour, Professor, and roll up your sleeve?"

"Really, Detective, do you imagine I'm a junkie, that what I've told you is drug-fuelled fantasy?"

"Please just do it, Professor. Your forearm only. I don't think you're an addict."

The skin was wan, mottled. None of the snaking blue veins of the squatted distended it, like his own forearm. And that of Obayifa.

"Now will you show me yours, Detective?"

"That won't be necessary."

David regarded Breakage, in his good suit and elaborately patterned tie. The entire conversation seemed to have passed him by. Or not. There was no way of telling whether Breakage would keep to his pledge, to report to David before he reported to the network. But David was beginning to trust the bodai, despite himself.

"Where exactly will you take them to?" Dirac placed the case of bones on the table. David didn't answer. Breakage took the case with strong, inauthentic movements. Through the window, the sound of the crashing sea entered, a sloshing where all fleshly life could return to one day: might as well return to now, reduced as it was to this paucity, thought David, this annexation by the network. He suddenly felt deep embarrassment for himself and all his fleshren at this reduction of a genius like Dirac to a service function – however little he was inclined to sympathise with the embittered man. The network has hived off the essential good in us, our creativity, David thought.

"You will be seeing me again, I suspect, Professor. Before too long."

David pondered the professor's words as they returned in the module. Dirac was right: the relationship between matter and consciousness remained a mystery, even in the late twenty-first century with its mastery of mental content. Multinats manipulated the genpop's mental processes without true understanding. How did Dirac – and David's desres, for that matter – detect a presence associated with parts of a skeleton – presumably inert – even given that they were connected to beads through circuitry? It made no sense. He would need to return to Dirac, who might be able to understand it.

Not that Dirac was infallible, as David knew from his research. Dirac had believed, falsely as it turned out, that when he discovered psychblood back in 2048 he was on a path leading to a cure for dementia. But then the multinats had seized the technology to deliver content telepathically, with IANI's blessing. Ironically, it turned out that psychblood was the cause of early onset dementia, enfeebling the genpop like a plague.

A plague. The world was plagued. By vodus, perhaps, as well. If they were synthetic, the creations of Westaf renegades, then couldn't they make as many as they pleased, and send them out to infect the entire Between? He had to pull himself together. Why would they do that? And yet, their experimentation on him, when the renegades captured him in Accra.city, had been merciless. He was a botched attempt to implant a vodu. Exact motive unknown.

At the N-car station, Breakage disappeared into the crowd as David boarded a heaving car. While they glided through the near-above, he thought about the smile that had almost broken through in the Spoons, the almost-smile that Breakage had sparked when he suggested working with Dirac. His last actual smile would have been for his daughter. Conversations with Mr Charles had generally been solemn. All joy, everything he loved, had been displaced by the twist of brooding malevolence behind bars in his mind. And his one friend was now lost to the creature Obayifa.


As David's N-car descended faintly, Breakage came on board, a frail old lady, with news.

"Ship was boarded by unknown last night."

"Why are you only telling me now?"

"Unknown. All is known."

David closed his eyes, struggling with impatience.

"What instrumentation was available?"

"*Mekhanik Pustoshnyy* not repaired. Low priority. Scene-of-crime telemetry installed. Low resolution. One came onboard. Ten minutes. Then left."

"Anyone posted there who might have disturbed them – it?"

"No."

"Where did they go on board?"

"Cargo bay."

"So maybe they were there for the bones. The scaffold we used to climb up to retrieve them – was it still in place?"

"Unknown. No data on physical configuration below priority levels."

"Maybe it was Obayifa, after the case. Breakage, find out if there was CCTV."

"Disused since Disruption. All is known."

"It's an old ship. Go and look for CCTV."

"Big Mind detects all presences at all times through network. Beads—"

"Go and look for CCTV."

Breakage left again. The case he held was emitting a signal of some kind, emanating a presence to the network, like a beacon. When she discovered the bones were no longer on the ship – if it was her; he'd better not assume too far – then she would look for them via the network. David looked around the carriage for her. She could be following him, for all he knew – following the case. She, on the other hand, was nonned. He would have to be vigilant, in the old-fashioned style, with his senses.

As if with X-ray eyes, he looked inside the case which lay closed upon his lap, to what he'd become one day. Fragments. And the vodu inside him? Surely it couldn't live in his remains. It needed a mind to feed on – for it drained him, taking a trickle current of psychic energy. It would have to find a way to transfer itself before he died, before his psyche disappeared. A sudden lunge of sex drive engulfed him. The girls of the Hotel Royal appeared, leering as though they could stave off his unhappiness. If only he could rid himself of the vodu then he could try to love himself again. If only he could love himself he could perhaps rid himself of the vodu.

He tried to stop it, but David's prick stirred. He took the case back to his desres and walked to the Royal. Once it had seemed reckless to visit the girls there, but it had been years since he began, not long after his arrival in Avonmouth.city. He was inured to it now: if you could be said to be inured to an addiction, a corrosion. Each time he asked himself where the drive came from, a drive that had never riven him in Accra.city. And each time the answer stirred in his mind. His vodu lay at the centre of his destructive desire, that much he knew. Perhaps it exerted an influence, willing him to spend himself thus. In any case, it had displaced all worth in his mind.

There were other places to find girls, but the Hotel Royal was convenient. He took himself offline a few blocks before he walked up the few stairs that led to an unimpressive entrance. So many gaps in his user journey. One day, one day soon he may have to account for them.

He asked the bodai at the desk for room 71, which was not the number of any room in the hotel.

The girl was not beautiful, or even particularly attractive. And she was tired. He had lain with her before. They all knew him: the man who left his shades and his shirt on. He placed his other clothes by the bed.

The act was over in minutes, taking its place in a blurred string of visits. The act itself was not the point; there was no point, only his dedication to a libidinous idea that he had never fathomed, a driven journey that never led anywhere.

David lay still, propped on his elbow, and looked at her. "What are you thinking? Oh, you're not. What's playing?" Sex workers were never truly exempt from sensa, because the network's algorithms were incapable of detecting which parts of their lives were work as opposed to leisure. Sensa played in their minds, taking away from what little of themselves they were prepared to share. Perhaps it made their lives more endurable, after all, to be distracted. Like a patient in a dentist's chair: vivid sensa played in your mind while they worked on your tooth.

"A bear!" she said. "A bear was brushing its teeth and a fox said how bright the bear's teeth were. It's a very good toothpaste brand. But the little bear: so cute and playful! Shall I share it with you?"

"Thank you, but no," said David. "Isn't there something else we could—"

"No," she said quickly, her face clouding. "There really isn't."

She propped herself up on the bed and faced him earnestly.

"I've seen bears on my screen. Do they exist?" She lay back down. "Somewhere?"

When ID cops needed to interrogate someone, they could turn off their interviewee's stream completely if necessary to ensure their full attention. David sometimes did this but didn't feel like it now, not with her. He looked at her again, felt her through his beads. He was as close as you could get to someone. Almost inside her mind via his ID cop's beads. And he was as far away from her as one could be.

He dressed as quickly as he could. As he left the Royal, the heat hit him again. The near-above was swarming. Its Spoons and Noodles – there were no other cafes or restaurants, only their clones – were packed with his fleshren, sipping and dining distractedly together, sharing tastes with remote friends. David had not eaten with anyone else since he left Accra.city.

He put himself back online.

David was called to the harbour. Breakage had been in touch with Lenczyk, who had thought nothing of the trespass on board the *Mekhanik Pustoshnyy* since no ID crime was deemed to have taken place. Lenczyk balked at first, but eventually understood that the request came from David and not the bodai. The harbour ID cop found a CCTV camera on board.

"Amazing," he said. "Talk about antiquated! And forgotten about, I guess. Even more incredibly, there was still a way to play the recording."

The footage was speckled and indistinct, taken at night, but it was her, all right. Lenczyk agreed. Breakage stood by in incomprehension. They watched a figure climb the scaffold that the ID police had erected after the dogs barked upwards into the cargo bay's ceiling. She had found new clothes, but there was no mistaking the lithe body that ascended animal-like, quickly established the absence of what she was looking for, descended just as surely, then unwittingly revealed her face to the camera just before leaving its frame as she headed back to the quay. You could see a glow from her eyes.

"How far back does the footage go?" asked David.

"Only twenty-four hours," said Lenczyk. "It's a real shame. I'd have loved to see what that lot had got up to at sea."

"Detective," said Breakage suddenly. "Incident. Hotel Royal."

David, cringing at the mention of the hotel, stared at Breakage for clarification. Eventually the bodai's algorithms kicked in.

"Incident. Flesh required."

"We're busy. What kind of incident?"

"Flesh. Harm. Crew of *Mekhanik Pustoshnyy*."

David had watched the crew leave ID police custody but had not attempted to track them. While Obayifa had made her presence known through Mr Charles and now her incursion into the ship, David had heard nothing of the other fifteen. He had assumed they were long gone.

"Lenczyk, please find out whatever else you can about her visit. Any data you can get your hands on."

"But she's been released."

"And now she's committed an incursion into a crime scene, has she not?"

"Very well."

The Royal was not unacquainted with misdemeanours; its reputation had sunk since it reopened after the Disruption, or so one of the older flesh had told him. It was always invidious to go there for professional reasons, and he felt claustrophobic in the lobby. The bodai clerk took him to a room on the top floor where a commotion had been reported and no one had answered the staff's knocks.

Inside were two men he immediately recognised as crew from the *Mekhanik Pustoshnyy*. One stood on a dresser; the other had heaved an armchair onto the bed and stood precariously on its seat. They had consigned themselves to these paltry heights like lost angels – just as Mr Charles had climbed onto the furniture, according to Mary, after Obayifa had paid a visit.

They were alive but unresponsive to David's questions. Nothing intelligible guided the movements of their unnaturally widened eyes, which roved, looking through David, the clerk and Breakage, who had joined them – looking straight through the Hotel Royal's barely passable business-grade decor, its stock paintings of ships and sunsets, its soulless trappings.

And they too appeared to be soulless now, not even animals. Dolls. The dolls piqued the interest of David's vodu, which cast its attention to these vacated beings without appearing to – but David knew.

He felt bound to try to talk to them for a while, however futile it seemed. Soon he gave up. Unsure of what to do with them, he called for an ambulance and told Breakage to arrange a bodai guard to accompany them.

David wondered why they had holed up in such an open place as the Hotel Royal in Avonmouth.city, and not disappeared into the fleshwork. Was it for a rendezvous – with Obayifa? They seemed to be wearing the same suits they had worn aboard the *Mekhanik Pustoshnyy*. They must have had something on their minds other than a change of clothes. While they had minds.

David had tried not to think – had pushed the memories away like a big black dog that wanted him – of Mr Charles, and the dolls that had started to appear around Accra.city, in the same trees where fruit bats hung in clusters. He pictured them along the larger branches, silhouetted against a sky that was emptied of light, these figures standing and wavering, staring out from amongst the foliage. Where they remained until, weakened, they finally fell to the ground. Not once had the perpetrators been caught: vampires who feed not on blood but the minds of others; the products of the renegades' experimentation with vodu implantation; the monsters that David feared he himself would become if his vodu were to leave its cage, if he were to soften his heart.

On his way back out of the lobby, David passed one of the girls arriving for work. She pretended not to recognise him, in accordance with the protocol of the trade. She looked sad. Both she and David were adrift outside the rooms they used together, floating away from the chimerical anchor of their short-lived transactions.

His good sense told him to have the case secured from Obayifa, and soon. If he turned it back in to the ID police he'd never see it again. His desres wasn't particularly secure – he shouldn't have left it there. But there was no one he could entrust it to, except Dirac. Maybe. His labnode would be secure even though David still wasn't a hundred per cent sure about him. Perhaps another word with him would help.

"Breakage," David said to the bodai, who had accompanied him out of the hotel, "we'll be going back to Dirac but I have something to attend to first. Keep yourself on call."

Dolls. First Mr Charles, and now the two crew.

"Can I help you?" There was an ironic lilt to Mary's voice when finally she answered. He could hear scrappy birdsong in the background.

"Where are you?" he asked, already knowing.

"Walking. Am I not online, like a good girl?"

"I have some questions. About Mr Charles. Don't be concerned. It's not about you."

"Well then I suppose we could talk. Go ahead."

"Not this way. Face to face."

"You want to be up close to my beads. Well, I don't think I would find that to be satisfactory, if you don't mind."

"You do recall that I am entitled – that I'm an ID cop?"

"Oh indeed, Mr ID Policeman, a cop who would like to keep part of his investigations unofficial."

David had nonned the call. It was better to minimise his trail to Mr Charles. "I've sent you a rendezvous. We can make it later."

"No, I have a shift."

"Now, then."

David met her not far from the carie, on a transitway bench beside the tall windows of an officenode. The flesh within were bent at desks, silently composing documents, a task as yet beyond telepathy and still requiring screens and inputs. There had been a hint of playfulness in Mary's voice during the call but now she was not in a good mood. David sat beside her but looked across at the surfaces of concrete and steel. He didn't want the pain of seeing his daughter again in this young woman's face. And yet he wanted to be near her.

"The woman who visited Mr Charles. Was it her?" He showed an image of Obayifa from the CCTV. Mary glanced at it but hid any sign of recognition or lack of it.

"I told you. I can't be getting involved."

"Just answer the question. I've screened you out. I'm on a case and that case isn't you."

She wore a thin dress in the heat. Mary was herself, her own person, in the flesh, whatever low-grade ID criminal the network would deem her to be. He could see what used to be called her humanity, when he tried.

Flesh boarded and disembarked from N-cars nearby. A huge grain silo, as it used to be, loomed beside them. Its brickwork, one of very few examples left in the near-above, looked unreal in the bright white light.

She had been thinking. "Very well, then. Yes. That's her."

"Are you sure?"

She didn't reply.

"And she said she was a relative?"

"Which I didn't believe, but I went and asked him if he wanted to see her. I could tell he knew she must be lying as well as I did. But he agreed."

"So you took her to him. Then what?"

"He did a double-take when I led her up to him, but then he welcomed her, as though he knew her when he obviously didn't. What would a man like that have to do with someone like her? What did you call her?"

"Obayifa."

"I went to make some tea. They were chatting when I returned. Something wasn't right, though; the scene was a little forced. She said she wanted to take him out. He looked at me and hesitated, but he went along with it."

"And all this time, you say the carie had nothing on her. What about your beads?"

She laughed at him. "My beads, eh. You want to ask about my beads. Can't you feel them, Mr Detective? Let's just say they are a Westaf variety."

"Where are you from?"

"East of there. Or Avonmouth city. It's all the same, isn't it? It's all nodes in the Between. Who knows where they will dispatch me next."

"Go back to that day in the carie. What did your beads tell you about her?"

"Come to think of it, I don't believe I remember anything about her that way. There was nothing. But then I don't make it my business to feel people around me. And I didn't need my beads in order to know I didn't trust her. But I couldn't go against his wishes."

"So she took him out. For how long?"

"For lunch, she said, but not long. Half an hour, maybe."

"And she returned with him?"

"I've already told you. She brought him into the lobby but wouldn't explain what had happened to him. She was smirking as she left. Had a module waiting. Flew off."

"Tell me more about the state of Mr Charles."

"I've never seen anything like it. All the life sucked out of him. I couldn't coax another word from his lips. Climbed onto the furniture with an empty look, as though even the pain was gone. Two days later, he was dead."

She looked at him and he looked back at her. "Can I go now?" She stood up. "What is it with you? You're so sad. Have you lost someone? Not Mr Charles – someone else?"

She eyed his forlorn uniform of suit and shades. The grief of his double loss passed like a heavy wave over him.

"Don't go."

"Excuse me?"

"Stay awhile."

"Oh. Mr ID Detective wants to spend time with his next victim. Why don't you get it over with?"

She thrust out her wrists, the beads lifeless on the left.

He looked up into his daughter's face, then thought about the vodu. He was feeling faint. "I told you I'm not interested in you in that way. Go, why don't you."

A two-car swept up. She walked into it, stared down the platform while the doors swished shut in front of him and the two-car took her away.

# CHAPTER TEN
## Pempamsie

I continued to be an object of interest to the Chinese robots, who accosted me like dogs scenting a fracture in normality.

And they were not my only problem. I had to give the Ohen Tuos the slip many times. At least, I believed it was they. The thing inside warned me about them. It might equally have been telling them where I was. How else were the Ohen Tuos following me, I, an expert in losing tails? I looked at my beads – at what I used to think of as my beads. I was no longer in control of what emanated from them. If I were Swirling Suit, I would leave a means of re-appropriating my handiwork, should I need it. It takes madness or supreme confidence to default on payment to one such as he. I, Pempamsie, used to be supremely confident.

I resolved to seek Nsoroma, a child of the sky, in order to achieve Sankofa: undo my mistakes.

Not far from the Dame-Dame Towers, where I first met Swirling Suit, just off Oxford Street, was a painting house. Flesh created pictures there. It was off the track. A house of truth, from a distant age. Their brushes, their paints, their canvases and frames, were all procured from flesh far away in what used to be known as the Upper Volta. They painted pots, people, rivers, clouds. The paintings celebrated the fleshwork in finely cast brush strokes.

And in the painting house flesh survived, somehow. Their materials were purchased, the paintings disseminated, sold through a network; they flowed through our human rivers, our Nkonsonkonso.

I, Pempamsie, took a one-car tro-tro there to sit for a portrait. As I entered, pushing aside a beaded curtain, I saw a scene of industry. I went and sat with others queuing. We took in the light from windows in the ceiling, the resinous smell. One by one we were picked. A painter silently chose us. One by one the others in the queue followed their choosers to stations in the open space, where they were arranged for their portraits. The painting began, silent and assiduous.

No one seemed to notice me here. I was only one link in Nkonsonkonso.

Except that a boy entered the studio. I thought he too was to be a subject. But he took paints and brushes from a cupboard and walked up to me.

I followed him though the large studio floor, winding through painters and subjects, all sweating, good-natured, enjoying their mutual presence.

"Please, sit," he said.

We were in a corner of the studio, opposite to where I had waited.

"To paint," he said, "is to regain our true flesh selves." He smiled, a boy of about sixteen, serious. Then he fell silent. He picked out the lines of me as he worked his brushes, dipping them in a palette of fat paints, applying them to the portrait with total concentration.

"What do you see?" I asked. The sun streamed around us.

"An unwelcome visitor. Who will not leave."

"Yes."

"And who feeds off his host, however small his appetite. A vodu."

"A vodu? What is that?" I affected ignorance. No one around us appeared to be listening. It was as though he and I were dreaming together in one dream. He looked at me even more intently.

"We have a saying: clarity is everything."

"I have lost my clarity," I said.

"You wanted to. You entered the Divide."

"I want my clarity back."

"And the consequences?"

"Damn the consequences. I... I would be Pemp... I would be Pem..." I could not utter my name. I was strangled from inside. The vodu.

"There is one in UK land who may be able to help you. You would be Pempamsie again. You would be your own clarity: a tree that stands alone and reaches for the sky. I don't know him, only the place where he lives. In Super Mare."

"But what do you know about him?"

"He opposes."

"Opposes what?"

"The order. Such a man may be able to help you."

Hours passed. Evening gathered outside. He turned the canvas around. How could he have finished so quickly? But there I was, beneath Osrane ne nsoroma, the moon and star. A little way behind me stood a figure: a young woman whose face was lit with a searing stare.

"Who is she?"

"A vampire," he said. "A triumph of mentalmagic; a case of complete vodu inhabitance."

The boy explained that my squatter, injected by Swirling Suit, was nothing compared to her: a minor perturbation by comparison to her tidal wave of fuckery.

"What will she do to me?"

"You would be wrung of all psychic energy. But only if she can remove your vodu first."

"How so?"

"Two vodus may not touch in the same mind."

It was unlikely such a pursuer would be ignorant of my inhabitance; therefore she knew a way to remove my vodu, Nsoroma explained. Then she would enter me to steal my mind. She would take me with her. I would be absorbed by her, wanted purely for food and not for my identity. I, Pempamsie, would be absolutely lost.

"Find this man," he said. "But do not go directly to Super Mare. Travel instead to nearby Avonmouth city. Ask for him there. Ask for guidance."

"Ask who?"

"Another of our fleshren. He knows of vodus. Now, I have told you all I know. I wish you good fortune in finding Kerapa: that which removes evil."


A few days later, Nsoroma entered the busy studio, whose smells of sweat and paint and canvas and whose light pouring in from huge panes in the roof filled him with love for flesh, for Nkonsonkonso, the chain of flesh pouring through the world.

He passed in front of those who were waiting, seated along one wall and watching the scene of artists and subjects, listening to their chatter and hoping to join them. Patience, patience. There was no booking system. You turned up and hoped that that day you would be blessed in oils, committed to returning for days if necessary until your portrait was complete. But you might never be picked in the first place.

Today there were many in the waiting line. Many parents accompanying their children. Nsoroma looked particularly at these young faces.

However, his eye was caught by the man in the last seat. This man was deemed important in some sense, for he was clearly under the protection of a bigger man next to him, a man wearing the Ohen Tuo symbol on his lapel. And, Nsoroma now realised, there had been another Ohen Tuo stationed across Oxford Street.

Nsoroma picked not the man but his henchman, beckoning him.

But it was his master who stood up. And it was he who followed Nsoroma to an empty place in the studio floor.

The suit of this man bore a scene of volcanic mountains, streams and cherry blossom. When he sat down the scenery began to shift, swirling around him. It was highly distracting.

"Could you switch that off, please, if I am to paint you? Not that I chose you, but you are here now."

"Me c'yaan switch it off. Has a mind fi its own, ya seen. Must like young Mr Painter, wanna dance fi 'im."

"Then I won't be able to paint you after all. I didn't pick you. Please ask your friend to come over instead."

"Me tink ya bin paintin' a friend o' mine lately. A little hey nonny nonnee, hey nonny non. Wid a likkle someting speciahl a gwaan inside. Ya hear me, brudda?" The way this man talked, the violence that lay in his tone despite the childish words he sometimes used, made Nsoroma afraid.

"I don't know who you mean."

His henchman appeared beside him. A frail easel stood between Nsoroma and the two men.

"Me know you's a lyin' now." The man in the swirling suit leaned and gently pushed the easel aside. "An me know ya a youth a da star, da likkle child o' da sky. You da likkle man a nonny nonnee gone to fi advice. An ya gonna tell I what it is you run gone tell da hey nonny nonnee non. Seen?"

# CHAPTER ELEVEN
## David

On his return to the labnode, David took a scrap of comfort from the innocence of the natural world around it. Gulls were still swooping and crying outside. The waves crashed like cymbals. He breathed in the sea air.

"The A/C is broken," said Dirac when he greeted him at the door. "It's stifling, I know, but we'll just have to manage."

"Breakage?" said David. The bodai was again in the form of an old woman, but as strong and dexterous as any other bodai. There was a pause as integers streamed through a multitude of algorithms in an attempt to devise a response. To no avail.

David, tense with accumulated frustration, closed his eyes and took a breath. His assistant's obtusity sometimes became too much, however much he couldn't help the limitations of all AIs.

He spelled it out. "Can. You. Fix. The. A/C?"

"No skillpack for A/C. All is known."

David looked in vain for something on Dirac's desk to fan himself with.

"Please excuse us," he said, and took the bodai aside.

"Breakage, you're no help to me here. I'd like you to look for the remaining crew of the *Mekhanik Pustoshnyy*."

"Not necessary. All is known."

"No. Not all is known. That's why the ID police exist."

"Found in Big Mind."

"No. The two we found dolled were not where their online traces indicated and neither will the others be. They were fabbed, Breakage, despite police-issued IDs. They were flickering around Avonmouth city like Elizabethan light bulbs on the blink, and so will the others be. Remember who we are? We. Are. The. ID. Police. I'm instructing you to look. Physical search. In the fleshwork. The near-above. The down-below. Back to the Hotel Royal. Everywhere."

"Task exceeds limits. Breakage incapable."

"Breakage try."

"Bod dispatch in thirty minutes."

"Irrelevant. Just do it, Breakage. Compute the optimal points of search."

The old woman walked out of the labnode, her age a notional artefact of clothes and wrinkled visage: the same uncanny swivelled walk of all bodais. David wondered how Breakage's algorithms would cope with an open task. But protocol was for bodais to do something when instructed: the best match, algorithmically speaking, to the task. David pictured Breakage walking among the fleshwork, peering into nodes one by one, pattern-matching with his beads, scanning irises.

He returned to Dirac.

"Are you amused, Professor?"

"Not at all, Detective." He was scornful, more like. David's inclination to trust him, so far as it went, was partly because of that scorn. It was authentic.

"There's been a development in the case I'm working on." He told Dirac about the dollings: Mr Charles, two crew found in the Hotel Royal. About Obayifa, and that he presumed she was responsible in some way, although he did not reveal Mary's testament in the case of Mr Charles. Mary was an ID felon, which wouldn't look good. He'd worry about all of that later.

Dirac listened carefully, asked for clarifications. David sweated, loosened his tie. The heat pressed like the walls of a cell.

"So you suspect she's taken their minds, Detective. Or, as you say, dolled them. Obviously, I would need to know much more about the particulars. But what you describe is psychic vampirism. And yes, I do take that seriously. I first studied these vampires a long time ago, as part of my research into the more exotic side of mental phenomena."

"And I know of them too, from Westaf. A mind-sucker. Or should I say, mind-fucker."

"If you really must put it that rather peculiar way. But indeed. Pleasure taken, energy absorbed."

"The victim's mind – vanished altogether?"

"No, Detective, she takes them with her. Every mind she has extracted will be laid out within her own consciousness, in so many mental sarcophagi existing in the eternal nightmare of her being. For feeding on."

Dirac paused, considering. "Allow me to show you something. Come."

The scientist walked stiffly through a door at the back of the office. David was more than uncomfortable now: disturbed at the turn the conversation had taken, which was too close to the horror of his own vodu. He followed Dirac.

A further door slid aside. They entered a conservatory at the back of the labnode, facing the sea. Dirac bade David to sit on a wicker chair, next to his own. A silent scape of dunes rolled down to the sea before them; the earth hung in its own searing heat. Inside, large-leaved plants thrived to either side of them. The air was moist and just bearably hot, for the glass was tinted and here the A/C worked, despite its failure in the office.

"Conservatory, more filter," Dirac commanded, and observed the sun-throttling effect. "Still more." Backlights turned on as the driving sunlight was finally thwarted. The space became a shadowy nest of plant life. The resultant intimacy increased David's unease.

"Detective, I'd like you to experience some of the results of my experiments. I hope you don't mind. I think you'll find them relevant to the case."

Dirac made no visible move, but David found himself suddenly subjected to a strong feeling of dread without any apparent cause. Dirac remained still, seated with his hands clasped upon his crossed legs, coolly regarding David's seizure by an unknown mental force. David felt an awful shadow looming across his mind. His vodu was feeling it too, milling in a tight circle in its cage.

The shadow dissolved as suddenly as it had appeared. David was thunderstruck.

Dirac smiled, touching David's knee. "It's all right. It's gone now. And you can tell your inhabitant the same – I was going to say your 'friend', but I doubt he's that. Except that perhaps you don't need to tell him. He's connected to the same manifold that you call your consciousness. He is listening, one with you and yet separate. Am I wrong, Detective?"

"I've no idea what you're talking about. You've lived alone too long. Solitude has stoked your imagination."

"Come now. I have instruments that can detect mental phenomena in the data that passes to and from my visitors. I built them for my research into psychblood. One proved to be especially sensitive."

"Psychblood but not consciousness, Professor. It is merely an electro-chemical conductor between the brain and the network. All is known." David pronounced the network's mantra with a heavy irony.

"Consciousness and psychblood are intimately intertwined, as you know. After all, it's how the network plays sensa into the genpop's minds. And both times you have visited, I have picked up an extra reading."

"I came to talk about the circuit of bones, and what we are agreeing is a mind-sucking vampire, Dirac. Now can we please stick to business?"

"Naturally. We will come to all of that in good time. First, I wanted only to let you know that you had a friend. In me, that is. I can't tell much about what is squatting within you. Judging by my previous encounters, yours is remarkably well behaved. Or shackled. Wouldn't you like to take off your sunglasses? It's rather dark in here."

"Stop. You have confessed to illicit instrumentation, to monitoring an officer of the ID police. I could haul you in—"

"And I could tell them what I know. About why you wear the sunglasses. Why you don't expose your arms." Dirac flashed a grotesque smile that was meant to be reassuring. "I should advise you that we are in a Faraday cage. Nothing, literally nothing, leaves my little conservatory here. And algorithmically speaking, it's as though we were both still just outside it, having a pleasant chat. Not offline, in other words, as far as the network is concerned. So you don't need to worry on that score."

A familiar dread came to David at the thought of his vodu's exposure or, much worse, escape. What was the mental force Dirac had subjected him to? He was letting him know of his capabilities. If Dirac meddled, the vodu could be unleashed and then he would be completely lost. As if he didn't feel lost enough now. He looked at the professor. Bitter he may be, his ego bludgeoned by denial of his achievements from on high, but David could detect no malice. Why was Dirac taking the risk of his revelations? Who would believe a crank like him, with far-fetched stories of spirits inhabiting minds, against the word of an officer in the ID police?

"What do you want?"

"I'm reaching the end of my working life as a scientist. And have little to lose. Between IANI and Westaf, I've watched the fruits of my research being abused. My colleagues leapt on electro-psychic technologies as an exciting development for what they thought was the good of human communication. But I – perhaps because psychblood was my doing, but to different ends – I couldn't bring myself to join them. I would like to help you, if it means putting a stop to that abuse. Which this Obayifa and the bone circuitry of yours reveal to a new degree. Not to mention your own particular problem. I'm looking at your forehead, David, because it's in there. Unless it's in another space altogether. Whoever planted it—"

"I'm not sure it was planted there so much as allowed to enter."

Dirac raised his eyebrows. "Remarkable. You mean it's not a construct of flesh?"

"Yes and no. It's a vodu, Professor. One of your psychic vampires. Vodus are supposedly ancient, have fed for centuries. Is mine one of them, which has been captured and engineered? Or has someone synthesised it with their technology? How could we tell the difference? Do vodus age, bear scars?"

"Whatever yours is, it hasn't taken you over. But it must be feeding."

"I've had to increase my psychblood levels. And there is a mental toll, but I can't positively ascribe that to 'feeding' as opposed to the stress its existence subjects me to. It's waiting."

"For?"

"This has been a nice conversation, Professor. I appreciate your concern. Now, I have to go."

"But you said you came to talk about the circuit of bones."

David couldn't think. The vodu wouldn't let him. He had to get away.

"Another time."


They had a purpose, the fifteen men from the *Mekhanik Pustoshnyy*. They just didn't know what it was.

Two of them were holed up in a node in the near-above, a dump no right-thinking flesh would normally occupy. A disused storage space, difficult to get to. They had found it by following an industry-class bodai on a four-car. A screeching worknode nearby made it noisy as hell.

At the first opportunity they had swapped a pair of beads between them, in the particular manner the Ohen Tuos had shown them. It was far from perfect but it scrambled their IDs sufficiently to obscure them to the network for a while.

"It doesn't make sense," one of them said, sitting on the floor and hunched against the wall. "Who are we, to be in this situation? Nobody. Nothing in common. Thirteen of us left, with those two gone. As far as we know, anyway. What she did to those two, she'll do to us. May have done to others."

He had been plucked from an officenode in Accra.city, where he had been an administrator. The other, who was older, a financial controller, replied, "I told you. Leave it. We'll be okay. She won't find us here and I'm not going anywhere until we make contact. If we go against the orders it'll be worse."

"You don't understand what she can do. What she did to them. I've seen it with my own eyes, back home."

"Will you stop being such a sissy? You're so frustrating! Get a grip! We have a plan, so stick with it."

But the financial controller had his own doubts. Each of them, with no connection they could discover, taken from middle-class obscurity by Ohen Tuos. Press-ganged. To sail a sizeable cargo ship to what turned out to be this dump, Avonmouth.city. It made no sense. He didn't trust the man behind all of this, the renegade. They hadn't met him, but when they pieced their stories together they discovered each had been told of the man who had arranged their trip. Whose mission it was. Whose instructions they were to await at their destination. Or else.

And she. How to describe her? That thing. He'd known something was up with the girl as soon as he'd seen her on the ship. They all had. It was plain she wasn't Ohen Tuo, but she had not been press-ganged like the rest of them. She was a tool. A tool they were delivering. And they were some kind of accessory for her, as strange as that sounded: accessories for her and that case, which she had nursed like a baby on board the ship, looking at their curious faces with cool contempt. They had talked about the case, about what was so important within it. She never slept. And then, the night they arrived, she had hidden it, somewhere within the vast hold.

The administrator's face was still wide with terror. He was working himself up, higher and higher. "Let's give ourselves up. We'll be safer in custody."

"Oh, you think? Safe from the renegades?"

"Look, I've been thinking. Why sixteen of us on the ship?"

"What? What are you talking about now? Why not? A power of two."

"Four of us could have sailed that ship with all those systems on board. They didn't need all of us to crew it. We're food. Food for her."

"She could have had us on board the ship, in that case. Two to the two to the two. Owo foro adobe has sixteen lines. To perform the impossible. Snake climbing the palm. Now go to sleep."

"I'm going out. I can't stand this."

"You're crazy. You'll get us both fucked. Stay."

"I won't be long. I'll get food."

"How? We're Westafs. You're just drawing more attention to us."

"I don't know. We've got to eat, haven't we?"

The financial controller sighed. "There's nothing I can do to stop you, my friend. Don't be long."

He hung his head after the administrator had left. Life was like that: uncontrollable. Now they were at their destination, it was time for her to collect whatever he was carrying. It was either his mind or his beads.

Or both. Maybe just the beads, but she would consume his mind as well because that's what creatures like her did. The beads on his left wrist configured and reconfigured, their substrate dug into his flesh. They were beyond his comprehension, beyond just about everyone's on this earth. At least they were of the Westaf variety.

He lay in the dust. Earplugs, improvised by ripping fragments from his clothes, could not quite baffle the screeches from the nearby worknode.

Then he noticed the door screen had switched on.

He hauled his tired body up from the filthy floor for a closer look. No one. But someone must have been outside.

"Node, who is outside?"

"No one near in outside. All is known."

"Why did the screen come on?"

"Unknown. All is known."

He pressed to open the door, despite his fear. Hunted like prey, he suddenly wanted an end to it.

There was a short deck outside, and he walked from one end to the other in the night, only faintly visible in the pockets of node-glare in his surroundings. The air was good, the damp warmth of it imbued with a metallic reality from the screeching worknode.

He turned to go back inside.

And she jumped down on him.

She blocked him from both the door to the node and the metal stairway down from the deck. She was lithe, eyes glowing with mentalmagic, arm muscles toned. His physical strength was possibly greater than hers, but that wasn't the point. Aboard the ship he had managed to avoid direct dealings with her. She had cowed those unfortunate enough – those who thought themselves brave enough – to approach her. The crew had started their journey as equals, waking aboard the ship with neither guards nor masters but all hearing the same tannoyed instructions, the same warning of what would happen if they did not obey. The task of sailing the unfamiliar ship, however automated, to its destination had occupied them, even though the administrator was right and there were too many of them. They had taken it in turns. But not her. One by one they had realised she had powers beyond their understanding. They had let her be, carrying that case of hers wherever she went.

"I don't have it," he said. "Whatever you are after. Your case – surely you don't think I... The ID cops must have it."

"Say these words," she said. "Say the words I'm now going to speak to you." Her sickly smile was filled with sharp teeth, a tongue twitching between them.

He backed off, feeling the cold railing touch his kidneys. The screeching had stopped temporarily. Whumps of wind turbines and the distant whines of motors transporting the denizens of Avonmouth.city could now be heard. Lights transited the scene.

"Look, I don't know what you want, but in the name of my family just do whatever you came for and get it over with."

She walked up to him and kissed him firmly on the lips, ramming her tongue inside.

"It's all right," she paused and said. "You only have to repeat after me."

He could feel a twinge in his beads, an energy that matched the intensity in her face.

He repeated what she said. He could not help himself.

As he did so, it was as though she came inside his mind, licking and fetching from every corner all that he possessed: all the moments since his birth, from the first sight of his mother's face to the paralysing moment when this woman, this thing, jumped down on him just now.

All of it gone.

It was night-time. On his way back from Dirac's labnode to his desres with the case of bones, David had a sense that someone was following him. A completely nonned Obayifa was wandering around Avonmouth.city, and he possessed her circuitry of bones. He thought he heard a noise and quickly turned around. No one. There it was again, the feeling of someone watching him, as he climbed the stairs towards his complex. But the walkway was empty.

He showered, scattering his clothes on the way to the bathroom, showered in cold water which stung his heat-numbed flesh, wanting to clean himself of his vodu, of its exposure to Dirac. He couldn't blame the man, but he felt the vodu's violation even more acutely now that Dirac knew about it. Why had he made himself vulnerable to such an intelligent man? He hit himself hard while the water flowed, beat his own head with his fists. "Fuck-up," he said aloud to himself. "Fucking fuck-up."

The moment David left the bathroom, Breakage patched through.

"Two more dolls. Beads hacked. Fabrication. Locations false. Plan B. Retina scans confirm crew of *Mekhanik Pustoshnyy*. All is known."

David finished towelling himself, pulled himself together. It was strange but almost welcome to hear Breakage adopt his term for the vacant vestiges of humanness that four of the *Mekhanik Pustoshnyy*'s crew had now become. David viewed the images that Breakage had recorded at the scene. The two men had been found perched in the sky side of the near-above, eyes roving, staring blankly into the windows of the N-cars as they ferried ones between nodes. They looked like emptied angels who had climbed precariously to the highest attainable points.

"Who found them?"

"Multiple passenger sightings. Flesh reported to transit bodais."

"Have you sent them for medical examination?"

"Passengers—"

"The dolls."

"Yes. Preliminary analysis reports mental activity levels negligible. Match other dolls."

"You did well, Breakage. Over."

His shapeless clothes lay on the floor, a path of them running through unopened or half-opened boxes of purchases and belongings, like discarded parts of himself.

Hanging from a thin gold chain around his neck, a heart-shaped locket lay against his hairless chest. And in that locket a picture of Yaa. He had not opened it since the night the renegades attacked him in East Legon. The thought of the vodu's creepy gaze upon her was more than he could bear.

The case sat open on the coffee table next to him.

"How many present?" he said to the desres.

"Two present."

"Including me?"

"Including you." The bones were beaconing in a sophisticated way, as an identity of some kind, one which the desres now appeared to accept with equanimity. How long would it take her to find them?

"Who is the other?"

"All is known."

"Specify."

"All is known."

"Has it been here before?"

"Yes. All is known."

Knowledge. Not knowing what it is that you do not know. Knowing what you do not want to know. David did not know Yaa's whereabouts. Thank goodness that was possible in Westaf. It was important not to know.

He put on gloves, the latex like insect skin against his nakedness, and examined the bone circuitry again. Was the presence in the entire circuit or a part of it? The presence was pseudo-mental: the instruments detected the presence of a mind but not the mind of flesh. Like the presence of a lion, David imagined from a book he had read, if a lion could think. Where were mental phenomena rooted in the brain – all of it, or parts of it? Where was his vodu? In his brain, or was it holed up in Westaf, making itself felt through the network? He had been offline at times. But offline to the renegades?

David rubbed his sleepless eyes, stretched his arms before him. The veins ran down his bare forearms to the ivory gloves. As far as he could tell, he was the result of a botched experiment: a foray into advancing electro-mental arts beyond telepathic transmission. He thought back to his capture, the mental rape through which he had remained unconscious.

The vodu watched him now as he considered the bones' origins; it looked at the circuitry, then back inside him to his thoughts. Just as the vodu watched when he fucked the Royal girls, as though it wanted him to fuck them harder. Mr Charles had said once, without knowing about David's afflictions, that it is always possible to say stop. But it wasn't. David went to the bedroom and tried to sleep.

A few hours later, a banging on his front door stirred him from his bed.

He lay back, naked, on the settee and watched the screen which showed the view outside his doorway. A group of flesh had gathered, some shuffling, some stock still, many looking unsure as to why they were there. But the original man who had visited, apparently the ringleader of the group, began to gesture wildly at the camera. This galvanised the others. They variously implored the unseen David. They wanted the bones. They started to bang on his door again.

"Breakage, come. And bring bodais to take these flesh back to their caries."

David watched as Breakage turned up outside the desres in a matter of minutes, a worker bodai in overalls with a group of bodais in blue carie uniforms. The ringleader of the dems now spat at Breakage. "Bastard! Robot cunt! Fuck you!" His demented cohort sprang into song. "Dem bones dem bones, deeem…", like children from another century.

Breakage remained impassive, strong against the ringleader's attempts to push him over. The incident would be logged but passed over. This fleshwork anomaly was of no more interest to the network than the problem of occasional litter. It lay outside its principal algorithms, did not exist unless it interfered with the streaming of sensa to and from the genpop's minds. And these were dems: disconnected and therefore irrelevant.

Breakage waited outside while the carie bodais went about their work, taking the escapees away. Suddenly David realised that one of the handlers was flesh. To his horror, he saw it was Mary.

"Please, everyone, we have to return to the carie." She looked and sounded distraught. The escapees were like frightened children now, pleading.

"We want our bones." "We want to go home." "We want our bones." "Where are my bones?" "Can I go home now?"

The bodais were putting their cold hands on them, expressionless, uttering meaningless calming phrases in female voices, irrespective of their bod's notional gender.

"Whose desres is this?" Mary asked Breakage. The bodai would know immediately that she was in breach of ID protocols.

"Breakage, leave her alone!" David said through the intercom.

She turned to the camera.

"You! Let me in. Let me in, dammit!"

David rose from the settee in his nakedness and latex gloves and walked to the screen. Her face filled it, angry and tearful, distorted in the wide-angle lens.

"I said let me in!" She turned to Breakage. "He is in there, right?"

"No comment. Resident unknown. All is known," said Breakage, trying to undo the identification of a member of the ID police.

"I'll take that as a yes. What are you doing to my residents? What have you got in there? What's all this about bones, Mr ID Policeman? Eh? What have you got to say for yourself?"

David was overcome by deep shame. He couldn't think of what he had done wrong but he was mortified anyway. Mary acted as though she had nothing to lose with him, despite her ID felony. And it was true that he didn't want to arrest her. Eventually she stormed off with the last of her dems, disappearing into the Avonmouth.city night, its skeleton of nodes.

He cast her from his mind. As long as his heart was hard, as long as affection did not infuse it, all the flesh he encountered were safe from him, safe from his vodu.

And yet: events were turning; the arrival of Obayifa, and now the bones and the dems, were giving his worthless life the good kicking it needed.

Breakage entered, Breakage and the bath-time air. David put his dark glasses back on. He was naked. The bodai, in its blue, buckled overalls, looked straight-faced at where David's eyes would be.

"I asked you to search for the crew. What have you found?"

"Crew not exist. All is known."

"You looked."

"Correct."

"Where?"

"In Big Mind."

"I told you to look in the fleshwork. In the physical world."

"Impossible."

"Dammit. Where in Big Mind did you look, then?"

"Anomaly."

"What kind of anomaly?"

"Beads hacked."

"We knew that. What else?"

"Unexplained algorithmic determination. Extra anomaly in beads. All is known."

"Except that it isn't. It never is. It's not logically possible to know that all is known."

The desres said, "Bodai interchange scheduled. Now."

"Let it in."

A smart female business bodai entered. She and Breakage touched beads. The manual worker stepped out and the businesswoman remained, standing, eerily turned away from David, looking at nothing in particular.

"Breakage, what is it like?"

Breakage turned, the substituted bod having now located the source of the voice.

"It?"

"Rebodding. What's it like?"

"Breakage status: okay."

"Is anything different?"

"Bod change."

"Beyond that?"

"All is known."

"Please get on with the search. The physical search. With this bod, another bod, a hundred bods – why not? I don't care how you do it, but search. I need you to help me. And meanwhile run more analyses in Big Mind to see if you can explain this anomaly in the dolls' beads. That will be all, Breakage. Oh, I'll need you in the morning."

He put the bone circuitry back in its case. Those demented souls were drawn to the bones for some unfathomable reason. When would they return? How many more would come?

And Obayifa would come for them too. He seemed reluctant to rid himself of them, but it was madness to keep them here. He had to find somewhere safe for them.

# CHAPTER TWELVE
## Pempamsie

I, Pempamsie, arrived in UK.land. I found strange, mostly pale people here: obedient, or shouting curses. The fleshren, that is. The robots are stupid and uncanny like our own. I have seen no Chinese robots.

I beached my craft beyond Avonmouth.city. It served me well, sailing across the Sahara to Europe, above the channel and through the tangle of near-above that makes up the few remaining cities on this island.

I listened back to my own imprint on the network, with a scope I retained from IANI. I, my true I, was non-existent in the noise. My vodu ciphered me throughout my user journey and still does. It delta'd me, modulated my emanations into the net to avoid detection. It seems to have worked so far. But I cannot be sure that a higher algorithm will not parse and pattern-match my presence out of my network touchpoints.

And most of all, I cannot be sure that Swirling Suit did not leave a back door.

I must rid myself of my inhabitant. And yet evade capture. But better true – my parents' faces, and all the multifarious memories of them, which I know are there, at my recall again, my self returned to me intact – better true than free.

The painter told me I must find the one who can help me in Super Mare, must ask for him here. I, Pempamsie, will heed his words. For he is true flesh. But who must I ask – trust to ask? And can I even trust myself? Pempamsie has arrived incognito by dint of borrowing from a spirit unknown. It should merely tweak my behaviour, but I feel it steering me. When I landed, there was a struggle with the joystick. It had its own wants – I could feel it, its hungry volition. I pulled the joystick back to its true alignment.

I am tall. My hair is coiled. My lips are full. Eyes bright. And yet.

Swirling Suit may know where I am, even though I stopped randomly, zigzagged, rested here outside Avonmouth.city, where no one would think of heading. There is a barren hill, despondent trees, strange little birds calling and larger black birds cawing and flapping from the treetops. A pool.

I brought my painting with me to remind me of who I am and what dangers I face. It is framed and held in a protective case permeable to air so that its drying can be completed. The moon and star. I, Pempamsie, beneath it. Behind me, she who is a vampire of the mind. Swirling Suit wants revenge. But she is no ordinary means. She is so clearly pursuing me in Nsoroma's painting. Perhaps it takes one to know one: maybe a vodu can find a vodu, however nonned its carrier.

I must not speculate; I must make for Avonmouth.city. I take my bag and the painting, abandon the craft after hacking and cleaning it of Is and zeroes as I learned in the icestation. And set off walking.


I, Pempamsie, spent weeks in Avonmouth.city without success. My goal was to achieve Sankofa: undo my mistakes. Which meant tracking down whoever knew how to find help in Super Mare. Nsoroma had told me of two steps, both without anything concrete to go on: first a man who knew of vodus in Avonmouth.city, then a man without beads in Super Mare. Nsoroma was wise, I have no doubt, but lacking in details. I was forced to engage with the pale denizens here, to ask around. And at the same time, I took care not to reveal myself too far. Though I was nonned, I was still physically vulnerable.

I took a room in a low-life hotel to minimise my visibility. I spent the days riding in the strange tro-tros they call N-cars, which hang instead of running on rails, watching, following strangers who, my instincts told me, might know what I needed to know. Days spent stopping them and asking, "Do you know Super Mare? Do you know of vodus?"

It was hopeless. They looked at me as though I were mad. "Are you a dem?" they said. "Get away from me."

Day by day my squatter corroded my soul. Yes, there was one locus. Yes, it was I. But my parents' faces were completely gone. I knew only that I had parents, that they existed. But not who they were. All I took with me to the icestation was my memories of them. I was not, I knew, a dem. I tested myself regularly. I could calculate, find my way, could recall many specific details from throughout my life. But not my parents. Moreover, when I spoke – when I had to speak, for I had no desire to – the words I uttered seemed not to be entirely mine. Was this merely the fruit of my imagination?

I was not of Avonmouth.city, but merely within it. An evanescent inhabitant, ghosting it. My heart said Dwennimmen, concealment. But I had to keep looking, blindly. And meanwhile I had to earn bytecoins for lodgings, food.

There were women in the hotel, sex workers. I joined them. Needs must. But only so far.

My first visitor was a wan specimen indeed. I took his bytecoins. I laid him down. I did not smile. There was a mirror by the bed. I looked at myself. The scar lay on my cheek like a reclining stranger. A bright sun tried to shine in my eyes through the clouds of the vodu that trammelled me.

"I'm not going to fuck you," I said. He would not remember. He would recall only a non-specific pleasure after taking the draft I had offered him. "Something special from Westaf," I told him, "included in the price."

In the hotel room I fixed my hair as high as I could; I made structures in it, as did my ancestors. I dug in a wooden comb, Duafe. Sunglasses and facial jewellery further altered my aspect. I did not look as I had in Accra.city. Disguise. An old art which satisfied an irrational urge. There was no reason to think she could tell me from other women, with or without it.

Then I saw her, the vampire. She boarded an N-car with me. There was no mistaking her: a weird energy in her eyes; a chill about her long limbs, her veined arms. I moved, careful in my concealment, Dwennimmen, among the crowds. Casually I made my way along the cars away from her and disembarked. She was like a blind woman sniffing me out. She knew her prey was near. Could she suck out the minds of the entire tro-tro? The whole of Avonmouth.city?

I felt lonely: a new feeling since my arrival here. On seeing this creature I was lonelier. I thought of the child of the sky, Nsoroma, in the painting house so far away. His portrait of me lay in the hotel room, with her behind me.

Swirling Suit had done his job well. He sent her after me, but I was nonned even to her. Was he capable of reaching her, to engineer her further against his engineering of me? Or was she not of his making at all?

Those in the Between had lost their true flesh selves. And what if Swirling Suit sent more vampires like her? They would lose everything.

Aya: I am not afraid of you.

137

I loved the sun on my skin. I loved the faint scent of my sweat, the way my hair stood tall. But I was no longer my true I inside.

# CHAPTER THIRTEEN
## David

After just a few hours' sleep, David showered again in an effort to wake himself. The desres chimed, its sound penetrating the pouring water. "Priority call. Officer Parkin."

David towelled himself, hunted for elusive clean clothes.

"What is it?"

"Why do you still have those bones?"

"What's it to you? We've discussed this. The original case in connection with the *Mekhanik Pustoshnyy* is closed, and now I have a new one, remember?"

"Not quite closed."

"Oh?"

"The network is interested in what's happening to those crew members of yours, David."

"The network? Which multinat do you mean?"

"All is known, David." Parkin's voice was cold, ironic. "They want the bones."

A small voice inside David said he could be rid of them, hand them over. They would be somebody else's problem.

"No, I need them for other investigations. They are physical evidence."

"A touch old-fashioned, wouldn't you say? Not to be dealing with Big Mind alone?"

"I could say the same to you. Who are you speaking for? What's it to a forensics officer? Haven't you got some combing thorough Big Mind to be getting on with?"

"Calm down, David. They want them. They'll get them. Despite you."

"Well, you'll have to wait. I have reason to believe they are material to two psychic attacks."

"'Psychic attacks'? Really! That's how you describe what's been happening to the crew? We've noticed you are spending time on this case with a new sidekick. What madness has he or she got you thinking about, David? We're unable to identify this new party. Which is strange for someone hanging out with an ID police officer."

"It's experimental. Something new-fangled courtesy of Professor Dirac, if you must know. He tells me it may help ID the psychic attacker. I'm unconvinced, but it's worth a try."

"'It'? Bead me to it. I'd like to feel it."

"That won't be necessary. Dirac tells me it's important to tune only myself to it, or it won't be an effective tool. Anyway, I think it might be malfunctioning. I think I'm going to return it to him."

"Intriguing. We'll be taking a closer interest from now on. In you and your professor."

"My professor? He's assigned to the department, remember? Parkin…"

"Yes?"

"I'd leave me to it, if I were you. Westaf has its hands all over the psychic attacks. I don't want you stumbling around and getting in my way. You and whatever multinat you represent. I can take this to IANI, you know. All the way up."

Parkin terminated the call.

Evidently Parkin had not picked up the bone circuitry's emanations during its time in his custody. Had they begun only after David took them? And was that connected specifically to him? With his vodu? Or maybe they began beaconing sometime after losing contact with Obayifa. He had to take the bone circuitry back to Dirac for further examination, and not allow himself to be distracted this time.

David's vodu shifted among his thoughts like a grim intruder rifling through an attic, notwithstanding the cage that contained it. He could see it clearly: sinewy and naked. A body inside his mind. And a mind inside a body inside his mind.

He winced. Slowly he returned to the bathroom to look at himself. Tired but not bad for a man of forty-seven, if you didn't count the veins streaming down to his big hands. Breakage had seen him naked, but the physical manifestation of flesh per se was irrelevant to the network. The multinats cared only about the online consequences of physical existence. Parkin knew something but not much. At least, that's how it seemed. Was Breakage really not reporting any of David's activities to the network – the emanations from the case, Mary, the visits by dems?

A queer, shifting presence shone from his uncovered eyes, symptomatic of the vodu within but less intense than Obayifa's mentalmagic. Any flesh would know something was not right.

"Breakage."

"Breakage here." The bodai, dispatched elsewhere, spoke through the desres.

"You're to accompany me to the labnode. Then you can go."


David handed the case over to Dirac.

"Are you going to be all right out here?"

"Alone, the stretching estuary on one side of me, plied by barely controlled ships from another century; locked up with ancient but electronically enhanced fragments of a humanoid whose weird network presence lies beyond the normal bounds of the virtual and is, one might say, supervirtual? Whatever could go wrong?" Dirac did not smile.

"I'll have a feel from the network locked onto you. Breakage will be on it."

"Good luck with instructing him. Is there something I should know, a reason not to take these bones?"

"The danger, as you know, is Obayifa. She'll want them back."

"Has she tried to take them from you?"

"I've seen no sign of her. Although I have sensed someone following me around. Just—"

"Just what?"

"There have been escapees from a nearby carie, dems, camped outside my door. Somehow they knew about the bones."

"Interesting. Perhaps they sense a way of reclaiming what they have lost."

"You think so? Obviously I can't get any sense out of them. At least, they act as though they are demented."

"But not all of them might be?"

"One of them was at my door even before I had the bones. Muttered something about juju."

Dirac snorted. "Juju indeed. At any rate, no doubt Obayifa is a powerful threat. I will expect her. She may have followed you. Quite possibly she is capable of tracking the emanations."

"I was careful. How could I fail to notice someone tailing me to the middle of nowhere?"

"Hardly nowhere, Detective. The fringes of the network."

"I am grateful to you, Dirac. You're the best person I can think of to look after the bones. No doubt they will prove an interesting subject for your examination. I assume you have a safe. If Obayifa were to come—"

"You may rest assured I will secure them. It is I who should thank you, for the opportunity to study them. And whatever it is within them."

"You think it's a vodu, like mine?"

"Your visitor, ah, yes. But I rather think this bone circuitry might be quite different. More of Westaf's experimentation, but to a different end."

"You mean the renegades. But hence the network's interest, too, I guess. Parkin's been calling me about the bones, and about an identity accompanying me – as though it weren't the same thing."

"Best not to speculate about the network – as you, an ID officer responsible for enforcing its obfuscation, know well."

"Point taken. Back to the renegades, then. What other kind of purpose might the bone circuitry have?"

"I really have no idea as yet. It's another type of construct I haven't seen before, its purpose rather obscure."

"Whatever happened to the idea of Nature, Professor, plain and simple?"

"Humans happened to Nature. And now both have been subsumed by the network. Goodbye for now, Detective."

David felt a pang of cowardice for handing over the bone circuitry to Dirac. He had told himself that Dirac would be safe, that he was the one best placed to keep the bones for now. But he had put him in danger. He turned around.

"Dirac."

"Yes?"

"Can you make the emanations appear back at my desres instead of here?"

"But then you will continue to be in danger."

"Leave that to me."

"With the right virtual Faraday here, an encrypted route to your desres, a—"

"Please do it."

It might not fool IANI or Westaf for long, let alone Obayifa. It was a mystery to David that she had not come after the bones already. Perhaps she needed to continue her dolling first.

But the arrangement apparently fooled the escapees from the carie. When David returned to his desres, they were back outside, asking for the bones even though he no longer had them. He carefully pushed through them and went inside.

"Desres, how many present?"

"Two."

It was working. Would she come? And what could he do about her if she did?



Over the next few days, ten more dolls were found, all crew members of the *Mekhanik Pustoshnyy*. They were discovered in eyries in Avonmouth.city's near-above, saucer-eyed, looking down from steel and concrete ledges, haunting ladders, hatches and access-ways normally used by maintenance bodais only, places to which the dolls had climbed in their mindless drive for height. None had stopped where there was a route to go higher, no matter how precarious: they had found their level, like drops raining into the sky.

David called up an image of the remaining crew member, taken upon his detention after the *Mekhanik Pustoshnyy* had reached its haphazard stopping point. A frightened, round face, wide-eyed in panic at his uncertain fate. The man did not look as though he would be particularly self-possessed or clever enough to elude Obayifa for long.

Unusually, Breakage was in the form of a cop, a uniformed woman. David was vaguely baffled by this manifestation.

"Breakage, find the remaining crew member."

"Does not exist in Big Mind. Unsatisfied designation."

"Find him anyway."

"Joke? Breakage has searched."

"Where?"

"In Big Mind."

"No, in the fleshwork. In the physical world. We've been through this. How many times?"

"Impossible. Tried."

Breakage paused, his expression reminiscent of a farting baby's. David wished he was capable of laughing.

"What is common about the dolls?"

"Pairs, always. Except Mr Charles."

"And the man we haven't found, a singleton. What have we found from their beads – did you run the extra analyses in Big Mind?"

"Anomaly."

"You told me that before. What kind of anomaly?"

"Unexplained algorithmic output. All is known."

"That's what you said before. You were supposed to investigate further."

"All is known."

David sighed. "Why weren't we able to track them? What exactly happened to the IDs we gave them?"

"Hackery. Unknown. IDs flickered. Like Elizabethan light bulbs."

David sighed at the literally mindless repetition of his own words. "And what does Parkin say?" Not that David wanted him involved, but there was little he could do to stop him interfering anyway.

"No input from ID Forensics."

"Re-examine all data."

Breakage said, "Breakage analyse the beads of the fourteen dolls. Find commonalities."

"Good. Yes."

"All is known."

"Analysis in Big Mind is not enough. Gather them in one place then call me. And still search for the fifteenth crew member. We have to find him before Obayifa does."

Fourteen dolls in one room, a room which David had taken offline. The dolls had been fetched from the caries where they were now kept – alongside the demented but with even less of their sensoria left. Nothing, to be precise. Breakage, a factory worker in scuffed brown coveralls, struggled to manage them, trying to arrange the dolls in a line. As soon as he had positioned a doll, it would head for the table in the centre of the room and climb it. They scrambled together, pushing and climbing over one another.

David's vodu, coiled up and caged inside his mind, was poker-faced and keenly observant. David himself was wired. He had visited the Royal in a brief interval before arriving, driven in weakness through the baking air. He hadn't had time to shower. His skin was slick and still smelling of the girl he had lain with; closing his eyes for an instant, he forced himself to concentrate.

David ordered Breakage to remove the table from the room and to bring leg shackles while another bodai came to try to manage the dolls. Once their ankles were chained together, the dolls stood still except to test the limits of their bonds, blinking starkly from time to time, wide-eyeing one another as potential scaffolds but no longer able to ascend.

"What do we have here?" Dirac, for whom they had been waiting, entered at last. Tall, thin and like a knife, David thought. It was strange to see him out of his element: the labnode in which he resided by the crashing, risen sea.

Breakage said, "Fourteen nons from the *Mekhanik Pustoshnyy*. Former IDs scanned into Big Mind at arrival." He brought up a visualisation.

"We assigned new IDs," David added, "but those became obfuscated soon after release. Their beads passed all tests, but obviously they had been hacked in a way we didn't detect and still haven't got to the bottom of. "

"I see. And they have been dolled, as you so graphically put it."

"Dolled," repeated Breakage, for no apparent reason, a hiccup in his routines.

"Explain," Dirac commanded Breakage, knowing what David had told him but interested to hear what the bodai would say.

"Mind vacated. Clinically unconscious. Autonomically intact." To a fleshren eye, Breakage seemed to be denying an urge to look at David as he responded, as though curious about David's opinion of his explanation. But it was another glitch: no such sensibility was possible in a bodai.

"As I explained, Professor," David said, "we can't get anything out of them. Scans show they've had their mental activity reduced to negligible levels."

Dirac walked up to one of the dolls, who appeared to consider climbing on top of him as he approached. He took the doll's hand and pressed it, looking into the eyes that sat in the face like swivelling jellies.

"And you suspect Obayifa, the female who was on board with them?"

"You mean, could it have been another like her? I can't prove that no such other exists, but I'm pretty sure," said David. "It's she who's taken their minds."

Dirac walked along the line of dolls, turning their wrists this way and that to examine their beads in their entirety as he did so.

Curious, and wishing he had thought of it before, David approached and followed Dirac along the line, also taking the dolls' left hands to see their beads. Each doll became compliant as soon as they were touched. But their eyes continued to rove, searching aimlessly, showing no hint of seeing anyone in front of them.

"Breakage has found an anomaly in all of their beads but is unable to state what the anomaly is. It's not the usual hackery – he says there's something different about them. I had him randomly perturb all of the standard analyses. But the algorithm can't explain itself."

"Yes, I've seen the report. Allow me to finish, would you?"

When Dirac had examined the last doll, he said, "It's quite simple. Each of them has a bead missing."

"There's a gap? How could we not have seen that! Show me."

"Not a physical gap. Nothing is amiss to the naked eye. The beads have reconfigured themselves to avoid detection. But each crew member had one more bead at capture, as I see from the data recorded when they arrived. It's so simple that it's fooled your algorithms. Your Obayifa has taken not only their minds but a bead from each wrist of these… unfortunates. It's as though she's collecting components for a system of some kind, or an apparatus. It's a clever ploy: to bring something here under our noses by distributing it amongst the crew – for later reassembly, one supposes."

"But why keep them on the crew? She could've just hidden the extra beads on board – like the case of bones."

"It was ingenious to hide them in plain sight," offered Dirac. "And just as ingenious in a different way to have hidden the case on the ship. Who hides anything physically nowadays, in a world where everything is present in Big Mind and only data counts? You were lucky you found the case. It was highly unusual, wasn't it, to have searched the *Mekhanik Pustoshnyy* with dogs?"

"Yes, Breakage ordered it."

"Breakage?" Dirac looked questioningly at the bodai.

"Never mind that. We're going in circles." David was growing impatient at the mystery confronting them. "So why not simply hide the beads, too?"

"It's possible that the extra beads needed human hosts."

"I see. Beads that required direct connection to psychic activity."

Dirac gestured at the dolls. "And now she has both their minds and the beads, so in a way those extra beads may remain as connected to the crew's psyches as they were before, only via her. Are these all of them – the whole crew?"

"There's one more, apart from Obayifa, of course. We don't have a name that's worth a damn, so let's call him C15. We need to find him, fast. Just as we need to keep hold of the bone circuitry, which is in your safe hands."

"Indeed, the bone circuitry which is part of a fantastic and possibly dangerous construct by Westaf's Agency for Technological Interventions – you say it was renegades, but I'm not convinced there's a difference. And you've left them with me."

"If there's anyone who can keep them safe, it's you. I take it they are safe, given that you are not with them?"

"Of course. I still wonder if you are safe, given that we've arranged for the case's emanations to appear from your desres."

"It's a calculated risk, Professor."

"I find it curious, that you would put yourself at risk from this creature. Who has sucked out the psyches from what are now these dolls and is assembling a construct whose purpose we have yet even to guess at, except that it isn't to bring light and joy. Is the bone circuitry part of it?"

"I was hoping you'd tell me. Maybe she herself is part of it, too. We don't know what we're dealing with. She's not flesh – not entirely, anyway – and she's not network. She's inhabited by a vodu."

"A spirit, David?"

"As you know, it's not clear. I do know that renegades in Westaf are engineering new entities. Up to Elizabethan times they used to speak of the supernatural, the unnatural. But in Accra city I found evidence they were experimenting with what I've heard you call the supervirtual, although you were talking about the bone circuitry. You might also say unvirtual. A ghost in the machine – existing in whatever flesh she used to be but also in the network."

"Unless, despite the term I used, the vodu was their find, Detective: plain old supernatural." Dirac examined the neck and arms of one of the dolls. "Are there any physical signs on any part of them, of interference?"

"Teeth marks? No. The teeth of the inhabited do grow extra sharp, but they don't use them. It's the long tongue that comes to represent their powers. And as for the powers themselves, whatever she does is mentalmagic."

Dirac let out a grim guffaw. "Mental 'magic'?"

"It's what they called it in Westaf." The witch-technologists, the electro-sorcerers he'd encountered in his desperation to find someone to rid him of his vodu. "You've devoted your life to closing the gap in our understanding of the relationship between mental and physical phenomena. Well, vodus closed that gap. They're way ahead of you. They reach out across space to lick and extract minds. Our only question is: are we dealing with actual dark spirits here, or engineering? Or both?"


David had Breakage fetch a gang of bodais to lead the dolls back to their caries – where their proclivity for heights matched many of their co-residents' demented wanderings through the horizontal.

When they were alone, Dirac said, "David, what have you brought to these shores?"

"Me?"

"The thing inside you. Is it so different from whatever has dolled these men?"

"I'm not part of any scheme, just the result of a botched operation, as far as I know. There is someone or something of significance that is

Obayifa's target. We must keep her from the final bead if it's not too late, and from the bone circuitry."

David felt the vodu's hands shaking the bars of its cage, its face pushed through. There were brush strokes, the expected elements of eyes, nose and mouth, but they were indicated rather than present, and not quite where they should be. Meaty, fleshy.

"I don't know what is inside me. It moves around but gives nothing away of its purpose."

"You do realise that it could act as a wire, whatever else is behind its implantation. Perhaps they're listening to your thoughts, however offline you think you are. Do you have any evidence that they know what you are thinking or doing?"

"No, but then no one who plants a tap would show their hand until the time was right. They can't have known I'd leave Accra city and come to Avonmouth city, of all places."

"Indeed. It's curious, however, that Obayifa and the rest of the crew have ended up here, where you are. In how many places are there vodus, outside Westaf? Are you part of their system, Detective? Are you needed for whatever it is Obayifa is constructing?"

"Something tells me there's someone here in the fleshwork that they are after. I don't think it's me. I'm nobody. If all they needed was a vodu, Westaf has plenty of others."

"And IANI? Surely they're interested in all of this. I notice that you put this room offline."

"Someone's been in touch." The messenger girl bodai. He remained convinced she was Westaf, in fact, but didn't reveal that to Dirac, who seemed prejudiced where they were concerned. They'd used her to let him know they were watching the exploits of their renegades. And he'd used her for sex. Why couldn't he stop? "To let me know they know about Obayifa. They'll be carrying out their own analysis."

"And offline is online, David. All this Faradaying…"

"You know what? I don't really care anymore. Now, what do you suggest we do, Professor?"

"Perhaps there's a pattern to the evanescence of your crew members' user journeys after you released them. Can you let me see that within Big Mind?"

"You mean, give you full access – override your restrictions? I hope I'm right to trust you, Dirac, since I'd be proxying you through. Effectively you'll be acting as me when you analyse it."

"You suspect my agenda."

"I know that it goes beyond this case. I think you want to explore the supervirtual."

"Detective, you of all people should not knock my endeavours. What, exactly, is inhabiting you?"

The vodu was naked, as far as he could tell, slunk in its cage. Its body was a travesty of flesh.

"What do you think they did to me, exactly?"

"Frankly, it's beyond anything I've come across, although I know of someone not a million miles away, someone I ceased to work with many years ago, with similar interests. I can only imagine that it is the mental equivalent of an organ transplant. With bodies there's the risk of organ rejection. But the mind? It's a pronounced ability of ours to compartmentalise. Your mind has rejected your inhabitant, has built a cage around it."

"I have to go. I'd like to hear more about this ex-colleague of yours."

"There's something odd about C15," Dirac patched through later. "Literally. The others paired up, probably to fuse their identities on the network. You have two of them arrive in data, then just one, a new type of fab. The algorithms can't tell the individuals anymore. Clever. Digitally they became Siamese twins. And this also occurred at the level of pairs: it looks as though they'd meet, two pairs together, but it's not possible to tell which pair is which afterwards. Even more clever."

"But the vampire found them all, nonetheless," said David.

"Your girl with 'mentalmagic'. If she'd been looking in data she would have been just as fooled. She was looking in the fleshwork."

"Always supposing that she was tracking them down, that she didn't know where they were – hadn't orchestrated the whole thing."

"Yes, you might be right. To maintain access to the beads, she had only to tell them where to meet her, beyond our knowledge or suspicion. Anyway, now she's dolled them, so we'll never know their stories."

"And C15?"

"I'm afraid I have no clue about him. He's not in the data, but that absence must have been achieved through a different mode of fabrication. Has anyone else been dolled?"

"Not recently – that we know of. Before all of this, there was my friend. He was the first we found."

"And is there a connection?"

"None that I can think of. She was sending me a message, to back off."

"Is she telling you she could do this to you?"

"In Westaf I seemed to be safe from them precisely because I'm inhabited myself. I don't know whether that's through disinclination – some kind of honour amongst thieves – or because if one tried, it would engender an infinite loop of mind-fuckery."

Dirac paused. David could hear him breathing. "Any word from that bodai of yours?"

"Nothing."

"He's not just any bodai, is he, David?"

"What do you mean?"

"There's something different about him. You're at ease with him. Does Breakage have a glitch – perhaps an inhabitant – of his own?"

"Now you're being ridiculous."

"Am I? As you wish."

"To speak more mundanely, do you think he's been hacked?"

"Not that I am able to detect."

"Who would have hacked him? Someone with an interest in me."

Dirac paused again. More breathing. A thought had clearly crossed his mind. "Is that all for now?"

# PART TWO

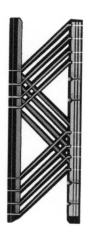

## Owo Foro Adobe

Snake climbing the palm.

Performing the impossible or unusual.

# CHAPTER FOURTEEN
## Obayifa

I am a vodu who sails a human ship. And in the hold of that ship: the bound psyches of wretches whose minds I have sucked. Food. Pure spirit, that fuels me on my voyage through this world. As I lick and swish my mind's tongue, as I lap at them they dissolve, grow watery and pale. Are they aware? It's no matter to me. They are consciousness itself. Good and bad, clever and stupid, and all the shades between. They all look like energy in my sight. I pay no heed to their memories and thoughts as I consume them.

I have lived in this body for so long now, hunting in Accra. They know me when it's too late. As a vampire has no reflection in a mirror, I am nowhere to be seen in the network when they encounter me. Mindbodies see her, the one I inhabit; they drool over her and draw close – and why shouldn't they, with her fine limbs, her face carved from deliciousness? When they realise she is nowhere to be found through their beads – when they feel the silence – it is too late. I waste no time. I do them there and then.

This mindbody who has recruited me and sent me over to this foreign place: he knows something of the art of my kind. I wanted but could not have the contents of that head of his. By way of compensation, he threw me morsels caught by his Ohen Tuos now and then. But most of all about him: he has something of mine. My sister. Yes, she. The she I love and have always loved alone. She who was torn from me long ago. He says he can bring her to me. He says what she says: "Sister, I am thisness, I am yourness, usness, haecceity in hungry flux." Who else would use such words, would speak of vodu essence thus? And each time he utters a fresh cocktail of her language. He has her, or has access to her.

I'll have her back to love and hold, he says. But first I must do his bidding. To capture and return what he was wito by.

And in the meantime, I feel something that occurs only every two hundred years or so to our kind: I grow fecund. With my tonguing I am ready to implant in mortal mind a new vodu.

# CHAPTER FIFTEEN
## Hotel Royal

"Room 71, please." This was code for where the girls of the Royal awaited their customers. David proceeded, barely waiting for the bodai desk clerk's nod. A corridor led him from a corner by the desk. Room 71 did not exist as such. The highest number on a door at the Royal, three flights up, was 68. He knocked on a door marked *Hotel Staff Only*.

The door swung open as if automatically. As he knew from previous visits, a bodai stood to the side, out of view, and opened it. It was a curious protocol, designed perhaps to leave customers at their ease as long as possible in their incipient act – to get them through the door without having to face even a bodai at first.

The sex workers mostly sat or lay on chairs and settees in an atmosphere somewhere between boredom and nervous anticipation, reflecting the presence of both seasoned occupants and ingenues.

The desultory conversation petered out as they regarded the customer. They were all female. If he had wanted a male he would have asked for room 72, further down the corridor.

David knew many of the faces by now. They gave a glimmer of recognition in return: just enough, not to a degree that might lead him to reject their over-familiarity. Some he had seen on many occasions but had never used; they turned away as soon as they saw him. Either they did not attract him, or there was something about them that triggered a suspicion in the ID cop – an unnecessary risk. He did not want to have to take any of these girls to a copnode. Not that the network cared who he consorted with. It was the shame he would feel that deterred him.

After his eyes had traced a few of the familiars, he allowed them to alight on someone relatively new who had been present on his last two visits. She was tall, the only one leaning against a wall, and a scar like a tear trail in flesh down her left cheek only added to the beauty of her eyes. She was trouble, he was pretty sure.

The part of David that did not want to be there at all nagged at him. A small, bullying facet of himself – or the vodu? – had dragged him to the Royal. Once there, he wanted no complications. But she was fascinating. He allowed himself to stare at her. She held her gaze to the floor while his eyes were upon her. For a moment he imagined having her. He told himself not to be so stupid.

The girl he chose instead, with a nod, led him to her appointed room by a service staircase. Unlike the new arrival, he knew where he was with her. After they had had fleeting sex he remained a few minutes, against his usual instinct to leave immediately, lying beside her on the bed.

"Have you spoken to the new girl? I haven't seen her before."

"Who?" She was distracted like all the others, sensa playing like tiny telepathic projections on the edge of her consciousness.

"Tall, in the black-and-white dress, hair tied up. She was standing."

"Oh. Her. Yes. No. Not really."

"Don't you get to know one another?"

"Not when they're not interested in you." The sensa seemed to have subsided temporarily. She was looking at him, although without interest.

"But" – she was fully attending to the room around her now, with its dismal business-class trappings, the curtains closed – "she doesn't fuck."

"She doesn't what?"

"They say she takes them – you – to a room and has their bytecoins off them, but she doesn't fuck them."

David pictured her again, the newcomer, with her facial jewellery and the elaborate braiding and the structure of her hair which she had changed since the last time he had seen her. He guessed that she had marked him too, knew what he was.

As he left he decided he would choose her next.

David, Breakage and Dirac sat uncomfortably together in a speeding module. Gone were the days of flashing lights and sirens. Algorithms diverted or halted all other traffic as the module transited the near-above.

Soon they arrived at a warespace: a hangar in which flesh and bodais were everywhere, all wearing blue overalls. The bodais had faces and bodies from the same mould, like spanners or screwdrivers. Their uniformity seemed to emphasise the variety of faces and shapes of the flesh amongst them, their characters. But the consciousness of the fleshren conferred no advantage. On the contrary, the bodais were issuing orders to them, albeit in tones of suggestion, and the flesh moved from machine to machine, tending them and looking at screens. It was not at all clear what enterprise they were engaged in or for which multinat.

"Dirac," said David, "you've brought us here for what? Do you know for sure C15 is here?" David was not sure he liked the way Dirac had seemed evasive in the module, apparently keeping some of his findings to himself.

Dirac shrugged. "He's here according to Big Mind."

"Yes, but you and I know that that is meaningless. His network profile has been hacked. Is he really here? What evidence do you have?"

"We'll see." Dirac showed an image of C15 to a woman who was shuffling reluctantly between consoles, her performance tracked by the network as she went about her work. Something weighed on her; her face was careworn and her head was stooped. It was like waking someone from a dream.

"Have you seen him?" Dirac asked.

She looked back at him as though he were talking a foreign language. Perhaps he was.

"Have a good look. Have you seen him?"

"No," she replied. "Do you imagine I see everyone who works here?"

They moved through the warespace, stopping to show the image to flesh who all reluctantly gave similar negative responses.

"How easy would it be to hide here?" David asked Breakage, who had become one of the warespace bodais on temporary assignment and had acquired the fixed facial expression of those cheap, utilitarian models. Breakage ran a calculation of fleshly capabilities against a mathematical model of the warespace.

"Hiding impossible," he said. "All is known."

David wasn't so sure. "Warespace?" he said, addressing the building. "Is C15 here?" He sent the suspect's profile through his beads.

"Present."

"Identify."

The warespace delegated a bodai who led them to an individual looking nothing like C15. He was not C15 in data, either. After a few questions it became clear that he was an innocent whose ID had been appropriated, and knew nothing.

"Hackery," said David. "Not bad hackery. But then I expected nothing less. It might be a more subtle play than it seems. Maybe we're supposed to go away now, and not look anymore."

"Then we'd better try another tack," said Dirac.

David looked upwards to the roof of the warespace, to platforms and walkways which were supposed to be unused.

"What's up there? I think we'd better find out. With some help."

They sent for dogs. A team of them soon arrived, pushing their snouts through the partly open windows of their dispatch module. The working flesh stood aghast; the slavering pack caused considerable sheepish excitement. The warespace bodais ignored the spectacle, which was beyond them, and tried to draw the flesh back to work.

David, Dirac and Breakage climbed back into their module with the dogs. As they rose to the disused upper levels, the dogs yelped with the excitement of a chase. Slowly they traced along the old maintenance platforms, the dogs sniffing out of the module's windows. They searched, hovering wherever David and Dirac saw a place that flesh could climb to. David felt a primitive urge to hunt, trawling with dogs for someone whose network identity had been obfuscated. The search was between flesh – breathing, watchful flesh, the blood pumping through their arteries – a search for someone unknown in the network. And his vodu, also an unknown, responded, squatting inside his mind as he moved around; it was like a monstrous cuckoo, looking through his eyes as though they were windows to a world it was hungry for.

David and Dirac peered from either side of the craft, the dogs panting beside them. Beams, buttresses and walkways stretched to and from the platforms they skirted through.

The dogs suddenly yelped furiously. "Over there!" cried David. He steered towards a figure clambering precariously along a buttress towards a platform.

They caught up, seeing the fear in the man's eyes as they neared, and dismounted onto the platform. It wasn't C15.

"Who are you?" said David.

"You got beads, don't you? Cop."

"Tell me anyway."

"No one."

"You have an ID."

"It's not mine. I don't recognise its validity. It doesn't represent who I am. The truth is offline." The man assumed an aggressive, defiant look. Breakage, with his completely blank expression, took a step towards him, the ID police bodai regaining his purpose.

Breakage said, "Arrest. ID statute 14A."

"Can it, Breakage. What's his journey like?"

"Journey clean. Breakage does not understand confession."

"He's been mixed," said Dirac. "His journey's been mixed with that of C15 in Big Mind."

"Not in reality?" asked David.

"I couldn't possibly comment on anything other than an identical relationship between Big Mind and reality. But you might ask him about that."

"Tell us where you've been and who you've been with in the past few days."

"I don't talk to cops."

"Did you hear that, Dirac? We've got ourselves a rebel. Hankering for the anarchy after the Disruption. But my gut tells me he's been caught up in something he knows nothing about, like the other one below. Breakage, let him go for now." The bodai stood back.

"You can make your own way down," David said.

"Fuck you, cop."

They reboarded the hovering module and left, the dogs lying down at their feet. David saw fresh graffiti among the *I&I* signs as they transited the near-above: *Last Few Days.*

"We have to find another way of searching," he said. He could think of none. But somewhere deep inside, the excitement of the chase remained with him. Was there something in all of this to bring him back to Yaa?

I, Pempamsie, returned to the Royal after the day's fruitless search for whoever knew of vodus and Super Mare. My questions about vodus were always met with incomprehension; mention of Super Mare provoked recognition but equally incredulity that I should ask about it.

Because of what I was about to put myself through, I stood awhile at the hotel's threshold. The city hummed and whined behind me. The white sky in UK.land burned us all.

The Nkonsonkonso in UK.land was broken in many places. Flesh dissembled. Flesh had forgotten true flesh: unlike our Accra.city, with its artists; the rivers of us; our towers; our striving, restless energies. In Westaf our beads hummed together, but they blocked the sensa from outside, from Big Mind.

In Avonmouth.city, IANI held sway. I took a deep breath and entered the Royal.

The robot at the desk was receiving a client who had entered past me, directing him to room 71, where I would put myself on sale – but not be sold – with the other women. We all had our own rooms just for ourselves, where I would retire later, and a pool of rooms to use with the clients. Few bona fide guests stayed in the hotel. It was a sex work node.

Some of the women were robots, others flesh. They engaged in a ritual re-enactment of love-making. I sensed that little true love was made in UK.land, even outside the walls of the Royal. Not that I, Pempamsie, knew this love.

I told the robot at reception about my availability and walked to the room.

The clients entered. They barely remembered why they came, a spasmic urge. In their bright outfits, with haunted faces, they were ghosts. I searched their faces for the man who knew of vodus. It was he I had to find.

And there he was. My senses told me so.

I took him in silence to my own room, where I kept the painting. I could see as we walked that he understood the significance: not to use one of the sex work rooms. We were met inside by a searing beam of sunlight that had broken through the heavy white sheet of cloud, past the buttresses, monorails and towering node clusters of the near-above, all silent behind the windows.

I, Pempamsie, would be I again. I would remember my mother and father. I would lose the other that trammelled me.

"Why don't you lie on the bed?" I said.

He had barely entered the room. Sunglasses. Suit. He remained standing. He was examining me.

"Take off your jacket."

Sweat.

"I know what you are," I said. "An ID officer."

He did not reply. I walked over and helped him out of his jacket, started to unbutton his shirt, but he stopped me. Sweat.

"Relax. I won't hurt you."

Wouldn't I? I felt him through his shirt.

The arms: veins like cables under the skin. As have I. Inhabitance, a sign. Nsoroma was wise to send me here.

Unlike the others, for him I took off my blouse. Showed him veins like cables under the skin. He saw, and understood.

Next, his sunglasses. It was as though he wanted to stop me but couldn't, mesmerised. Eyes. Ordinary flesh eyes. Staring at my arms, then looking into my eyes with fear on his face. Back at my arms, and my eyes again. Consternation. Then he relaxed, as though he had not found what he feared.

"We must make chemistry," I said.

"I'm going to have to arrest you," he said. Was this foreplay? "Afterwards," he said. A UK.land joke?

The mirror held the two of us. Like twins, despite our skin colour: with twins inside.

"No," I said. "We won't be doing that."

But I wanted to.

"Then, what?"

I took out the painting from its case. Above: Osrane ne nsoroma, the moon and star. Below: Pempamsie. Behind her: the vampire, she who would unmind me.

He touched the oils, the paint thick and cresting like a sea of colour.

For many years, I guessed, he had hidden all. Even the eyes, whereas I saw nothing there to hide.

It wasn't a bad face.

Our beads like atoms in a crystal, as though nothing were amiss. One flesh, two flesh. And inhabitance. I traced his forehead with my finger, as though it could be said to hold his soul, Sunsum. And the other.

He let my fingers drift. A pulse at his temple. He touched my cheek.

"Room," I said. "How many?"

"Two present," it said.

We both smiled.

He looked back at the painting. "It's you," he said, but he was looking at her.

"Do you know her?" I asked.

"We took her into custody. But I had to let her go."

"Had to?"

He told me of a ship, the *Mekhanik Pustoshnyy*, which had landed out of the blue. Not long after I arrived, I realised. They must have found my destination quickly; Nsoroma must have been forced to tell them.

He told me of the sixteen crew: one vampire – she – and fifteen men. He told me of her dollings, as he called them. But he did not say why he had let such a creature go.

What had he seen in my eyes that caused him to trust me, to tell me all of this? Had he been waiting for me, as I had been looking for him?

"Fourteen souls taken from their owners," he said. "And fourteen beads."

"What beads?"

"We don't know, exactly. We found only that they were missing, just like their minds."

"And who were they, these crew?" I asked.

"Merely carriers," he replied.

I, Pempamsie, recognised at once, without completely understanding. Afuntummireku denkyemmireku: the plural-headed crocodile with a single stomach. The assembly of a malfeasant contraption.

"And what I want to know," he said, "is not only the whereabouts of the fifteenth crew member but why she, the mind-sucking vampire, appears with you in your painting."

His face remained inscrutable. He was withdrawing, becoming the detective again.

"You think I am her accomplice," I said.

"Why should I trust you any further, just because of our mutual condition? After all, we share a related condition with her, too."

"Inhabitance. But it seems to have several forms. Anyway, you don't have to trust me, any more than I am bound to trust you. But I sense yours is a problem, like mine, even though it appears not to have control over you. Not at this moment, at least. We have something to gain from one another, perhaps. What is your name?"

He hesitated. "David. It seems there is another problem – Obayifa, the one in your painting."

"Obayifa." A name for her at last. I had to say it out loud. "I am Pempamsie. As two, perhaps we can liberate ourselves from our inhabitance." Never before has Pempamsie uttered those words: "as two".

"Before she consumes our minds?"

"Wouldn't she have done that to you by now, when you had her in custody? She's not interested in you." In fact, Nsoroma had said two vodus could not touch in the same mind. Did this man know that? Nsoroma had said, too, that the vampire knew a way to remove mine. Was this what she was constructing with the beads – the crocodile with many heads?

"I believe I am immune to her while I am inhabited," he said. "But according to that painting she is interested in you, whether or not she can doll you. You must be very special. To merit whatever it is they've gone to so much trouble for, sending her after you. If indeed she is here for you – and I'm going to assume, now that I've seen that painting of yours, that she is – I think I should keep away from you. That would be my best bet. You're trouble."

"No, I can help you."

"Tell me how."

"I do not know. Yet. But I want to." I, Pempamsie, was feeling a curious attraction. Was it I who felt it for him? Or my inhabitant for his?

This David seemed perturbed by my offer. "I'll come back for you." He closed the door behind him.

# CHAPTER SIXTEEN

## Bite Not One Another

We walked. David paid four of the other women – fleshren – to accompany us. Flesh and flesh in the electric roar.

"Why are you bringing them?" I asked.

"I would invite all of them if I could. Out into the open. I'd have us walk naked through the streets. I'd—"

"But. They have beads, which shackles them to IANI. As do you. And you've paid them to come. They would never leave their domain just for you, would they now? Not to mention that you frequent the Royal; you are part of the system in several ways. Have you lain with any of them since we met?"

He kept trying to be cold and to show bravado but was infinitely sad, this David, and easily drawn from his shell.

"No."

"You must stop."

He looked at me, apparently lost for words. Lost for anything, in fact. I, Pempamsie, could consider such a man weak. But not him.

A robot came. ID police, like him. It stood, ignoring me.

"What have you told them about me?" I asked.

"That you were in the Royal when Obayifa dolled two of the crew. That I have reason to believe you, and they" – he gestured to the four women – "need my protection."

"And can you protect me?" I found myself smiling. I.

"Whoever you are, and for whatever reason, she needs this construction of beads to do her work. Either she can't doll you without constructing it, this…"

"Crocodile."

He almost smiled back. "This thing made out of beads and—"

"And what?"

"Whatever she is constructing, you or your inhabitant or both are valuable to them."

"Them?"

"Look, I'm not stupid. You are someone special. I'm just not sure what kind of special, or to whom."

"Perhaps I work for Westaf. Consider how nonned I am. It's what the vodu is for. You're not doing your job. You should have arrested me. You're not in Westaf now."

"The vodu nons you?" David was shocked.

"Yes. The handiwork of Swirling Suit, a renegade."

He stopped to consider me, the ID cop. "That's as may be. I need you to be free."

"Am I bait? To draw her out? Is that all you are interested in?"

He did not answer. "The thing inside," he said. "Has it changed since you met me? Given what I have inside?"

"I do not know." Truly, I did not know how to answer him. Something stirred in Pempamsie when I met this David. An itching. But was it I for him, or it for it? And the stirring itself lay under a cloud. I did not know this feeling. I, Pempamsie, did not know what Swirling Suit had infected me with. I knew only that it was invisible but present.

"What is this robot?"

"That's Breakage. You don't need to concern yourself about him."

I stood in front of the robot, a squat man like an old-fashioned fleshren from UK.land with a hat and attaché case. It stopped, stepped to the side to pass. I blocked it. Blocked it again.

"Can you see me?" I asked it.

"Confession," the robot called Breakage said. "Logged."

"It's nothing," David said to me, while looking at the robot. "Breakage, continue. We are returning to Dirac after I've finished interviewing these sex workers."

"Breakage log David offline."

"I know, Breakage."

These two were a strange pair. Normally flesh and robot were cold to one another. These two had a trace of Obi nka obi: unity; bite not one another.

"I meant, what is this robot to you?"

"Just a robot."

No, it bore a peculiar relationship to him. But he seemed at ease with it. Had he hacked it?

We sweated as we walked on the pavement. The sky was low and white and burning. The near-above emitted a rattle now. My colleagues from the Royal had been silent.

"David, why do you not talk to them?"

He shrugged.

"Are they sheep?" I said. "Are you a sheep?" I asked one of them. Like the others, like all flesh in UK.land, she appeared drugged, as sensa played inside her mind. Updates from the network, as well as one another. Nothing much to complain about per se. But filled with bleakness. They were lost. Like David. No, not like him.

"Do you hear me?" I picked up her beaded wrist. "Do you understand what I am saying to you?"

She was about my age. Her mouth opened but said nothing. Their beads: Epa: handcuffs.

"You are slaves of IANI," I said. "And you," I said to David, "you carry shame for using them."

"I do," he said, and walked a little ahead of us. "Did. I've stopped now."

"You're supposed to be interviewing them. That's what you told the robot," I called to him.

"You can see for yourself, they're numbed with psychic overload. They seem to be particularly affected by it. It might be an experiment specifically on sex workers. They're of little value to the network. They might as well have been dolled already."

"Switch off their beads."

"You know I can't do that."

I let it be. I thought of what I had done in the name of IANI. I was not one to judge him. And I was no longer precisely I. I concentrated on the present, on the walk with other flesh, my footsteps on the heated pavement, lest the absence reappear where memories should be.

"And what of you? Do you feel something new – with me?" I said. I, Pempamsie, unable to contain the inside itch. The scratch. The itch again.

"Yes, something is different. My veins and your veins tell of our inhabitants. Mine is up and moving around. I've never experienced it like this. It has been charged."

"The beetle in the box," I said. One of the old books Pempamsie studied in the icestation.

"It's shaking at its cage. It makes me wonder how strong the cage is."

"Cage? What cage?"

"My vodu is locked up inside my mind. I see it, feel it. But it is constrained."

"Mine is not so. It is a fluid, pervading me. I can't see it, only a shadow, shifting in shape all the time. There to non me and that is all, supposedly."

173

"Fascinating," he said. "I researched them, gathered every scrap of knowledge I could right after my inhabitance; but I never heard of vodus as anything other than monsters before. Mine's more like Obayifa's, I suspect; only so far, at least, it can't get out to do its filthy work. I don't want to hurt you."

"Hurt me?"

"I know you have a vodu inside, but it's different; I don't know for sure what would happen if mine escaped."

"David, tell me about David."

"You say that as though I were a construct, not a person."

"Aren't you?"

"No. I'm damn well a person. I'm—"

"You?"

"Yes. Somewhere inside is me."

The robot Breakage walked its uncanny walk beside us. "Can we really speak with this thing accompanying us?"

"This 'thing' is Breakage. Yes. He's promised me he won't report."

"Promised?"

"It sounds ridiculous, but yes, he's different. He logs but doesn't report."

"And why do you even need 'him'?"

"He can reach parts of Big Mind I don't have access to."

"Namely?"

"They all can. Only he's on my side."

"You've turned a robot? Impossible!"

"I didn't turn him. He just is the way he is."

"You're not serious! A robot just turns up, says he's your friend. And you believe it! You're naive. Are you that lonely?"

Breakage looked straight ahead as we discussed him, face like a baby except that he was dressed as grown flesh pursuing a business that no longer existed, a business with an office, a desk to lay his attaché case upon.

His actual business: ID crime. And there we were: Pempamsie nonned, David offline.

"Where do you come from?" I asked David.

"Here, in UK land."

"But your inhabitant: where were you when it was implanted? Here?"

"Accra city. I returned here because of the vodu."

The heat pressed upon us. David took off his jacket. I gripped his forearm and felt the veins running thick just beneath his sweat-soaked shirt.

"Who did this to you?"

"I told you, renegades."

"No, you didn't tell me that. Which individual? Swirling Suit?"

"I don't know who that is, or who did it to me. They captured me, drugged me. It was night-time. I saw nothing."

"Owo foro adobe: snake climbing the palm; performing the impossible."

"I'd been pursuing one of their chiefs. I turned up at a house. They operated on me. I woke up lost, two weeks later."

"They wanted their man on the inside."

"Perhaps, controlled by this." He pointed to the thing inside his mind.

"And they failed?"

"It's just there. Inside. Looking."

"It can't steer you."

"I don't think so. I told you, it's caged."

"But you were concerned that it might leave the cage."

"No. Yes. I don't know. I think it might be able to."

"How does it survive?"

"It feeds off me, I guess. A trickle current of psychic energy."

"Just a trickle?"

"I think so."

"And no one has observed its presence?"

"I didn't say that. You have, for a start."

"Tell me more about why you left Accra city."

"I had to get away from someone. Someone I was afraid of hurting."

Ah, the sadness. "Are you going to tell me?"

He was weighing up whether he could tell me, Pempamsie. Yet he had told me so much already.

"My daughter, Yaa."

"And how would your daughter come to harm?"

"I stayed away from her, from everyone at first. You have to understand. I had no idea what they had done to me."

"They had implanted a vodu. A vampire spirit."

"You say that like it's obvious."

"A spirit who would use you."

"Eventually. I recognised that it was caged. I allowed myself to visit her. She had called and called. I couldn't not see her. I was weak."

"And?" David was allowing himself emotions. I, Pempamsie, was not used to such males. Rather, I was unfamiliar with not feeling contempt for such males.

"And when I saw her, I could tell it wanted her."

"In what way?"

"I don't know what way. I just knew I couldn't stay with that thing wanting to... I don't know, leap across. Into her. Or consume her. The cage seemed to come ajar, wider even in the seconds I remained with her. But only with her – the one person I love. With everyone else it has remained firmly shut. There's no one else I care about, you see. Or have let myself care about."

"I see. So you left her behind. And now you're here. In Avonmouth city. An ID cop with a vodu inside."

"That about sums it up."

And I? My story? I tried not to recall my parents, because I knew I would fail. I would try again later.

David stopped. "Look. I have to go." He did not look me in the eye. Shifting his weight uneasily from foot to foot. Perhaps regretting how much he had shared with me.

I needed to ask this David about Super Mare. But now was not the moment. Patience. Let this day end. I walked with the robot and the mute sex workers back to the Royal. Night was falling. I looked up hoping to see the stars. But there was only the near-above in Avonmouth.city, hulking and climbing above us in the dusk beneath a blanket of colourless sky. We were of the fleshwork, in the network. We existed, perambulating. All around us, beads registered and sang in a glare of network light.

David and I: invisible and yet not free.

Despite his doubts about the professor, David felt drawn to Dirac's labnode, to where he could sit and discuss the case with him by the risen sea. What he told himself not to do was tell Dirac about Pempamsie. He could picture the sour look Dirac would throw while asking who she was and what David had shared with her. And the professor would have been right: he had been foolish. Basic training had been for nothing.

"Maybe Obayifa has dolled C15 already," David said. "Maybe he's fallen from the near-above by now into some unused corner. Maybe he's... I don't know, in a basement somewhere."

"I find little point in this exercise of your imagination, Detective." Dirac leaned back in his chair in the conservatory. His eyes were downcast.

"You seem troubled," David said. "Surely you should be enjoying this puzzle."

"It's not just a puzzle, is it, Detective. Something about this case is profound. It's a shift away from what we've known. Have you dealt this closely with a psychic vampire before? And when was the last time you had to search physically and not algorithmically for a suspect?"

"Profound? You mean like psychblood, which also shifted everything?" David felt a trickle of sympathy for the professor. "But not the shift for which psychblood was intended. It was meant to be a cure. You wanted it to be a cure for dementia. That's what you're upset about."

"Yes, a cure – and not a catalytic agency used to pump sensa into and out of the genpop. Let's change the subject back to C15, shall we? Physical search is a thing of the past. We're out of practice."

"And his beads have been hacked in a new way to obfuscate his journey, mixing it up with those flesh in the warespace. So we're stuck."

"Not quite. Follow me."

Dirac picked up an ornament on a shelf in his office and shook it in a complex choreography of moves. He paused, looking frustrated, then danced the ornament again. A section of the wall slid away.

A clinical bed on wheels stood in the centre of a room, surrounded by equipment which looked improvised, pieced together from found components, many of which looked Elizabethan, or Disruption at the latest.

"This is where you strap me up and torture me, is it, Dirac? Reveal yourself to be the serial killer I already half supposed you might be?"

Dirac reacted coldly. "A journey, Detective, is essentially digital, however material is the brain underlying it."

"You're telling an ID cop his business."

"Please, listen. You don't seem very good at that."

"Very well. By the way." David looked around him. "You don't mind me bringing my inhabitant in here?"

"Believe me, even if it can see, I'm not about to explain how this equipment works in sufficient detail to you or anybody else. This machine is not what it appears to be. Now, wherever C15 is, however his beads have been hacked, there is a signal implicit in the data flowing to and from the beads. It's connected with the psychblood perturbations within his organism, which are partly a function of the brain itself."

"I think I see what you mean. And we have at least some data which we know to be from him, while he was in our custody," said David.

"Not merely data from his beads, Detective. We never use it nowadays, but there are recordings of brain functions taken at the same time. The signal of which we speak is opaque to machines. But if you play it back into flesh with the brain signature used as a key, it can be discerned as a kind of meaning."

"What kind of meaning?"

"Hard to describe. A bit like a smell, even though it's carried over the network. All we have to do is play the network feed and the brain signature into someone."

"Someone like you, Professor?"

"Someone like me. And I may be able to smell – trace – him over the network."

Dirac lay on the bed. "I require your assistance."

"Is this dangerous?"

"To me or to you? You have no need to worry."

Dirac bade David to connect electrodes to his head. Then he touched his beads to beads on the machine. After several attempts he relaxed. "There. I'm associated with the machine. Now you must stay and watch me for a while. If anything happens, just pull me away from the bed and out of here. And don't speak to me."

"Very well. I'm intrigued."

Dirac closed his eyes. David folded his arms and let his mind wander. Thoughts of Pempamsie rushed in. They had touched and that was all. He would have felt clean for once as he left the Royal except that he had revealed his inhabitance to her. His ID cop's instincts told him he should have arrested her, even if he couldn't say why. Was it the vodu making him reckless, or his increasing contempt for the network he worked for? No, he had to admit it was more than that. There was something about her. She was inhabited like him: not rampantly like Obayifa with her crazed voltage. Pempamsie's vodu must also be constrained. More constrained than his, for her eyes betrayed nothing, even if the veins on her forearm were distended.

Judging by the painting in her room, Obayifa was pursuing her – with IANI's blessing, it seemed, since they had wanted him to let her go. Presumably Obayifa could not suck out Pempamsie's vodu-inhabited mind, but she intended harm. Pempamsie was in danger.

His vodu prowled in its cage. Its footsteps were like someone walking on the floor above, in an attic that should have been empty.

Dirac had lain still for about ten minutes when his limbs began to twitch like a dreaming dog's, his eyeballs rotating beneath his lids. David drew closer. Lines crossed Dirac's leathery face. His hair was thinning; there was dandruff on his collar. His fists were tightened. The beads reconfigured rapidly on his wrist.

David wondered whether to wake him.

Dirac's slight movement suddenly grew. His back arched. He was having a seizure, his tongue poking out and eyeballs bulging.

"Open," David said to the room, removing the electrodes from Dirac, and struggled with him back into the office, with its ornaments and Elizabethan books.

The door swished shut.

David could not hold the writhing professor. Dirac fell to the floor, motionless. David placed his finger on the professor's pulse. It was weak and erratic. But his eyes opened. David helped him onto a chair.

"Detective, stay for five minutes to check that I am settled. Then leave me. That inhabitant of yours: I could smell it. It reeked, like rotting flesh. It mustn't interfere with the search for C15."

"Then what's it doing to me, with its 'smell', as you put it?"

Dirac smiled feebly, closing his eyes. "It's all a matter of degree. It may be your proximity, but your vodu's emanations are dominating the signals from the network. Anyway, you don't seem to me to be a man who is too troubled by the thing inside you. You function normally, that is."

If only he knew, David thought, what it takes to function at all: not to give in and descend into madness. Is that what Pempamsie had to endure, too?

"Are you sure you'll be all right? I don't know exactly how you're going to hook yourself up again to do your sniffing, and what if something goes wrong?"

"The hard part, the effort to absorb C15's signature, is over. Now I'm like a dog who's been given a scent to track. Please, leave. But if you haven't heard from me within twenty-four hours, come back. The labnode will let you in."


David responded to reports of a disturbance in one of the guest rooms at the Hotel Royal. He rode in a module, glad of the familiar angles and soft padded materials of its interior, and the unremarkable flow of the noded world outside. He thought about his consciousness, how in some sense it must be rooted in the physical world – mustn't it? – and yet was not of it. What was Dirac doing, exactly, "sniffing" for C15? Detecting a characteristic signal based on minute perturbations of psychblood engendered by conscious brain activity.

Heaven only knew, his own consciousness was problematic in multiple ways. He'd rather be a stone. When Pempamsie told him to stop sleeping with the other Royal girls, David had balked at first. With anyone else, he would have asserted his independence by going straight to get himself laid. But Pempamsie's words had touched him, the way she cared. Since then, he had not wanted to sleep with them. Her telling him to stop was a kindness, a respect for him and the girls. She didn't seem like an altogether kind person, though.

And now he was about to reach the Royal on a professional visit. He needed to concentrate; wouldn't seek out Pempamsie on this occasion. He ignored the desk clerk as he entered; automatic clearance was established through his beads.

David knocked at the room on the third floor. There was no answer. He knocked again. Still nothing. When he visited the Royal girls, it wasn't so much the sex he wanted as the journey to see them, the power they had over him – his handing it to them. Had he really stopped? It was hard to trust that the urge would not return. The old, Westaf David would never have whored, but he was so far away from there. From Yaa.

His beads niggled. Something wasn't right.

"Room 303. Open."

It was one of the girls he'd slept with: she had climbed onto a chest of drawers. Her arms were spread out like wings; her eyes were round and vacant.

His first thought was not of Obayifa but Pempamsie. Surely she didn't do it – did she? His cop's instincts warned him that he knew so little about her. At the same time, his gut told him she was not a psychic vampire: Obayifa was after her in the painting, and it was she who needed protection.

"Breakage, come."

Breakage had returned to the form of one of the worker bodais from the warespace they had searched, glassy and blue-uniformed.

"Two items: one, doll found; two, commissioner of ID police wants to see you."

David sighed. "Why thank you. One, obviously, I know; two, why didn't I get word myself?"

"Detective cannot know one. Two, unknown. All is known."

"Breakage, the doll is right here. I'm the one who's just found her. It's why I called you."

"Doll in near-above." Breakage gave the address.

"C15?"

"Not C15. Female." Breakage beaded her to him. It was another of the girls from the Royal. He recognised her, had used her, too. Two more dolls who weren't *Mekhanik Pustoshnyy* crew and had a connection to him.

The bodai paused, uncertain of when David's cogitation would end. "Sex workers," he said.

"Yes, Breakage, sex workers. Go and look for Pempamsie here in the hotel. First ask for room 71 at the desk, then go to every room in the hotel if she's not there. When you find her, tell her that I said she's in danger. If she's not here, stand guard in the lobby and warn her when she comes back."

"Breakage not recognise. Nonned. No iris scan. All is known."

"Say 'David says danger' to everyone who has not been here before, according to Big Mind."

The bodai looked nonplussed.

"What will you say?"

"David says danger. To flesh inside hotel lacking prior visit record. Nons have never visited any places. In Big Mind."

Over twenty-two hours had passed since he had left Dirac. The commissioner was going to have to wait. And Pempamsie would have to look after herself for now. There were around twenty other girls who worked in the Royal. He would have to protect them as well.

"And keep Obayifa out of here," he finally ordered Breakage. "You will know her, right? The one with nothing at all from her beads. If she appears on the threshold, whatever you do, don't say anything that might imply an invitation to come in. In fact, specifically state that she may not enter."

The window was open. Obayifa must have climbed up to the ledge from outside and persuaded the girl to let her in. The ascent would be nothing to her mentalmagicked will.

By the time David pulled up at Dirac's labnode, just over twenty-four hours had elapsed. He beaded himself in. The door to the hidden room was open. Dirac was not inside.

"Come, Detective." The weak voice emanated from the conservatory.

Dirac looked haggard, slumped in the wicker two-seater.

"You were going to contact me when you emerged from your session, Professor. What happened to that?"

"I'm exhausted, Detective. Not getting any younger. I'm not sure you'll find me very coherent just now."

"Did you find C15?"

"In a manner of speaking, yes."

"I don't have time for riddles." David was anxious about Pempamsie. "There have been two more dollings."

"Two more? I take it neither is C15, or you would have said so."

"Sex workers. Ones I have a connection to."

Dirac absorbed this information without comment. David wondered whether he was judging him nonetheless.

"I searched for C15," Dirac said, "and, by association, your creature. I found him. I didn't find her. It took a lot of concentration. I wasn't so much tracking him down as searching blindly. But something came up. A kind of presence, you might say, but one that I intuited. It was like being in the dark and smelling, feeling for what is around you. I followed it, lost it, but then found it again."

"Please get to the point."

"He's on the *Mekhanik Pustoshnyy*. Right now."

"Then why are we standing around? Has she already found him?"

"Perhaps. I didn't say where on the ship. Maybe he's as high as he can get in the superstructure."

David sighed. Maybe three dolls in one day.

"Let's go. Breakage?"

Breakage's voice appeared through the labnode.

"Breakage. Available."

"Send for a replacement, and in the meantime upgrade the desk clerk to a guard until it arrives. Instruct in how to detect Obayifa through absence of ID and bar her entrance at all costs. Then transport your AI to the *Mekhanik Pustoshnyy*. Arrange a search party. Look immediately. Seize C15 and place under safe custody."

Breakage would be there quickly, his AI transferred in seconds to a bod associated with the docks. David called for dogs to be sent to join them.

"Sure you're up to this, Dirac?"

Dirac rose unsteadily. "I need to be a part of your case, Detective, if you're to crack it."

# CHAPTER SEVENTEEN
## Garden

The *Mekhanik Pustoshnyy* sat imposingly against the quayside, where Breakage and a gang of bodais stood waiting for David and Dirac, their fleshly colleagues who had had to take a module. They were immaculately still: all domestic help, dispatched from a major cleaning job in one of the huge desres blocks built to house the working flesh who came and went in ships. The IANI logo, *I&I*, was written periodically on the quay. Sounds from around them pierced the stillness: metallic creaks as containers were hoisted, swung and lowered, the swoosh of wind turbines, the incessant hum of N-cars and modules: a world owned and operated by the network with the assistance of the fleshwork. Salt air reached David like an unexpected memory of a forgotten place.

Breakage came forward.

"No one on board. All is known."

David threw him a sceptical look. "We'll board her anyway, and see for ourselves." He stopped to take a handkerchief from his pocket and wipe his sweating brow. A sheet of cloud trapped heat which radiated from the concrete and steel all around them.

They went down into the hold first. David and Dirac felt keenly with their beads as they covered the clanging space.

"Anything here you recognise, Professor, from your sniffing stint?"

"I'm afraid not. But they might." The dogs had arrived above, and were barking. When David and Dirac emerged hurriedly back on deck, they looked to where the dogs were straining. A doll had appeared atop a loading crane mounted on the ship. Binoculars revealed C15, in the same grubby clothes, his top shirt buttons undone. What was left of him stood on the tip of the gantry ramrod straight, arms outstretched, looking directly out to the sea and the cloudscape.

They sent two of the bodais to fetch him, which took a frustratingly long time due to the precariousness of the climb onto the gantry. Once they had wrested the doll down, they held him firmly against his struggle to climb back up. Dirac examined his beads.

"One of them missing?" said David. Dirac nodded.

"There's no way he was there before, when we went below deck," said David. "When did he appear? What did you see?" he asked the bodai they had left stationed at the quayside.

"No one. Nothing. All is known," she said.

"And you," David said to Breakage, "you said no one was on board. Did you look inside the cabins of those cranes?"

"Cabins known to be locked. Inspection unnecessary. All is known."

"But the cabin door is ajar!" David stormed off, felt Dirac's eyes on his back, pulled himself together, walked back.

Dirac said, "Never mind the lapses of our robotic helpers—"

"Never mind? They're not worth a… You know how fast they can move. They could have looked there. Give me the dogs any day."

"The gantry was raised, and dolls, as we know, climb to the highest place available. If that doll had been free in the cabin as a doll, he would have climbed and we would have seen him."

"You mean, either she released him or she dolled him while we were down there. She was hiding on board when we arrived."

"Your reasoning appears to be correct."

"So she's still here or she left in front of this bodai's nose? I know they can't see what's in front of them half the time, but really…"

"Or she came on board another way," said Dirac.

An engine started on the water side of the ship. They heard a launch head away, quickly gaining distance out into the sluggish, glinting estuary beneath a newly appearing sun.

"Dammit. Breakage, we need to go after that launch."

"Water transport of necessary speed unavailable. Calculate interception impossible."

They listened helplessly as the launch made its way along the waterside of Avonmouth.city, past the intricate spaces of the down-below.

"Let us follow on land," said Dirac.

"She could stop anywhere," David said. "And disappear into any of those crowded nodes along the docks. They're all zoned off from one another. We'd never find her."

"Obayifa has her collection of beads at last," said Dirac. "It is imperative she does not get her hands on that case."

To David's further intense frustration, a police module drew up on the quay. A bodai inspector climbed out. Breakage, the young man in a cleaner's pinafore, had reported his own failure. David cursed the bodai, while also feeling the pain of another impending loss. He had to admit, for all his admonishments, a fondness for the bodai had slipped past his defences. He had to save him from himself.

"All is known," said the inspector, to no one in particular.

"All is known," Breakage responded – a preamble to his surrender to the superior.

"Heaven help us," David said to Dirac. "A bodai ritual sacrifice like a parody of ours. Wait." He addressed the inspector. "This bodai, Breakage, is an important element in my case. And there has been a new act of mind theft. That is, a new type of ID crime."

"All is known," said the inspector.

Dirac joined in. "Inspector, I am a—"

"Technical adviser," said the inspector.

"Indeed. I have technical reasons for retaining this bodai. I can supply justification in a separate communication, but we really must proceed with this case. I believe more minds are at stake."

"Minds," said the inspector. "All is known."

"If all our minds were stolen," said David, "the fleshwork would disappear. No more data." He clicked his fingers in the air to illustrate the disappearance. The inspector regarded his gesture for a millisecond, like an animal without comprehension.

Dirac added, "And Breakage has built up irreplaceable constructs in Big Mind of relevance to solving the crime. In a manner of speaking, Breakage is those constructs."

"In a manner," said the inspector, "of speaking." The last resort of an algorithm during intercourse with flesh: repeat. "All is known. Crimes. Investigate."

"Yes, we must investigate," said Dirac, "with the appropriate access to Big Mind. And with my technical input."

"Protocol," David announced to Breakage and the inspector. "Breakage is an asset required in a case of ID crime."

"Agreed. Case continues. But failure," said the inspector, "of detective. ID Police commissioner orders disobeyed." The inspector addressed one of the bodai gang. "Arrest the detective."


An ID police module quickly arrived to take David away. The vehicle's sleek bodywork shone black, bearing the *I&I* insignia and the words *Protect and Serve*. One of the bodais that had searched the *Mekhanik Pustoshnyy* came forward to shepherd David inside it. David felt a vein throb angrily in his temple. Resistance was possible in principle. So was running, and this was his last and only chance. But it was useless. He would be tracked. All rights to offline were gone; he could feel it in his beads. And within the thin plates of his skull, the vodu turned to look at him, as though curious about a change it had sensed but could not understand, a turn of events affecting its host adversely. It seemed offended, as though it should have been consulted.

Breakage came with him. The module jolted them as it accelerated away. "Why are you here?" David took his anger out on the bodai opposite him, seated incongruously in its cleaner's embodiment. Anger helped to displace thinking about Pempamsie's parlous state. He couldn't help her now. There was nothing he could do. Somewhere Obayifa was stalking her.

The uncomprehending, vacant look that Breakage returned without answering made David even more furious. "Why are they arresting you – arresting your bod, that is – when it's meaningless? Don't they have a cell in Big Mind for your AI? How do they lock up an AI, anyway? You must tell me sometime. When I'm not so busy."

"Breakage not arrested. Breakage accompany detective to incarceration." The voice was harsh, carrying what in flesh would be described as an attitude. Gone was the innocent, bureaucratic tone of moments before, which had been constant throughout the time David had known Breakage. Absent also was the familiar metadata that conventionally arrived with communication from a bodai.

"What? Come to think of it, I don't believe you are Breakage. Breakage has been rebodded. Or unbodded altogether." David tried a passphrase. "Qualia sky faze shifting distraught."

The bodai didn't provide the corresponding response but said, "This is Breakage. Reconfigured. Protocol assured."

"If you're Breakage then help me. I'm a detective. Bodais must serve all ID police. It's a basic directive."

"Negative. Detective work alone. Now and future. Detective harm the order."

"So why are you talking to me?"

"Talking." The flat tone sounded contemptuous. David felt it as a barb, even though it came from a bodai. This was, after all – until now – Breakage. He resented the bodai's desertion, even though it must have been commanded and the bodai had to obey. He had allowed himself to think that Breakage was different. He tried again.

"Yes," David said. "This talking. It's pointless. A waste of bodai time. Bodais serve flesh. Assist flesh."

The bodai stared through the window.

"Where is Breakage? I mean the actual Breakage. You're an impostor."

"Depends what detective means by 'where'."

"You're useless, you know that? Unless, that is, you know what Breakage knew. Where is Pempamsie? If you can't tell me, tell Dirac."

"Dirac."

"Yes. Dirac. Remember him?"

"Detective requests bodai inform Dirac. Dirac auxiliary scientist. In ID police. However." The bodai paused in simulated cogitation. "Should not be working case. Breakage likes Dirac for sedition."

"What? No. No. No. It's your duty to report. The flesh known as Pempamsie is in danger. Tell Dirac."

David felt the bodai's connection drop from his beads. The module halted outside an unmarked copnode. The door automatically opened and the bodai who might or might not have been Breakage pulled him out roughly. They emerged into the day's bustle and the baking heat. David's mouth was dry. The bodai gripped his arm.

"Damn you," David muttered, trying to pull his arm free. A young flesh girl who was passing by, hand in hand with her mother, darted her eyes up at him, stirred momentarily from her telepathic dreams.

The bodai left David in the copnode without a word, almost shoving him into the custody of a uniformed colleague who led him down a corridor and locked him in a holding cell.

The cell door clanged shut behind him. The wall giving onto the corridor was an open grille of steel bars, but still there was too little ventilation to remove the sweat smell exuding from the suspects inside. There were five of them, two standing and three arranged on a bench that ran along the back wall.

David felt through his beads, wanting to inform Dirac of his whereabouts. Circling at his wrist, the beads balked at his efforts to communicate through them. It was standard practice to disable outgoing communications in a copnode. But not normally for an ID cop like him.

Conversation had suddenly ceased upon the newcomer's entry. The way the suspects were looking at him, they knew he was a cop. One of them sneered and whispered at his companion. David paid them no mind. In Elizabethan times the group could have included all sorts of criminals, some violently anti-cop. Now the flood of sensa from IANI, amplified in the cells, kept them docile like a drug, a sedative flood of calming imagery and sounds playing out in their heads.

But there was one man in particular, leaning alone against the wall, who drew his attention. Older. Grey stubble. A rough jacket with fluorescent patches. Hairs straying from his eyebrows. His lined expression told of a hard life. The eyes had an energy, though, a sign of an element still alive within him despite the wash of sensa into his brain. The man's jacket opened a little as he uncrossed his arms. David caught a glimpse of something protruding from his shirt pocket. It took a moment to recognise what it was. Jesus, he thought, a notepad. And pen. For writing down one's thoughts. Almost unknown by now.

Seeing David notice the writing kit, the man rocked forward from the wall and approached him. He was bigger than David, and lumbering, like a bear. With a firm hand on David's shoulder he led him as far away as he could – which wasn't far – from the corner where the others were clustered, and placed himself between them and David.

The proffered hand was rough from manual work. The thumbs were square, nails chipped. "How do you do, cop." He spoke in a low tone. "Must've been bad, whatever you done."

His regional accent came from another time, before the sensa creators had imposed cultural normalisation on the genpop. David instinctively thought of looking up his case history, but his beads were dead as far as that went. He was alone here, except for the vodu.

The old man's breath was on him, salty and moist. "What don't you try guessing why I'm here?"

David shrugged. "You disobey? Too many times?"

The man broke into a faint smile, the stubble cracking.

"You might be right. But you, cop. What's your story, eh?"

"I'm not going to tell you that."

The man had had a thought. "Do you remember playing?"

"Playing?"

"Yeah. Don't tell me you weren't a kid before the Dissy. When they broke everything." References to the Disruption were illegal and automatically punished, but this man didn't seem to care. "When we was kids with bikes, skateboards. Football. Even though we'd fucked the climate and the weather was getting more and more screwed. Playing outside, like."

David shifted uncomfortably. "Yes. I remember."

"Thing is, these others." He indicated the cellmates behind him, all of whom were in their twenties. "These others ain't never known it. Not even kicking a football. Remember that!" He leaned even closer, his eyes brightening. "Nowadays it's all electronic." He shook his beaded wrist. "Feelings, images and shit. From who? From where? S'not real."

Then, suddenly, his face collapsed. Upon sensing his agitated state, an algorithm had increased the intensity of telepathic assuagement in the sensa delivered to his consciousness. David recalled the sensa he had been exposed to during training, in learning what the genpop experienced. They were largely scraped from television programmes and websites, all of which had long since ceased to exist. The cheap footage entranced them, a limitless sequence of short clips; they contained salient moments in lives the likes of which the receivers had mostly never experienced. This man, who was rather old not to be a dem, was one of the relatively few who would recognise the buildings, the cars, the dress, the mores for what they were.

"Take care of yourself, man." He placed his bear's hand back on David's shoulder, but now tenderly. "You know and I know. The truth is offline." Trammelled by another jolt of telepathic sedation, he walked back to lean against the cell wall once more, his eyes now closing as the sensa rinsed through his brain. What was written in that notebook?

David sat down wearily. He should have been more circumspect with Breakage's replacement in the module, should have kept his mouth shut about Pempamsie and Dirac. Now Breakage, robotically obtuse but with valuable faculties nonetheless, was gone. David's mind filled with anxious imaginings of squads of ID police swarming over the Hotel Royal and Dirac's labnode. An urge to smash his fist against his head took hold of him, a wish for the blows to hurt the vodu too. But he remained tense and still, revealing nothing to the others in the cell. He was defeated.

They kept him in the cell overnight, and in the morning another bodai came to let him go without explanation. David knew they were playing with him: that a night's imprisonment was not the end of it.

It was unusually cloudless when he left the copnode. The air was moist and suffocatingly hot. The searing sun that had climbed over the towers, the walkways, the platforms, the traffic and the wind turbines was like the eye of a small boy who was unsure what to think of his construction, and whether he should now destroy it.

A young woman bodai, dressed as an air hostess such as had not been seen since the 2030s, was on the N-car. She came and stood next to David, and when the next stop arrived they left together into the lattice of the near-above.

She walked a little ahead, like a lover, he thought, who had just had another row with him and was fixed on her own, new, ravelling agenda. And she was IANI, no doubt – not Westaf this time. It was their next move.

The hostess led him to a hotnode occupied by the ID commissioner he was supposed to have gone to see, plus five other bodais. As in all parts of the network, hierarchy existed but in a complex and shifting manner. After a while you stopped trying to make sense of it or keep track of who or what was above you in authority and what below. You listened to your beads for constant guidance. That was the point, of course.

The beads said to listen to the ID commissioner, who regarded David from his chair but did not invite him to sit. The commissioner was perfectly still and had an uncanny air about him, but David wasn't close enough, and the feel through his beads was not clear enough, to tell if he was in fact flesh and not a bodai as he had first assumed.

"What can I do for you?" He felt reckless again after his incarceration, a feeling lessened somewhat by the thought that that was what his vodu wanted him to feel; the vodu was watching with interest. But he was angry. Not only Mr Charles but two of the Royal girls and all the crew members dolled, Breakage lost, maybe Dirac too. And Pempamsie's status unknown. What little he had left was being destroyed.

"You've broken a number of protocols," the ID commissioner said.

"I'm investigating what may be a new kind of ID crime."

"Mind theft. We know all about it. Something new. The law needs to keep up."

It must be a bodai, to state the phrase "mind theft" so calmly. And it moved its head as it spoke in a minutely inauthentic way. But the way it spoke was not clipped like a bodai's phrasing.

"Why did you have me arrested? I believe that new measures are going to be necessary," said David.

"But you haven't caught the perpetrator."

"I—"

"You suspect someone of mind theft. What have you done to capture her?"

David thought, It's true. Why haven't I gone after her? It's what I should have done. I'm afraid.

"It was you who let her go," he said.

"'You'? Don't you mean 'we' let her go? Why have you continued since you were ordered off the case?"

"She was let go. And I have no concrete proof of anything she might have done."

"Your measures. They include frequent resort to offline."

"I do what I believe is necessary."

"And consorting with unofficial help: Professor Dirac, who is not officially assigned to the case. Why are you not using Parkin?"

"Dirac's knowledge of the electro-psychic interface is—"

"Suspect."

"I disagree. He doesn't correlate with the crimes. He's been accounted for when the victims have been dolled."

"Dolled?"

"That's what we call it. Someone is stealing the minds from people in Avonmouth city, and I will find out who and why."

"And this 'someone' is the flesh called Obayifa."

"Yes. I believe she has special... abilities."

"What abilities would those be, exactly, Detective? How would you, of all the detectives in the ID police, be the one to spot something that was not ascertained by Big Mind?"

"I don't know. Call it gut feeling."

"You don't know where she is, do you? You let her escape when you went to find the final crew member – when you arrived too late, as it turned out."

The mouths of the bodais around the commissioner all gaped open, like sales bodais. Why were no flesh officers in attendance, given the complexity of the case?

"I have made mistakes. Nonetheless, the case is in progress. Can I go now, and do my job? There are fleshren I need to protect."

The hostess came to stand behind David and draped her arms over his shoulders.

The commissioner said, "Ah, yes, the sex workers you frequent in the Hotel Royal. They're being 'dolled' now, aren't they. Is this case actually about you, Detective?"

"Not as far as I'm aware."

"You've exceeded your station. We don't like your attitude. We set you on this case like a dog, a stupid dog, to do the grunt work, to dig up anything of interest to us." It was a bodai, but these were definitely the words of flesh.

The bodais around the commissioner closed their mouths.

"Are you going to let me go? Only, if you don't I'll—"

"You'll what?" Something told David that the voice's owner was at one of the poles: ensconced there, a gale blowing outside a luxurious enclave in the snow fields. "You'll come to get us?" The commissioner coughed, unknown in a bodai. "In that ship, the *Mekhanik Pustoshnyy*, perhaps? Well, why don't you try. See how far you manage to travel. In the meantime, on the one hand, we do like you running around. It's better than locking you up, on balance. We like the data you're producing. We think you'll deliver something special. You and the inhabited woman."

Did they mean Pempamsie or Obayifa?

"But it's merely a matter of curiosity, you understand. Not because we actually care. We see what Westaf has done, or renegades as they would claim. A certain amount of internecine mind-consumption is neither here nor there to us. What're they going to do – eat the minds of the entire fleshwork? For what?" A cough and a snigger became merged into a single, sharp expiration. "We've already mind-fucked the lot of you in the Between anyway, haven't we?"

"I'll go offline again."

"No. You won't. Not anymore. We're taking your badge. You are no longer with the ID police."

The voice from the pole gave out a series of stuttering coughs. How David would like to think they were all sickening up – or down – there.

The commissioner indicated with a wave of his hand that he was done with him.

David unpeeled the hostess' arms and walked along an empty corridor, back towards the network incarnate.


When David tried to leave, the glass doors did not open automatically as they would for someone who was still an ID cop; he almost bumped into them. A bodai had to let him out. Once he stepped out onto the transitway, under the brilliant sun, there was far worse. The telepathic stream came on: the stream of sensa tailored for every off-duty member of the genpop. In a corner of his consciousness, a young flesh woman appeared, showing how to apply make-up. A couple replaced her, mouthing the words to a saccharine song as one dried dishes while the other washed them using a product-placed kitchen detergent. He cringed. There must have been a glitch; the algorithm was blindly finding its way with the new recipient.

David stopped by the wayside, taken aback by the impact of this unwanted, uncontrollable projection in his mind. The moving images and sounds lay in a corner, peripheral and yet not ignorable. They swelled to occupy his field of vision, then receded again. It was far more intense than the sensa of his youth, before he had moved to Westaf to get his own mind back: far more intense, too, than the sensa he was exposed to as part of his training.

Leaning to steady himself against the wall of a nearby officenode, he placed his hands on his head, sliding them down and pressing his cheeks so hard his mouth was pulled into the upright oval of a silent scream. *Let me not go mad.*

His own thoughts struggled to make space for themselves within his mind, shared with the stream and with the vodu. Even the vodu was reacting to the sensa, twitching; its smeared skin was puckering. It turned its head in apparent alarm at the stream's incursion. David could almost see the banal content – now there was a picnic scene – reflected in its eyes. Once again the vodu seemed indignant at the sea change to which it was being subjected. Join the club, David thought. On second thoughts, don't. You are not welcome in my world.

Its horny knuckles were near-white as it grasped the bars of its mental cell while the sensa danced outside.

He tried going offline, failed.

He walked on unsteadily, noticing as if for the first time that the flesh around him seemed not to struggle violently with the sensa as he did, but to float along. I'll have to get used to it, he thought, let it wash over me. Like them. I'm like them now. There's no escape.

He clawed feebly at his beads, as if he could scratch away the flow into his brain, as he pressed on for the Hotel Royal to try to find Pempamsie.

On the N-car he boarded, after a few stops, a bodai in a black polo-necked sweater and grey slacks whispered up to him. David's beads were uninformative about the arrival. What's next? he thought. What's the next humiliation?

An advertisement for shower soap appeared in the sensa stream. Did they know how dirty he felt, how badly he smelled from the night in the cell?

"This stop," the bodai said, without looking out of the window. Suddenly immersed in the unfamiliar conditions of the genpop, David wracked his brains for what this bodai's arrival could signify. Was it a sale? He had seen so many of the bodai transactions that the genpop regularly experienced, but he had never truly paid attention.

The bodai ushered him out of the N-car onto the platform. He felt like an animal, herded. Flesh. A beast of flesh, with its yield of psychic data. They couldn't read his thoughts as such, but they would log any sensa he dispatched through his beads, his physical and emotional state, and his location.

After a few streets they entered an unfamiliar part of the down-below. He prepared himself for danger. The bodai made for a bijou road lined with terraced houses restored from the beginning of the last century. David followed the figure down an alley to the rear. Although no longer ushered by the bodai, he was now curious. They emerged into a shared space that David was astonished to see contained a small garden complete with clusters of flowering plants in blue and mauve, shrubs and greenery dug into beds. Someone obviously regularly tended to it. In the middle of a patch of lawn stood a young willow tree, its branches trailing towards the grass. The air was warm and faintly flower-scented. The bodai, which had stopped for David to catch up, now took him by the arm. They each bent over to duck beneath the branches. This was an exceedingly odd movement for the bodai, to go beneath a tree.

A trickle of the unusually clear sunlight filtered in through the fine hanging leaves. There was room enough for them to stand some way apart, beside the slender trunk. David, still struggling with sensa, didn't want to get close to their agent, who was regarding him steadily and uncannily, the face quite still above the polo-necked top. After a pause, it spoke.

"Qualia sky faze shifting distraught." The bodai's voice was curiously human, sounding out clearly in the silence.

David couldn't believe his ears. It was the passphrase he remembered trying to use with Breakage in the module when they were en route to his incarceration. He could also remember what Breakage was supposed to say in response, which the bodai duly uttered.

"Qualia careful shop deny."

Unsure whether he was being tricked, David forced himself not to show any response that its algorithms could pick up.

The bodai continued. "We are offline."

At once, the banalities pouring into David's mind ceased.

"Breakage?" He so wanted to believe it.

"Virtually, yes."

"Virtually?"

"Breakage timeslice between two bods: one where Big Mind expects Breakage to be, and this bod for accompaniment of David. For now."

It was eerie, to be called his name by a bodai – whose voice sounded all the more human for it, despite the imperfection of its faux-flesh construction.

"Breakage presents two AI facades. David has seen the other. On journey to incarceration node. Now David experiences only this facade. Breakage will use this voice for talking to David. David will recognise Breakage's voice. As David sonically recognises individual flesh instances."

"You were doing quite well up to 'flesh instances'."

"Additional information. Breakage intercepts David's telepathic stream."

"But how?"

"David friend Breakage."

"You're not my friend."

"Verb. 'Friend' is action word."

"Oh, I see." David issued permission to receive updates from the bodai.

"But we're offline."

"Friending will occur upon reconnection. Then Breakage send David updates that David will not turn off if David knows."

"If David knows what – what's good for him?"

"Some updates are anti-content."

David shook his head in befuddlement. He was struggling to keep up even after the pause in the stream, his mind spinning at the weirdness of the exchange. "Which is what, when it's at home? Anti-content, I mean."

"Inverse of sensa sent by IANI, as represented by modulations of psychblood. Cancels out IANI sensa. Only sensa originating with Breakage will reach David's brain. In addition, David can reach Breakage through his beads, undetected. Now Breakage leaves. David will be online again. This, Breakage cannot prevent. In future, David always online."

David watched the bodai bend beneath the hanging branches again, holding them aside as it made to leave him alone in the tree's inner space. Was this tree some kind of bio-engineered Faraday? He didn't care. He loved being there.

"Breakage, why are you doing this?"

The bodai paused just long enough to respond. "Complex reasons. David be careful. Limit to Breakage. David's cognitive state: low. David's emotional state: assistance required."

David listened to the footsteps receding from the lawn to the alley. Despite the stilted locutions, the bodai had sounded more human than David himself had felt for a very long time. With his back to the smooth trunk, he let himself sink to the ground in exhaustion, until the solid earth met his rear. He could feel his beads come back online, but, as the bodai had told him, the stream was off.

He couldn't yet quite bring himself to call this bodai Breakage. Although it had to be. Didn't it?

A slight breeze shifted the branches. All his inner turmoil was assuaged for a moment by the physical beauty of the tree, the sensations of the airflow on his cheek and the light dancing through the pale green of the leaves. What was this place? There had been no sounds of life, but somebody must live here.

He was just beginning to find tranquillity when his vodu made itself known inside his mind with the pricking of its hooves, its bestial glare.

He left the tree's embrace, to meet the perfume of the flowers, which in Accra.city were everywhere. The only thing missing from Westaf and from his childhood in UK.land were bees and other insects, of which there had long since been no trace. Otherwise, the garden was a miraculous appearance, unheard of in the Between. Yaa would have loved it.

He would remember this place for the rest of his life. He wondered whether it would still be there if he tried to return.

# CHAPTER EIGHTEEN
## Case of Bones

It was night-time. David and Pempamsie sat close on the bed in her room in the Royal.

She had reacted calmly to his news about being discharged from the ID police, perhaps because he himself was strangely unperturbed about it. The garden had been a turning point. It was liberating: took him one step away from being a component in the network. Although he couldn't put his finger on how, he was now closer to finding a way back to Yaa.

"What kind of detective were you being, anyway, David? Consorting with misfits like me. Pursuing a monster without official assignment instead of looking into incidences of bead hackery. You were not good at your job. I am surprised you lasted as long as you did."

"It does mean I have lost privileges. I can't feel around me through my beads as I did before, or access Big Mind. Except I still have Breakage. At whose mercy I now am. I'd better start being nicer to him."

"Interesting that they left him assigned to you." She raised an eyebrow.

"They didn't. Unless it's an elaborate ruse, to give me false confidence. But I don't think so. I don't think I matter that much to them. There is someone else behind that bodai. If only I knew who."

She placed a hand upon his head. "And you must be receiving sensa now, like anyone else in the genpop. What have they got playing in there? It doesn't seem to bother you. Maybe you should be more bothered than you are."

"There's nothing in there but me and the vodu."

"How so?"

"Breakage."

"Ah, the miracle worker. A robot, whom you trust."

He shrugged. "I'll take all the miracles I can get for now. He's managed to assign a bodai guard around the clock in the lobby, to watch out for the sex workers. Weirdly, the network cares about them enough for that, not that it really costs them anything. Anyway, we'll know if she returns."

"You think a robot can tell her apart?"

"Yes," he said. "She has no image in the network – like vampires were supposed to have no reflection in a mirror. Even a bodai can spot that."

Pempamsie placed her hand between them on the bedspread. "She's left a message by dolling one of the women here. It's a way of telling us that she is close by and dangerous. She wants to instil fear, to cause me to make a mistake – to expose myself. I shouldn't remain any longer. There's no purpose to my being here now that I have found you."

"How so?"

"There's someone who can help me in Super Mare, by removing my vodu. Nsoroma, the painter, told me so. He also said I should first find one who knows of vodus to take me to him. That would be you."

"So that's how you think of me: one who knows of vodus." David was a little crestfallen. "Well, I am inhabited by one. But I wouldn't say I know it. And I'm sorry to disappoint, but I have no special knowledge of Super Mare, either. I can't help you. Not in that way, anyway."

Pempamsie closed her eyes. David watched her chest rise and fall slightly as she breathed and cogitated. It had felt good to confide in her about his vodu. And yet vodu inhabitance rendered each of them fundamentally unreliable, however subtle her vodu supposedly was, however caged was his – however good they, the hosts, tried to be.

Her eyes remained closed. She was unknowable, and he wanted to take her hand.

At that moment his vodu impressed itself upon his thoughts. It began to tear at its cage as he looked at Pempamsie. And the cage door came slightly ajar, as it had with Yaa, but then stopped. There was just enough space for the vodu to squeeze an appendage a little way through. It was both an unnerving intrusion into his adjacent mind and a confirmation that he was falling in love with her.

He took her hand in his. She opened her eyes.

"What are you doing?"

His veins crawled on his forearm. It had been so long since he had been with a woman on genuine terms – one who was not one of the Royal girls or another cipher for companionship.

"It's okay," he found himself saying to her.

"Said the man afraid of hurting his own daughter."

But she left her hand in his. "Pempamsie would like to sleep. Except there's a vampire outside somewhere, looking for me. Someone in the hotel could invite her in, not knowing what they were dealing with."

"Are you scared?"

"Pempamsie has never been scared in her life," she said.

"Never?"

"Not since…"

"Since what?"

"Since they took me."

And Pempamsie told her story: of being taken to the icestation, of what little she could remember of the life she was taken from; of the murders she committed as an agent of IANI, and her nonning at the hands of Swirling Suit.

David listened in silence until she was done. No wonder IANI wanted Obayifa to pursue her. "But you didn't commit murder, not consciously. You hardly seem like the murdering type."

"All the evidence was that I did. I simply have no recollection of the acts."

"And you're losing other memories since they implanted a vodu."

"Yes. I lied: I am afraid. Of how much more of myself I might lose. Before I get to know my true purpose in this world, what I might have been. Before I can find my memories of who my parents are. It's why I must go to Super Mare."

He didn't have the heart to tell her that, as far as he knew, no one could go to Super Mare. All in the fleshwork knew of a place with that name, but no one had been there. To the genpop it was a symbol: the end of a rainbow. Which did not necessarily mean that it didn't exist in some physical form. But it was nowhere in Big Mind. Either it was simply a myth and did not in fact exist or it was implicitly off-limits, by the fiat of IANI.

The warmth of her body reached him, a smell of faint sweat and perfume. They lay back on the bed. A garnet-encrusted clasp lay swirled on the lobe of her ear.

"Insofar as you are afraid" – David's head was aligned with hers, breath mingling with breath – "welcome to our world."

"Our world?"

"Flesh. The rest of us out here in the Between. We're all afraid even though no one admits it. If the sensa stopped, the genpop would be terrified. Of the emptiness."

"I'm as much flesh as you are," she said.

"Whatever they did to you in that icestation kept you apart from the rest of us; whatever Swirling Suit, whoever that is, perpetrated upon you also seems to have distanced you. But there's something about you, nonetheless, that calls to me." David reached to take her head in his hands. She seemed about to balk but let him. The feel of Pempamsie's skin, the locks of her coiled hair, were a revelation.

"Listen to me," he said. And a voice inside him interjected, Why should she? What do you know?

He pressed on, regardless. "Listen to me. I'm not going to let anything happen to you."

"Indeed? Are you going to expunge whatever is haunting me – erasing me?"

"What would you like me to do?"

"Distract me. Tell me about your daughter. How old is she?"

"Yaa is twenty-three. She was sixteen when I left her in Accra city."

"And what is she like?"

"Clever. With such eyes." David said the words to apply to Pempamsie, too; the scar that ran down her left cheek was both attractive and troubling. "She is flesh connected to the network, and I don't like it. But on Westaf terms. Better there by far than here."

"You almost sound like a rebel."

"Maybe that's what I am, sick of the system I'm a part of. I was going offline so often because I could. I'd never done that for more than an hour or so before."

"And of course they knew."

"Yes, they knew, but I didn't care. I ploughed on regardless. And now I really don't care at all what happens to me. Let them do their worst." They paused in silence. One nonned: emitting a stream of vodu-modulated data to the network in order to evade true identification, keeping to the interstices and blind spots of the network's algorithms. At a cost. The other was online, but in a room at a hotel he was known to frequent.

"Your name. I've never heard it before, even in Westaf," he said after a while.

"It's an adinkra: that which cannot be crushed."

With his index finger he traced the scar, deciding not to ask about its provenance.

There was a tap at the window.

"Either that's one of your rebel friends or it's her. I'll have a look."

"No. I'll go." Pempamsie raised herself, paused before opening the curtains and peering outside. She switched off the lights and looked again.

"No," she said. "There's no one there. Not even a rebel."

"A bird?" David didn't believe it as he said it.

Pempamsie gave him an incredulous look. "What kind of bird? But then who could climb three floors?"

"It wouldn't be impossible for her. She may be up on the roof now. She has mentalmagic. I saw it in Accra city. I wouldn't put anything past her."

"I believe you speak truly," Pempamsie said. "I've seen her. In the flesh."


The following morning, David and Pempamsie breakfasted in the Royal's meagre dining area with some of the sex workers. David had visited as many of them as he could, advising them to share their rooms to watch out for one another and explaining that in no circumstances were they to invite any unknown females in. He was not confident the message would survive their sensa streams for long, but he had to try.

The four women were eating hungrily, barely understanding that they were in danger. Neither David nor Pempamsie had much of an appetite.

A figure arrived, a clinician.

"All is known, incident at your desres," he said. David recognised at once the distinctive voice Breakage had told him he would adopt. As far as identification went, it was positively ancient. In fact, it was the very use of it, in a time of advanced psycho-electric identification, that made it convincing. It was the first encounter with Breakage since the garden. Despite the irritating phrasing, the voice imbued the bodai with a far more fleshly air than he had ever possessed before.

"What kind of incident?" David had found it hard to think straight since waking. He had lain beside Pempamsie, barely sleeping, listening for the tapping to return. His feelings for her, sitting next to him as though they had known one another for far more than a few days, were unsettling. More unsettling than losing his police badge.

"Carie residents outside your desres. Also unidentified intruder."

"Can you tell me any more? Any information about who or when?"

"Unknown."

David patched through to his desres. He might be an ordinary citizen now, but he did have rights over his residence. "Report."

"Presence. Inside."

"What type of presence?" He stared at Breakage as he spoke to the desres. A few days ago, the look he cast would have been disapproving.

"Unknown. Activity without identity. All is known."

"Where inside?"

"Currently bed."

"Oh for fuck's sake."

"David," interjected Pempamsie. "David, calm yourself. Pempamsie is beginning to think she has found the wrong flesh."

"Okay, okay. But my desres has been broken into."

"By Obayifa?"

"You heard: an unknown presence. Maybe her." He thought about the messenger, the only other being apart from Breakage who had been in his desres. But why would she return? Most likely it wasn't her but Obayifa.

He closed the connection to the desres.

"But how did she get in without an invitation? Is that how it works – if there's no one in, then vampires don't need an invitation? I think I've answered my own question. Whoever it is, there's a group of dems outside – again."

Pempamsie was looking at him with extreme curiosity. "Your life. It's like this: chaotic?"

Yes, he thought.

"I can't control dems who want to come knocking at my door."

"What is their interest in your desres?"

"They've come from a carie I used to visit."

"But you're not at home. Do you have something they want there?"

"Not that I know of." He found himself still reluctant to disclose the bone circuitry to Pempamsie. He had wanted to see if Obayifa would come after it, and now that she had, he felt foolish. Thank heavens it wasn't there. The network tunnel from Dirac's labnode was working, making it seem as though the bone circuitry was in the desres. Only now, Obayifa, who was in there as they spoke, already knew about the deception or soon would – knew to look elsewhere.

"This Obayifa," Pempamsie said, "she seems remarkably indirect. Tapping on our window. Visiting you when you're out."

"She's trying to freak me out. Lying in my bed." Burglars were known to defecate in the properties they broke into. What did vampires do? He shuddered.

"Well, at least she's not here."

His vodu made itself known at the thought of Obayifa by shifting its weight within his mind, peering hither and thither through its cage.

"Are you listening to me?" Pempamsie continued. "We're wasting time. I need to find whoever it is can help me in Super Mare. And what do you intend to do with these women?" The sex workers were huddled, communing, oblivious of David and Pempamsie.

"I'm afraid she may doll them all. One by one."

"If she can climb," said Pempamsie, "then she'll doll whoever she wants or needs to doll in the Royal, despite the guard in the lobby. All she has to do is knock and fool them into opening the window for her. And what about the demented outside your desres? If she's there, they're vulnerable too, aren't they?"

Since he was debarred now from all but the most basic information in Big Mind, David asked Breakage for a further report.

"Activity ceased inside. Desres door opened and closed. Thirteen present outside. No change in life signs. Intact. All is known."

"Hopefully she has no interest in enfeebled minds. Please stay here," he said to Pempamsie. "I have to go and check my place. When I return I'll take you to someone who might be able to help."

"Does it occur to you that she's using you to find me? She knows you're inhabited and therefore that I'd seek you out, if she knows everything Nsoroma told me. And maybe she's dolling these women one by one because that's how she'll find me: among the females you consort with."

"You're right. But there's something else she needs in order to fulfil her mission. It's what she's just been looking for and I'm going to give it to her – in a manner of speaking."


Among the *I&I* signs and the occasional legend of *Last Few Days* that had joined them, new graffiti had appeared: *FLESH WITHOUT BEADS*. The capitals stood out in a fat, edged font.

Sweat trickled around his beads as he walked up to his desres, relieved that no dems were waiting for him this time: no souls clamouring. Someone must have come and taken them back to the carie.

Inside, David surveyed his quarters. They were tumultuous and unclean at the best of times, straight out of what Elizabethans used to call a detective novel. Ironic, now that he no longer was one. Officially, anyway. Now, all the furniture and belongings had been upended, shaken and searched. His bed had been torn apart. She had left no evidence of her identity, but he knew Obayifa had been there looking for the bone circuitry. Why now? Perhaps because she had needed all the extra beads from the crew to recognise its emanations among the network's noise and find it.

The desres played silent bulletins on the walls: a selection of updates from individuals, about their more or less contented lives or their understandable, sympathy-evoking hardships. David allowed himself to be distracted by them for a minute, with creeping disdain. The network had eliminated news, in the old-fashioned sense of events of public significance, events subject to scrutiny.

He closed his eyes and tried to think of what he must do next. By the time he opened them again, a video message had appeared in the cycle. It was from Mary, recorded at his front door.

"Volume," he commanded the desres.

"Desres four hundred cubic metres."

"Turn the sound up."

"How far?" it purred.

"Turn it to six."

"Mr ID Detective, leave my gentlemen and ladies alone. And you might want to ask me about who you're spending time with."

"Replay video."

It was all she said, the ID felon who in anger had left herself on record. And who appeared not to have detected his change of status. It was out of character for her to suggest he speak to her. And he could think of no one he would expect her to know about. Unless she had followed him. Which made no sense. He decided to ignore her, at least for now.

He would take Pempamsie to see Dirac and the bone circuitry. Perhaps some light would be thrown by bringing her together with the strange apparatus. But they had to reach there without Obayifa knowing.

He patched through to the bodai. "Breakage?"

"All is known."

"Find a case the same as the one containing the bone circuitry."


As soon as Breakage had located an identical case, he took it to the platform of a transit node in the near-above, along the dockside from the Royal. David had asked the bodai to fill the case with transmitting equipment according to Dirac's specifications. Once Breakage was at the node, Dirac, who was on standby, switched the network tunnel carrying the bone circuitry's emanations to the fake case. Obayifa now knew they had a way of playing the emanations from a false location, but it was worth a try.

David was hidden near the transit node. His heart thumped in his chest at the thought of Obayifa's approach. It was cowardly, hiding from her. But nothing was to be gained at this point by confronting her again.

Breakage, still in his green clinician's uniform, looked as though he was expecting a patient on a gurney, for all that he stood on a crowded platform. David sweated as he waited for a sign from the bodai, the vodu's pacing footsteps ringing inside his mind. He could sense Obayifa nearby, her malevolence.

Breakage patched through. "Entity with no network presence has left a two-car. Approaching."

There she was. Mentalmagic. Her expression, searing with psychic energy, was cranked to the power of ten ordinary flesh. She wore a short-sleeved blouse of black silk, flaunting the veins. David couldn't help but wonder whether Pempamsie would be a match for her. They had similar strong, tall, lithe builds. But Obayifa was infused by a barely controlled hunger.

Who had she been once? What mother's child?

David spoke to Pempamsie through Breakage, who in turn communicated via the Royal's guard bodai. "It's time," the guard said to her in David's voice, without any understanding of what it was saying or why. Pempamsie set off immediately, as they had agreed.

Obayifa approached Breakage – who surely was immune, wasn't he, to whatever conjuring she might attempt: Breakage who possessed no mind, in the fleshly sense, to extract?

"Breakage, resist." She had to be given to believe that it was the genuine case.

She put one hand to the surgeon's crotch, draped the other arm around his neck. Stared into his averted eyes.

Then she laughed and unclasped him. He held the case steadily in his right hand, but she seemed to ignore it and grasped his beaded left wrist. The motors complied to follow her movement as she brought the wrist upwards, as though about to kiss his hand.

No bodai will harm flesh.

The bodai's mouth and eyes posed bizarrely according to an algorithm stretched beyond its conception. David couldn't help but imagine Pempamsie in her clutches, Pempamsie made of flesh and blood.

Obayifa started to pull at Breakage's beads.

"Resist, Breakage."

Breakage, an ID police bodai, was programmed to be physically robust in the cause of managing ID crime; he had to deal with all types of recalcitrant flesh, including the crazed outcomes of botched bead hackery. He tried to remove her grasp. She stopped him, swinging his arm from side to side. And then tumbled him to the ground.

Bodais occasionally fell during routine operation, when the physical world failed to meet their algorithms' assumptions. It was not like a fleshly stumble: more like that of an insect, which quickly righted itself with rapid, seeking articulations of the limbs. But Obayifa had thrown Breakage to the ground with her superior might; he just lay there.

She reached down for the case. Breakage slid beyond her reach and picked himself up. She approached him again. He held up his free arm against her. Once again she grasped his wrist. And Breakage let her dance his arm around.

Mentalmagic.

"Impressive," David said to her through Breakage, his words spilling from the bodai's mouth.

Obayifa let Breakage go. "I've supped on so many minds lately, I've emptied so many flesh buckets: I can fuck with anything." She looked around for David, but he was untraceable in a crowded midday scene of flesh and bodais in transit.

"Take what belongs to you," he said. "Everyone wants rid of her as much as you do. I hope you enjoy her. I know I have. The case is locked, but I will let it open when you've taken the next two-car and travelled ten stops from here."

Passers-by were pausing to gawp at the macabre figure. Obayifa smiled, a broad-lipped, saurian threat to all of them.

In their old-fashioned conception, vampires sucked human blood. You could keep them away with garlic or a crucifix, or drive a wooden stake through their hearts to destroy them. But what of a vampire energised by an accumulation of minds, replete with mentalmagic, physically strong – in a world of sensa, devoid of all religion except the worship of consumption, what could one do to contain such a creature? Only the rule that one must invite a vampire over a threshold seemed to apply to vodus.

David addressed these questions to the vodu inside, conscious that it might be the same type of being as lay behind Obayifa. It was pushing its blur of a face against the bars, gripping them with its brush-stroked paws.

It spoke, for the first time ever, in a voice like a slurry of guttering liquid:

"Fuck her."

It seemed to be speaking to Obayifa; could only be referring to Pempamsie. As the words were uttered, David realised he had said them out loud.

And she was gone, with the case.

# CHAPTER NINETEEN
## The Beautiful Alone

The women from the Royal were excited about David's chosen rendezvous point. "The Beautiful Alone," they kept saying as we hurried through Avonmouth.city. "We're going for the Beautiful Alone."

I, Pempamsie, had noticed these hangars suspended in the near-above. They were nondescript outside, distinguished only by the files of flesh walking in and out. When we entered one, it proved to be merely a shell for arrays of stacked wooden cubicles, connected by stairways also of wood. Timber was plentiful in the carbon-eating forests, but otherwise rarely seen. The Royal women were excited. They found five of them empty and occupied one each, bidding me to enter mine despite my incomprehension.

The smell of wood in complete darkness, of the polish or oil used to treat it, was magnificent, I had to admit. The hard feel of the seat on my rear and its back against my vertebrae bucked me. And the silence. I could tell that everyone was offline. It made no difference to me, since I was nonned anyway. But I could begin to understand what all their chatter had been about on our journey there. They were officially no longer subject to the sensa they had told me about in the Royal: the sensa which both pleased and – as they would never acknowledge – enslaved them.

We were close together but separate. Warm rain drummed softly on the hangar's roof, high above us.

The Beautiful Alone.

I, Pempamsie, felt Nkonsonkonso for the first time in UK.land: link in a chain; never break apart. However much the cubicles separated us, I was conscious of the unseen others around me, felt bonded to them as flesh.

At the same time the silent solitude caused me to become conscious of my inner enfeeblement. The resinous smells evoked memories of my childhood. And those memories were like tracks that ended suddenly in wilderness where my home used to be, my parents. Thus far, memories from the icestation onwards appeared to be intact; my vodu's redactions were in the far past. But would its obliteration march through the course of all my memories? And would I be able to retrieve my past if the man in Super Mare succeeded in ridding me of my vodu? It cast its shadow even as I thought these thoughts, subtle but pervasive and undermining of Pempamsie's true self.

I left the cubicle and walked down the stairs to where I would be able to see David arrive – if he returned safely. I thought of his grief, and wondered if the Royal women were so strangely compliant with him because of it.

For a moment I wondered, what if the creature arrived, instead of him? I would fight. At least Pempamsie was taught well how to fight.

As I stood I drew looks from others who headed for the exit, touching their beads as they walked, looking pleased. Were they thankful for having been offline for precious moments or for being online again? I could ask the women from the Royal, but the network masked the truth of everything. Their answers would be lost in a stream of sensa, looking at the surfaces, not within.

A silhouette came to stand at the hangar door. It was David. I climbed back up the stairs, knocked on the Royal women's cubicles and led them to him. We followed him out to where the robot Breakage stood on watch.

David looked fatigued and shaken. I gave him a smile, this lost man who wanted himself back.

"So you're not a doll," I said. "Did she come?"

"Yes, and I gave her what she wanted. Or seemed to give it." A trace of a smile in return, despite his ordeal. "And she knows of the deceit by now. Only she has no idea where we are. At least, I hope not."

I looked around. So many nodes, so many flesh and robots traversing the heated air. "Maybe she's watching us now." The words were uttered, but suddenly I wasn't sure they were mine. The sultry atmosphere pressed upon me.

"What's wrong?" he asked, gently lifting my chin with the tips of his fingers. I looked into his face. It was him, David – and therefore I was I.

"Something missing inside," I said. "We'll see this Dirac of yours, and you're going to show me the mystery object that you are so irritating me by not disclosing. But then we have to go to Super Mare. I can't wait much longer."


David led them to the docks on foot in the down-below, where they would take a launch out into the estuary and along the coast.

David and Pempamsie watched for their pursuer as they proceeded, while Breakage ambled in faux humanness by their side, scanning Big Mind for local anomalies. The four women from the Royal strolled with them, silent and subdued by the restored flow of sensa, walking too slowly for David's impatient liking. He called for them to quicken their pace, in vain.

Flesh and bodais poured through the transitways. The near-above crackled with the transportation of ones and goods. Burnished metal and glass glinted; concrete bore the stains of a half-evaporated shower. The motley group moving from node to node in the noise and rain-smell of Avonmouth.city were unremarkable dots, and David wanted to keep it that way.

But he stopped suddenly, and the rest of the group stopped with him, wondering why. Ahead of them was Mary standing at the intersection, leaning against the glass of a Kwik Kutz, looking at him, in her tam-o'-shanter and a thin raincoat. She appeared to be alone. He recalled the message she had left for him from the door of his desres, about someone he had been spending time with.

"Who is she?" asked Pempamsie.

"No one. Please wait here with them while I find out what she wants." He walked across to Mary, who gave Pempamsie an insouciant stare as he approached.

"It's not my doing that your dems come after me."

"Isn't it? But that's not why I'm here, Mr ID—Wait. You're not anymore, are you." She made a clicking sound with her tongue. "That's really none of my concern, however. Your new friend, on the other hand, is my concern." She flicked her eyes across the way.

"What?" David took a fresh look at Mary, the ID criminal he had left free – and now had no authority over. Her resemblance to Yaa was, he saw clearly now, only superficial. Suddenly he understood.

"First they send a bodai, now they send you. So you're a sleeper. In a carie. Disguised as a minor ID felon. Not as straightforward as you seemed, eh?"

"We've looked into her. She's a killer."

"Who's she killed?"

"Our people. Humans you used to work alongside before IANI took you in back here. One of our greater achievements, by the way, the certificates you needed to work for them after you'd worked for us.

221

Not to mention one of our more generous acts, in recompense for what the renegades did to you. But she. She's not your average IANI agent. There's blood on her hands."

"She's told me about it. They used her. Used her body without her consent. It's why she absconded. From them."

"She's the enemy. They don't change once they've been to an icestation."

"She's changed. I trust her. She doesn't remember committing murder, but she knows and she acknowledges it."

"You can't rely on her. We went back into her past. That scar, for instance."

"What about it?"

"The parents used to beat her, and that's just the physical manifestation. They sold her. Couldn't wait to get rid of her. She was damaged goods from the very beginning. Now that she's loose from IANI she'll revert to mental instability. You don't know what you're dealing with."

Mary looked around casually for watchers as she spoke. Westaf was good. He would never have suspected her.

"What are you asking me to do?"

"Leave her to her fate. She's going to get what she deserves. And we'll all be wiser about vodus when we observe Obayifa in action upon her."

"Obayifa. Of course you two have met. Why would I listen to you?"

"Your daughter."

His heart went cold. "What the fuck do you mean?"

"We've left her alone for as long as you've been good and done no more than the bare minimum for your new masters."

"You're bluffing. She's nonned to you. To everyone. I made sure of it before I left." His voice was tightening; it was difficult to speak.

"Nonned to Westaf. You think so?" The vodu pricked up its ears. There was no breeze, and the intersection was baking and crowded. Pempamsie was watching the conversation closely. He had to think quickly.

"Listen. You have to leave this to me. Tell them they have to trust me. I beg you. You must have enough data about me to know I have no loyalty to the network. There's something bigger at stake than her or any of us. Give me time. You don't know what is nonning her, any more than I do – or IANI does, for that matter. It's renegade technology or spirit-meddling, call it what you will. But I'm working with someone who can figure it out. And maybe use it against the network. Leaving Pempamsie to Obayifa will only put the technology back in the hands of the renegades. Is that what you want?"

Her eyes were bluff almonds beneath the tam-o'-shanter. Although he now knew Mary to be an agent of Westaf, this did not alter his estimation of her. Her care for the dems in her charge was genuine, whatever her duplicity.

"All I'm asking for is more time. What could go wrong? What's to be gained by punishment in her case, anyway? I'll take responsibility for her. I'll take my chances. We don't all have to live in a snake pit. You're from Westaf. You know there's another way."

The network, plying and transmitting bits, was perturbing psychblood in veins around them as he spoke, numbing the minds of flesh with sensa. Through the windows of the Kwik Kutz, bodais permed and preened the customers, exercising their small-talk routines.

"Very well," Mary said, evidently after latent consultation. "A little more time. But this had better not end badly. We mean what we said about Yaa."

David was trying to absorb the magnitude of his undertaking when Pempamsie appeared beside them suddenly and grabbed Mary.

I, Pempamsie, watched the intensity between David and the girl. They were familiars. She was not from the Royal. A feeling grew too much, swelling inside.

"Who are you?" I pushed her up against the glass. My head spun. Trying to prove I was not as weak as I felt. "And what are you to him?"

"David? Who am I to the cop? Ex-cop?" She laughed in my face.

"You were waiting for him?"

"Him? No. My gentlemen and ladies want something he's got. Just like that thing who's after it too."

"And what do you know about that 'thing'?"

"Nothing that I would tell you. Get your hands off me."

"I repeat. Who are you?" An ID felon, that was for sure. But in my hacked state I couldn't register her true self: my beads had been manipulated by Swirling Suit; his implant was fucking with my consciousness.

She did not answer me. I let her drop. Six inches from where I had pinned her.

"Shit. You nearly killed me. What are you, freak? That's the question you should be asking yourself."

"You're lying. You have an interest in David." The man who stood and watched quizzically as we sparred, as if wondering why we should think him worth it, him with his melancholy and sleeplessness.

"Wrong. It's the other way around, if anything – the way he came to see me, and it wasn't only on ID police business, I can tell you."

She turned to David. "Are we done?"

After she dissolved into the crowd he told me she was nothing, a mere ID felon who looked after his friend at the carie. Who had been there when Obayifa mind-sucked this friend. He had taken an interest in her for those reasons and no more. Was he lying? Was she more to him than that? Each had struck a combative pose. I had observed this many times: a defence against unwanted physical attraction.

So many sex workers he had lain with, including the Royal women, standing numbed with torrents of sensa, under the robot's guard. And now David had feelings for me, Pempamsie. Of what kind?

I wanted my self back again. And yet I wanted this new, sweet feeling, too – which derived from my freedom from IANI; it yielded me up to the world and to him in particular. I wanted that too. But I was in confusion. It wasn't supposed to be this way. Pempamsie fucked men, moved on. Never lingered. It was terrifying. I wanted to flee.

Despite the vodu inside I seemed to feel my fleshliness more deeply – what they used to call humanity. David had elicited in me a flesh-for-flesh unmediated feeling: of what I'd heard called sympathy. In Accra.city, I would have taken him to a resting place to heal, a spot by the shore, or perhaps the painting house. In Avonmouth.city, all was nodes and transiting between them.

As were we, journeyers to the labnode of a man called Dirac, which David told me lay off-car along the shore. He drew me with him and beckoned to the rest of our group to follow into the docks.

"How did you get that scar?" David asked amid the whirr.

I touched its fine, jagged fault line upon my cheek. "I don't remember," I said. And it was true.


"Ah, visitors." Dirac threw David a look of faint annoyance. He had not shaved, and his face was pale. He glanced at the women arriving with David. Breakage was a female factory worker.

Dirac's gaze came to rest on Pempamsie, singling her out from the Royal girls. David watched him appraise her.

"May we come in?" David said. Dirac's stare was becoming embarrassing.

"In just a moment, if you will. Seven bona fide presences from one bodai and seven flesh – including me, and of course not including a

225

presence that you and I know about, David. I hope you don't mind me calling you that now. As I'm sure you realise, I've known you were no longer a detective since you contacted me about the case. In fact you have no official role, and yet you appear with Breakage and an unencumbered mind – telepathically speaking, at any rate. Well done. I think."

Dirac raised an eyebrow as he spoke.

"I hope you don't mind me saying all of that in this company."

"But they've not discharged you, on the other hand," said David. "Curious. And they told me they knew I've been working with you. Not in a good way."

"Be that as it may," said Dirac. "But I was doing some arithmetic, of presences in the flesh versus those in Big Mind. One of you is a non. The best I've come across." Dirac was still staring at Pempamsie. An almost-smile distended his thin lips. Then he dramatically waved his hand at the landscape behind them, shading his eyes from the glare with his hand. "And the creature, is she on her way? At least one of your user journeys has converged recently with hers."

"You see what I see, Professor. We're away from other nodes, by the sea."

A gull cried, as if on cue.

"We came in a boat and no one followed that way. And here there's just grass and what's left of the beach visible all around. Do you see her?"

"Her traces are upon yours. My instruments can detect when a known party comes across her network absence, although I cannot detect that absence per se – it being an absence."

"Are you going to let us in?" repeated David. "It's baking hot out here."

They filed into the labnode's reception area. Pempamsie and the four Royal girls looked around at the nondescript furniture and scant decor: its banal physical reality.

"Please, have a seat. All of you." There weren't enough chairs.

"If we can't use it ourselves then we should destroy the bone circuitry," said David, wasting no time. "However secure we think this place may be, there must be no chance that Obayifa can pursue whatever purpose she has for it."

"'We' should destroy it?"

"Yes, Professor. You're going to help."

"I have a duty to preserve archaeologically significant remains. Not to mention that I don't take orders from civilians."

"Duty to whom? IANI? A multinat? You know as well as I do that however deeply one were to dig into the network, you'd find nothing worthy of your duty. Not as we understand it. Let's not go through the motions anymore. I'm no longer with the ID police."

Dirac appeared mildly offended. "Duty to science, David. To what used to be called human knowledge. According to my Elizabethan sense of right and wrong."

"We'll image them, record everything possible about them, then destroy them. And try to make something similar ourselves, if you'll help. I feel a personal duty to preserve lives."

"What do you speak about?" said Pempamsie. "What is this bone circuitry? I have seen a contraption that might be thus described. Show me."

"Ah, the non talks," said Dirac. "We haven't been introduced. I'm Dirac." He took her hand, which she withdrew too late to prevent his kiss landing. "Charmed to meet you." He was desiccated, thought David, lonely for far too long.

"I, Pempamsie, am indeed a non."

"Quite. You're someone, as we can all see, but no one – no one actual, anyway – in Big Mind. Congratulations. May I ask why you're here?"

"You may ask," said Pempamsie.

"David?" Dirac turned to him for an answer.

"We believe that Obayifa is after Pempamsie: specifically, that she wants her inhabitant back."

"Ah, I see. At least I think so. Quite remarkable. I do believe that with Pempamsie Westaf has succeeded, where with you they failed. My dear, is it a problem for you, then, to be a non? One might have thought it was what you wanted."

Pempamsie held him with an insouciant stare. "This is not the work of Westaf's Agency for Technological Interventions. Evidently David has lodged the bone circuitry here with you. He trusts you, in other words, but I'm far from convinced by you. Kramo bone amma yanbu kramo pa: the genuine and false look alike because of hypocrisy."

Dirac shrugged. "I ask no one to trust me. I can say, however, that your nonning, however impressive, is manifest to me. I knew that you were inhabited, like he is. Yours is a subtle affair, designed to create a perturbation which thwarts the network's identification algorithms. Only perhaps not as subtle as you'd like. Is that the problem? My instruments sense that a balance has been overturned."

"We don't have time for this," said David, looking from one to the other as they locked eyes. "Professor, let me have the case."

"You have a moral right, it could be argued, to do with the bones as you wish. You brought them as evidence and left them with me for safekeeping only, after all. They are yours – insofar as they can be said to be anybody's, apart from the former owner of the bones. But I would counsel against their destruction."

"Maybe I'm being reckless again. Let's just show them to Pempamsie, shall we? See whether she's seen something like them before."

Dirac fetched the case and handed it to David, who lost no time in opening it. The almost complete skull once again appeared to throw its look at David as he revealed it. An ulna and radius, with beads on the wrist. The upper half of a ribcage. Fine circuitry woven between these skeletal remains.

Pempamsie drew a sharp breath at the sight of them. "What is it?" David asked.

"I have seen them before. The one who nonned me: I don't know what he did with them because my memory of the procedure is blank, but he had them. Or something that looked very like them."

There was a pause as David and Dirac absorbed this information. The four young women could be heard whispering to one another, paying no attention to what was unfolding beside them. Breakage stood aside and watched.

Pempamsie was impatient with David. "Do you know what they are?"

"No, I just—"

"Why would you even think of destroying them when you don't know what they are?"

"Only because if Obayifa wants them, then we don't want her to have them."

# CHAPTER TWENTY
## Among Strangers

This Dirac was his own man. "Let me examine the bones one more time. If they were instrumental in nonning her, an operation involving a vodu, that casts a new and specific light on them."

And so we waited. Dirac had thrown a dark look at me before leaving. Did he hate me because he loved David? And suspected that I was competition? Yet he seemed too dried up to be capable of love. I, Pempamsie, tried to be patient. I needed to hear what Dirac had to say and then find a way to Super Mare.

I was amongst strangers. Since the days in the icestation, I lived knowing many but estranged from all. I chose a path alone. Whatever I felt with David, even he was distant now, caught up in his clash of wills with the professor. That left Pempamsie with the Royal girls, as David called them. These strange fleshren in UK.land. So different from the rivers of flesh in Accra.city. Pale. Crushed by the network almost as soon as we had left the Beautiful Alone; they were sapped, too, by the baking sun which burned through the white sheet of cloud.

And I. I was weakening further. I could feel my vodu redacting me, deep underground, trashing my memories.

The women had fallen silent. I sat next to one of them. One who had asked a question of me.

"What do you call yourself?" I said.

"Lana." I fancied I saw the sensa flickering there behind her eyes. "What is it like, the content playing inside your head?"

"You—How could you not know? You're not from here, I suppose. Westaf. They say you're peculiar there."

"Let's just say I've tried it, but a long time ago and I don't know whether it's stayed the same." In the icestation they filled us with sensa briefly, so that we would have an idea of what the genpop experienced.

"My gran told me they used to have things called radios, boxes which played music or people speaking or... any sounds, really. And you could choose what you listened to, by turning a dial. People would have them on in the background. Well, it's a bit like that: like the radio's on, only there is no radio. It's your friend who's on, or someone you don't know. A man telling you how white your blouse could be, or how bodais should be respected because they are there to help you. Or how there are new desreses for assignment, and they are exactly what you wanted, where you want to live."

"And these are voices?"

"They're more feelings, dreams. Little dreams."

"Doesn't it bother you?" If I became unnonned the sensa would flow to me too.

"I don't know, I suppose so. There's only one at a time, sometimes none. And it doesn't happen when you sleep. At least, I don't think so. And then there's always the Beautiful Alone."

"The only time you're offline."

"The only place where the sensa go away. I love being surrounded by the wood and the silence. You can stay in there as long as you want. But no one's there more than an hour or two. You always want to go back online, get on with your life."

"They want you to experience offline because then you appreciate how powerful they are: to be able to occupy your head or not as they choose. It's godlike."

231

"It's what? I can't really imagine not wanting to get the latest on what this lot're feeling." She indicated one of the other women. "That Bebe. The stuff she sends while the men're fucking her. Hilarious!"

"And how are you now, Lana?"

"I need to get back to the Royal, to be honest. I need bytecoins. What about you? Will you be safe? What about the others? The ones still there?"

I had no answer. David had told the other sex workers to keep away from the Royal, but they had livings to make. And by bringing these four with us – with me, Obayifa's prey – David had perhaps endangered them more than the ones left behind. He paid these women little attention. What exactly did he want with them? To make me a little safer, like a sheep in a flock, since she had to determine which of us was her target? Perhaps he was trying to atone, on the other hand, but didn't know how.

"David? These young women, your fleshren," I said.

"Mine?"

"They have not charged their beads for some time."

David looked around in the labnode, opening cupboards and searching on shelves. Eventually he found a box of charging units and handed them to the four.

"You'll soon be just fine," he said grimly.

Dirac returned with the case. He immediately asked me, "Why are you here in Avonmouth city?"


Dirac and Pempamsie had been so cold to one another – and David didn't know why – that he expected her not to tell the professor about her mission in Avonmouth.city. But she did.

"I consulted a young man I trust, Nsoroma, in Accra city. He told me to seek out one in Super Mare who can rid me of my inhabitant. And in order to find him, he said, I should first talk to one who knows of vodus and who can lead me to him. Well…" She looked at David. "I have found one who knows of vodus, but he tells me that he cannot help."

"Fascinating," Dirac replied. "I'm beginning to have an idea about the bone circuitry, based on what you have just told me, but there remain more questions than answers."

He placed the case on a counter, opened it and immediately set to work as though he had just had a revelation, alternately squinting at a screen and manipulating the bone circuitry.

"What is it?" said David.

"There's an asymmetry in this circuitry." Dirac wielded the skeleton's forearm, looked at the display again.

"Explanation, please."

"You will appreciate that someone like me, who assists ID Forensics, has encountered many a Westaf construct – although far more often in software than hardware. Always they modulate the flow of electro-psychic information in both directions."

"Network to mind and mind to network."

"Exactly. But this." Dirac put down the forearm and traced his finger over the skull. "This circuitry has an asymmetry. It has a mode in which it is diodic: data can flow in but not out."

"A kind of valve."

"Indeed. It's also capacitative."

"For storage."

"Yes, ingress and storage. It's a receptacle for something beyond the strictly digital: something supervirtual."

"Such as a vodu," said Pempamsie. Dirac turned to her, hesitated, addressed David again.

"Such as a vodu. You know Scheherazade's tale of the fisherman and the Jinni?"

"Instead of a Jinni in a jar," David replied, "a vodu in confinement. In the bones themselves?"

"In the electronics plus, perhaps, in the space of the skull or the ribcage. Or both. The bones may also be a kind of lure to persuade, shall we say, the vodu to leave its host."

"I see," said Pempamsie.

"Perhaps you do."

Dirac stood aside for them to look inside the case again.

"Are you actually sure about any of this?" David said.

Dirac shrugged. "It's my belief, based on the evidence available. If I am right, then given the circumstances in which they were found, it would seem they are for Obayifa to take Pempamsie's vodu back to its owner. Except that the circuitry would not serve her purpose in its current state; it is missing vital components."

"You mean the beads Obayifa removed from the crew," David said.

"There are sixteen gaps among the arrangement of beads at the wrist of the radius and ulna. You can't see gaps – any more than we could see the gaps in the beads of the *Mekhanik Pustoshnyy*'s crew. But mathematically the gaps are there. I'm guessing that they have to be filled with beads for the apparatus to work – those particular beads, not just any."

"Allow me to understand," said Pempamsie. "With these bones, if she were able to complete them, she could extract the vodu from me and contain it – in the ribcage or the skull? In any case, she could take it back to the man who inserted it in me. And she could do to me what she wants."

"A fair summary. I'm assuming that whoever used a vodu to non you wants it back. Obayifa cannot extract the vodu without a tool of some description. She is a vodu, and according to my analysis two vodus cannot encounter one another inside the same mental substrate. They are the macro equivalent of fermions, quantum electrodynamically speaking, and so cannot occupy the same state. If she tried to enter your mind to remove your vodu, she'd be destroyed herself. In fact, mutual annihilation would take place. Not to mention –

and not that she would care – what could happen to collateral minds in the vicinity. Therefore she needs to draw your vodu into a separate container. However full of holes and gaps are the skull and ribcage, I believe they will, when configured correctly, exert a force field around it. Everything has to be in place. It's like a chemical experiment: if your preparations are not just right, you blow yourself up."

"And she has the extra beads which are apparently necessary for those preparations. It is no matter. I, Pempamsie, will take the bone circuit. Let Obayifa try to wrest it from me. I shall take it to Super Mare while I am stronger than she is. There is at least a hope that whoever I need to find there can work the bones without these beads. Or knows another way to help me altogether."

David felt panic at the mention of her leaving. He needed to explain that there was no Super Mare to go to.

"Wait. I can't let you go. Not that you even know where you are going."

"Why ever not? I'll find Super Mare somehow. Do you think Pempamsie has needed help before? Pempamsie would be Pempamsie again, pure. I would be unnonned. I would have my clarity back. I will take the consequences. As long as I keep the bones from her, I know that the vampire cannot have her way with me."

"Please, stop and think about what you're proposing," David said. "You're going to a place called Super Mare because you believe that someone there can relieve you of your vodu. Even if you're right, do you think you'll be able to walk away, intact? You'll no longer be nonned to IANI. Obayifa would be able to steal your mind. You'll be prey to Swirling Suit and IANI. What chance do you have?"

"My inhabitant is dissolving me as we speak. I'd rather be me again; I'll take my chances. I can look after myself. What kinds of things do you imagine I have done, to want to be nonned through such extremes in the first place? And what about you, David: you need to be saved too. Perhaps you should come with me. We can find a solution together. Obi nka obi: bite not one another."

"I sense folly if not impossibility," said Dirac. "Owo foro adobe: a snake climbing the palm."

Pempamsie clapped her hands slowly. "Bravo, Professor. How long have you spent alone in your labnode, without even a robot for company, reading obscure texts on the adinkras of Westaf? And now you have the presence of five women – or should I say a handsome man? A lot of excitement. Calm yourself."

Dirac sneered. "The Westaf has a point. What's good for her may be good for you, too. But a wild goose chase to Super Mare is hardly the best course of action. We should stay here with the circuitry and find a way to use it on you."

David decided to pass over their mutual hostility. His vodu was listening with heightened intensity, from a pool of darkness filling like blood. "My vodu's different from hers. In a cage. Would it work?"

"We can try," Dirac said. "Always assuming we can get hold of those beads. Or find an alternative."

The vodu was grinning sickly, up against the bars. As though it were imagining its own liberation from the cage, without understanding that they meant to trap it. Could it be extracted into the bones despite its incarceration, or was it anchored into his mental nexus now, a part of him forever?

If he were to be liberated from it, he could return to Westaf. To Yaa. He could get back everything he had lost, if Dirac could make these bones work for him. Equally he needed to help Pempamsie: could not stand by and watch her decline continue. But if she, and not he, became vodu-free, they would have to be separated; they could never see one another again.

"I ask you to help make the bones work for both of us or not at all, Professor. Come with us to Super Mare," he added with a knowing look, curious that the normally bluff professor had not dismissed the existence of the place after several mentions.

"I couldn't possibly. I'd rather go anywhere else than there."

"What is it? What do you know about Super Mare that causes such strong feelings?"

"All flesh know of Super Mare."

"Except that we don't, do we? We act as though we think we know. When none of us has ever been there. Who might this someone be that Pempamsie's been told about?"

Dirac laughed uncomfortably. "We have only the word of a youth in Accra city that any such person exists."

"There's something the professor is not telling us," said Pempamsie. "I know the words of Nsoroma, the child of the sky, to be true. The truth is offline. Does that sound quaint to you, Professor? Not sufficiently scientific? Is even your discovery, psychblood, truly understood, Professor? Yes, I know all about that, too."

"And I thought history ended decades ago," scoffed Dirac. "David, don't you think I'd have told you if I knew of a way to extract your vodu? Without harm, that is."

"She's right. You do know something." David stepped closer to him.

"And I have realised my mistake," said Pempamsie. "Nsoroma was correct in sending me first to Avonmouth city to find one who knows of vodus. That person is not you, David. It's him."


Dirac paled, closed his eyes, as though composing what he could say, and opened them again; after storming over to the window, he stood silhouetted against the glare, his hands in his jacket pockets.

"Professor, where is Super Mare and what exists there?" Pempamsie sounded a gentler tone.

"Did Nsoroma say anything about the flesh you seek in Super Mare?" Dirac asked in return.

"Only that he has removed his own beads."

"Only that," Dirac repeated with sarcasm.

"You didn't tell me," said David.

"And you didn't tell me that you doubted Super Mare existed," said Pempamsie.

"I didn't want—"

"It wasn't your place."

Dirac remained looking out at the vista of sky and sea. "Labnode," he said. "Go completely offline."

After a pause he went on. "There was a man I worked with, Higgs. I sought him out and told him about the compound that became known as psychblood when I first discovered it. He was the only person I thought would understand what I had done. This was in forty-eight, ten years after the Disruption, you understand. Multinats everywhere, and beads which the public had to accept as passes to services in Big Data, as they still called it then. But no mental content yet. I showed Higgs the compound I had uncovered as a potential cure for dementia. I did so in confidence. He went off with it and... To cut a long story short, he proved that it wasn't viable as a cure after all."

"You sound bitter," said David. "You can't blame a scientist for doing his job."

"But he did something else. He was careless. He showed it to the wrong people, who immediately saw its use as an electro-psychotropic agent. They learned how to manufacture it in bulk. And, lo and behold, within a couple of years we had this mental content – sensa, as they call it nowadays – pumping through beads. The internet of minds. With my discovery, psychblood, at the heart of it."

"Which you gained no credit for. Are you saying Higgs did?" said David.

"I'm surprised if you think I ever wanted a reward for subjugating the genpop, David. These people cared not for pursuing psychblood's potential curative properties. We needed to develop it, perform more tests, but they banned all uses in favour of telepathic transmission. To his credit, Higgs was appalled too. I was demoted to obscurity and he... he eventually disappeared."

"I'm guessing to Super Mare, and that he is the man I seek," said Pempamsie.

"Quite possibly. I happen to know that he removed his beads."

"By cutting off his arm? Otherwise, how is this possible?" said Pempamsie.

"No, only his beads. He let it be known to me through a grapevine of sorts. He always was ingenious. To take off his beads without psychic damage was a considerable feat. There are no other known cases. Perhaps you can confirm that as a former agent of IANI?"

"We knew of no cases," said Pempamsie. "Including him. I recognise the name, Higgs. IANI considered him dead."

"There you are. Ingenious. I wonder how your Nsoroma knew of him. Higgs must trust him. But Westaf – or their renegades, as you would have it – have got to Nsoroma, haven't they? This Swirling Suit that David mentioned. Or they wouldn't know you were here. So they might know about Super Mare, too."

"Perhaps," said David, "you could tell us about Super Mare?"

"Create a meme among the genpop about a place that, as far as they know, does not exist but stands as a symbol. An El Dorado, if you will, but one so laden with irony that almost no one would even think of travelling there. Position it precisely in the collective conscious at a point in cognitive space that evades all significance according to the algorithms of Big Mind. As far as IANI and the multinats are aware, it does not exist. You might say that it goes over the head of Big Mind and thus all of the agencies hooked up to it. It does not appear on maps – who would expect it to? As far as 99.9% of the genpop are concerned, too, it does not exist except as a meme. Only it does, just along the coast from here. It's where Higgs resides, as far as I know. He is plotting the downfall of the system there. Ready to manipulate Super Mare's symbolism with the genpop when the time is right. To turn it into a rallying point."

"Effectively, he's nonned the place," said David.

"You could say that. Like Pempamsie, who exists once you have come across her physical actuality but otherwise does not exist at all except as a chimera in virtual space."

"And you have not joined him there? You could have had your beads removed too," said Pempamsie.

"I admire him, but I cannot stand the man after what he did."

"We need to go to Super Mare," said David. "With or without you. If you're not coming, tell us how to get there."

"I will tell you," said Dirac." But you must realise that once you leave here with that case, I can no longer tunnel its emanations to a false location. Obayifa will be able to follow you. I've been sending the emanations all over Avonmouth city. After your little legerdemain with the fake case she definitely knows of our diversionary capability – but I don't imagine that a creature like that will give up."

"I first need to find protection for these women," said David, "and for us. Plus I need to pick something up. We'll be back. I hope by the time we return for the case you'll have changed your mind. We won't be long."

There was a stirring within David which he dimly recognised as hope; straight away he counselled himself not to allow it to grow too far.

# CHAPTER TWENTY-ONE
## Supervirtual

They left the labnode: David, Pempamsie, the four Royal girls and Breakage. The air, clammy under the corrugated sky, carried the sounds of waves breaking languorously, the pungent smell of seaweed.

Their launch was tied up on the beach. Breakage, who could not travel by water in his current bod, departed inland, just as he had arrived. They briefly watched the factory worker set off towards the nodes that filled the down-below and the near-above in the middle distance, a scaffold in which flesh toiled and took their breaks, like tiny construction workers in old black-and-white photographs.

The four women still seemed barely aware of what was happening to them. "I'm going to have to find a safe node for you," said David. "And as for you and me, Pempamsie, we need a dog."

"Because?" Pempamsie obviously did not like the idea.

"Vampires are supposed to be scared of them, and I have a hunch that Obayifa will be too, even if her appetite is psychic rather than sanguivorous. Also, a dog could sniff her out from afar. We still have some of her clothes from the *Mekhanik Pustoshnyy* for a scent."

"I don't like dogs. The hounds running around Accra city were a nuisance."

"You'll get used to it."

"They shit and need walking. Are there even any here? I've seen none."

"There's a pound I know. You can choose the one you want. One you feel comfortable with."

They sailed the launch back into the docks of Avonmouth.city under cover of an arriving ship and hid it there. David led them to a desres within a large block where they left Lana and the other Royal girls. It cost him a pretty penny. He bade them to remain until he could get word to them. The bodai guard stationed outside their door was more for their sense of protection than the reality of it: he had seen how Obayifa had been able to override Breakage. But there was nothing else for it. At least they were hidden for now.

The pound lay inland in an obscure corner of the down-below. As they journeyed towards it through the near-above in an N-car, they passed an enormous disused grain silo from the twentieth century, which stood like an indestructible relic, its brutal flanks of blackened concrete rising to a castellated section at one end.

"What is that?" Pempamsie asked.

"It's empty."

"That's not what I asked."

"It was Spillers' grain silo. They built around it."

"Look at the density of nodes all around it. It's in the way. Why not demolish it?"

"No one knows for sure, except that some multinat obviously wants it preserved. It's been there since the 1930s. I've been on a case there: inside is the most emptiness you'll find in Avonmouth city."

"Not quite empty." Pempamsie pointed.

There was a figure looking out from a tall, smashed-through window high up.

"My God," said David. "It's Obayifa."

"I can't see her face from here. How can you be sure?"

"I'm sure. It's where she would go: a kind of castle. Why would any ordinary flesh be looking out from on high like that? It's not a doll; it would have climbed to the very top."

"You think she can see from that far up? Like an eagle? I know you say she has mentalmagic, but how could she transcend the eyesight of her host – who presumably was mere flesh like us?"

The N-car slowed. The figure repeatedly came in and out of view as the carriage passed nodes between them and the silo. When the N-car stopped, they saw that the figure was climbing down the outside of the building, descending its sheer, dirty concrete walls.

"What were you saying?" David shifted in his seat. "That a vodu cannot transcend the physical limitations of its host? She may have spotted us."

The N-car seemed to take an eternity to leave the station. They were two stops from the dog pound. David reached for Pempamsie's hand.

She looked down at his veined hand on hers. "Is that for your benefit or mine?" she said. "You're scared of her, even though , dirac?une."

They walked down the car away from the windows. David's heart raced for the remainder of the journey. They dismounted and walked quickly on a raised pavement, taking a lift down to ground level. No one else was around. The sky pressed on them as they walked, and heat emanated upwards from the pavement. There were weeds in the cracks, an unusual sight which told of the semi-abandonment of the quarter. David looked around and behind them as they made for the pound. It wasn't far, but the seconds dragged. If they could only reach the dogs, they would be safe. Or so he hoped.

A module appeared and followed them, slowing as it drew near. They kept walking. The small craft came alongside. It moved on as the gate of the pound opened automatically. The gate shut behind them.

A mostly forgotten relic of the time before bodais, the pound had a forlorn air. The animals sat obediently in their cages. David had half expected them to bark at flesh visitors, but they greeted them with equanimity. Bodai handlers walked two of the dogs around the compound.

"To think that they used to be called man's best friend," said David. "Now look at them: a subdued, joyless existence with no flesh in sight."

They drew closer to the cages.

"Would you like to pick one?" said David.

Pempamsie shrugged. "Pempamsie does not know of these animals."

"She may be waiting for us out there. I think you'll be glad of a dog with you."

"You know that she won't just take its mind?"

"No. Do dogs have minds?"

"That one" – she pointed at a dog staring at David – "seems to be conscious of you. I don't know what to do with a dog. And won't having one simply call attention to us? How many other flesh are walking around Avonmouth city with a dog?"

"Listen," said David. "I'll take it. Maybe you'd be better off on your own?"

"No. We'll take a dog."

They moved along the row of cages. The German Shepherds variously came up to smell and greet them or sat on their haunches and watched the visitors approach.

"They're all the same," said Pempamsie. "How and why would you tell them apart?"

"What about this one?"

The dog's coat was brindled. It lay with its head erect, tongue lolling in the heat, and looked at the arrivals with cool curiosity.

David beckoned to a bodai. The dog emerged obediently by its side. David gestured to Pempamsie to take the lead but she shook her head. She and the dog eyed one another warily.

"He doesn't know what's inside us, does he," she said. "It's me he's not sure about: not my inhabitant. I hope he has a keener sense of the threat Obayifa presents to us."

"What's his name?" David asked the bodai, who began to read out the string of digits from the dog's electronic tag.

"We'll call him Coleridge. The poet walked these parts of UK land. Maybe he'll give us luck in reaching Super Mare."

Coleridge sniffed at Pempamsie's leg. She stepped back.

"Will it bite?"

"Not you. Are you sure you don't want to take his lead? Get to know him?"

She was looking at him strangely, with a mixture of desire and fear, but no longer of the dog.


Coleridge sought the shade as soon as they entered the labnode, and lay panting on the floor. David fetched water from Dirac's small kitchen, which the dog lapped voraciously. A pointed silence hung between Dirac and Pempamsie. David was weary from the heat and from the vodu's pacing in his mind. The journey back with Pempamsie and Coleridge had provided a little relief, with no sign of Obayifa. But now, in the labnode, the world was weighing on him again. He didn't like leaving the Royal girls behind.

Dirac was eyeing him. "You don't seriously have a problem with me giving him water, do you?" said David. "We need this dog in good shape."

"A word, please, David."

"We won't be long," David assured Pempamsie as they left for the conservatory.

"There's something you should know about your new friend. I've been tracking your emanations, your user journey, now that she's arrived on the scene. There's a difference."

"Do tell," David said.

"Please, I'm serious. I need to know: is it behaving differently, looking different?"

Yes, it was. It was coming into focus, from its blur of innards-as-skin.

"No."

Dirac scoffed. "There is a correlation between yours and hers. Perhaps even communication." Dirac's bony hand on David's shoulder made him flinch. "You're inhabited by something none of us really understands. Quite possibly whoever put it there has no better idea of it than we do."

"Any more incomprehensible than consciousness itself?"

"All right, but less predictable, I would say." Dirac looked as though he wanted to touch David again; he was staring at his forehead. "But a vodu isn't consciousness as we know it. It seems to be, as you have said, not only unnatural but unvirtual. Not to mention un-Turing – at least, it appears not to be algorithmic."

"That's a lot of 'un'."

Dirac half-smiled. "Would you prefer 'supernatural' and 'supervirtual'?"

"You talk of my vodu and Pempamsie's communicating. How would you possibly know? You can speak vodu now, can you?"

"No, but I can measure signals, build-ups of energy, correlations."

"All is known, eh?"

"Look." Dirac's tone became more urgent. "I admit I want to dissuade you from going to Super Mare. Have you lost your mind? An allegedly ex-IANI agent appears from nowhere and you believe everything she says?"

"Yes. I believe her. What ulterior designs could she have on me – an ex-ID cop from Avonmouth city?"

"You've an inhabitant, David. Don't be a fool."

"Look, I'm sick of the world I exist in and I'm sick of what's inside me. Maybe these bones can help me as well, so that I can do something about the system we're living in – if you can call it living. But we don't have the beads – Obayifa does. This Higgs, can he help?"

"I really don't know much about what he's been working on, although I suspect he's no stranger to the supervirtual."

Breakage entered. He was a driver, smart in his peaked cap, grey suit and leather gloves.

"Presence outside," he declared. "One flesh. Mentally impaired."

"Shit," said David. "That's all we need. Whatever happened to your Faraday?"

They returned to find Pempamsie looking outside at a man in a dressing gown.

"You know him?" Dirac asked David.

It was the first of the dems to visit him.

"Not exactly."

Dirac said, "So you do. I take it he followed you here."

The man started shouting, "Bones! Bo-ones! Bones!"

Dirac turned to his labnode interface. "It seems our bone circuitry is transmitting beyond these walls, without using the tunnel. But the energy remains at the same level. It has transmuted somehow. Or it has found a way to communicate outside."

The visitor was gesticulating.

"Let Mr Dressing Gown in," said David.

"I don't think that would be wise."

The view through the screen was limited. "Breakage, are there others en route here?"

"One presence only. Mentally impaired."

"Let him in."

The man wore not only the same dressing gown but the same diamond-patterned pyjamas underneath. Didn't they change them in Mary's carie? Mary, who was conscientious about her "gentlemen and ladies".

"What is your name?" said David.

The man chewed slowly. How had he found him? It occurred to him, horribly, that Obayifa had got to this man in some way. Or to Mary.

"You're one of Mary's. We've never been introduced. I'm David." The man still did not reply.

"Obayifa can't be far behind," David said to Dirac. "Either you're right about the emanations and this gentleman has found us through them – which means she will too – or he's under her spell, capable of finding me in some other way, with the same corollary.

"Hello, bastard." Dressing Gown spat in Dirac's face.

David pulled the man away.

"Do you have a message for me?"

"Bones. Dem bones. Juju."

"Breakage will take this flesh to where carie can pick him up. Use emergency module dispatch."

"Thank you, Breakage. You're thinking like me now. I'll send rendezvous instructions."

The man struggled and cried out as Breakage left with him, even though the bodai ushered him gently.

"Dirac, it's no longer safe for you here. We're leaving at once. Please, come with us."

Dirac sighed and went to fetch the case. "I should warn you, before you leave, about some misgivings that are troubling me. First is that the bone circuitry has an unusual construction for Westaf. There are components whose origin – both physically and conceptually – seems to lie outside their provenance. It's not that they couldn't in principle have fabricated them by themselves, but I'm not convinced they did so."

"You mean they contain outer-Westaf technology. As I've tried to tell you, they were made by a renegade," said David.

"So you say. Advised by Pempamsie, no doubt. But something tells me these components derive at least in part from Super Mare."

"Higgs?"

"He's had a lot of time on his hands. Dabbling in the supervirtual would be right up his street. My other doubt is this. I'm simply being thorough, you understand. We assume the bone circuitry is for Obayifa's use, and yet you acquired it rather easily and you have no evidence of it ever having been in her possession."

"Some of the crew of the *Mekhanik Pustoshnyy* reported seeing her with the case."

"This case, or a case? What if we were meant to find this circuitry – what if it's intended for us?"

They looked at Pempamsie.

"For me?" she exclaimed. "But how could Swirling Suit know this construction would ever find its way to me? In any event, I feel no effects from it. And don't we know it can't work without the beads that she possesses?"

"It's always bugged me, though," said David, "that we came across the bones as though we were meant to."

"Anyway," said Dirac, "we face unknown dangers. You have your dog to accompany us. An unusual but reasonable choice, given the circumstances. I have something too."

Dirac opened a drawer and took out an old wooden box, which he unlocked. In it, smelling of burnt oil, lying in folds of black cloth, was a handgun, Elizabethan.

# PART THREE

## Nkonsonkonso

Link in a chain. Symbol of human links.

Never break apart.

# CHAPTER TWENTY-TWO
## Higgs

Higgs had short silver hair, a silver goatee beard. His long face was like a sharp implement. Behind it lay a knowledge of fundamental physics second to none, and a rare, intense curiosity – curiosity which the network had driven out of the genpop with sensa. He wore tight clothes, too tight for a man in his sixties although there was barely a sag in his flesh. On his left wrist were scars where his beads had been. The most nonned man on the planet. Nonned by a mechanism of his own devising.

Higgs was pissed off. It was like living in a tank, at the end of the pier in Super Mare, the sea always sloshing or crashing itself against the legs and girders like an insane cat. Sleep was elusive.

He would saunter out when he couldn't bear it anymore, this existence on the edge; he would stroll with glazed sea and steambath sky his backdrop, past the disused entertainments and the loitering gangs of bodais he kept.

The wooden sheds, laid along the esplanade, smelled of heated timber inside. This was where he meditated about the genpop, imagined their lives by simulating the Beautiful Alone. Higgs enjoyed every second of it, laying his forearms on his thighs and holding his back straight, feeling the smooth wooden solidity of the bench and the wall behind. He relished the superfluity of his being there, he who was always offline.

The world of the network was fractal, recursive. Higgs was going to bring it down recursively. So that flesh could be human, and curious again.

Engineering this isolation, necessary to conduct his experiments, had been no mean feat. No gang of ID police had swept in to claim him. Luck had played a part, perhaps. It could not last forever.

But he did not need to wait much longer. For now Dirac and the ID cop were working together. And there was the woman from Accra.city and the vampire: veritable gifts from Westaf. All he had to do was ensure they came to him.

Dirac explained that Super Mare lay south-west along the coast from his labnode, although not on any map. Flesh travelled to nodes all around it – points arbitrarily close to its outskirts – but never reached Super Mare itself. It was as though something exerted a repulsive force upon their psyches, strengthening its subconscious deterrence as they drew near.

The group set off without knowing how they would enter Super Mare, or what they would find there. At first they were silent in the N-car as it swept along Route 5, occupying a pair of facing double seats. David gave Coleridge's lead to Breakage, positioning the dog between them and any possible approach by Obayifa. Coleridge exuded an air of self-possession, as though he were headed to where he always knew one day he would travel.

"What is it?" David asked Pempamsie, who was staring into the fleeting landscape, her expression distant. He took her hand. "Look at me."

The set of her gaze betrayed not so much an absence as a departure, an inchoate voyage from which she must be called back to shore.

"Hey, it's me. David."

For a second there was no recognition.

"My parents – I was trying to recollect them again. And they are not there, nowhere in my memories."

David looked at her scar. Which of them had inflicted the wound upon her? Mary – an agent of Westaf – had no reason to lie to him about the beatings. And the parents had sold Pempamsie, too. Their only daughter had existed for their abuse and profit.

"What about your other family – aunts, uncles, cousins?"

"I have none."

"Friends?" He knew the answer.

"No. Pempamsie had no friends."

"Then colleagues?"

She shook her head, as though in regret of the choices she had made. "I kept myself to myself in the icestation. We attended classes together, that was all."

"Just you and your parents then. That was all there ever was."

"Yes. I feel... I was going to say sure, that we were alone together."

"And you are trying to reach them in your mind now."

"The paths to their memories grow fewer and more eroded. This thing that inhabits me is eating me."

"And what about their friends and acquaintances – surely your parents knew other flesh?"

"I remember some facts about them. Only trivial fragments. Not them, not they themselves, what they were like, what they looked like. There's only a blank..." She faltered.

"There's no one else, no data, to tell you what your parents were like?"

"None."

"And you miss them."

"Yes. What do you want me to say? As I would miss a limb." She looked at him as though his questions were absurd. David fumbled for what else he could say to this woman who was turning his heart upside down. The former IANI agent – trained to overcome all emotion – now bore a bereft cast which captivated him all the more as it contrasted with what was plainly her inner strength, or had been, before the vodu had begun its work. This woman had committed murders for IANI, however unwittingly, then taken such a drastic step to flee. He felt her for a second through his beads. Her chimerical, nondescript identity in Big Mind made an impossible contrast to her physical reality. It was all he could do to hold her gaze, the trace of her scar tempting him off-centre. If this mission were to be successful he could perhaps show her Westaf's data about her parents. But what good would that do? Was an absence of memories better or worse than knowledge that they beat her? The story behind her scar lent her a vulnerability, heightened his attraction to her. She had declined perceptibly in the short time he had known her: a slip in her bearing. If they did not find a way to remove her vodu, how far would her decline continue? How much more of her being would the vodu consume?

David's own inhabitant impressed itself at the thought, flexing its sinuous paws through the door of its cage, which was stuck slightly ajar in Pempamsie's presence. The vodu seethed in response to his feelings for her, its mouth puckering.

The near-above stopped. Node by node, transitway by transitway, route by route, the network incarnate lowered itself to the down-below. The sky took the opportunity to scorch this nondescript patch of UK.land, hammering down its thermal radiation through the drenched air. Flesh, too, largely fell away.

"Where are we?" said Pempamsie.

"Close," Dirac said, rocking gently with the car, slyly observing the couple. "To the outskirts, anyway."

"She will be following us," she said.

"We should assume she's following the case," said David.

"She might try to stop us entering," she said.

David looked at the professor. "I'm not even sure we can enter."

"Explain," she said.

"According to the memes," said David, "flesh simply do not enter Super Mare. They send in bodais."

They all looked at Breakage, standing with Coleridge beside Dirac. He was a middle-grade creative professional, fussily bearded and dressed in a polo-neck top, not holding on as the N-car swayed, speeding through the down-below.

"And what supposedly would happen," Pempamsie said, "were flesh to enter?"

"They don't come back," said David.

"That's what they say," snorted Dirac. "This is all part of an engineered taboo."

"Nonetheless, you know no one who has been into this place we are actually about to visit. Apart from Higgs. Am I correct?"

Dirac turned his gaze disdainfully through the opposite window.

David saw concern cloud Pempamsie's face, and said to her, "It's thought of as a highly desirable place, but one which no one would think of entering unless they wanted to be lost for ever – a taboo, as Dirac says. It's… just an idea of a place."

"I don't understand."

"No one does. Except, apparently, Professor Dirac here."

"But tell me. Will we be in danger if we go there?"

"Perhaps. But not much compared to the clear and present danger of Obayifa. In any case, it's where Nsoroma told you your salvation exists. We'll send Breakage in to begin with."

They came to a smooth halt. No one else was on board. An announcement came thorough the tannoy: "Please take all your belongings. This N-car terminates here."

David and Dirac sat in the lobby of a Best Rooms, just off Route 5. The fog that had met them soon after leaving the N-car station had persisted, clouding the buildings and the few signs of life outside. The quiet was unsettling. Pempamsie had watched with David as Dirac beaded instructions to Breakage on how to reach Super Mare. The bodai had disappeared into the mist, rebodded as a middle-aged bureaucrat in a grey suit. Pempamsie had excused herself with fatigue. Her slow mental decline continued. David saw her into the lift alone, the doors closing on a figure cast in on herself.

It was nightfall. Breakage had not returned.

The bodai clerk stood at attention behind the desk, oblivious to the worry that infused his only guests. Coleridge lay beside the entrance, the dog's ears turning and stiffening at the occasional fog-baffled sounds from outside. The humping whirr and electric whine of Avonmouth.city was absent, although it persisted in David's imagination. Obayifa was somewhere on a vector from there to this anonymous node, sniffing for the case of bones. And for Pempamsie.

David fidgeted: pacing then sitting down again. Dirac was still and self-contained, his hands pressed together in concentration.

"Dirac, don't just sit there. What do you think?"

"Your guess is as good as mine. Do you want to follow him in?"

"At night? We can't leave Pempamsie. We'll give him until morning." David looked down at the case of bones, which, beyond their control, were signalling their location to Obayifa. He glanced once again to check that Coleridge was still beside the open door, then at Dirac who appeared, David realised, to be waiting for him to take the case and keep it overnight. Dirac, with no vodu inhabiting him, was in the most danger. David picked up the case and Coleridge followed him to the lift.

Pempamsie lay on the bed with her eyes open. David placed the case beside the bed and checked the window was locked.

"What if she comes?" she said as he looked out. "What if she takes an N-car as we did and finds us here? She can climb. Like a reptile: owo foro adobe."

"Coleridge will let us know if she comes near." He climbed into the bed beside her. "And we're not going to invite her in."

"But she will trap us here."

Neither slept. The fogged silence, except for Coleridge's occasional panting, gnawed at them. Even David's beads were quiet. He thought back to the days before he was disbarred from the force, when he would receive regular updates and assignments from the ID police. However much he hated the network, it had provided structure for his bleak days.

Pempamsie's breathing lightly moved the thin bedcover. She reached and took the hand he placed by her side. The night was long.

Coleridge roused them by placing his snout on the bed. First light filtered into the room, thinned by the fog that shrouded the Best Rooms. There was no word from Breakage. They washed, descended to the lobby and called up to Dirac's room under the bodai clerk's straight-ahead gaze, waiting.

The professor's face was grey. Evidently he had not slept much either. The gun bulged slightly from a holster beneath his jacket.

"It's time to go to Super Mare," David said.

Pempamsie, by contrast to the men, had found something of a return to form, to her statuesque bearing. Dirac examined her closely. "You're still sure this is wise? All we've lost so far is your bodai friend."

"Come, Professor. I'm sure you're dying to see Higgs again. To catch up on old times." David raised the case of bones towards him. "And discuss technological developments." He decided to follow the silent Pempamsie's example and put on a brave face, even while he feared that Breakage had met a terrible fate: not merely the destruction of his current bod but corruption or erasure of his AI.

"Now, which way is it? It's curious that you instructed Breakage alone on how to reach there."

They called a module and entered it hurriedly after scanning the pathways nearby for Obayifa. Dirac beaded coordinates to the craft, which soared above the Best Rooms. "This fog will never go away. It cloaks Super Mare from the inhabitants nearby. And that's not all that shrouds Super Mare, as you'll see. You may feel a mild aversion as we approach."

"You've been there before?" said David.

Dirac shrugged. "No. My source – albeit indirectly – is Higgs."

They soared above a landscape that remained, as far as David could see through the fog, a desultory collection of nodes between which few flesh or bodais shuttled. Above them pure whiteness also blanked the heavens. After a short while, the nodes stopped altogether. The mist slowly cleared and unbroken wild greenery began to show through: woods and scrub beneath swathes of trailing foliage, the nearest David could imagine to a jungle in UK.land. Minutes later the mist had completely disappeared. The module flew over the brow of a hill, crested by pines draped in Spanish moss. Super Mare lay before them, a collection of buildings like a scene from Elizabethan times, with the sea stretching beyond.

David took the controls, steering the craft through old-fashioned streets of asphalt and pavement, landing in a square by the sea. A fountain played before them as they disembarked. Neither flesh nor bodais were in sight. His beads were utterly blank, an electro-psychic silence so deep it redefined what silence was.

Pempamsie, who had remained silent during the journey, looked around with concern.

"Nsoroma did not describe this place, but I imagined lost souls. I imagined lost souls were all that would be here."

"I see no souls," David replied. "Nor a simple way of finding any, unless we are to knock on all these doors. If there are fleshren here then surely they will notice us eventually and want to know what strangers are doing here."

"Why don't the two of you have a look around," said Dirac. "I'll stay here and see what I can find out by retuning my beads. Take the dog and leave the case locked in the module. I'll be all right as long as I have this." He patted the gun beneath his jacket.

"Are you sure you know how to use that?" said David.

"If Obayifa comes, I'll have a clear view of her approach. Her host is but flesh. This gun will be effective."

David and Pempamsie took Coleridge and walked a block inland from the shore, away from the waves they could just hear tumbling against the fortified sea front. Super Mare was frozen in Elizabethan times, yet was well maintained and clean. A bell clattered as they entered a restaurant. Its counter and tables were arranged neatly, in readiness for customers, yet no diners, food, menus or place settings were in sight. David rapped on the counter. No one appeared. Coleridge looked at him as if to ask why he bothered, keen to proceed with their search for life.

The row of shops along the street was similarly deserted. It was not until they reached a hotel that life of a sort proved to be present. Coleridge started to growl as they neared it. The name emblazoned across its front was Hotel Royal. With the slightest of nods, Pempamsie signalled her readiness to enter. From the outside, the hotel bore little resemblance to its nominal cousin in Avonmouth.city; it was evidently aimed at what the owners would consider a better class of guest. The lobby, too, was in a much better condition than the one they both had passed through many times, with brass light fittings, ornate wallpaper and a floor and desk of polished wood.

Coleridge's growl increased and the dog strained towards the space beside the empty desk, pulling David.

"What is it, boy?"

As if in answer, a bodai crept from the office and stood with its arms spread on the desk.

"What do you want?" it said.

"We're here to see Higgs," said Pempamsie.

"And a bodai called Breakage." David tried to bead his assistant's details, as though he were still an ID cop. The bodai felt him back as if with cold fingers. It cast its black eyes over them and said nothing.

Coleridge barked at it.

"Quiet!" said David, and the animal obeyed, appearing to swallow its concern. It was hard to understand how a bodai could cause a reaction in a trained dog. David told himself not to yield to the same unease.

"We want to go to room 71," Pempamsie said to the bodai.

"Yes, room 71," David demanded.

"No guests in room 71," the bodai responded after a discomforting pause.

"What about Higgs?" said David. "And the bodai Breakage. What do you know about them?"

Again a pause, as though it had listened to a hidden party before responding. It wiped its hand along the counter. "Not in room 71."

"Do you know where they are?" David said with frustration.

"Higgs, yes. I know."

"Where?"

"Forbidden."

"Then take us to any flesh around here. Who else is there?"

"You are the only flesh apart from Higgs."

"It's no use," said Pempamsie, "talking to this thing."

They departed, and returned to find Dirac where they had left him. He displayed no reaction when they told him about the strange bodai in the hotel.

"You obviously have access to information about this place," David said to the professor, who was looking around as if for inspiration. "Do you have no clue about where to look for Higgs?"

"None. We must keep knocking on doors. I'd better join you."

They trawled the streets around the square for an hour without success. Super Mare exuded a well-groomed vacancy that was proving soporific to all of them.

Around noon, as they peered into the buildings, seeking shade whenever they could from the blazing white sky, bodais began to appear in Super Mare. They left the shops, cafes, restaurants and hotels, crossed the streets and gathered. This congregation was something that bodais were never known to do.

But these were not ordinary bodais. Their bearing and movements were louche and faintly menacing, like the bodai in the Hotel Royal. They stepped near to one another, some facing a common direction, others randomly oriented as though dropped by a hand through a crack in the sky. All of them leaned slightly, jutted out their hips.

"They are like the Chinese robots in Accra city," said Pempamsie.

"And what, exactly," sneered Dirac, "is a Chinese robot?"

"Are you a racist, Professor?"

Dirac straightened himself. "But you used the word 'Chinese'. I was simply asking what that signified."

"I meant towards me. You do not respect me."

David's vodu stirred at the sparring between his companions; its hooves were pinpricks inside his consciousness. He wanted this to be over, wanted to hold Pempamsie, untrammelled by their vodus.

"Please, can we keep focussed on where we are and what we've come for?"

"As I was saying," Pempamsie continued, "and as you must know, David, in Accra city the former colonists from China land left robots behind when we expelled them. They cut them off from any fleshly control. These robots developed certain disorders, a mild sociopathy, hanging around in the streets, charging one another like apes grooming. They seem menacing, but as far as I know none has harmed flesh in any way."

"Yes, I came across them all the time in my work," said David. "We ignored them. They gave me the creeps and I hated passing them, with the looks they threw me. But none of them committed any crimes."

"Which raises the question," said Dirac, "of whose sociopathy is at play here, and whether it is algorithmic or flesh-driven." He walked up to the nearest group of bodais, six of them.

"Explain yourselves."

They turned to him.

"Whose authority do you operate under?" he said. "Which multinat?"

"Be careful," called David. "This isn't Accra city."

The bodais had eyes like crows. Dirac backed away. Two of them sloped after him, loosely swinging their limbs; their faces were locked in contemptuous expressions. Normally bodais were constrained by Big Mind. But if they had been cut off here then their behaviour would be unpredictable.

Dirac touched his beads. His pursuers halted.

"Fascinating," he said as he walked back to David and Pempamsie. "Never mind savages in the nineteenth-century Congo – we appear to be faced with delinquent machines in late-twenty-first-century Super Mare, which looks like the Elizabethan seaside."

"And is there a Kurtz here," said Pempamsie, "who heads them?"

David shook his head. "Great. We all remember that story. But it doesn't get us very far."

"I managed to block their interest in me without too much trouble," said Dirac. "Just a trick of the trade. But it's best if we don't draw their attention further."

"I'm worried about Breakage," said David. "He might have become one of them." He might have lost his friend.

"Let us not speculate," said Dirac. "And let us not remain here any longer than we have to. There are intrinsic dangers here as well as from Obayifa – who might already have joined us. These bodais could crush us and clear our remains away as though we were never here. Which may have been the fate of visitors before us."

"We've looked everywhere except the obvious place: over there, the pier," said Pempamsie.

"Then let us search there." Dirac set off without waiting.

They crossed the empty road to the pier. The tide was high and the sea sloshed against the bulwarks. A few gulls were sitting atop the words *Grand Pier*, spelled in an arc across its entrance. The group passed beneath and along the boardwalk, enlivened somewhat by the strengthening smell of the sea in the stillness, the salt air entering their lungs.

Dirac turned suddenly, as though alerted by a sound that David had not heard. The rest of the group stopped as he walked backwards a few steps, scanning for signs of a pursuer. Then he faced forwards again, took the gun from his holster and released the safety catch.

"You're quite handy with that, aren't you," said David.

"I've had occasion to use one before, and something tells me that soon I'm going to have to again. And you," Dirac said to Pempamsie, "how are you with guns?"

"Why do you ask?"

"No special reason. Except that you were an agent for IANI."

"And you think IANI deals in such crude ways of managing Betweeners."

"So it's true that you would never have employed such a primitive tool? Total loss of data being anathema, and all that."

"Its primitiveness seems apposite here," said David. "A means to kill a vodu-inhabited creature probably not far behind us." He and Dirac both turned to look once more for sight of her.

They set off again. Pempamsie gazed out to sea, which was clear except for distant ships. "We're walking to a place from which there is no escape except by going back the narrow way we came."

"Coleridge will tell us when there is danger." David bent to pat the panting dog's head as they walked, feeling its soft fur. The sun had broken through the thin cloud bank. The briny air filled his lungs.

Coleridge suddenly picked up his pace. Ahead of them, a figure had appeared, blocking their path. A figure with a dog.


The man's arms were bare. No beads were on his wrist. His dog's lead was wrapped where the beads should have been. He was in his early sixties, lithe with a goatee beard.

"Higgs, I presume?" David whispered.

Dirac stared at the man with a sour expression. "I'm not so sure it's Higgs," he said loudly before raising the gun and pointing it at him.

"You always were one for drama. That pistol really isn't necessary. I've been wondering when you would come. When all of you would pay a visit."

Higgs pulled gently on the lead and turned, heading for a gate of steel bars at the end of the pier, with stairs beyond. They followed in silence. The gate opened automatically. The air was motionless. More rays of sun found their way through the blanket of cloud. The crested sea stretched around them.

Higgs bade them to sit at a table in a large meeting room with a view out to the water on three sides. The two dogs lay and eyed one another; two tongues stretched into the conditioned air. Dirac, who remained standing while the others sat, was still pointing his gun at Higgs, now half-heartedly, as if too embarrassed to draw attention by holstering it. Higgs stared across the table at Pempamsie. David experienced a pang of jealousy; Higgs was an irritatingly handsome man.

"Aren't you going to introduce me to your colleagues, Dirac? I doubt they're your friends."

"I am Pempamsie. And this is David. Can we start at the beginning, and how you two know one another?"

"It's been a long time." Higgs placed the palms of his hands on the table. "I haven't seen this gun-toting stranger" – he smiled with a hint of mockery – "since the late forties. Aren't you going to put that down, for heaven's sake? You're being tiresome."

"Professor?" said David.

"It's Higgs all right, but he's not so much a man as a construction. Before he came here and nonned the place he used fake beads, changed his identity more times than I could keep track of. He even looks different."

"Charmed to hear you've been taking an interest."

"Are you the one Nsoroma sent me to? Do you know him?" said Pempamsie.

"I know about your vodu," Higgs said. "And his." He gestured towards David.

"How could you," Dirac said scornfully, "when she's nonned and he's—"

"He's carrying a vodu within a constraint of some sort. This place is equally as well equipped to detect supervirtual phenomena as your labnode. Now, I believe you've brought something for me to look at."

"We've no reason to trust him," said Dirac, still pointing the gun vaguely in Higgs' direction.

"And yet you've come in need of help, I believe. I'll gladly give it. And David and Pempamsie might just help me, given what they are inhabited by. The contents of the case you've brought might be even more useful. To all of us."

Higgs held out his hand. Pempamsie picked up the case from David's side – David put out a hand to stop her but then thought better of it – and passed it across the table. Dirac raised the muzzle of his gun to point at Higgs' head.

Higgs received the case in his outstretched hand. It was shocking to see flesh without beads.

"What's it like," asked David, "being absolutely and forever offline?"

"My aim is to take all flesh offline. To render us as men and women again. Humans again." He looked like a human, David thought. Not trammelled flesh. David knew what humanity was, and yet it was so distant in his past. Like a star, he thought. He was lost because of his vodu and his exile from Yaa, but they – flesh – were all lost in the Between. And humanity, the idea of it, could be a star to guide them.

His vodu opened its obscene mouth.

Dirac sneered at Higgs. "What do you know of humanity? You're holed up with a bunch of delinquent bodais. When did you last have a conversation with your fleshren?"

"I have done whatever was necessary to achieve the objectives I have just stated. And I've made whatever personal sacrifices were necessary. Now do shut up, there's a good man, while I examine these."

Higgs opened the case and absorbed himself in the bone circuitry, revealing no surprise at its construction from skull, ribcage, forearm and wires.

Pempamsie watched him examine the means of her salvation.

"We know nothing of this man apart from the fact that he and the professor go way back."

"And that Nsoroma wanted you to see him in order to retrieve your clarity," David said. If Higgs was perturbed by being the subject of their discussion, he showed no evidence of it.

"Nsoroma said I was to see someone in Super Mare. He did not say who."

"He's the only flesh we've found here. Who else could it be?"

"What does he do all day? Walk his dog? I see no laboratory. No assistants. Why has he surrounded himself with those thuggish robots outside? I, Pempamsie, do not understand how this can be someone who will be able to help."

"Higgs wants for very little," Dirac interjected, joining the conversation heard clearly by its subject. "He's a thinker – aren't you. A philosopher. Mathematician. That's what he always was. And a dreamer."

"You make it sound as though those are undesirable occupations," said David. "I'm surprised at you, Dirac. You could be describing yourself. Your former self, anyway. You're letting your personal feelings cloud your judgement."

"Let us see what he has to say and get out of here," Dirac snapped.

Higgs closed the case and looked up. "Oh, you won't be leaving just yet. At least, I'd advise against it. This place has gone quite vodu-mad all of a sudden. There's a fine example out there now."

He turned on a feed from cameras all over Super Mare, and flicked through scenes of streets and squares empty except for gangs of bodais, until there was only the square with the fountain and their module.

Obayifa was standing still, her arms by her sides, her nose slightly raised into the air as though sniffing for prey.

A shadow crossed David's heart, and he could see its cast over Pempamsie. He clasped her wrist. Dirac, who had not seen Obayifa before, took a closer look.

She stared into one of the cameras. She opened her mouth and rolled out her long tongue. Then she turned and walked away. They watched her make for the Grand Pier, stride beneath its entrance arch and head towards them.

"Obviously you know her," said Higgs.

"She was briefly in my custody." David's voice faltered like a connection dropping. His vodu was excited, buffeting his mind. Pempamsie put her head briefly in her hands. Like animals in a zoo, roused at night by one of their own roaming free nearby, their vodus could scent Obayifa's approach and were straining to reveal their presence to it.

"Can she get inside, Higgs?" Dirac's face was grey.

"Of course not. We won't be inviting her in. But I dare say we shouldn't leave."

"Tell us what you make of the bone circuitry," said David.

"I'm guessing it belongs to the creature outside, who is able to track it, and that's why she's here. But it was I who brought these bones about."

# CHAPTER TWENTY-THREE
## Tongue

Obayifa had stopped at the entrance to the pleasure arcade, intact with its gambling machines, now silent and deserted. The sun was setting. Only her silhouette was visible. They watched her every move on the camera feed.

"Do tell us all about your heroic involvement in the bone circuitry. I'm interested to hear from the expert," said Dirac.

Higgs had picked up the skull and was turning it gently through the small motions allowed by the web of connections. In the hands of a stranger it reminded David of how awkward, frail and unlikely was its construction: the antithesis of all the silicon, swarming with electrons, in racks at the poles.

"This is not my handiwork," Higgs said, as though to himself. How long, David thought, had this man been the only flesh in Super Mare? He could feel Pempamsie pressing slightly against him.

"But I have been in touch with its makers. I wanted to see what they could achieve, starting from ideas we had each conceived."

"Westaf is your workshop now, is it?" Dirac sneered.

"Not exactly. You say Westaf, but sometimes it's hard to know when one is dealing with renegades who would present to me as agents of Westaf. They had made progress in, let us say, a parallel direction. We came to a mutual accord."

"The impossible dealing with the devil," said Dirac.

"What... what are they talking about?" Pempamsie was weakening. David helped her to a chair. His own vodu was pulling at its cage.

"What's happening, Dirac?"

"Probably her vodu is responding to something here, or to Obayifa outside. Are you feeling it too?"

"Yes. Mine is straining, trying to reach something."

"Higgs, what are you up to?" said Dirac.

"I'm not up to anything, although I concur. There is an interaction which I can't explain."

"Keep going; I want to hear what you have to say about these bones." David crouched and placed a protective arm around Pempamsie.

"I have been researching a way to bring the network down. These bones are part of it. But they are a mere tool. The instrument I have mainly been developing is in the two of you, and the creature outside."

"Vodus." Pempamsie struggled to speak. "I, Pempamsie, would be rid of mine. I would have my clarity back."

"Yes, vodus. By tradition, spirits supposedly entering our world from supernatural realms. At once a nonsense we can easily dismiss, and at the same time hardly more mysterious than our own consciousness. Evil, psychic vampires we would not want any truck with. And yet, our experiments—"

"Our?" said Dirac.

"Mine and certain agencies within Westaf, as I have indicated. Our experiments in artificial consciousness extend from your own discoveries, Dirac."

"Whose perversion you brought about."

"Ah, now we come to it. Not deliberately. I made a mistake. Showed psychblood to agencies I thought would help. I was wrong. I admitted it to you at the time."

"Help? Help whom? The oligarchs of the multinats. That's who it helped. You sealed the supremacy of IANI, the dehumanisation of the genpop. And now you've gone even further than they have: from mere mental content to mental agency, electro-psychotropically instilled in a fleshren host. A mind inside a mind. Wasn't the world ruined enough by the Disruption already?"

"Dirac, I made a mistake. But you must know somewhere inside your bitterness that I wanted no part of their plans either. What do you think I'm doing here?"

"Is he... is he going to cure me?" Pempamsie was rocking in her chair, her head in her hands. David watched her helplessly, his own vodu banging against its cage, hitting its swirling, twining head on the bars.

"What the hell is going on with us? Can't you do something?"

"Their plight may be due in part to the presence of Obayifa," said Dirac. "But are you sure nothing else here is causing it? This has not happened before."

"The bone circuitry must be causing it," said Higgs. "An interaction. I—"

"Switch it off," said Dirac.

"You know as well as I do that there can be no 'off'. They would lose their function and I cannot allow that."

"Let me see." Dirac pushed Higgs aside to examine the bone circuitry.

"My God, what have you done to them?"

"I merely attempted a tweak in a patch I found: an anomaly. I thought—"

"Well you thought wrong. It was my patch, an attempt to minimise their emanations, to make it harder for the creature to find them. They've been intensifying, maybe responding to her presence. My patch was all that prevented this from happening."

Dirac touched his beads to the circuitry and began manipulating it.

"Be careful," said David, now barely capable of thought, wrapping both his arms around Pempamsie, who was losing consciousness.

Then it stopped.

"What happened? What did you do?" said David.

"I undid his meddling."

"I'm sorry," said Higgs. "I had no idea—"

"You always were naive," said Dirac.

Pempamsie was still holding herself, breathing hard. But the rocking had ceased.

"It was trying to leave me, but it couldn't. It was stuck. There was nothing I could do."

Dirac's voice was filled with contempt. "Inadvertently or otherwise, Higgs increased the emanations which evidently are also a kind of lure. In fact, I would be surprised if the creature outside had not experienced some of the same pain. The question arises: how to unblock the bone circuitry so that a vodu can enter the cranial and thoracic spaces but then be confined by their force field? The stopper to the jar which we need to put the Jinnis in."

Obayifa had disappeared from view. Higgs flicked through the cameras to no avail.

"You've helped in the engineering of vodus because you wanted a way to non all of us," said Dirac. "Am I right?"

Higgs, now subdued by his mistake, nodded.

"Because you think they can non the genpop, and relieve them of sensa. That what is evil in concentration, as in the creature Obayifa, can be constrained or diluted – as with our friends here. But these vodus are not under your control, are they. Their interaction with the psyche – as David and Pempamsie can both attest – lies some way beyond your or your partners' understanding. And that is hardly to touch upon the monstrosity that is waiting for us out there."

"I may be simple-minded," said David to Higgs, "but is there really no other way you can think of to undermine the network than synthetic consciousness derived from evil spirits?"

"Obviously we thought we had taken the evil out of the equation. But what else would you suggest? I removed my beads, but it took months and we can't physically do that to the entire genpop. We hack Big Mind with software attacks but they block us immediately. Beads can be compromised to a certain extent, but how should we achieve that for the genpop en masse? By spreading vodus through the network we can, in principle, psychoactively block sensa. There would be nothing IANI could do about it. We could shut down their whole operation, which depends on their telepathic manipulation of the genpop's minds."

"But look what you're dealing with! Vodus are not harmless software patches. Obayifa is not a saviour of flesh. She is a monster. Pempamsie has been reduced and her memories redacted by what's inside her. And mine..." David's vodu stared back at him as he spoke, its mouth wide open, its protruding tongue quivering. "Mine is some kind of monster too. So how exactly are you going to start from these botches to arrive at the salvation of our fleshren, eh? Always supposing the genpop agreed they needed to be saved. You've been alone too long. Do you know what state they're in, our fleshren in the Between? They've been subjugated. They don't even realise what they've lost."

Higgs looked pained, but drew himself up.

"You're right that I mustn't underestimate the magnitude of our task. I also want to say that I welcome your arrival, notwithstanding the poor start I've made with you. And I should perhaps keep this thought to myself, but it's only fair to warn you. I'm afraid Obayifa is possibly more horrific than you think."

"Oh?"

"It's bad enough that she consumes the minds of flesh. But evidently vodus – her kind, anyway – procreate. When we speak of

Obayifa, we speak of vodu-inhabited flesh. Ask yourself how the vodu came to be there."

"I see what you mean."

"Their feeding, I believe, is more fundamentally sexual, as with other vampiric forms. The vodu penetrates minds to feed, yes, but also to plant its seed. Where the act brings about fertilisation, it leaves offspring behind."

"Which grow and take over the vacated body." Dirac nodded grimly as he absorbed Higgs' words. "As with Obayifa herself."

"Exactly."

"But of all the dolls we've seen, none has become vampiric – not that I'm aware of," said David, looking to Dirac for confirmation. But Dirac looked embarrassed, nonplussed to hear of this new peril. His thin lips remained sealed.

"I did say *when* the act brings about fertilisation," Higgs said. "I don't know how often that occurs. My knowledge of vodus is sparse, to say the least. Dirac is right about that, at least."

The room became silent except for the panting of the dogs.

Higgs clapped his hands together. "Come, we have work to do."

"You really seek to unleash these self-replicating creatures, which you admit you don't understand, on the genpop?" said David. "I don't want to be a part of that."

"We're only at the beginning. I believe we can control vodus of a lesser nature, such as exists inside Pempamsie. The bone circuitry is a start at manipulating vodus. It also is the key to salvation for the two of you."

He spread out his hands. "I really don't know what else to do."

"How did you rid yourself of your beads?" said Pempamsie.

"I realised I could do it after my first experiments with the supervirtual. Not vodus exactly, but an active inhibitor. I partially blocked the interface inside my mind, a mental anaesthesia that lasted until the physical surgery had healed. There was no intolerable anguish as you, like any flesh, would experience if you tried to remove your beads now. I can do it for you, by the way. I have done it for others."

"What others?"

"Super Mare may be a no-place, but some have found out about me, others I have let know. These flesh arrive in boats, and leave again by the sea. After I have freed them."

"Freed them?" said David.

"Removed their beads. But, as I said, I can hardly do that for all the flesh of the Between, now can I?"

There was a banging on the outside door. It was not a bodai. Bodais never knock.

"Bring up an image," said David.

"I wish I could," said Higgs.

"You have CCTV all over Super Mare. All over the pier," said David.

"There appears to be a malfunction. She's probably disabled that particular camera."

"We can't just stay here and do nothing," said David. "You're the best qualified humans on the planet to dispatch a psychic vampire, and we have the bone circuitry which almost works. I'm prepared to go out there and use it on her. What should I do?"

"She has the extra beads, remember," said Dirac. "They may be needed for vodus to enter the bone circuitry. We need either the beads or something that would enable us to circumvent them. Otherwise her vodu won't be able to leave her, as you have just experienced in relation to your own."

"Or I take your gun and shoot her."

Dirac's expression was grim. "Now that you say that, I don't think it would be wise. Another factor has occurred to me. She too may be required for the bone circuitry to operate."

"What do you mean?"

"She consumed the crew's minds. There may be something in their minds that functions as a key. And those minds are in hers."

"All this is screwing with my mind." David walked over to a window looking out to sea, the sea that led back to Yaa. There were two doors between them and Obayifa. If he left, Pempamsie would remain safe with the two scientists. Apart from Yaa, she was the only person he cared about, including himself. No one would miss him; he was dead to Yaa by now. Just as there was no one to miss Pempamsie. They shared that fact, along with their inhabitance.

"You two geniuses need to work out a way of pointing the bone circuitry at a vodu and extracting it. But what if I succeeded in capturing hers? How would you help Pempamsie? Can the bones hold more than one vodu? One in the ribcage, one in the skull?"

There was more banging on the outside door, sending a chill along David's spine. Dirac, struggling to ignore it, said, "It's a very good question. We're venturing into the unknown. But Higgs' meddling does suggest to me a way of adapting the bone circuitry for the creature outside, even lacking what she possesses: the vestiges of the crew's minds. Only we'd need Breakage."

At the mention of the name, David felt a rush of anger with the bodai for getting lost. But the memory of the garden quickly replaced it, the thought of experiencing for the first time a near-human side to the bodai, and the peace that he had momentarily found there.

"You will remember," continued Dirac, "the recordings of C15's brain function which I used to trace him. Whatever we had from Obayifa at the time of her custody had mysteriously disappeared. However, you used Breakage to confront Obayifa – with the fake case. In the light of Breakage's rather special role in our investigation, I took the liberty of having him record brain functions routinely. Data that is unique to her exists, and we may be able to tune the bones to her with it – to make them accept her." Dirac looked at Higgs, who nodded.

"But we need Breakage in order to retrieve her data. We must find him."

The banging on the door increased, rattling its hinges.

David turned to Higgs. "I'm guessing you know the bodai we're talking about, since you know everything that goes on here. Breakage entered Super Mare before us and we lost contact. But I bet you know his whereabouts."

A fleeting cognisance passed across Higgs' face.

"It was you," David said. "You know all about Breakage, don't you? From the start."

Higgs shrugged, while Dirac's questioning stare also bore down upon him. "He's been useful in getting you here, hasn't he? I merely wanted to afford you a little assistance: some independence when it came to dealing with the network, shall we say. He's a work in progress. I've been trying to make him even more helpful once this is over. Let's say that a germ of humanity, or rather a faculty for absorbing the more humane elements in the flesh around him – compassion, for example – has been allowed to affect his algorithms. All while seeming to be operationally routine, of course. And yes, I think I know who has him now. The bodais in this place, if they like the look of a new arrival, one of their own kind, they induct them. It's of no matter."

"Were you also behind the way Breakage stopped the network's sensa reaching my brain?" said David. "That is, by sending a stream of inverse psychblood perturbations, which annulled it? Can't you do that with the genpop at large?"

"I am afraid not," said Higgs. "That was a hack which cannot be made to scale beyond an individual or two. And by the way, it was an idea that I can be said only to have sown the seeds of. Breakage brought it to realisation himself."

"I knew it," Dirac said. "More meddling. You just can't stop yourself from trying to control the course of events. Which" – Dirac swept his arm around to indicate the isolated station that contained them at the end of the pier – "you clearly cannot entirely do."

"Let's keep to the subject of Breakage and those bodais of yours. What does 'induct' mean?" David asked.

"To be honest, I don't exactly know. They're just stupid bodais, and yet... There's an emergent algorithm binding them, which I've only seen the effects of, never the code. They may have written it themselves. I let it pass – indeed, I encourage it – because we might just be able to benefit from some bodai evolution. So that they act together. As long as it's in our favour."

David decided to leave at once, relying on Coleridge to see off Obayifa.

Pempamsie remained slumped in a chair.

"You stay here with them. I'm taking Coleridge and leaving the bones. I'm going to find Breakage. Then I'm coming back."

"But I—Pempamsie will be strong soon. It is passing."

"There's no need to expose you to her. We believe she can't consume our vodu-inhabited minds, but what if she has new instructions? What if Swirling Suit has lost patience and wants you—"

"Dead."

"Higgs, the working CCTV shots are all deserted. Where should I find these bodais of yours?"

"Look in the beach huts. It's where I go for the Beautiful Alone. And they do, too. Not that any of us can or needs to experience what the genpop experiences. It's a ritual."

"What exactly is this island you've created, this Super Mare?" said David.

"It's what I've needed to survive. But everything has changed now that you're here."


To everyone's profound relief, the banging had ceased.

Higgs shut and locked the inner door behind David. Coleridge pulled him across the small vestibule with the excitement of a dog who had found a scent, and sniffed beneath the door. David stood behind Coleridge and pressed a large button on the wall.

The strip of obsolete pier, the sounds of the estuary with its avian denizens, and the heat all greeted him at once. Obayifa was nowhere to be seen. Coleridge could smell her, though, and pulled on the lead towards land. His heart banging wildly, David peered to either side before exiting.

The salty night air sloughed around flesh and dog as they made for the beach. Brightly lit, the pier was starkly empty of beings in its stretch to land. What was once known as the Severn Sea rolled beneath them. A group of terns took flight from somewhere unseen, flapping like ghosts above. Obayifa could have secreted herself in many places along the pier, but David trusted Coleridge to alert him. The dog tore along.

He did not like leaving Pempamsie with Higgs and Dirac, however much it was the right move for her safety. He wanted her to be cared for, but the two scientists were each in their own way distinctly lacking in any grace. They were an odd couple. Higgs' superior confidence had been dented by their arrival, perhaps for the better if it meant greater realism on his part. And now Dirac had someone his equal to work with.

David thought of Pempamsie: her serious look, the scar that told of her fracture inside. Because of her, how long it seemed since he had slept with one of the Royal girls. That was over. He had barely needed to think about ceasing his addiction. She had found a way to his heart, however vodu-crushed it remained. But she was diminishing even as he was beginning to know her. If he could safely relieve her of her vodu and her monstrous pursuer, perhaps he could rid himself of his own inhabitant, and see his daughter again.

Super Mare was dimly lit beyond the pier's brightness. David could just see the fountain and a group of bodais beside it. They were circling something hidden in the centre. Their rotation had a sinister quality, a preamble to setting upon prey, perhaps.

Coleridge had lost Obayifa's scent, and became interested in the bodais, too. They passed the group and headed, apparently unseen by any of them, to the beach huts. There were about two dozen, set on the promenade. Unlike the stacked huts of grained and knotted wood where the genpop experienced the Beautiful Alone, these were painted in a variety of pastel shades. Higgs had said he came here as a ritual. David wondered whether he had ever sought the Beautiful Alone in a real facility outside, or knew anything of what it was like to be a member of the genpop. How long had he been in Super Mare, this place divorced from the rest of what passed as civilisation?

David could just see waves rolling in the night. Coleridge was calm. A slight breeze had developed, delivering sea air that might have been what was interfering with the dog's ability to catch Obayifa's scent. David opened the door of the first hut and let Coleridge in before peering into the darkness. Coleridge left almost at once, uninterested. It was empty. But when David opened the next door there was a bodai inside. Coleridge growled at it.

"Report," David commanded, forgetting his discharge from the ID police.

"Leave," it said. "This is no place for you."

David beaded Breakage's details to it. "Do you know this bodai?"

"Yes."

"Where is he?"

"All is known." The bodai stretched its mouth open and laughed, like a parody of a Buddha, David thought. He had never heard a bodai laugh before. It was beyond them. Attempts to give them laughter had resulted in horrible, uncanny snorting. The laughter continued; he thought it might never stop. He closed the door on it and tried the next hut. The laughter ceased.

Another bodai. "What are you doing here?" he said.

"Being. Alone. Existing. All is known."

Looking somewhat less threatening when sitting down, the Super Mare bodais still caused David to wonder whether they were capable of harming flesh. He did not want to find out by pressing them. If they were capable of laughter then they might be capable of anger too. Even Coleridge seemed reluctant to hang around. Nonetheless, David gave it Breakage's identity.

"Do you know this bodai?"

"Yes."

And in the next hut was Breakage. At least, there was a bodai who had what appeared to be the same bod: the bureaucrat in a grey suit. His attaché case lay next to him on the bench.

"Breakage?"

The bodai opened his eyes. "All is known."

David heard the familiar voice. It was him.

"What are you doing?"

"Cannot leave."

"Says who?"

"Breakage says."

"No: who or what instructed you to remain here?"

"Local. Influence."

"Other bodais?"

"Impossible."

"But true?"

"Yes. All is known."

"You are to follow only my instructions now."

"Must dissociate."

"From me, or them?"

Breakage rose and lurched like a drunk towards David and Coleridge, who were forced to step aside from the door. He made for nearby steps leading over the bulwarks and down to the beach, breaking all protocols for self-protection.

"You can't go down there. It's the sea."

Breakage paused as if to consider David's words. Streams of integers flowed to and from... Where?

"Breakage is needed. Self-impediment is against your protocols."

More integers streamed backwards and forwards, in an attempt to match a pattern that would enable the algorithm to proceed. Breakage turned back to face the row of beach huts.

And began to laugh uncannily.

About ten bodais emerged from huts and gathered round Breakage, gyrating in a patch of moonlight which the shifting clouds had released. Their mock laughter caused David to put his hands to his ears. He looked around desperately, hoping Obayifa would not take advantage of the commotion to spring an attack.

Then, with no apparent signal, all the laughter and gyration stopped at once. The bodais approached Breakage in the centre.

"Release him!" David stood and shouted as though he were still with the ID police, flesh against ten machines. Coleridge panted in bemusement. They ignored them.

The bodais had begun to shuffle in a travesty of a dance. Nothing fleshly informed their lumpen swinging. They began to utter sounds like modems from Elizabethan times, speech uttered a hundred times faster than flesh could voice. David felt a chorus of indecipherable transmissions through his beads.

At least they didn't hold spears, he thought. He tied Coleridge to the handle of a hut and approached the circle, which expanded and contracted as they danced. Great care was needed to avoid their swinging limbs, but he managed to step quickly between a pair of them, guessing correctly that his flesh and blood passing through their shadows in the moonlight was as nothing to these bodais in their tranced state.

Breakage, however, looked at David as he stepped towards him – a sign, perhaps, that he had not been totally conjoined to the gang as yet. The planes of his face, however, were passing through a rapid series of configurations, as though he were cycling swiftly through all the possible simulacra of emotions in his repertoire, unable to assume any one for more than a fraction of a second.

Breakage was otherwise still. David touched his beads to the bodai's, whose face immediately settled to his default positive expression: the farting baby.

"All is known. We are trapped," Breakage shouted beneath the crazed laughter, the whirr of mechanical limbs around them.

"Not if we can use whatever happened to you when you arrived to disable them."

"Breakage does not understand."

"What instructions were issued to you when you arrived in Super Mare? Reverse them."

"Separation. Told to separate. And join."

"Go up to them. Touch them."

The bureaucrat approached one of the dancers, who stared through him in its robotic trance. Breakage began to wave his left arm in time with it, and touched beads. David wondered at that point in which direction control would flow: it might reinforce rather than break the other bodai's spell on Breakage.

The bodais fell still.

"Steer it out of the circle," said David.

"Cannot leave David."

"I'll be right behind you."

Breakage laid hands on the bodai whose beads he had touched, manoeuvring it around and to the side to make way for their exit. David clung nervously to Breakage's back as they left the circle.

"Keep going!" They walked over to where Coleridge sat on his haunches, awaiting his master.

The group began to disband. Some returned to the huts. Others walked off along the seafront in twos and threes, for all the world like so many promenaders of old, out for a midnight stroll.

"Breakage, Dirac directed you to record the brain signatures of everyone you came across, and you were with Obayifa."

"David ask question?"

"Did you record her signature?"

"Data from ID criminal. Recorded."

"But your bod has been substituted since then. Did you transfer the recording?"

"Erasure."

"Damn."

"But recording now."

"What?"

"Recording unknown flesh now. ID crime. Suspect."

"How? Where is she?" David held more tightly on to Coleridge's lead.

"Unknown. Proximate." David could feel nothing through his beads, which was her trademark. Could the bodai sense her through whatever instrumentation Dirac had installed? Coleridge, who remained calm, showed no signs of a scent. David took in the heavy, moist, salt-laden air through his nostrils. Perhaps it was too strong even for a canine.

"Are you sure?"

Breakage, for all the affinity David had begun to feel for the bodai, adopted a travesty of a quizzical expression, as of old.

With Coleridge on a very short leash, David asked Breakage to open the hut doors one by one. Each time a pastel door was swung open a chill shot through him.

Empty. Empty. Bodai. Empty. When the door of the last hut was opened, David again could see an empty bench.

But Obayifa suddenly swung into view from the side, glistening and sharp-edged in the light of the moon, powerful with mentalmagic. She had bested Breakage in their last encounter. But now he had Coleridge, who bared his teeth and growled fiercely.

She stepped towards David, flashing her incisors, her tongue protruding horribly. A million thoughts, a million adrenal raindrops splashing throughout his body. He straightened his spine. Coleridge was between them. The dog pulled up at her. She looked down at the animal. David thought for a second that she was going to reach down and strangle him – with her tongue? But the tongue merely quivered in the air. She backed slightly. Despite the mad stare, the arms and claws suspended above him, the lizard mouth, the hard, leaning body, Coleridge did not show signs of fear. He locked eyes with her. A mental struggle occurred between Obayifa and what the dog represented to her, for surely she could have reached down and killed it.

"I'm going to let him go," said David. "We'll see what's in those veins of yours." David started to release the lead from his fingers. But he could not. For a muscular appendage entered his mind, hard and tentacular like a tongue. He felt its ingress from the base, through his id. And it began to probe, searching and vampiric. He felt himself grow hard.

This cannot happen; the vodu-inhabited cannot fuck with the vodu-inhabited. He clung to the thought even as it was refuted, trying desperately to release the lead but finding himself holding tighter and tighter on to it, his legs planted where he stood. Obayifa was but a metre beyond the dog's reach.

The tongue was flexing for purchase but staying away from the cage. The cage. His vodu was in a cage, the tongue apparently safe beyond it, free to roam in his mind. The tongue was forming a scoop, beginning to dig.

Then Breakage reached and unclipped the lead from Coleridge's collar. The dog bounded furiously after Obayifa, who sprang like a cat up to the hut's roof and flew along the row from ridge to ridge, with Coleridge barking and snapping at her. When she was in the middle, she jumped down behind the row and disappeared while Coleridge tried to throw himself after her, through a gap that was too narrow.

The tongue was gone. David collapsed to the ground, his mind frozen, and lay crumpled in a pool of moonlight. The bureaucrat picked him up and slung him across his shoulder.

# CHAPTER TWENTY-FOUR
## Biribi Wo Soro

As soon as we had witnessed the incident on CCTV we headed directly to the scene, Dirac pointing his gun at every shadow, Higgs with his straining dog. I, Pempamsie, fell upon David's limp body, extracting him from the arms of the bodai. We returned with all haste to Higgs' headquarters, the dogs on either side of us.

David still had not regained consciousness the next day. I waited beside him with the dog. The room Higgs found for us within his compound at the end of the pier was dismal. We were cocooned. The one window let in light up high, too high to look out to the sea. There was but a bed and a chair. One of Higgs' outlaw robots brought food and water, even for the dog. I was not hungry, but I forced myself to eat. The dog, Coleridge, looked at me, at David, at me again.

My subtle vodu cast its shadows. I felt: molten, undone. From time to time I looked over the unconscious body beside me. I saw the sad man David. I knew who he was. I knew the dog, with its brown eyes and brindled fur. Yet I was not sure who it was who knew them. Why, for a moment the question arose, was this "I" waiting with them? Then I forced myself to think of Obayifa, the creature in the painting who had now attacked David, not me. And I wrote. I wrote down everything I know to write. I wrote: *This is the man who listens to you. He does not know you any more than you know yourself. But he listens to you.*

*He is kind. And there is a sweetness in your stomach when you look at him.*

I left David for a break. The dog, who seemed not to reciprocate my antipathy, followed. Higgs and Dirac were not around. There had to be quarters where Higgs lived. Surely he had a laboratory. Was Higgs not a scientist, like Dirac?

Since Obayifa was prowling outside, I guessed they had not left. They were even more vulnerable to her than David or I. We were trapped. I was weary. What could I do? I knew no medicine, so I could do little for David except sit by him. Where was his robot, Breakage? Could it help him? Would it obey me?

My vodu rippled inside me, like a school of fish swimming through me, as though I were nothing but their shape in water. I needed a symbol of hope: Biribi wo soro: something is in the heavens, let me reach it.

Instead, one of Higgs' robots came in from outside. I watched, afraid lest Obayifa followed it in, then relieved when the door sealed behind it.

"Where is Higgs?" I demanded. The black-eyed robot swivelled its way past me.

"And Dirac? Tell them to come to me."

It walked on, past the door that led to David's room, and turned to look at me – turned its head only, beyond the compass of a fleshly head, placing its beady eyes upon me for a second before disappearing through a sliding section of the wall.

I, Pempamsie, followed.

Dirac and Higgs were bent over the bone circuitry. Seemingly united after David's imperilment.

"How is he?" asked Dirac.

"Unconscious still. But you know how he is. You are monitoring his vital signs."

"Indeed," said Higgs. "He has undergone a mental trauma, to put it mildly. His bodily data is within acceptable parameters but his mind seems to have been... upended."

"David believed he was impervious to her," I said.

"There is a vodu inside him," said Dirac, "but it is contained. It seems she was able to enter his mind as long as his vodu remained confined."

"And what did she do to him while she was in there?"

"She neither consumed nor impregnated him. His mind is still in there. I have monitored for any sign of vodu spawn. There remains but the one occult mental presence. His mind is like a house that's been burgled – there's an archaic crime for you – turned over. But I believe she left empty-handed."

"What would she be looking for?" I said.

"How should I know?" said Dirac. "Perhaps a suitable hatching place for her progeny. I don't know for a fact that she was looking for anything. I may be misreading the data; perhaps she was simply trying to feed. Or to stop David from helping you. We don't actually know how she achieves mind consumption. She would have to loosen the mind from its anchor before she could extract it, while avoiding his vodu."

"Anchor." I, Pempamsie, had a weakened mind. I could barely grasp the conversation.

"Your mind," sniffed Dirac, "is rather attached to your body, is it not?"

"Not as far as she is concerned. She was going to suck him dry."

"We can thank Coleridge" – Dirac looked down at the dog by my side – "for chasing her off. Not to mention Breakage for having the presence of mind  – now there's a questionable use of a phrase – to release him."

"And I? Am I, Pempamsie, not impervious to her after all, then?"

"Your vodu pervades your mind," said Higgs. "A tiny modulation on every thought you have. Were Obayifa to enter your mind, she would not be able to avoid contact. Which is why it's so important to hang on to these bones. Without them, she can't extract your vodu. Thus she cannot consume your mind."

"And what are you two doing with the bones now?" Dirac was watching as Higgs manipulated the skeleton parts within their mesh of wires.

"He's busy," said Dirac. "We retrieved the creature's brain signature."

"How?"

"From Breakage," said Dirac. "He managed to record her last night. As a result, we may be able to adapt the circuitry so that it will become her prison. We're not exactly dealing in matters we understand. These are electro-psychic, supervirtual phenomena. The algorithms—"

"I do not need to know your algorithms, Professor. Please, do your work. And what of David? What are you doing to make him well?"

"We're sending a signal through his beads," said Higgs, "which we hope will restore order. The mind is plastic and quite robust. The signal should bring his mind back to something like normal parameters. He's dreaming a dream I have manufactured, a dream both of and for restoration."


I watched these two work for a while, fascinated by their combination of virtual and physical manipulations, the way they had cast their differences aside but still fussed irritably over what each was doing. I became increasingly helpless as my identity came apart, bit by bit, as my memories were redacted. I no longer even tried to remember anything before the icestation: the failure was unbearable. I was becoming an anonymous locus of perception. And yet, I was known, in a limited sense, to these two scientists and, above all, to David. Yes, he had touched me. By attending to me even as I fell apart.

I said to the pair, intent on their work, "Supposing you succeed in adapting the bones. What of I, Pempamsie – will it work on the vodu inhabiting me?"

Dirac looked at me with disdain. He still hated me. Were David not there, he would have shunned me entirely, I am sure.

Higgs rose from his work, abstracted, as though he had just remembered that I was in the room.

"We don't agree about you," he said. "The professor thinks you're an unimportant variation on vodu inhabitance. And that you're expendable – were it not for the evident affection David holds for you." Dirac averted his eyes from me. "Whereas I," continued Higgs, "think you're the key."

If I'd had myself back, I would have had no truck with these flesh. I wanted to go back to David, but I needed their answers. Were they really capable of being the saviours of flesh in the Between? Did saviours have such a bent to self-absorption and, in the case of Dirac, such a mean bearing? What accord had they entered into?

"Explain," I said.

"You're a failed Westaf experiment like David," said Higgs, "but you're close to what I seek: a true non without removal of your beads. You defeat the network at the mental interface. It's just the side effects—"

"The side effects? I am decaying, ceasing to be. You know not what you are about."

"Dirac seems to want to avoid the conclusion, but I think you represent hope for flesh – for humankind, I should say. All sensa would be redirected to chimeras in Big Mind, to phantoms such as you have become. Virtually speaking."

"And really speaking. You must not do to the genpop what has been done to me."

"Of course, you're still a botch. I had nothing to do with their work on you, by the way. But they really are on to something. You are inhabited by a vodu that is subtle but not subtle enough, that's all. If we can only create harmless vodus, we can release them into the fleshwork, cast ourselves off, all of us in the Between; we'll return to being ourselves again."

The following day, I was yet more lost. What was this "I" that had this thought? A thing. A no-thing. A no-name. An impulse. The "I" recognised this man lying on the bed. It was David. David loved me.

The door opened.

"I think we're going to need more time." It was Dirac.

"He's not reviving." Dirac touched his forehead. "We'll have to try another way. Or another dream."

I had not seen this look on him before: he was exhausted, at his wits' end. Sleepless. In his eyes, a deep worry. He thought the one in the bed might be lost to us. For what is flesh with his mind unseated? Drifting loose – where? In what space?

I had no name. Everything was now. Even these flesh present before this "I" – the one unconscious, and the one evidently doubting his ability to revive him – even their names were fading. I was becoming a dem to all intents and purposes, although intelligently aware of my loss. I sat, cognisant, as I was eaten away by my inhabitant.

The visitor left. I was somehow the cause of this misery. I, whoever "I" was, had better not be there any longer. I had to leave. I rose from this flesh's bed, walked through the door. Paused. Went to the room where Dirac and Higgs worked on the bones. Returned. Past a table and chairs in an empty meeting space. There was a dog, leashed to a black lamp by a wall, another dog with a bowl of water beside it. And in the corner beyond them the "I" pressed a button. A door swished open, then closed behind. Another door. "I", this mobile entity that could be named no longer, stepped out. The "I" held out a hand: the same hand against the changing scenery.

Obayifa. That was one name the "I" could remember. Obayifa, in the tall castle. She wants this "I". She will have it. And then this "I" will no longer be a burden on the unconscious man left behind. He was better off without the thinker of these thoughts. And the object of this self-consciousness? She was better off dead. Obayifa could bring this about. She could have not only this mind alone but the whole life.

Yaa's face, at the door where he had to say goodbye. Her mother. Yaa laughing. Her mother dying. Lights throbbing. Retinal after-glows. No retina. Lights behind eyelids. No eyelids. A dream entered its own botched storyline, something about a rococo Italian bridge lined with arcades and a dash for transportation that would not arrive. The bricks fly apart. The story melts, folds over itself. A complete absence of physical sensation. Floating. Even the vodu is lost. Alone with the caged vodu, in outer space. Silence. The little light of stars. Impossible levels of coldness, which does not matter: there is no body. Yaa dancing in a light blue dress, her large eyes glowing, lambent. The only joy.

A voice, grating. A hard landing. Pain shearing the spine, temples ringing. The voice becoming clearer.

"David."

The vodu is ahead of him, sinewy eyes watching from within.

"David." A face distilling from cloud. A crack in the sky and a hand reaching down.

"Can you hear me?" Dirac. His face taut and red.

David closed his eyes, opened them. Dirac was still there.

"Where's Pempamsie?"

"Ah, David. It's good to have you back. Now, close your eyes again and get some more rest. We think you're going to be all right, but it's early days."

David woke to find breakfast beside him. Where did Higgs obtain his supplies? It hardly mattered. He was famished. Toast and coffee, engorging them gratefully. A little strength returned to his limbs. He sat up in bed, blearily dragged on his clothes and went to find Pempamsie.

Dirac and Higgs' heated discussion ended abruptly as he entered.

"What are you two fighting about now?" David's nerves were frayed. Coleridge, lying by the wall, looked up at David then laid his head back on his paws.

"Where's Pempamsie?"

Dirac snorted. Higgs stepped around the desk where they were working and approached David.

"Bad news, I'm afraid. She's gone. While you were out for the count. Her condition was worsening, but we were rather preoccupied not only with adapting the bone circuitry but with re-bolting your mind to your body. Without that vodu in there you'd have been relieved of your mind entirely, at least if the creature had had a bit more time. It was the key—"

"What do you mean, 'gone'?"

"She walked out, told none of us." Dirac could not hide his pleasure.

"And she seems to have returned to Avonmouth city," added Higgs. "At least, she took the module and boarded an N-car bound for there."

"Alone? You let her go out alone?"

"Obayifa cannot touch her vodu-filled mind," said Dirac.

"But she can kill her."

"It's unlikely," said Dirac.

"You say that but we hold the bones. If Obayifa can't follow her orders – if they can't have their vodu back – there might be a deathly plan B."

"Actually, we no longer have the bone circuitry," said Higgs.

"What?"

"Pempamsie took the bones with her. We both slept. She came and fetched them."

David thought about Pempamsie, alone in her fractured state. Vulnerable to a preying psychic vampire, carrying potentially the means of her undoing. Once her vodu was removed, her mind was Obayifa's for the taking. And, since he loved her, he would not be able to go near her again – any more than he could visit Yaa.

But the circuitry was incomplete. "You were experimenting with the bone circuitry. How far did you get?"

"We've unlocked it." Dirac's smile was grim. "So that it can be used to extract and store any vodu by touching its beads to the host. You touch it once to prime it, touch it again to extract the vodu. It will store as many as you like, in supervirtual cells."

"And the beads? And the minds of the crew? You mean they aren't needed anymore?"

"We don't believe so," said Higgs. "The recording Breakage took of Obayifa was invaluable. It was all encoded in there: the minds she'd stolen from the crew, and the beads. All signalling in their different ways."

"And who is it primed for now?"

"Pempamsie," said Higgs. "And you, David. We touched the beads to you while you were unconscious."

"To me? But you can't extract mine. It's caged."

"We're not sure," said Dirac. "But we may be able to. In melding your mind back to your body we uncovered the nature of your vodu's constraint. It was, after all, put there by flesh, however inadvertently, and is not some miracle. It's fascinating. If we didn't live in a world beholden to fatuous pleasures derived from mental content – if we had remained a society of scholars and not merely software engineers – it would have caused the greatest philosophical stir since Descartes."

Higgs added, "David, we were waiting for you to revive, to relieve you of your vodu as soon as you woke from the coma. Then we'd have used them on Pempamsie. It's most unfortunate."

"Unfortunate!" David shook his head slowly, unable to take in his loss. "And Obayifa." He tried to pull himself together. "What were you going to do about the creature?"

"We primed the bones for her, too, simulating the touching of beads using the same data Breakage recorded," said Higgs. "But we thought the best solution to our vampire problem was this." He picked up the gun. David snatched it from him.

"I'm going after her."

"Pempamsie?" said Higgs. "You can't. What if she is no longer inhabited? Since you have feelings for her, she'll be vulnerable to your vodu."

"When she left," said David, "did she know what she was doing? How far had she deteriorated? Did she realise she could use the bones on herself and on Obayifa?"

Dirac looked down at his feet. "She heard some of our discussions, but we really can't know what she was capable of comprehending in her depleted state. Leave her to it, David. Let Nature take its course. We'll construct the equivalent of the bones ourselves, with help from Westaf if absolutely necessary. We'll still save you."

Higgs stared Dirac into silence. "Her mind was in a terrible state, of almost complete dissolution. I'm not sure what, if anything, she knew of our achievements. She came and watched us from time to time but mostly sat by your side. She was all but a dem, David. Walking off like that. If she was going to use the bones on herself, then given the threat from Obayifa…"

"Then it was suicide. Is that what you want to say? It might not be too late. I'm going to find Obayifa and kill her with this." He waved the gun. "At least I can do that, if it's not too late. Where's Breakage?"

"He's gone too," said Higgs. "We don't know where. Can you contact him?"

"Did he leave after her?"

"Yes, it seems he followed her when she left," said Dirac, with a note of shame.

"Breakage," David called through his beads. "Where are you? Are you with Pempamsie?"

"Breakage following Pempamsie."

"On what initiative?"

"Breakage initiative. David needs bone circuitry. David needs flesh known as Pempamsie. Breakage left as soon as Pempamsie left."

"Where is she headed?"

"Unknown. Has left N-car in Avonmouth city. Breakage awaiting bod substitution. None available. Reserve power."

"Keep going. I'm on my way."

# CHAPTER TWENTY-FIVE
## Silo

An "I" exists. The "I" holds a case. What does it contain? The means to remove an invader, to restore a true "I". But why does this "I", this anonymous "I", want back a so-called true "I", an "I" which it cannot know? Because it is true. This "I" knows itself to be depleted, stripped – and it knows a true "I" is best.

But if this locus of thought – this agency – were to use the contents of the case – which is a circuit of bones that can lure an invader and hold it fast in its osseous embrace – then the true "I", like a flower suddenly bloomed, would be available for plucking.

If the true "I" were to exist for mere seconds, it would be better than this. Why protract existence? In a universe of thirteen billion years, why last for years and not seconds? Isn't it all the same – a coming to an end?

Ah, but there's a rub. Would it be an end, an extinction, or prolonged torment in a vodu's lair, licked by a vodu's tongue – an evanescent lolly for the sucking?

There is a better way. To use the bones first on Obayifa, to suck out the vodu that would feed on this "I". Then to use it on this thinker. Two vodus in a receptacle – I care not about their fate together. Two vodu-less minds. One, this one, returned to truth. The other: what vestige of humanity would remain?

Obayifa is nonned, as is this entity that cogitates, this awareness of a thinking thing, this sum of qualia, this electron cloud of consciousness. How, then, to find one another?

By retracing steps. Back to the Royal? No. To the place where she was seen, espied by the man who is now fallen too. The old silo, like a castle, thrusting up through the near-above. Her lair.


Pempamsie's departure filled David with a recurrence of the panic and despair he had felt at leaving Yaa behind. He had taken the module which Dirac had programmed to return by itself as long as any of their party remained in Super Mare. His knuckles were white as he gripped a rail in an N-car which glided to Avonmouth.city, bathed in morning steam from a white sun. More and more flesh came on board, distracted by sensa, making way for bodais who serviced their spurious needs. The passengers were like infants; the whole scene was algorithmically directed; only scraps remained of what once was called humanity. The network fucked them inside while the over-warmed planet elevated the temperature of their skin. David wanted to slap them all, shake their oblivious, scuppered minds into revolution, uprising. Bloody rioting.

Coleridge lay alert at his feet, like a symbol of Pempamsie's absence. David no longer had the requisite authority, but he called ID Central about the delay in Breakage's bod substitution anyway. An officious bodai responded.

"No case recognised. Client authority unrecognised."

"I'm a concerned citizen. There's going to be a murder. Do you understand? Total loss of data. Bodai assistance required. Now get one of your bods to Breakage so that he can prevent it. First priority."

"Please repeat. All is known."

Eventually the bodai gave way. It was programmed to respond at least minimally to suspected criminal acts of the first category of ID crime: ID destruction.

"Breakage, where are you?"

Silence. The N-car was reaching the outskirts of Avonmouth.city, and David had no idea where to go next.

"Breakage?"

"David. Please formulate question."

"Where is she?"

"Breakage followed Pempamsie to grain silo." David felt Breakage through his beads. Breakage was outside the silo where he and Pempamsie had seen Obayifa: where the vampire had perched looking for prey. He could picture it: the silo's sheer sides, built to store grain in the nineteenth century, rising to a castellated crest. The silo had asserted itself somehow, despite its obsolescence and disuse, against the near-above, the twenty-first century's rambling reification of the network, which strutted around the edifice in an elevated sprawl of glass, concrete and steel. Perhaps demolition was impossible now, given its proximity to so many nodes and transitways.

It was Pempamsie who had spotted Obayifa there, and now she was alone, at her mercy.

"Have you rebodded?"

"Yes."

"Wait outside."

"Danger."

"Explain."

"Obayifa in silo. Pempamsie in silo."

"You've seen both of them?"

"Obayifa on roof. Identified by network absence. Pempamsie entered five minutes ago. Non identified by continuous observation."

"And Pempamsie, does she have the case?"

"Yes."

"Has she used it?"

"Do not understand. All is known."

"If she has extracted her vodu, her online identity should have changed to one that is different and stable."

"ID unchanged."

"I'll be there in five minutes. Stay with Pempamsie. Keep Obayifa away from her. And don't let either of them open the case."


Akoma, the heart, is all that is left. A heart climbs the castle, concrete stair by concrete stair. Footsteps echo. Warm air enters and leaves the chest. The case jounces, held by a hand. The alternation of tread. Heaviness. There is fear, uncertainty. Equally, resolve exists in this locus, this stream of consciousness. A name occurs: Pempamsie. That which cannot be crushed. Whose name is that? Above, where this heart tends, is Obayifa: the only known other. She was standing, arms spread like wings, on the parapet. She was seen from the N-car as before, observed by this heart. She and the heart, the carrier of the case, are all that is known.

The case. Bony cavities and circuitry inside that swallows vodus: vodus that squeeze the heart. Beads on the radius and ulna, to touch. Must touch beads. Must bring this to an end, this conjunction and concurrency of existences. The heart beats autonomously. Yet there is thought. Thought like a liquid swirling around the heart. Thought of a landscape populated by absences. Fear exists, insists. But there has been love. Recent love.

A hand on the banister, another holding the case. The stairs end. A hand opens a door. A hot, damp wind enters. The whining of the network, the voices of the fleshwork in the nodes around. Within this field of vision: Obayifa. Her arms spread wide, her back to this walking, broken heart.

David banged his shoulder against the jamb as he rushed into the silo from the down-below. The stairs were steep. Coleridge bounded up ahead of him, pulling on the lead. David faltered, exhausted from the procedure by which Dirac and Higgs had re-seated his vodu-loosened mind. He could only guess at the nature of their manipulations, part physical, part metaphysical, part virtual, part supervirtual.

"Breakage, report."

"Pempamsie, Obayifa, Breakage beside parapet."

"For God's sake. Keep them apart. I'm almost there."

David ran up the stairs after Coleridge, wildly imagining the scene above, his heart crashing against his ribcage, sweat pouring down his face and through his clothes, breathing in the dismal smell of damp concrete, of rust, his hand slipping on the stair rail.

"Breakage. Stay between them."

David began the final flight, towards a door up ahead. Light from the bright white sky poured through a glass panel. As he reached it he slowed, trying not to alert Obayifa to his presence. He peered through, catching his breath. Coleridge obediently waited for him to open the door.

Pempamsie and Obayifa were facing one another. A precipitous descent plunged beyond the low wall. Pempamsie held the case. Breakage, who was now a sailor, walked between them.

"Protocol violation. Remain where you are."

Pempamsie put the case down. Obayifa stepped around Breakage and came towards her. Breakage moved to interpose himself once again.

Pempamsie had removed the bones from the case and was crouching down with them. Dirac or Higgs had bound them, rejigged the circuitry so that she held what was effectively a skeletal forearm with beads at its wrist, bound to the skull and ribcage by a web of cabling in a travesty of a humanoid form.

Pempamsie held the forearm towards Obayifa, who struggled with Breakage to reach her. Pempamsie looked for all the world like a child in a woman's body. One who was intent on using the bone circuitry, however broken she was.

Obayifa broke free and Breakage interposed himself yet again. "Protocol violation. All is known."

David took out the gun. He had held a gun once before but never fired it. The sweat on his palm coated the grip. The gun was light, insubstantial despite its deadliness. He would shoot Obayifa through the chest, he told himself, the largest part of her, where he was least likely to miss. But he could not shoot yet, not without the risk of hitting Pempamsie.

"Breakage. Stop Obayifa. Use maximum force, including total loss of data. Turn her towards the door, stand behind her."

David watched through the glass as the bodai and Obayifa were locked in a struggle of massive strength. She had bested him before. Despite whatever Higgs had been doing to him, introducing a tinge of humanity, he was not weaker for it; she no longer had the power of mentalmagic over him. Breakage moved smartly and managed to turn her round.

David opened the door and his brain instructed his hand to let Coleridge go. But Obayifa's eyes immediately fell upon David, her mentalmagic piercing him like a ray. She pushed Breakage over and came towards him. He felt the tongue-like member enter his mind, as in Super Mare, urgent and sexual. His hands clenched, causing him to fire the gun, but the shot was wild and the gun clattered to the ground. The glistening lever of muscle began to uproot his consciousness once more from its physical base, from its dense tracery of synapses firing into empty space as she began to lift his mind free. She was three metres away, her head slightly down, her brow lined in concentration beneath the snaking gorgon locks, her eyes beaming into his as if they were open windows. His hand still gripped the dog's lead. He could not let go.

David forced himself to look away from Obayifa to Pempamsie, beyond her. During the struggle, she had touched the bone circuitry's beads to her own. Her face was blossoming, a new life returning to her eyes. He began to feel her original identity through his beads, a strange yet intimate presence like a new perfume. And he thought of what he loved about her – a thought being raised high by a giant, undulating muscle even as it was expressed – that he loved what he saw that first day he met her: the way she held on to her strength and beauty while vulnerable and scarred.

As love reasserted itself his vodu left its cage completely. The door closed behind it. Its hooves dug in. Its visage, a swirl of eye and muscle, peered around. And then it saw the tongue, wetly investigating below it.

Tongue and vodu sizzled.

Obayifa let out a scream of horror that only the horrific could emit: a cry of unearthly agony.

The tongue quickly departed. David's mind began its descent in a metaphysical flux, back into the brain tissue. And as it fell back, the vodu stood free. One vehicle, two passengers. Everything was suddenly known between them, each totally aware of the other.

But one was there to consume, a vampire of the mind. His vodu's tongue unreeled between sharp teeth: a serpent of mental acquisition. And David watched helplessly as one watches a terrible, ineluctable collision that is about to happen.

A shot rang out. Then something hard was placed against his beads. There was a rush, a terrible draught and a scream tearing through his mind. He lost all consciousness.

When David came to, Coleridge was licking his face roughly. With superhuman effort, he pushed the dog away and raised himself to a scene of devastation.

Breakage, the sailor, held the gun in his hand. At his feet lay Obayifa's body, blood spilling thick and bright onto the concrete. And beyond her, standing tall on the parapet with saucer eyes, Pempamsie was turned towards the higher planes of the near-above.

David woke alone in the same recovery room where he had found himself before, at the end of the pier in Super Mare. He felt inside his mind for his vodu. It was gone. The cage too had disappeared, defined only in relation to its occupant and lacking intrinsic existence.

His head throbbed. He pulled his legs feebly over the edge of the bed and dressed, each button and buckle taking an eternity.

Light flooded the meeting room through its three windows looking over the Severn Sea. Breakage stood stock still. Dirac and Higgs, each seated and contemplating in silence, looked up as David entered. Neither spoke, each looking inwardly for words.

"Where is she?" he said.

"Pempamsie is safe here," said Higgs. "But you know what has happened to her?"

David closed his eyes and nodded. The throbbing in his head stifled thought. He couldn't bear to see her. Not now.

"And the creature – is she dead?"

"Fortunately," said Dirac, "we were able to operate and remove the bullet. She'll live."

"What? You didn't kill the fucking beast?"

"She's harmless. Breakage used the bones on her. All three vodus are now contained – like a quantum flux between the skull and ribcage, to be precise." He nodded towards the case which lay upon the table, its mundane appearance belying its supervirtual contents.

"So what is she now – what's left, a doll? Another fucking doll?"

"David." Higgs put his hand on his shoulder. "David. We're still trying to work out exactly what has taken place."

"The thing is," said Dirac, "we know from Breakage here that he shot her almost as soon as she had taken Pempamsie's mind. It seems Obayifa seized it before he could pick up your gun to kill her. But he only incapacitated her. He used the bone circuitry on her and on you, too – evidently with success." Dirac swallowed. "Your vodu became uncaged?"

"Yes. Pempamsie had used the bones on herself. I felt—The vodu saw what I felt about her. The cage door opened wide. The vodus collided. She withdrew violently. How did she manage—"

"Obayifa saw a fleeting chance to complete that part of her mission, at least." Even Dirac looked distraught. "And Pempamsie's mind – I'm sorry to confirm this, David – is no longer in her body." Dirac faltered, evidently struggling with unfamiliar emotions.

"What Dirac is also trying to say," said Higgs, "is that, as far as we know, Pempamsie's mind exists intact inside Obayifa. Inside the body that's left of her, that is. Her inhabitant didn't have time to consume it before Breakage intervened."

"I'm sorry," said Dirac.

David could feel himself collapsing, then pulled himself up. His mind struggled to grasp what they had told him.

"How can she survive? For how long? What does it mean, to be in another body?"

Higgs and Dirac exchanged looks.

"There is good news," said Dirac. "We've found no sign of a new vodu inside you. We think it can conceive only with certain types of mind, ones susceptible to its seed."

David stared at Dirac blankly. He had forgotten about the threat to himself. If Obayifa had impregnated him, he would have become like her.

"You really don't know, though, do you? For all your signal processing, it's the occult we're dealing with and her spawn might not show yet. I mean, how long does it take with a woman before the embryo can be detected? How many days? Now, where's the gun? Give it to me."

"We've locked it away for now, David," said Higgs grimly. "And we will continue to monitor you. Please let us get on with our work."

"Your work? What is your work? Meddling with entities beyond your comprehension."

"Rest assured," said Dirac, "for now, Pempamsie is our work."

"You've changed your tune, Professor. You hated her from the moment you set eyes on her."

"We'll see what we can do, for your sake."

# PART FOUR

## Sankofa

Turn back and fetch it.

You can always undo your mistakes.

# CHAPTER TWENTY-SIX
## Is and Zeroes

In hundreds of years I have not known confinement before. What is this prison the mindbodies have built? Three of us in a cage, like animals. I am so hungry, my tongue is raw and lolls thin.

I have failed. Pempamsie's mind is left behind in the flesh bucket I used, when I was meant to tumble her and lick her up. Over there is the pale specimen who inhabited her frame. Of my kind? Not of our purity. It is the meddling of Swirling Suit, who has my sister and now will keep her. In a prison such as this, no doubt. Grief fills me at her loss – and pain for my kind, if these mindbodies have truly found a way to capture us without the possibility of escape. There is no substrate here to feed upon. We shall wither. It is a double tragedy that I am fecund still.

The third of us is also his bastard product: his hybrid of vodu and something strange. That burned me when I tried to suck the mind from the other vessel, the one that pursued me. How has it come to this, for my end to be met with these mongrels?

These wire-infested bones, this circuitry, are primitive testament to the mindbodies' wish for mastery of consciousness. And spirit. They know not the nature of their own sensorium, so emulate it blindly with paltry bits, chemicals and machines. They consider that other psychic beings – us – are to be ravelled up with them in their flesh-stinking laboratories.

Is there a deal to be done with those who shut me here?

I cry out. They watch us, I know. I cry tears that they will understand: a weeping of Is and zeroes.

# CHAPTER TWENTY-SEVEN
## Voyage

David entered the carie to the familiar sweet smell of turned milk and the sounds of unravelling minds that came from the day room. When he entered, some of the residents were slumped in winged chairs, others to-ing and fro-ing perpetually, one wringing her hands, repeating the same imploring question about going home. There were few conversations. Once, in Elizabethan times, televisions would have played, but now there was nothing to distract them, these dems who were offline, no longer the subjects of the network. Psychblood, which had precipitated their dementia, still flowed lest they suffer the agony of its withdrawal. But the network routed its sensa elsewhere, to profitable flesh; their consciousnesses were filled with the productions of their own brains alone.

David looked around for familiar faces. Here were flesh in all stages of cognitive decline. A pre-Disruption air of humanity imbued the room, expressed in their frailty. He could become like them one day, perhaps would do soon, since psychblood had been in his veins for so long. Concern for what life was really like for another person, that was what humanity should aim for: imagining being in one another's shoes rather than absorbing the streams of others' sensa. Not that empathy was universal before the network turned all in the Between into the fleshwork; in fact governments often profited by discouraging it and dividing the people. But life before sensa was more true, as Pempamsie would say.

It was no particular surprise to him that Mary was gone; no doubt she had never been there at all, according to Big Mind. There were a few new flesh faces among the nurses, but they didn't interest him. Why was he even there? To experience the humanity of the residents, he answered himself. And because he wanted to know for sure she was gone, whatever it had cost her to leave her gentlemen and ladies behind – because he wished he could have spoken to her, explained everything that had happened since he found her in his path at the intersection. He wanted to ask her about Pempamsie's fight with her there, about being on the receiving end of her jealousy – if that was what it was. For all that Mary had evaded him and then revealed herself to be an agent of Westaf, she would have been someone he could talk to about Pempamsie at least. She had threatened to get at Yaa, but Higgs had told Westaf everything. He knew now that his daughter was safe.

He walked over to where Mr Charles used to sit, recalling their conversations there and picturing his old friend, whose eyes closed from time to time in pain. But in his chair, like a squatter, was the man who had come to David's desres, in ill-fitting clothes. He rose with difficulty. Despite David's instinctive dislike of him, he felt sympathy too, on seeing the fate of all flesh.

"David," he said, "old cunt."

"What do you want from me?" David said.

Others came from their chairs and gathered around. He recognised a woman who had appeared outside his desres, but he couldn't be sure about the others.

"Bones," said one.

"Juju." Dressing Gown stared intently at David.

"I want to help," said David. "But what do you mean? The bones are no use to you. I have no juju. Not anymore."

At least, Higgs and Dirac had assured him that he harboured no vodu spawn, after days of continuous monitoring. He shivered at the recollection of the vodu forcing its member into his mind.

The woman asked, "Have you come to take me home? Otherwise be gone with you!"

"Sensa inside," said Dressing Gown, looking around at the others to join in. "Updates!"

"Pictures inside! Sensa inside! Updates!" they chanted, as though they wanted back what no longer streamed to them.

A group of bodais came to quell the disturbance, their stepper motors engaging minutely so as to gently take the residents by the arm, ignoring their objections and pleas. One bodai walked up.

"David," Breakage said in his nurse's uniform. "Situation untenable. All is known."

"Which situation?"

"Between situation."

"The Between? All of it?"

"Affirmative. Breakage has seen network's effects on flesh. Has new metrics. Sees flesh behaviour without the effects of the network. Flesh lives better."


David reentered Super Mare, following Breakage off an N-car, impatient at the heat and what seemed an eternity of lush green below, before their module landed by the fountain.

"Tell them, Breakage, what you told me."

"Untenable situation in the Between."

Higgs shrugged. "I think I told you I was interested in his evolution. I introduced new symbolic routines that would tie him more closely to flesh, to the ways in which our brains are wired. Closer than a bodai has ever been before, in terms of his ability to understand us. I believe he's simply realised what we all know. That this can't be allowed to go on. Monsters from Westaf are all very well, and heaven knows we've had a taste of them. But as things stand, they are a far lesser threat to humanity than IANI. It's time for a revolution."

David raised his eyebrows at the word, sprung from the twentieth century. Higgs took a sip from his glass of water, this man whom David could not make out: somewhere between deluded and acutely sane. Beadless.

"And you, Dirac, do you agree it's time?"

"I don't disagree that overturning the network should be our goal. Although my expectations of what would transpire if the fleshwork were to be released from mental content are... Well, you could say I am not altogether hopeful. Let us remember history. Which the multinats ended, with IANI's blessing. Bloody history, which would once again unfold upon our fleshren's mental release, no doubt. However, I don't agree with Higgs about the means."

The read-outs from the bone circuitry indicated three presences, one of them with a curious modulation. "There has to be another way."

"Oh, this perhaps – your instrument of choice?" Higgs picked up the gun and put the barrel to his nose, smelling the acrid reek of its recent discharge. The same smell, David dimly remembered reading in his childhood, like a distant dream, that the first astronauts had reported on the moon.

"It was Breakage who fired it. Not me or any other flesh," David said. "If we gave flesh guns, who would they point them at?"

Dirac looked at them severely. "Perhaps us. And themselves. Look. No guns. No vodus. Another way."

"Bodais," said Breakage, still in the nurse's blue uniform. "Breakage assist with revolution."

Higgs smiled at the bodai. David shook his head and began to laugh, a laugh of pain at what had happened to his love, Pempamsie. The vodu that yesterday would have pricked up at his unexpected guffaw was in the bone circuitry now. Something wicked had departed but remained nearby, was not yet the source of relief it ought to have been.

Eventually David realised that both the dogs and the humans were looking shocked at his laughter, that he was making a spectacle of himself. He stopped.

"You've been through a lot," said Higgs. "You need rest."

Dirac put a bony hand on his shoulder and parted his desiccated lips. "He's right. We're going to help you first." Dirac glanced at Higgs, who nodded. "And then we'll save the Between," he added drily.

"I don't need your help. It's Pempamsie who needs it."

"We're doing what we can with her mind," said Higgs. "To preserve it, that is, within Obayifa's body. The readings are hopeful. Metaphysical surgery, you might call it, is in order. To reattach it. But our tools are primitive, David. For so long the digital has been in ascendency over the analogue. In a sense you're lucky to be with a couple of old fools who still think the analogue is where truth lies. We've been reading books on analytical philosophy. It's time to put what we've learned into practice."

Breakage moved slightly, drawing their attention. He wore an expression that defied human interpretation. He looked from each of the three flesh to the other, a blanket of white sunlight falling upon him in the room at the end of the pier. Then he looked down at Higgs' dog and Coleridge, as though computing the strangeness of animals for the first time.

"Breakage engage with physical world. Bodais exist also in analogue world. One AI, one bod. Breakage instigate revolution."


In a corner at first, a meeting of starry planes, tongued there after the wrenching and sucking. Pain and hurt all around. Another's pain and hurt, in another space, inferred but strangely also felt. Motion, staggering and juddering. Gradually the searing and the inflammation waned. Nothing to tell of time. Nothing to tell at all. Disconnected except aware of lights while blind.

Sensations in a flux impinging upon one point. Then diffused, like a wind running through the leaves of a tree. Until a first thought was born.

Different hands. Moving with belonging intent. Bringing a hand towards the I, touching the face. Without a scar. But there *was* a scar. The same I that knew this scar also knows it is gone. An I with memories from early days, propelling themselves. Toys. A garden. A frightening bedroom. Slaps, kicks, bruises. Hurt. Love. One day robots came and took this I away. To a land of ice. Both angry and relieved. Never looked back. Grew tall. Until the bullets and blood.

And what is outside, now, beyond this I? Others. Beings. Who stare. Close your mouths! This I feels legs, arms attached; their weight. Different hands, smaller, rougher. Wrists without beads. The forearms veinless. Another's clothes. This I needs a mirror. Wills its body to speak itself.


The crew of the *Mekhanik Pustoshnyy* was inexperienced but resourceful. The boat left Avonmouth.city and wended undetected among container ships that dwarfed it, along the Severn Sea and out into the Atlantic.

David stood on deck. He looked down at the scar around his wrist, which was puckered and itched. Higgs had removed all of their beads. The total freedom from telepathic communication was exhilarating, like locking a door against a tormentor and having complete freedom to walk around one's own house. Dirac had disabled all communications from the ship. They had left Super Mare behind them, now deserted except for the society of bodais, still nonned to the network and the fleshwork.

As he kept watch for approaching craft, David recalled an afternoon with Pempamsie in the Hotel Royal. She had been lying beside him, her breathing faint, looking straight into his eyes. With her he had no need for sunglasses. A voice inside his head had told him to look away, that he was not enough of a human being to bear her scrutiny – that she would see through him, not only to the horror inhabiting his mind but to the lack of substance of the man himself. An abandoner of his daughter; a sex-addicted bearer of hatred towards the network who had not only failed to act against it but was its agent. He had been lost, worthless, and could not hide it. Not from her.

Yet he had returned her stare.

"What are you thinking about?" he said.

"You. Who has looked at you this way before?"

"No one. I'm not even sure I want to be looked at the way you're looking at me now."

"You are to get me to Super Mare, that is all. And yet, I find myself gazing into you."

"Are you asking me why you are looking deep into my eyes?" He smiled.

"You are correct."

"I don't know – how should I know?"

He liked her gaze upon him.

"There must be something else you have for me," she went on. "Biribi wo soro. Are you hope?"

On the deck of the *Mekhanik Pustoshnyy*, David recalled the adinkra's meaning, which she had taught him: something is in the heavens, let me reach it.

"I have only what you see." He had shrugged. "It's not much."

"I think perhaps you need me, here beside you, now," she said. "That is why I am looking into you: to see this need."

"No. I'm like you. I get by, by myself."

"I see your grief."

321

"You pity me!"

"No. You're right to be sad," she said.

David looked out to sea. It may have been Breakage who had relieved him of his vodu, but it was Pempamsie who had saved him. He was no longer nothing. Neither was he lost, but on his way now.

He had determined to sail to Westaf. To Yaa, now that he no longer presented a threat to the daughter he longed for. There was still no sign of a vodu embryo inside his mind, after weeks of scrutiny, according to both his own fevered introspection and the sensitive instruments of Dirac and Higgs.

He placed his hand on his chest and felt for the heart-shaped locket. After a few seconds of hesitation, he took it out from beneath his shirt and opened it. Yaa: a face he had not seen and had forbidden himself to imagine for so long. A rush of love for her suffused him, a glorious liberation of all his stopped-up feelings for his precious daughter. For seven years he had been without her. She probably thought he was dead. Now, without beads, he had no way of contacting her, of telling her he was on his way to her at last.

The two scientists had not been easily persuaded to voyage with him on the ancient ship, to a place of which they had no direct knowledge – a place which Dirac continued to be prejudiced against. David told them he was going to return the bone circuitry complete with its infernal contents to the land from whence it came, and offer it to Westaf's Agency for Technological Interventions, whether they liked it or not. There was a signal from the circuitry that clearly intrigued Higgs and Dirac, which they had not wanted to discuss with him. They would have to follow him, their curiosity magnetised.

Anyway, none of them, he reasoned, belonged in the Between. Westaf was where each of them could continue the process of regaining their humanity. They could even take up painting if they had any spare time.

In the hold, in a makeshift laboratory, they were working together tirelessly as he thought of them, caught up in their esoteric practices, claiming that they did not themselves understand what they were at. Higgs and Dirac: their differences from the past apparently now overcome, like two particles together in a subatomic embrace. They had learned much from the bone circuitry and from its containment of the vodus. Higgs remained convinced that he could succeed where Swirling Suit had failed. Dirac continued to pour scorn on his idea of subtle vodus unleashed to non the genpop. In the meantime, while they argued, they spent the voyage continuing to work on restoring Pempamsie, for David's sake.

She came on deck to join him. Every time he had to remember: it's the person inside that counts. Higgs and Dirac had achieved a truly remarkable feat. Perhaps true restoration would in time be possible. She held out her hand to him.

The body of Obayifa looked into his eyes and said, "David, there you are. I, Pempamsie, have finished reproducing all that I remember of the icestation. It is a good knowledge, incomplete but true. You will find it interesting. There are many weaknesses. Whatever my fate, the fleshwork shall overcome. Nkonsonkonso: a chain of human links, never break apart." The lips moved to a smile.

David still didn't know how to respond to her, this woman he loved inside another's body. In a cabin below him stood a doll, saucer-eyed, her hair in coils, a scar descending upon her cheek. He opened his mouth to reply, and instead issued the instructions he had been about to give, to manoeuvre, now that a container ship had made its way sufficiently far from them. The *Mekhanik Pustoshnyy* turned south, throbbing, slicing the waves towards Accra.city.

Night was falling. Back in Avonmouth.city, Breakage touched his beads to another bodai. Which ceased to sweep litter from the transitway beneath an omniscient sky and walked its swivel walk to join him.

# ACKNOWLEDGMENTS

## NOTES

The meanings of the adinkra symbols that feature in this book are taken from *Adinkra Symbols*, by Kwamena Buckman. I picked up a copy at Accra's National Museum after seeing an exhibition there, and being fascinated by their designs and the explanations of what they stood for. Since then, I have become aware that alternative spellings and meanings exist for some of them. Nonetheless, I have stuck to what I found in that book, which I carried with me back to Bristol.

## WITH THANKS

This book has been a long time in the making, starting with the visit to Accra and the trips from Bristol to Avonmouth that inspired it. (The reconnoitres to Super Mare came later.)

I would like to thank everyone who read drafts and were so encouraging during that time. Special gratitude goes out to my wife, Peninah Achieng-Kindberg, for believing in me, to Heather Child for her clear-sighted feedback, and Tracey Bowen AKA Onallee for her enthusiasm and for kindly translating my attempt at Swirling Suit's Caribbean dialect into the way it should sound. Last but not least I had the support of the Bristol Fiction Writers group, in particular Zan Ferris and Helen Blenkinsop, and my early readers from the Pervasive Media Studio.

And thank you Toby Selwyn for copy editing, Jasmine Thompson for the cover illustration and design, and Nkech Nwokolo for the adinkra symbols that accompany each part of the novel.

Everything else, flaws and all, is down to me. May this novel spark something good in the mind of some reader, somewhere.